Spoils of Olympus
By the Sword

Christian Kachel

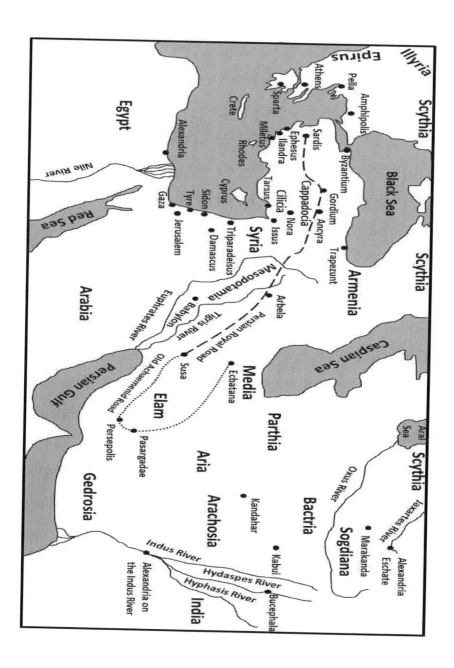

Chapter 1

The dream is a recurring one but I wish it were more frequent. I'm visited by my father and we speak of where he has been. I'm told of the horrors death has in store for the unrighteous and he urges me to always defend my house and enjoy life's pleasures. My father certainly lived by the latter, sometimes to the detriment of the former, but I decided long ago that, overall, he was a good man.

I hear familiar voices now…then laughter…something jostles me…I'm awake. My head is heavy, my mouth is stale. The events of last night pass through my mind's eye as a procession of chronological debauched images: meeting my mates to drink wine- that explains my hangover; a few rounds of dice- that explains my light purse; a fist fight that I believe we won- that explains my sore cheek; a quick hop over to our favourite brothel for a victory romp- that explains the warm body next to me; and now my mate is half drunkenly recounting our exploits- that explains my consciousness about an hour too early. All in all, a good night- father would have been proud.

"How's your cheek feeling lover boy? I can't believe that peasant decided to grow a pair and sucker punch you," taunted Patrochlus.

"Aren't you supposed to be looking out for things like that while I'm predisposed fighting some deviant on your behalf?" I weakly responded.

"Don't worry, I broke his nose about three times over after I stopped laughing."

Patrochlus is the mouth of our wretched little band- a mediocre fish in the mediocre sea of Ilandra, a city on the Ionian coast of Asia Minor. He'd gotten us into altercations before, knowing full well his mates would be there to clean up the mess. I can't say we necessarily minded; the problem being it was always at a time of his choosing- nothing like a surprise fist fight to make the night lively.

Hearing Patrochlus' voice, Alexandros walked in from the adjacent bedroom with the slimmest of cloth covering his groin and added, "That little imp needed a stepping stool; we should buy him a drink next time." His stout physique needed all the room the narrow doorway allowed. With more body hair than a bear cub, Alexandros was truly a sight this early in the morning. He was short, stocky, loyal, and jovial- all in all, a good friend. Seeing him standing in the doorway with his bulbous features and impressive gut hanging over a piece of cloth stretched to its ripping point brought a smile to my face.

"Did you wake to find you pissed on your whore again Alex?" I retorted.

"The way she screws, I should have. Like fucking a warm corpse," he responded laughingly.

"Poor girl," I thought to myself. "Where's Nearchus?"

"He went home last night," Alexandros responded.

"You know what happens when Leanna finds out he's been here with us," Patrochlus answered. "The lad's pussywhipped with nothing to show for it- forced to return home to a cold bed with only his hand for comfort." While Patrochlus' characterization would sound mean spirited to most, he was truly saddened by our more responsible friend's celibate situation. Someone not doing exactly as they wished was inconceivable to Patrochlus- he would have called himself a true epicurean, if he knew what that meant.

With that our bedmates began stirring, "You boys still talking about that stupid fight last night?" Patrochlus' female companion asked, sounding a bit annoyed.

"I'm a lover not a fighter, let me feel good about my rare feats of soldierly."

"If you love better than you fight, your victim must have been a sickly Persian eunuch," she quipped.

"Of the most deformed kind my dear," he laughed as he gently smacked her half-exposed rear.

For all our bantering, the four of us really did enjoy each other's company and waking up recounting the previous night's antics were some of my favourite memories growing up. We all understood our lower lot in life, and our mischievous adventures made it all quite tolerable. I got out of bed and threw on my tunic. This wasn't the first time I've woke up here. The room was sparsely decorated with two beds side by side and a small table between them gingerly

6

supporting an old vase with dying wildflowers from the coast. A faint hint of their pleasant odour could still be detected among the cheap perfume permeating the small room- masking the sordid acts which frequently transpire here. At the foot of each bed was a chest containing our bedmates' personal items along with our payments from last night to be sure. I stretched, thanked my female companion, and the three of us began our familiar walk home. As we exited, the head of the house, Eurydike, saw us out.

"Good night I trust boys?" she asked with a jealous smirk.

"It would have been better had I the pleasure of bedding you last night my lady," said Patrochlus with his usual insincere charm. Eurydike was the kind of person it worked on best.

"In my day you young pups wouldn't be able to handle a siren like me, not even the three of you at once." She was probably right. Walking down the alley she yelled, "You boys remember who takes care of you and don't be going to those disease-ridden shacks down the street- You'll wake up pissing lava."

These types of establishments are never in nice parts of town and ours was no exception. We stumbled and laughed down the dirt streets moist with dew, emptied chamber pots, and brackish water. The buildings were mostly wood with the filth of the dirt street staining their outer walls up to the height of a man's knee. The food sold in the carts on either side of the street was spoiled to the point that even Alexandros wouldn't touch it. It was now the middle of summer and the flies were everywhere. They mainly swarmed around piles of livestock dung throughout the streets. As children, we would wait till a member of our group wasn't paying attention and swiftly nudge them directly into these steaming messes as a joke. Many of the faces we encountered in this neighborhood had the true look of despair that only years of utter destitution could bring. Their clothes dirty and in tatters, their frail, weathered hands extended out for alms. Some of them were ex-prostitutes left caring for a child. They would nurse these crying infants, sometimes covered in grime, along the streets during our morning walks home. To say we didn't sometimes look at these unfortunate souls with some introspection would be a lie. I wondered whether my recent bedmate knew this horrid fate was more than a possibility for her.

7

The cacophony of misery combined to create a pungent odour that began to wreak havoc on my already fragile stomach. Alexandros and Patrochlus were talking about some type of thievery scheme, as they are apt to do, when I made the mistake of looking one of these vile street creatures in the eye. Seeing an opening, he shoved a rancid piece of goat meat in my face and asked for a coin. I immediately gagged and vomited- to the delight of my two companions. After the laughing subsided, Alexandros gave the urchin a coin for the spectacle and we continued on towards our homes.

Leaving the seedy neighbourhoods behind, we entered the neatly drained thoroughfares of Ilandra proper. The city is quite pleasant, with a number of public fountains and baths, a small amphitheatre, various outdoor markets, columned building facades, temples to Zeus and Poseidon, and a deep water port. A hint of salt water brought a distinct character to our coastal air that lost its potency the further inland one travelled. We passed by a familiar fountain to grab a drink, splash water on our faces, and make ourselves somewhat presentable for our triumphant return home. It was about three hours past sunrise and the city had been bustling since before daybreak. Much of this activity was from merchants, fishermen, and travellers using the port on the western border of the city or the Ionian road connecting much of the coastline on its eastern edge. Ilandra was always prosperous under the Persian King Darius II and our Satrap, Spithridates, but the tangible atmosphere of the city, along with all the other Greek Ionian ports, was simply euphoric since the Battle of the Granicus River twelve years earlier featuring the heroic slaying of our Persian governor during Alexander's first victory over the Persians. He was one of us, and now, all the world was Greek. Alexander installed his father's trusted general, Antigonus 'The One Eyed,' to administer Asia Minor after the Battle of the Granicus, with Asander installed as our Satrap. We had known them as ruler for over ten years, but now the machinations of civil war were forming after Alexander's recent death, with Antigonus challenging Perdiccas, Regent for Alexander's two successors.

As children we made my older cousin, Leandros, take us to see the army of Greeks marching through Ionia after defeating the Persians at the Granicus River. Alexander's army marched south after their victory to liberate the Greek towns along the Ionian Road. Thirty thousand Macedonians and another twenty thousand Greek mercenaries and auxiliaries spanned a five mile distance, confidently marching towards a Persian enemy who, despite their initial defeat, had hundreds of thousands more men to field against them. On our way, we could see the dust being kicked up by the moving serpent of warriors miles away. We first came upon the army about three miles into its five mile procession, running about two miles non-stop to get a look at the head of the snake. There, we saw first the heavy Macedonian phalanx of veterans with their eighteen foot long sarissas disassembled in tow. These hellish weapons formed a combined instrument of death when assembled for battle with the front row of the phalanx bristling with spear points from the next five rows behind it. Foes that dared face this leviathan had to first hack their way through a thousand-toothed monster while avoiding impalement and trampling along the way. If they were formidable or fortunate enough to pass through this gauntlet of wood and iron, they found themselves standing opposite a heavily armored veteran of the Greek wars, sword in hand, ready to bury it deep within the foe's stomach.

At the front was the elite Companion Cavalry, of which Alexander led at the very apex of the march. The Companions looked like gods to us with iron, polished brass, leather, cloaks, and plumes. Scurrying ahead we saw this moving weapon of destruction's leader. It was the first and only time I would ever lay eyes on the God King himself. Compared to his Companions, Alexander was short in stature, yet sat atop the proudest and most magnificent black beast any of us had ever seen. He was clad in a white linen and polished bronze cuirass, flowing red cloak and bronze helmet with red plume. An additional two ornate feathers upon his helmet were the only markers distinguishing him from the rest. No other show of human importance could ever match what we saw that day. All four of us, including Leandros, who was a teenager at the time, were ready to follow this man into the dark void of Hades. We shadowed the army for a couple more miles before Alexandros began complaining of fatigue and Leandros decided to take his gang of brats back home.

Later, we heard of all the historic battles after the Granicus and dreamed of being there with him at the planes of Issus, the siege of Tyre, the final epic battle of Gaugamela, the triumphant entrance through the Ishtar Gate of Babylon, the arduous conquest of Bactria and Sogdiana, and the battles at the edge of the world along the Indus river. Four years after the great army marched through Ionia, Leandros joined a mercenary outfit when he was of age and I bid him farewell at age eleven. We received occasional letters from him thereafter about his time in Babylon, his participation in the eastern campaigns, and his experiences in India. At first my mates huddled around every letter that came in, spending the rest of that day pretending we were there. As the years wore on, other extracurricular activities became more important to Patrochlus and Alexandros, but Nearchus and I cherished each correspondence. Growing up, Alexander was Achilles incarnate whose military feats would make Ares himself green with envy. Then, a little over one year ago, our Heracles died a death not worthy of a dirt farmer, let alone our God King.

News of his death spread throughout our world quickly via messenger, runner, horse courier, and fire beacon. Women wept in the streets. Every Greek town, village and city within the empire held their own funeral ceremonies to honour the most important man to ever live. Much confusion followed as to what would happen next and who would inherit the entire world. His generals, some childhood friends, others former companions of his father Phillip II, divided the empire between them with Ptolemy taking Egypt, Antigonus retaining Asia Minor, Antipater retaining control of Greece and Macedon, and Perdiccas taking Asia while acting as regent for the two Kings- Alexander's son, Alexander IV, and his half-brother, Arrhidaeus, renamed Phillip III, in Babylon.

As we made it to our neighborhood we came upon Theon, a vile creature from our youth that followed his family's trade of thuggery, thievery, and violence. Everything about him offended me; from his dirty clothes, his wild hair, his propensity for accumulating filth and canker sores around his mouth, and his facial tick that obligated him to lick his lips every few moments like some wretched lizard. Theon no doubt detected my disdain and returned the cold civility I strained to muster in his presence. Patrochlus found use for his lecherous tendencies on occasion and frequently associated with him in the hopes of establishing connections with Theon's older brother, Ganymedes. Ganymedes was a powerful criminal and someone our band all respected. Theon attempted to impress us with some exaggerated tale of recent indecency which received its usual response of disgust from me and dismissive silence from the rest. Theon was older than us and he and his band of menaces saw themselves as our superiors. Patrochlus saw his appearance as an opportunity to continue discussing his latest scheme with a dedicated criminal. The three continued to loiter while I took my leave towards home.

Chapter 2

My home was one of four apartments in a small building along a quiet street. I have lived there my entire life with my mother and younger sister Helena. Helena was fifteen now and becoming her own woman. My relationship with her progressed from sibling torture, to systematic ignoring, to now, one of fervent protection from any perceived outside threat. She did not share my affinity for irresponsible behaviour and was fast surpassing me in maturity despite her youth. I entered our home to find her busy with house chores. She looked up to greet me and quickly resumed her work. My older sibling aura was wearing off and she was beginning to form critical judgments about the brother she once looked up to. Despite these new developments, we had a loving relationship and we both could do no wrong in our mother's eyes, as long as we tolerated her overt affections.

Like many sons recently come of age, I felt my mother was too emotional and decided her public displays of affection were unacceptable. Like most mothers, she didn't care. Her overt devotion to us enabled some of my irresponsible behaviour, for she would rather me follow in my father's footsteps of debauchery and have me home with her, then see me getting any ideas of joining a military outfit participating in foreign wars like Leandros. She willingly turned an eye to my merry band's comings and goings, even extending her affection to them over the years. This was no easy feat given the amount reserved specifically for Helena and myself. My mother's acquiescence, coupled with my father's absence, threatened to stunt my maturity to manhood altogether had it not been for my uncle Argos, Leandros' father and younger brother to my father.

My mother always discouraged Leandros' talk of joining the fighting abroad and forbid Argos long ago about voicing a syllable of encouragement to me as he did with his own son. Over the years my mother received the arrival of a coveted letter from Leandros with joy to hear from her nephew and dread seeing Nearchus and I beam with envy over each scene recounted on the parchment. The threat of me leaving her began to seem more palpable now that I was nineteen and growing restless with the mundane repetition of working with my uncle Argos and raising Hades with my mates all inside the same ten square mile radius.

Our home occupied one half of the first floor of a two story wooden edifice. We shared the first floor with uncle Argos' wine and olive oil storefront. Our walls were primarily bare with intermittent patterns painted on them running parallel to the floor. Our floors were sparingly adorned with two eastern style rugs. Our front room contained two couches constructed of wood with a blanket thrown over each and a small table in between them. My mother always ensured incense burned in this front room to greet any unexpected visitors. Two bedrooms lined the far wall where my mother and sister shared one small chamber and I slept in the other. In the back of the apartment was the kitchen and rear courtyard that contained a small brick oven and shrine to Dionysius to ensure the good fortune of uncle Argos' entrepreneurial ventures. Argos never questioned his responsibility to care for his brother's family after my father's death and we owed our continued livelihood to his generosity. Argos provided for us while my mother and sister tended to his apartment located on the second floor of the building. They cooked for all of us each night and I worked with him most days at his storefront. My relationship with him grew after Leandros left for the great campaign and I became of more use to him with age- but his demeanour to me was always cold and condescending.

Nearchus and his family shared the second floor of the apartment building with Argos. Nearchus' father, Priskos, was a fisherman and lived with Nearchus' mother and three other children. Priskos was a famous drinking colleague of my late father and Nearchus, being the oldest, had assumed much of the paternal responsibilities of his family. Nearchus' elevated position was solidified when he began fighting off his father's drunken beatings to a draw. Argos was always the more responsible sibling and thus openly looked down upon my father and disliked Priskos as well. As an extension, Argos frequently criticized me, believing I was resembling my father, and complimented Nearchus, believing he was growing up to be the responsible one. Only familial loyalty precluded Argos from choosing to take Nearchus as his apprentice after Leandros left for the wars.

After drinking some water, taking a handful of whatever Helena was preparing for supper, and after receiving a playful slap for it, I gave her a hug and a kiss. She briefly smiled and then immediately pushed me away.

"You smell like women's perfume and your breath smells like a sewer drain. Did you have fun with your idiot friends last night?"

"Quiet you," I ordered sarcastically.

"Luckily mother is at the market. Go sleep for a while before Argos comes for you."

Most days I would be with Argos early in the morning to walk down to the piers and get first look at wine and oil coming in from the Greek mainland. Today we would take our cart east to the Ionian coast road where merchants established an impromptu market once a week. Argos was already in his storefront but would not call on me for another hour. I did want to sleep more but also did not want to hear about my lethargy for not rising at proper hour.

"Wake me up in half-an-hour," I ordered Helena, to which she consented.

As I turned to enter my chamber my mother entered the apartment with our basket half full of food items.

"Good morning Andrikos darling, please take this basket from me."

She handed me the worn nest of reeds and hugged and kissed my face. I instinctively turned my head and weakly returned the hug. My mother was a short, round woman over one head shorter than I and one half head shorter then Helena. She dressed simply but was adorned with several strategically placed items such as rings, make-up and a hair beret to signal that she was no commoner. She was considered educated for a woman and always assured her two prized possessions that we were superior than the average Ilandran peasant.

"What did you do last night?" she inquired.

"Out with Nearchus for a while." I always responded with Nearchus' name when this line of questioning commenced since he was beloved by my family and was generally understood to be the more responsible of the two of us.

"I saw Nearchus up early this morning with his brother and sister," she replied with delight knowing that I foolishly left an opening for follow-up questioning.

"He retired earlier then me, so I decided to stay out with Alexandros for a while." Alexandros was the next name I would fall back on because my mother loved his jovial demeanour and kind personality. She believed him to be a bad influence on me however, but didn't worry too much since she did not believe him capable of swaying my decisions.

"And Patrochlus?" she asked unassumingly, despite this being the true intent of her entire line of inquiry. My mother also believed Patrochlus to be a bad influence on me but unlike Alexandros, understood Patrochlus was indeed intelligent and willing to put his cunning to ill use. She figured the more I was around him, the more likely I was to be involved in one of his schemes.

"He was there for a while," I replied with a little annoyance.

"Hmmph," was the only utterance she felt worthy of the subject. Despite her feelings, she did treat Patrochlus agreeably when in his presence and he went out of his way to be polite. This latter fact may have contributed to her overall disapproval of him, however, given that he was not capable of warm overtures and thus any attempt at making them were artificial. This contrasted with Alexandros who could bring a smile to the most putrid wretch. My mother was highly skilled at detecting contrived sentiments which I was frequently reminded of when I only half-heartedly hugged her or told her I loved her.

"Are you working with uncle Argos today?" she asked despite already knowing the answer.

"Yes," I mumbled.

"Did you get enough sleep?" she inquired, again, already knowing the answer.

"Yes," I muttered.

"Make sure you're at your best when working with him, he was very kind to take you on."

"Yes mother."

It now became apparent I needed to retreat to my room or I would be subject to further examination and useless conversation.

"I'm going to get ready now."

"Be careful darling," she felt compelled to add, despite there being no danger on the short walk from the front door to my bedroom.

I took a small bowl of water into my room to quickly wash myself and collapsed on my bed for a short while. My room was simple with two blankets thrown over a wooden board sitting on four legs acting as my bed and a wooden trunk containing an unimpressive inventory of worn clothes and insignificant childhood possessions. My walls were dirty and my floor was bare. A diminutive window was the only source of light in the small chamber. Sleep was elusive, however, as I kept startling to the image of Argos entering my room and dressing me down for sleeping at this late hour. I finally summoned enough motivation to end this anxiety-riddled wave of consciousness and got myself up. I drank the brackish water out of the bowl sitting on my trunk and exited our apartment to the sound of my mother reiterating me to "be careful" as I entered Argos' storefront in the adjacent room.

Chapter 3

I entered the musky store front to find my uncle behind the warn wooden counter separating empty clay amphora to discard on our journey to the Ionian road market. The store was stoic and neat, like Argos, with a bare countertop separating the entranceway from clay jugs filled with olive oil and wine along the back wall. He would occasionally have other items that he was able to procure a favourable price such as produce or even meat. Argos was not a rich man by any measure but he worked hard and never asked anyone for anything. He joked that he was the neighborhood's lackey in that his job really consisted of trekking to the docks or the Ionian road to pick up everyone's wine and olive oil. He utilized his personal relationships developed over decades to secure profitable prices on wine or oil purchased in bulk. He would load his cart with his acquired wares and bring them back to his store where many local residents were happy to buy them at a reasonable mark-up.

Argos looked up at me and instructed me to load the empty clay jars on the cart.

"You spend the night with those idiot friends of yours?" he inquired despite already knowing the answer.

"I was with Nearchus," I answered timidly. Using Nearchus' name also worked with Argos but engendered a different judgment with him than my mother. Whereas mentioning Nearchus to my mother caused her to think better of me and put her mind at ease, it induced Argos to think less of Nearchus. I was more than willing to sacrifice Nearchus' reputation in the eyes of Argos rather than uttering Patrochlus' or Alexandros' name however.

"Nearchus was up early this morning being of use to people. He tried covering up for you when I asked about your whereabouts but he clearly wasn't with you at the end of your night. Did you pass out somewhere or did you find some whore?" asked Argos, only slightly annoyed. He was certainly a responsible man but he hadn't taken a vow of chastity either. As long as I was ready to work at the appointed hour he wasn't going to get too upset.

17

"I fell asleep at Pasicrates' tavern," I answered, thinking this answer was better than the truth. I quickly realized I was incorrect.

"So you're one of those types of drunks are you? Drinking more than your little body can handle and falling asleep in front of everyone. That's not how a man drinks. You're lucky you woke up with clothes still on your back. Pasicrates is not the type to attract Ilandran aristocrats to his dump of an establishment."

Argos was of course right and I saw the error in my answer. I made the snap decision that I would tell him the truth rather than him think of me in this light since I was both proud of my drinking prowess and very concerned about Argos' opinion. This might have been his plan all along: to elicit the truth by assaulting my ego. I of course played my role perfectly.

"Well, lest you think me a pussy and a fool, I *was* with a woman last night."

"Of course you were." I felt small for being so easily provoked into divulging privileged information and this certainly wasn't the first time Argos exploited my childhood stupidity. I usually learned from each beguilement, but Argos seemed to have an endless capacity to elicit information from me in different ways. On instances where I learned from these ploys, I made haste to perform the same mental manipulation on one of my mates. Alexandros was usually the easiest target.

"You know, people will begin identifying you and your associates as criminals sooner or later and maybe have you ostracized, then I can't help you. You're not going to be happy working here with me the rest of your life and your idiot friends will eventually get you into something you can't get out of. Besides, if Leandros wants to work with me when he returns, I'll have to give it to him."

This dose of reality created a knot in my stomach for many reasons. He was right that I had little prospects in this world and I understood that his first choice would be to give his business to his war hero son. Nearchus surely would have been second in line had it not been for Argos' sense of familial loyalty. It also reminded me that I didn't have a father figure looking out for me in this same fashion. And even if I did, my father was not respected by Argos- in the same manner which Argos looked down on me. This was what my mother and uncle did not understand about me. I yearned for a strong male figure in my life to provide caring guidance and champion my best interests. Barring that prospect, at least I could take solace in the companionship of my mates. The fact Argos held no real fondness for me used to hurt my confidence. Now I used it as a source of strength, believing I didn't need anyone's help in this world. I still longed for his approval but could now convince myself I was fine without it. In this same way, my mind immediately jostled me out of this train of thought and instructed me to stop feeling sorry for myself. I obeyed.

"What would you have me do in that case?"

"You could always join a mercenary outfit assigned to the Royal Army. I of course will remain here and continue looking after your family in your absence." This suggestion took me aback as my mother had forbid the subject and it was the first time he ever raised this possibility in a serious way to me. I certainly wanted to join when I was of age, but years of Argos' disappointment in me had created an insecurity and feeling of inferiority about whether I could withstand the rigours of training or the catastrophic violence of battle. The initial training time of a new recruit weighed heavier on my nerves than the prospect of combat. In addition, the fact the subject had been banished from me by my guardians had accomplished its intended effect over the years of removing serious thought given to the matter from my own mind. This pretext served as a mental barrier for me to pursue the endeavour which I now secretly doubted my ability to succeed in. Uncle Argos didn't help my esteem in this matter but I would certainly use this opening to extract a vote of confidence from him.

"Do you think I would be a worthy soldier?" I asked, my eyes showing that only one answer was acceptable.

"I think you have the ability to succeed in most undertakings but you're lazy and irresponsible. If you truly committed to the task you could prosper but you haven't committed to anything in your life other than loving your mother and sister. But you don't need to try and love them, that comes natural; even though you'd rather spend a night with your idiot friends than enjoy their company for the evening."

This wasn't exactly the warm endorsement I was searching for but, again, Argos was correct in his analysis. There was also a small nugget of praise in his cold assessment, however, and I would continue to pull on that thread to obtain more substantive support. My uncle was being uncharacteristically frank with me this afternoon. I suspected he felt this way about me but usually he appeared not to care enough to voice an opinion one way or the other.

"Did you not engage in youthful indiscretions at this age?" I asked.

"Your father did enough of that for the both of us, I was the one that stayed home and ensured everything was in order, our mother and sister were looked after and I rose at proper hour the next morning to begin the day's work. Youthful indiscretions lead to adult vice and it led to your father being found face down in a ditch, stabbed to death and smelling of wine." Many of Argos' cautionary tales end with the discovery of my robbed and murdered father found in Miletus, the next town over from Ilandra. This of course occurred before Alexander's destruction of that city for its refusal to pay homage to our God King shortly after his liberation of Ionia.

"Let us begin our trek," Argos ordered, perhaps believing he had overstepped by bringing my father into the conversation. As we began walking I again broached the subject of joining the army of Asia Minor. Argos now acted indifferent about the topic in hopes I would let alone the idea he had mistakenly put in my head.

"We live in very perilous times now that Alexander is dead. His two successors are not capable of ruling and there are too many powerful Macedonians throughout the world to cause trouble in the absence of a strong singular ruler. I fear Greeks will be fighting each other now that the lesser civilizations are defeated. It would be a shame for you to have missed the great conquests only to be killed by a fellow Greek on soil already conquered by Alexander." Argos, as most Ionians, loved Alexander because of his successful defeat of Persian rule over our coastline. He was a proud Greek before all other things and always resented the reminder of Achaemenid dominance over the Greek cities of Ionia in the form of Spithridates, the Persian Satrap. Argos, like most of us, believed the Persians, as well as all lesser races, to be inferior to Greek civilization and

20

culture. They no doubt felt the same about us. He would always support the successor to Alexander whom he thought had the most legitimate lineage to Alexander himself. As such, he would support the current dual- successors of Alexander IV, a half-Greek infant born to Alexander's Bactrian wife Rhoxanne; and Alexander's half-brother Phillip III, a half-wit only allowed to live because of his ineptitude. Alexander's general, Perdiccas, was to act as Regent for the two until Alexander IV came of age. It appeared all the major generals of Alexander had accepted this arrangement but Argos frequently spoke of looming civil war. Many Ionians wagered that Alexander IV would not make it to his second year.

"Would you not be proud to see me fight on behalf of Alexander's rightful successors if a challenge was ever made on their legitimacy?" I asked, seeing a chance to elicit the answer I had been searching for.

"Finally, a good question falls from your tongue. Maybe you aren't hopeless after all. The answer is yes, just as I am proud to see my only son fight with Alexander at the ends of the earth against the barbarians in the name of Greece, I would be proud to speak your name in defence of all Alexander fought for. You don't tell your mother that, you understand?"

"Of course not," I assured him with a noticeable grin. The thought of Argos speaking of me as he did Leandros brought a warm comfort to my gut.

Argos quickly changed the subject to business matters lest he show more of his true feelings to me. Helena minded the store as we made our way through the city to the Ionian road. I pulled the cart full of empty amphora as was the routine. Argos had lived in Ilandra his whole life and getting anywhere in the city was a time consuming process. He would talk to a multitude of Ilandrans about the latest gossip, local politics, world events, business matters and family. Argos informed me that I was fortunate to be living in these times since there was always something to be talking about after the coming of Alexander. The day's topic in Ilandra's agora was Asia Minor as I stood with the cart patiently waiting for Argos to conclude his political conferences. The men were discussing Lord Regent Perdiccas' latest effort to consolidate Greek rule over the rebellious Asia Minor regions of Cappadocia and Paphlagonia. These areas were bypassed by Alexander and had not been fully subjugated under Antigonus' rule. Perdiccas' general, Eumenes, was to lead this effort since Antigonus had refused to do so. The crux of the discussion centred on the competence of Eumenes. Many Ilandrans had a very strong opinion about his character and his familial background despite no one ever meeting the man. They derided the fact he had been but a secretary to both Phillip and Alexander, not a military commander. They accosted his background as a Thracian and therefore could never command the respect of Macedonian regulars. Argos was at the centre of this discussion on global politics for about half an hour before signaling me to resume our trek.

We came upon the mound of clay shards where Ilandrans discard their used and empty amphora and carelessly added ours to the pile. We reached our destination shortly after and came upon a number of carts hauling a myriad of different items. Olive oil and wine were my uncle's primary concern but he again used the opportunity to inform me of how lucky I was to be living in this age ushered in by Alexander where all manner of goods from the Greek mainland could be obtained in quantities never before seen. If the Ilandran agora was where local news was discussed, the Ionian road is where it was obtained. Men travelling from the north, south, and east all could be found on the road and information was freely passed. The rumours of Perdiccas and Eumenes bringing an army into Asia Minor were true, according to a merchant who had travelled from Cilicia. A Thracian informed us that one of Alexander's greatest generals, Craterus, had travelled through Thrace into Macedonia. Craterus was a name well known in the Greek world and any news of his whereabouts was welcome. Craterus joined Antigonus at the royal court of Antipater, the ruler of all Greek possessions in Europe in Alexander's absence. This news did not seem particularly important to me but uncle Argos saw this as an ominous sign.

We encountered an old colleague of Argos named Euneas, formerly of Miletus. He was decidedly my least favourite merchant as we had been meeting with him since I was a boy. This animosity stemmed from his general disrespect of me for an unknown reason.

Being of fighting age, he never wasted an opportunity to remind me that I was not doing my part for the Greek cause. He frequently utilized the discussion of current politics to convey his negative view of me to Argos.

Once wares were obtained and information gleaned, Argos and I began our trek back to the store with each of us taking an arm of the cart since it was heavily weighted with full jugs. Taking a more direct route home allowed us to circumvent the agora which surely would have impeded our progress. Walking down a narrow street we came upon Theon and some of his vile entourage. They aggressively stared me down until we came within a few feet and he uttered my name "Andrikos" in greeting and I uttered his back. I of course lost the staring contest approaching this group but my uncle Argos held his own with the small gang, even succeeding in diverting a number of their eyes. Growing up, Theon, his older brother, and the others he kept company with, certainly took advantage of some of my insecurities to bully and denigrate me on many occasions. I was too afraid to stand up for myself physically at the time, for many of them were older and bigger than I. When I attempted to make verbal counterattacks, words did not form in a confident and coherent manner, which further encouraged their feelings of disrespect for me. Now that I was older, I began to find the right words and my physical stature had surpassed many within their group and served as a check on the others who still retained an inch or some weight over me. This situation had contributed to my feelings of inferiority and I would always go over in my head what should have been said or done while walking home after an episode of humiliation or emasculation. The correct answer usually came to me during these introspective moments while walking down the narrow paths back to my home, but I could never summon my 'wit of the alley' at the time it was needed.

Nearchus did not fare better with this group although he did not seek their approval and rarely was in their presence. They viewed Alexandros as a sort of bumbling mascot for their group and thus tolerated him in their presence as long as he did whatever act of humiliation they found comical. Patrochlus always thrived in company such as this and was often able to produce his 'wit of the alley' at proper opportunity. They saw him as a younger version of themselves and thus treated him the nearest to their equal out of our band. Despite my uncle's feelings towards my close associates, he understood we had not graduated to the level of Theon's ilk. He also understood my feelings towards Theon, since I frequently came home in varying states of anger due to his torments over the years. He knew my little band looked up to his brother and frequently warned me that once it was generally accepted that we were associates of his group, people of Ilandra would forever think me beneath them.

We arrived back on our street and pulled the cart in front of the store where I began off-loading our items and Argos began logging them in his account book. Helena greeted us and returned to the apartment to assist my mother with the evening's dinner. Argos had purchased a few items along the Ionian road to add to the night's meal which I handed to Helena and gave her a hug. After dinner I remained in the apartment to build upon the good will I felt I had engendered with Argos and called Nearchus down to spend some time with us. We drank some wine and shot dice for a while. Once my mother retired for the evening Argos spoke of all the news we had heard today and provided an impressive number of strategic military scenarios it all could mean. Nearchus and I listened intently despite Argos' penchant for the dramatic from time to time.

Argos also imparted cherished new intelligence to Nearchus and I...Leandros would be home from the eastern campaigns any day.

Chapter 4

I fell to sleep with ease that night, where my father was awaiting me. I saw him as I was walking down a dark alley. He was holding a torch and signalling me to come to him. We embraced and sat on a portico where we shared a jug of wine. His demeanour was jovial and he was genuinely happy to see me.

"Argos has got you feeling ashamed of me again. And he's got your esteem down doesn't he?" my father asked warmly. It felt good to have an older male concerned about my well being and providing words of encouragement, even if they were from a spectre.

"Is he right about us?" I asked, hoping his answer would elevate my spirits.

"He's mostly right about me, your story has yet to be written however. You don't need to join an army so that your uncle will be proud of you. It's not necessarily *what* you do, it's the way you do it. Your uncle is no war hero but he has conducted himself with honour by dutifully caring for his family members. Many people will give you respect just for joining the Greek armies but joining does not equate greatness. Many soldiers will die nowhere near a battlefield for a number of disreputable reasons. Others will die with a spear in their back while retreating. Some will not conduct themselves honourably, while only a few will become courageous leaders of men. So while joining the Hellenic cause is a good start for one's name, you have years of hard times and hard decisions to prove to yourself you're worthy of respect. Sure, you'll always be able to inflate your prowess with the other retired veterans over jugs of wine- that is a soldier's privilege, but you will always know the truth deep down. Remember, an honourable man such as Argos didn't have to fight in great battles to gain respect from those around him."

I woke early the next day and tended the store for several hours. No wares needed to be acquired so my time was spent day dreaming in between the few transactions that occurred. My thoughts frequently turned to my father's words from last night and I made several vows that if I ever was to join the Greek armies that I would acquit myself with honour.

One of Theon's minions, Hipolytus, lived near me and his family frequented our store. He was one of our few patrons of the day to purchase olive oil. He was older than I and had committed several boyhood tortures against me over the years. I had grown larger than him by now yet, he still retained an heir of superiority in my presence. He would certainly be a candidate to physically confront one day should he attempt to belittle me again. Since his acceptance of my physical stature, however, he mostly ignored me.

"Two olive oils. We will be at Pasicrates' tonight, you going to be there? I think Ganymedes wanted to speak with you." His question resembled more of a command than an inquiry.

"I probably will be, tell him I'll be around," I responded as casually as possible.

Hipolytus paid for the items and exited. It was rare for Theon and his band to request my presence anywhere, let alone his older brother Ganymedes. I would see Patrochlus and Alexandros tonight and would discuss the matter with them beforehand. Shortly after Hipolytus' departure Nearchus came down stairs and propped himself up on the countertop. I informed him of Theon's request to which he responded, "Why do you listen to those swine herds? They don't even like us and associating with them is going to get us in trouble one of these days." He had a valid point and I always did envy Nearchus' apparent level of comfort with himself. He never seemed to care what others thought of him. That was a confidence my insecurities had never allowed me to manifest.

"Well, I'll be out anyway and it won't hurt to see what they want. Are you going to raise a cup with us tonight?"

"Not tonight, my father leaves today for a fishing trek up the coast, he won't be back for three days. He'll sail up to Ephesus and fish off the coast for a few days to bring their haul to the larger Ephesian market."

"Some good places to drink and some good company to find in Ephesus I hear."

"I'm sure that's why he chose to go, vice fishing waters off Ilandra for the next three days. Anyway, he'll be gone and my mother will expect me to stick around for the majority of his absence. Why don't you remain home with us tonight? My father forgot to bring a good jug of wine." His response was yet another glaring example that his level of responsibility and selflessness far exceeding my own.

"Say hello to Argos for me then, I'm sure he'll take note of your presence and my absence this evening."

"For the best then, Leanna has chosen another over me…I would not make good company tonight. She is to be wed to some Ilandran merchant," Nearchus announced with a nervous smirk and unsteady voice.

"I am truly sorry to hear it but now that she is no longer a possibility for you I feel compelled to give my blunt opinion that she did not deserve your favour. Had you two been married, you would never receive the affections you so desired. In fact, I think this a perfect night to forget such thoughts and drink heavily with your loyal companions."

"Let's just make a clean break from that whole gang of criminals. Patrochlus probably won't come but maybe we can convince Alexandros, and, if not, it will just be the two of us and the rest be damned. I know you don't want to stay here forever and now that my younger brother is coming of age, you and I can make our own way in this world. What do you think?" Nearchus made good points and I knew I could always trust him.

"Let's revisit this tomorrow, after I speak with Ganymedes. You know I would choose you over them any day but I am looking forward to some drinking and debauchery tonight anyway."

"Suit yourself; I'm off to the market. One day you need to put this behaviour behind you." With that, Nearchus departed and I was left to my empty thoughts once more. I nodded off on several instances, each time waking in a panic for fear of Argos catching me asleep. After several more hours dusk approached and Argos walked in the store.

"Any news?" he asked while looking through the inventory.

"Nothing," I answered.

"Book." This was his command to see the summary of sales for the day. I handed him the small, battered ream of papyrus leaves that contained an account of our sales.

"Alright, I'll close up. Tomorrow I'll open and we'll take the cart to the harbour around noon." I took my leave after being dismissed and walked towards Patrochlus' neighbourhood. Patrochlus lived in a busier part of town which suited his personality and probably influenced it as well. He seemed to know everyone and the street where his small apartment was located was one of the busiest in Ilandra. He was an easy individual to find since, if he wasn't out drinking and whoring, he was sitting on the portico with Alexandros talking to this person or that.

I began thinking about the unsolicited advice I had been given over the past few days from my uncle, my father, and Nearchus. I believed Leandros would come home some day and take on the wine store with Argos which would leave me without a means to provide for myself and my family. I agreed with Nearchus that we did not need to associate with the likes of Theon, his brother, and their gang of criminals; but I did have a relationship with them and they could provide a way to earn money- albeit an immoral one. It was pretty clear Patrochlus and Alexandros were heading in that direction anyway so I decided to develop my ties with them in the short term until I could find more honourable means. Lastly, my father's words about the Greek armies lingered. Just because someone decides to join does not immediately win them respect and honour. One had to work at it every day for many years to consider one's self a worthy soldier. Joining was an important first step however and I concluded that I should continue to keep it as a serious option.

I ended my daydreaming when I came upon Patrochlus and Alexandros talking with a few of the younger boys in his neighborhood who looked up to these two older criminals in training. I greeted the two of them and told the two boys to get lost.

"So Hipolytus came by the store today and said Theon's brother wanted to speak with me tonight. What do you think it is about?" Patrochlus kept his usual stoic façade when matters of treachery were being discussed so nothing could be gleaned from his demeanour. Alexandros foiled Patrochlus' best efforts of discreetness however by first looking surprised then shooting him a grinning stare. Patrochlus returned his gaze with a disgusted sneer.

"Hipolytus?" Patrochlus asked, regaining his composure.

"Yes, what do they want?" I reiterated, perceiving they both knew something.

"Ganymedes has made inquiry about us helping him in a scheme involving trade caravans along the Ionian road. I wanted to bring you in as well and told him you are familiar with this environment and may be of use. I hope you don't mind me speaking on your behalf but you were not present and this could be our chance," Patrochlus explained. "You're not going to blow this for us right?" Alexandros now stared at me with his dumb grin while it seemed Patrochlus was not sure how I would receive this news. We had always wanted to be contributing members of Ganymedes' brood but the nature of the plot was unsettling and Patrochlus' demeanour continued to be guarded.

"Why didn't you tell me earlier?"

"Ganymedes took us in his confidence so act surprised when he speaks with you," Patrochlus' answered. He was quick to change the subject and suggested, since we had time before the appointed hour, we spend it drinking a jug of wine one of the two younger boys had just presented to Patrochlus in hopes of winning his approval. As a reward, Patrochlus called them back over and allowed them to sit in our presence while we loudly enjoyed their tribute.

As the evening wore on, I continued thinking about my meeting with Ganymedes. Surely he knew people that were also familiar with the Ionian road, why take Patrochlus' suggestion and choose me? I realized Patrochlus must think he had done me the largest consideration possible by including me and doubtless felt I owed him an insurmountable debt. Despite not feeling totally sure of this sudden thrust into prominence, I appreciated it as a gesture of friendship from an individual who always put friends over morals and appreciated friends without morals best of all.

As Patrochlus and Alexandros continued drinking and hazing the two boys who delighted in their attention, a sudden thought came to me that immediately caused concern. Could Ganymedes be planning a scheme that would affect Argos? I couldn't live knowing I contributed to the ill fortune of someone my uncle and I had done business with for years. This notion continued to fester and as we began our walk to Pasicrates' it came to me that Patrochlus had offered my name because the intended target must be someone I am familiar with. This also explained his hesitance to tell me of the plot himself. My deliberations now turned to how I could extricate myself from this predicament without raising suspicions or otherwise being ostracized.

Additionally, I began attempting to deduce a rationale for not immediately informing my uncle of any intelligence I would become aware of tonight that may hurt him or someone we know. There was the cold disposition he held towards me, there was the condescension, there was the fact that he will choose Leandros over me- but I determined none of this was cause to spite the man that looked after my family upon my father's death. My thoughts now turned to surviving the night and taking Nearchus up on his offer of ridding ourselves from these dregs.

We arrived at our destination to find it filled with its usual cast of crude revellers. Pasicrates' was a spacious, two story structure that spanned the area of several apartments. The first floor was dedicated to drinking wine and gambling. There were a number of chairs scattered around sturdy tables and several wooden beams along the outer wall that served as a place to set cups of wine. The condition of the wood was old and warped; the smell was stale, musky, and rank. After a few drinks, however, the senses numbed and these foul odours were forgotten. The floor was compacted dirt which served as a capable sponge for spilled wine, blood, and vomit. A sectioned-off area in the rear separated by a wooden half-wall served as a storage area for wine jugs and casks that were dispensed out by a toothless, depraved, yet jovial looking imp who had been there as long as I had been a patron. This creature was protected by a local colossus in Pasicrates' employ because the imp dealt with rather large sums of money. Behind the imp's station was a back room where Ganymedes, Pasicrates and a select few villains spent much of their time. As the door to this room opened and closed one could catch a slight glimpse of its inhabitants. Growing up, this was a more important sanctum to our misguided band than the Oracle of Delphi. In another corner lay three gambling tables run by the establishment. These were guarded by a large Syrian brute and were usually the origin of any altercations that occurred somewhat regularly. Better-off patrons regularly gambled at their own tables but Pasicrates' tables offered Ilandra's destitute a chance to make wager with any small amount of coin that they begged, borrowed, or stole.

The second floor of this hole was for the women and consisted of multiple closet-sized rooms. The women that occupied these quarters fit right in to the overall atmosphere of the establishment. Their appearance was hoarse and weathered through years of mistreatment. Their manner was crass and devoid of warmth through years of abuse. Being familiar with the women Ilandra had to offer, our band rarely showed these unfortunate souls any attention despite a few drunken episodes that Alexandros woke up regretting in the morning. They would be down amongst the revellers, flirting with this drunk and that one until they found an interested party. New faces were always their prime target and since Alexander's conquest of the world, new faces were streaming through Ilandra and Pasicrates' on a regular basis. The stairs leading to these fetid dens was guarded by a third fiend from Pontus who clearly held no aptitude for any other line of work. His job was to ensure the customers paid and did not mishandle the merchandise in a way that would bring down their value.

Scanning the first floor I noticed the regular silhouettes housing familiar worn and tired faces. There were also fresh visages full of life in hopes of finding their fortunes abroad. For most, Ilandra was a one night stop along their travels east. Some would linger in Ilandra's brothels, bars and gambling houses a little too long however and find themselves without enough money to continue their journey. The lucky ones would sober up and find menial employment in order to one day continue their travels. The unlucky ones could not pay their gambling debts to establishments such as Pasicrates' and never left Ilandra. As the years wore on and Ilandra saw more travellers passing through, Pasicrates had to create a system to dispose of these unlucky patrons by discreetly transporting bodies to the harbour.

Arriving at our normal table we spotted Theon and his gang drinking at their normal table across the room near Ganymedes' lair. I pretended not to notice Theon nodded in our direction to his minions with a condescending smirk as we sat down.

"So do we tell Ganymedes we are here?" Alexandros asked.

"Just be yourself, they'll get us when they want us; they know we're here. The last thing we want to look like is three dogs sitting at Ganymedes' feet waiting for him to throw a stick," Patrochlus replied. He then ordered Alexandros to get us a round from the imp to which Alexandros obeyed. We always took Patrochlus' lead in these matters, myself included, as I was feeling nervous about the whole situation.

Patrochlus and I sat quietly waiting for Alexandros to return and casually took notice of our surroundings so as not to appear we were waiting to be summoned. The local drunks were either rambling to each other or drinking alone. Some new faces were enthusiastically arguing over the current state of the empire with some supporting Lord Regent Perdiccas and the Argead line of Kings, while others favoured Antipater and Antigonus. The current theme of all similar discussions taking place around Ionia at this time was the unknown variable of Eumenes.

Other young, unfamiliar faces were discussing their future as soldiers in the Greek armies and were passing through Ilandra on their way to the ancient city of Sardis to join mercenary outfits. I naturally listened to their deliberation for some time, making sure to remember routes to be taken, places to stay, and names and locations of mercenary recruiters in Sardis. Sardis was the Western most point on the Persian Royal Road, with the Achaemenid ancestral capital of Susa being its eastern most extent. An older Royal Road connected that part of Elam with the Achaemenid's second ancestral capital of Persepolis, and pushed further east to Pasargadae and beyond. Under the Persians, and now under the Greeks, Sardis was the hub for all movement of goods, travellers, and armies from the coastal Ionian cities eastward. Thracians and Macedonians usually travelled by road to Byzantium on their way to Sardis to join the mercenary ranks; while the majority of peninsular Greeks sailed to Ephesus, with a handful of wayward travellers passing through Ilandra and Halicarnassus on their way to the inland city. Even uncle Argos understood the Royal Road to be a marvel of human achievement, despite being constructed by Persians. The road ensured expedient communication and travel throughout the empire with countless outposts for couriers and travellers. Argos was always quick to add that Alexander had of course improved the Royal Road since his conquest which allowed him to reconcile his narrative of Greek superiority.

Alexandros returned with a jug of wine and three cups. The three of us began drinking and subtly looking over to Theon's table to determine when we would be summoned. Finally Hipolytus approached and instructed Patrochlus and I to follow him. Alexandros shot an excited grin to Patrochlus to which Patrochlus broke character and grinned back. I was not in a giddy mood making my long awaited walk through the sacred inner-sanctum of our youth. As we passed Theon's table I again noticed him murmur to his sycophants with a condescending grin in my direction. Hipolytus nodded to the colossus who walked back to the rear room and alerted the occupants to our presence. The colossus returned and motioned us to come forward. Patrochlus gave me a nod as we walked past the imp to remind me to maintain my composure.

Hipolytus opened the door and we followed him into Ganymedes' presence. He was sitting around a table with Pasicrates, two intimidating foreigners that were unknown to me, and two house women filling their cups and providing enthusiastic company. The room was about ten paces by ten paces with a rectangular table in the middle and a small table in the corner holding several jugs of wine and two candles. A lamp was also on the small table with unpleasant incense billowing out. The large table had a number of candles, several jugs of wine, and plates with bones on them that had been picked clean. There were not enough chairs for the three of us to sit so we stood awkwardly in front of this panel of villains awaiting directions.

Pasicrates spoke first and ordered Hipolytus out of the room in a demeaning manner which caused me great satisfaction. He did not tell Patrochlus and I what to do however so we continued standing awkwardly in front of the table not making eye contact with any of the seated men. Pasicrates was the oldest of those assembled and had been a friend of Ganymedes' and Theon's father. He was sleight in stature with a grizzled, wrinkled face and graying nappy hair that looked to have been recently slicked back with water. He was fairly bald on top and was missing a few teeth. The few he had left were crooked, browning, and brittle. His beard looked to have been shaved about one week ago and was comprised of black and gray stubble protruding like grimy shards out of his face.

Ganymedes spoke next. Looking directly at me, "you're Andrikos?"

"Yes," I replied.

"Son of the dead Iatrokles, nephew of Argos the wine merchant?" he inquired further.

"Yes," I answered, attempting to keep eye contact.

"My father was fond of Iatrokles, he didn't like your uncle," Ganymedes stated looking directly at me. I immediately dropped my gaze to the floor but could feel Patrochlus' eyes burning a hole in my side willing me to respond appropriately. It was apparent that Ganymedes was making a direct provocative statement to test my mettle so I quickly recovered my eyes to his and replied that Argos doesn't like me, my father, Patrochlus, Ganymedes, Theon, or Ganymedes' father. This engendered a slight chuckle and nod which apparently signalled I passed the first test. Patrochlus let out a small but audible exhale.

"You," Ganymedes continued pointing to Patrochlus. "Why are you here?"

Patrochlus cleared his throat, stood up straight and replied, "Hipolytus told me you wanted to see both of us."

"Hipolytus is a fool and a coward. Are you a coward?"

Again clearing his throat Patrochlus replied, "N...No. Shall I leave?"

"Do you know anything about the Ionian Road south of here towards Miletus?"

"No," replied Patrochlus weakly.

"Then leave," was Ganymedes' final order.

Patrochlus looked longingly at me as he exited the room to sit with Alexandros and the other outsiders. Ganymedes instructed me to sit in the last empty chair at the table and motioned for one of the women to bring me a cup of wine. I fidgeted in my seat for several seconds to attain a posture I felt best mimicked the rest of my table mates. As I laboured to look my new acquaintances in the eye and

34

act as though I belonged in their presence, I quickly realized I was at a social level considerably above my lowly station.

The individual to my right was the most intimidating man I had ever seen up close. He was a good three inches taller than me and twice as wide. He had two tree trunks jutting out from his tunic comprised of muscular definition and scars. These massive arms rested on the table, bent at the elbows, and came together where he was calmly passing a knife from one hand to the other. His skin was dark and weathered; his hair was long, full and black. He looked to be about seven years older than me and was clearly not from Ilandra, nor did it seem he was passing through to join the army. He had found his fortunes heading west as opposed to east, joining the criminal underworld in Ilandra to capitalize on the influx of naïve travellers passing through from the Greek peninsula. He did not speak during my audience with Ganymedes and I found out later he was called Meric.

His colleague, Druz, sat across the table from me and was mercifully a more manageable size. He was also of a darker color with long black hair and a sharply chiseled face resembling a snake which, for purposes of intimidation, more than compensated for his somewhat diminished stature. Several scars lined his eye brow, cheek, and mouth adding to his unsettling appearance. It was apparent Druz was from the same region as the giant to my right and was clearly the mouthpiece of their partnership as he made several unpleasant comments directed towards me which certainly did not bolster my confidence during this time of unwanted elevated prominence.

Sitting on either side of Druz were Pasicrates and an unsightly house girl trying her best to not look miserable at the prospect of spending a night with the criminal. Sitting at the head of the table was Ganymedes. Alexander is at the top of my personal Pantheon but Ganymedes always made a good showing. He had short cropped hair that stood almost straight up with a youthful yet serious face. He acted the way I desired people to perceive me; he spoke the way I aspired to speak. Growing up, I desperately wanted him to notice me and even now felt a strong urge to please him despite becoming less enamoured with his world as of late. The only thread of Theon's being I ever coveted was Ganymedes' relation to him. The thought of having a living blood relation so capable of looking out for me was the only strand of respect I allowed myself to give Theon. This longing of his approval was my primary motivation for sitting in his presence at this moment.

After my cup was filled by the house woman, insults levied by Druz, and enduring an insufferable lifetime of being stared directly at by men I considered my superiors, Ganymedes finally spoke. "So, do you know why you're here?"

"It appears you are interested in my knowledge of the Ionian Road but I am unsure why. I would also caveat that my knowledge of it only extends to the immediate north and south of Ilandra and my dealings with the tradesmen who travel it regularly."

"Tell me of these dealings. What do you know of it?" Ganymedes ordered.

I finished the cup of wine as I collected my thoughts. Ganymedes immediately motioned the house girl to refill it which she complied rapidly. "Well I assume you are aware of my uncle's industry and my involvement with it. As part of my responsibilities I accompany Argos to the Ionian Road every few days to purchase wares at the ad hoc market set up on the Ionian Road just outside of the Ilandran Gate. On certain occasions I have travelled with Argos north as far as Ephesus and south past Miletus." I finished my cup of wine and was immediately given another.

"Name the merchants you do regular business with," instructed Ganymedes.

"Um, on a regular basis, we primarily deal with Agelaus of Smyrna, Damastor of Sardis, Elpenor of Ephesus, and Euneas formerly of Miletus, now from points further south." As I mentioned Euneas I noticed Pasicrates and Ganymedes look at each other. I also noticed I was getting drunk after what had become a few hours of drinking.

"Tell me about Euneas," commanded Ganymedes.

I felt very uneasy speaking about Euneas with my present company but I did not want to raise suspicion. "He peddles mostly wine and olive oil. He was from Miletus until Alexander razed the city. Now he inhabits parts further south along the Ionian Road and travels as far north as Ilandra to trade and sell with his established customers." I finished another cup of wine to calm my nerves and it was quickly refilled again.

"Have you ever known him to act as courier?"

"On occasion he has told us that he is transporting items for a fee. These are usually from former residents of Miletus who were displaced and now are attempting to move to new cities."

"Does he have security?"

"Regularly no, but when he is acting as courier he will hire two retired veterans, usually the same two individuals, as protection utilizing a portion of his courier fee as payment." This last question revealed their true intentions which, in my inebriated state, only became apparent to me as I was answering it. I thought Ganymedes perceived this realization in me, causing me to squirm a little while finishing my answer, and began considering how I would answer going forward. I did not favour Euneas but I also did not want to be the cause for his misfortune given his long relationship with my uncle.

"Just the two guards? Is his wagon covered? Is there anyone ever inside the wagon as well when he is transporting valuable cargo? Describe his wagon to me," Ganymedes further inquired.

"Euneas' wagon is not sturdy but it is fully covered. You will know it by the worn red fabric he uses as curtains for the small windows located on either side. I'm unsure as to what security measures he takes within the wagon while acting as courier since I never saw a reason to ask." I knew he never kept additional security in the wagon but I was now trying to be as vague as possible.

"At what pace does he travel from the south to Ilandra? When does he arrive here? What is your approximation of his arrival passing through the Miletus ruins?"

It now was apparent to me that Ganymedes was planning to ambush Euneas at Miletus, using the once great city's ruins and desolation as cover. It was also strange that Ganymedes would choose to divulge such details to someone like me. "I believe he begins one hour before sunrise and arrives at the Ilandra market one hour before noon. If he is continuing north to Ephesus, he will spend the evening in Ilandra and depart the next morning at the same hour.

Assuming this pace, he will pass through Miletus approximately two hours past sunrise on his way to Ilandra."

"That's about all I need to hear from you about his particulars. I am curious as to your personal beliefs about the man. Do you favour him?"

I took another large drink of wine to bide some time before answering. I was unsure how to proceed. "Honestly, he does not favour me and has shown me great disrespect on many occasions. I am not implying that someone like me garners much respect, but his contempt of me has not engendered any feelings of loyalty if that is your meaning."

"Do you believe yourself respected by the men in this room?" Ganymedes asked with some sarcasm.

This inquiry did not sit well as it looked like he was about to twist my words. "I do not believe I have done anything to earn your respect, nor do I believe I've committed an infraction or displayed an incompetence which would provoke animosity," was my very deliberate answer.

"A good answer Andrikos. That is all. Oh and it goes without saying that this conversation is to be kept secret."

With this last response it appeared Ganymedes had extracted all necessary information. He motioned me to exit and I immediately stood up as if at attention. It was a clumsy attempt however since much wine had necessitated me to use the table for assistance standing. Druz let out a contemptuous utterance and I exited the room as deliberately as possible, passing by the colossus and Theon's table. As I did so, Theon again shot me a disdainful look and whispered something to a sycophant sitting at his table. Drink had emboldened my sense of self by now, however, and I returned his expressional dagger with one of my own. This was uncharacteristic of me and certainly got Theon's attention. I didn't linger for a response to this sleight and sat down at my table to find Nearchus sharing a jug of wine with Patrochlus and Alexandros. Alexandros could not contain his excitement to see me return, Patrochlus attempted to be uninterested at first and Nearchus appeared concerned as our eyes met.

Patrochlus spoke for everyone, "Well, don't keep us waiting."

"I can't really get into the details of what was said past the time of Patrochlus' exit. It's nothing important, don't worry about it." I could see this response was a blow to Alexandros' excited curiosity and a jab to Patrochlus' ego for being asked to leave. Nearchus' eyes caught mine again to inform me that he expected to be told the details of my encounter in the very near future. My eyes replied that he would indeed, for I was going to need his advice.

"You better tell us when you can," was Patrochlus' final words on the subject. "And now let us drink to the increasingly rare appearance of our most responsible of companions," Patrochlus proclaimed putting his arm around Nearchus. "Our band is not as intimidating without you brother." Nearchus looked genuinely happy to be out with us despite his broken heart and concern over my meeting. Seeing that I made it out alright and in good spirits, he relaxed and drank his fill.

As the night wore on, the islands of revellers sitting around tables became an intermixed sea of drunks yelling, singing, and enjoying life despite whatever circumstance they had awaiting them in the morning. Our band was absorbed into this sea, still retaining its integrity, talking to a mix of familiar drunks and new travellers. Eventually the outer shell of our band brushed up against Theon's group of miscreants. The crowd had thinned considerably by this time as the hour grew late. Patrochlus and Theon were the cogs that brought our two floating groups together and we found ourselves now enmeshed. Patrochlus and Alexandros engaged Theon's sycophants while Nearchus and I talked discreetly about the meeting.

"So what happened? Everything alright," asked Nearchus.

"I will tell you the details later, for now just know that he has a thievery scheme that I had little choice but to provide information for which will help accomplish it. Nothing to worry about tonight however, let us enjoy the evening." There wasn't anything to be done till at least tomorrow and wine had lifted my spirits to a point where nothing could interrupt my level of revelry. Like many times in my life, I would drink today and worry tomorrow. Thus when Nearchus suggested we retire I would hear none of it and encouraged him to continue in the merriment.

Our two groups continued conversing in this manner until I began overhearing Theon speaking loudly in what appeared to be thinly veiled disparagements towards me. I looked at Nearchus and he agreed with my assessment and turned with me to face the conversation. As we did, Theon was completing a diatribe about 'someone' believing themselves to be important when in fact they were below swine. Years of degradation and large quantities of wine acted as an irresistible inner force compelling me to confront the villain once and for all.

"And who is this fool you speak of?" I asked brazenly with a slight slur.

"No one worth wasting another breath on," was his barbed response. He was drunk by this time as well.

"No, please continue, you've sparked my interest," I said at a loud decibel. Patrochlus, foreseeing the coming battle, grabbed my arm and offered to buy another jug. I grabbed my arm back and again encouraged Theon to continue, this time I closed the distance between us to an uncomfortable proximity. His sycophants also realized the impending clash and now lined up in formation behind him.

"Why don't you back away from me you fucking nobody," ordered Theon. We were now so close I felt his breath and saliva hit my face.

"Why don't you make me, you scared little pussy. You know you're nothing without your brother," I hissed with a confident tone. My muscles tensed with this last taunt and I felt blood rushing to my head. Patrochlus then wedged himself in between us in the hopes that a rift would reduce tensions. Patrochlus' actions were in vain, however, for I had directly challenged and disrespected Theon to the point where he would have to respond lest he be disgraced in front of his entourage. He threw a well placed jab around Patrochlus' head and squarely connected with my left cheek. I was more stunned than hurt by the blow and Nearchus immediately got in between Theon and his sycophants, convincing them to let him fight me alone. They held such little respect for our band that they agreed and turned from opponents to animated spectators imploring their leader to kill me. Alexandros and Patrochlus were in such a state of shock that they became silent bystanders, not daring to outwardly support an opponent of Theon. Thus with both sides immobilized, the battle was joined.

Theon again took a wild swing at me, this time missing my face and grazing the side of my head. Initially, I was overwhelmed by the entire circumstance and all the repercussions it entailed- causing me to hesitate in retaliation. Luckily his fortitude was underwhelming and as he threw the third punch I closed ranks with him, tripped him down onto his back and fell on top of him. Realizing his disadvantageous position, he began scratching my face, punching the side of my head, and arching his back in an attempt to get out from under my weight. I quickly jammed my left forearm against his throat to create enough distance between us to bring down my right fist onto his left eye socket. Theon was clearly hurt by this strike and changed his strategy from offense to a defensive posture, pulling me closer to him to restrain my ability to bring another blow down upon him. We were almost nose to nose now and he was spitting on me, attempting to bite me and violently screaming "I'll fucking kill you! You're dead! Dead!"

He was able to remove my left forearm from his throat which created a fleeting window of space that I exploited to bring my right elbow crashing down on the bridge of his nose. This second blow was so instinctive it was as though Theon pulled it down on himself. Blood then splattered over my arm and Theon was temporarily stunned which created another opening for me to now bring the full force of my left fist down on his right cheek which pinched enough skin against the bone to open a fissure. As I pulled my left fist back from this strike blood splattered onto my face and fist. Sensing the strength leave his body due to semi-unconsciousness and an acceptance of defeat, I grabbed the back of his neck and unloaded three right blows in quick succession which broke multiple bones in Theon's face, opened more wounds, and splattered blood over both of us.

As I wound my arm back again, it was caught by Patrochlus. I looked up at him panting, covered in blood, to see that everyone had gone quiet and was no longer looking at our scuffle. I followed their gaze to see a lifeless body lying in a pool of blood. After brief scrutiny I realized the body was Hipolytus. I looked up from the corpse to see Nearchus standing over him with a bloody dagger. He had a jolted look on his face and then met my eyes. I was too busy thinking about the repercussions of my fight with Theon to even comprehend this latest catastrophe. Nearchus snapped out of his daze, grabbed my hand and the two of us ran out of Pasicrates'. The remainder of Theon's sycophants tended to their two casualties while one of them ran after us. I sharply pulled Nearchus down a small alley, took his dagger and ambushed our pursuer as he turned the corner after us. My frenzied attack consisted of clumsily, yet violently, stabbing him in the stomach before he even saw us. My hand immediately felt warm and wet with his blood gushing from the wound. This was not a debilitating injury in the heat of the moment however and he grabbed my wrist which was too soaked with his own blood to get a good grip. As he feverishly attempted to remove the dagger I violently twisted the blade, causing his grasping hands to involuntarily open wide with pain and shock. Using this opportunity I removed the dagger and impaled his neck, opening a gaping wound which caused his body to buckle and brutally fall to the ground. I felt the blade open the skin, slice through the trachea, graze off the neck bone, and exit out the other end of his throat severing multiple arteries. This attack was so instinctive it was graceful. His body began convulsing as his neck gargled on the blood spurting out in volumes. Prior to this night, I had never been in a real fight, never stabbed someone and certainly never killed someone. I apparently held talent in all of these skills.

I stood over the corpse looking into his eyes, watching the life depart them when Nearchus pulled my arm viciously backwards and we continued our flight. He looked at me while panting heavily and exclaimed "We need to get to Eurydike's, they'll hide us." It sounded as good an idea as any and we made our way there.

Arriving at our favourite recreational destination, Nearchus pulled me back from view of the entrance. "You look like a demon. Stay back, I'll talk to her, she'll listen to me. Wipe that shit off your face in the meantime."

I wiped off as much blood and gore as I could onto my tunic. Luckily its cloth was a dark brown which helped to mask the true nature of the stain. Nearchus rushed back to me after briefly explaining the situation and we ran around back of the establishment. Eurydike opened a back door and we found ourselves entering the kitchen. She opened a flimsy wooden door to a sparsely stocked pantry and the two of us stood face to face in this cramped closet trying to catch our breath.

"What the hell happened in there?" I gasped.

"Hipolytus came at you with a knife from behind once you started winning. I came in from the side and opened his stomach with a hole the size of my fist," Nearchus replied panting.

Understanding exactly what he had done, I hugged him, told him I loved him, and assured him we would get through this. "How long should we wait?" I asked.

"I don't know. I think we stay here for an hour or two until they stop looking for us in the immediate vicinity. Then we need to get back to our home to ensure they don't try and retaliate there. If we can avoid them till morning, we should be in the clear for several hours. These people don't make moves like this in daylight." Nearchus' plan sounded logical and the two of us sat down and waited.

"I don't think Ganymedes will retaliate against me for this. I seemed to have pleased him tonight," I stated after a long silence.

"What about me?" Nearchus asked sarcastically.

"I saw that Hipolytus means nothing to Ganymedes tonight so, unless Theon convinces him to move against you, you may be safe for now."

"What did he want with you anyway?" inquired Nearchus

"Apparently a friend of my uncle's will be couriering something valuable and Ganymedes means to attack him near the Miletus ruins."

"What are you going to do about it?"

"I don't know, let's worry about the immediate issue and we'll talk to my uncle about Euneas tomorrow." We sat in silence for another hour before we decided to sprint back to our house while we still had the cover of darkness. Nothing was stirring in Ilandra and we avoided all major roads. We came upon our building and entered my apartment silently. We figured if anyone was to come, they would arrive at my apartment first. There was still two hours till daylight so we opened a jug of wine, changed out of our blood-soiled clothes, and waited for the sun to rise. When it did, we retired.

I was roused from sleep late the next morning by a familiar form. When I opened my eyes I saw Leandros standing over me.

Chapter 5

Leandros' sudden appearance in my quarters did not register for a short while as I woke fairly hung over. Normally after waking from an evening where I committed some drunken transgression I have a second or two of peace before remembering my actions and dealing with the repercussions. Leandros' presence had interrupted my normal mental routine and I thought I may still be dreaming. I became overjoyed and hugged him rigorously, all while the evening's events cascaded over my mind, triggering a large pit in my stomach. It was early in the morning and I conveniently decided to enjoy Leandros' safe return with my family for a few hours before divulging last night's news to Argos.

I walked out of my bedroom behind Leandros to see him heavily favouring his right leg as he laboured to manoeuvre into our main room. I entered to find my mother, Argos, and Helena all standing with beaming smiles and cheerful laughter. I enthusiastically joined in the celebration lest anyone think something was wrong or that I wasn't elated to see my long departed cousin. I then declared I would go wake Nearchus for he too would want to hear the first recitation of Leandros' adventures with all of us. While this reason was factual enough, I knew I would need to calm him down and manage our grand disclosure to guard against him waking up, running down stairs, and blurting out our murderous night in front of my whole family in their time of merriment.

I ran upstairs and walked into Nearchus' apartment as I have been accustomed to doing my whole life. His family did not take much notice of my intrusion except to inform me he was still sleeping. His mother, sister and younger brother, Argeaus, were all doing some form of house errand when I triumphantly proclaimed that Leandros had returned, to which they all let out excited exclamations and made their way downstairs- which was my intent. I then walked into Nearchus' room and stirred him to consciousness. He woke with a melancholy disposition and I quickly advised him what had transpired. He agreed with my suggested course of action and we walked down stairs, took a deep breath, and joined our families in my apartment.

"Tomorrow I will speak with Ilandra's governing council and will have you officially recognized as a favoured son of Ilandra and war hero," pronounced Argos. "Perhaps you too will find yourself sitting on the council some day. Helena, go fetch us some wine."

"The good fortune of not dying does not render one a hero father," Leandros retorted clumsily with a little embarrassment.

"First of all, you are a contributing member of Alexander's great world conquest and the entire world is now Greek. Second, you are a contributing adult male in this extended family and we will all do what we must to elevate our status," Argos explained. This declaration was received with earnest nods by all in attendance. "I understand a man's desire to be humble but you must think of everyone that means the most to you now. But enough of politics, we have all assembled to sing your praises and listen to your adventures." Argos' plans for Leandros had certainly matured and were now a long way from him simply partnering in the wine store.

As we sat down I whispered to Nearchus to hold his tongue until after Leandros had finished because my uncle would most likely send the women to the market to procure items for a celebratory dinner in Leandros' honor. At that point we could send Nearchus' younger brother away and the four of us could discuss our predicament. Nearchus nodded his head in agreement. I added that we had waited so long for this day, let us try and enjoy it for an hour before the harsh repercussions from our actions take hold.

Leandros attempted to begin his tale in Babylon, the launching point of Alexander's great eastern campaign, but Nearchus and I quickly insisted he commence with his initial training. Leandros yielded and told of his harsh ordeal from early recruitment to finally joining the main force in Babylon. These recruitment outfits were run by Macedonian veterans of severe temperament whose job it was to provide trained bodies to the Macedonian juggernaut that could keep up with its rigours from the onset of their enlistment.

"The purpose was to take non-Macedonian clumps of shit like myself and mould us into something which could breathe the same air as the Macedonian regulars," explained Leandros smiling. "At least they considered Ionians Greek. Non-Greeks were treated like dogs and slaves." He went on to describe waking up before first light and toiling till evening; consuming meager amounts of food and water each day while being forced to conduct painfully strenuous activity; being subjected to harsh discipline and frequent beatings; the regular occurrence of new recruits dying or deserting; endless training with the heavy and cumbersome eighteen foot sarissa spear; marching countless miles; and the hours of drilling in formation under the hot Persian sun. Leandros' cruel narrative weakened my resolve for war and glory and my inner insecurities surfaced about my future prospects once again.

Leandros spoke of the journey through Asia Minor along the Royal Road with his detachment of recruits on their way to joining Alexander's army in Babylon. He told of leaving Sardis and marching to the city of Gordium where Alexander famously untied the Gordian knot. There he saw the famed burial mounds of King Midas and his father, Gordias, who had ties to Macedon. From Gordium Leandros' outfit marched east on their way to the northern Mesopotamian city of Arbela with its ancient citadel located on top of a large central mount. Alexander's legendary Battle of Guagemela had taken place just west of Arbela several years earlier. They departed the Royal Road at Arbela and travelled south along the Tigris River, finally reaching Babylon several weeks after they began their journey.

"My harrowing experiences of initial training ended when our group finally arrived at the outskirts of Babylon," Leandros reassured his captive audience. "There, those of Greek and Macedonian heritage who proved themselves competent along the journey were assigned to the Macedonian Foot Companion Phalanx. All non-Greeks and Greeks lacking fortitude were assigned to either the light infantry Peltasts or to support and quartermaster units. I of course represented Ionia well on our little trek and was assigned to a Phalanx Lochos. Several sixteen-man Lochos' made up a Syntagma. The majority of my Syntagma were men from the Pella region of Macedon, thus we were the Pella Syntagma. Several Syntagma cohorts made up a Taxis. Several Taxis made the Phalanx. Many of my new Lochos mates did not initially view me as their equal due to

47

my inexperience and lack of Macedonian heritage however, and I was treated quite harshly for some time."

"And what of Babylon?" my mother interjected impatiently, wishing Leandros tell us something positive about his experiences. "Is it the grand city we've all heard of?"

"It certainly looked like it was," replied Leandros. "The majority of phalangites making up the Foot Companions camped outside the city and were not frequently allowed within its walls, and if so, only in small numbers. Myself, being newly arrived and lowest among them, never stepped foot in the city. Babylon was a grand site however, encompassing many miles of urban buildings, parks, public spaces, temples, statues, and palaces. The city was surrounded by an imposing wall with temples to ancient gods and the central palace of Nebuchadnezzar jutting out over the city skyline. The Euphrates River ran through the center of the Babylon making it a congested thoroughfare of every manner of vessel- from the most decrepit dingy to the most royal flotillas."

"I arrived at a time of great activity among the army," Leandros continued. "Alexander was ready to continue his push east to conquer the remainder of the Persian Empire and capture King Darius once and for all."

"So did you see him?" asked Nearchus, apparently compartmentalizing our predicament quite well and getting caught up in the adventure.

"I did see him on occasion, but not yet," answered Leandros. "Because my arrival coincided with the final preparations for the eastern campaign, each day was filled training, drilling, equipping, organizing, and conducting every manner of human activity outside the city walls. When the day arrived to begin the march east, the army lined both sides of the city's Processional Way where we saw him exiting the blue Ishtar Gate, leading the Companion Cavalry out of the city. He looked the same as he did after the Granicus River those many years ago despite having sustained several injuries through hard campaigning. His Companions were followed by the Hypaspists, his elite infantry drawn from high-born Macedonians who also quartered within the city. The Hypaspists are now known as the Silver Shields since the India Campaign under the commands of Generals Nicanor and Seleucus. Our Foot Companion Phalanx fell in after the Silver Shields and was followed by the Macedonian elite light infantry Peltasts, Greek hoplite mercenaries, Cretan archers, barbarian mercenaries, siege craft, and finally the support soldiers, servants and baggage trains."

"Our march from Babylon to Susa was straightforward and no army was fielded to confront us. Alexander's army had a considerably small number of baggage and servants compared to armies of comparable size which allowed us to cover greater distances in shorter duration. We reached the glittering city of Susa, the winter capital of the Achaemenid Dynasty, in twenty days and found its doors opened to us. Our army confidently marched through the city's main boulevard and Alexander secured its treasury, instantly making him the richest man in the world. Where Babylon was remarkable for its sheer enormity, Susa was remarkable for its opulence. It was truly a royal seat of power not matched in the Greek world."

Leandros' description of superior Persian cities caused Argos to rustle in his seat, "a lot of good it did them," he growled. "Any woman can decorate a pretty home but it takes a man to defend it."

Leandros gave a condescending smile and continued his narrative. He clearly had been exposed to spectacles unimaginable to his audience yet still understood our narrow minded view of the world. "Yes father, they certainly cowered in our mighty wake."

"Once Susa was secured Alexander hurriedly continued our march east towards the other Achaemenid ceremonial capital of Persepolis where he meant to take the city before its vast treasury could be emptied. To achieve this goal, Alexander led an elite detachment on a direct route to the city while the main body, myself included, marched along the ancient Achaemenid roads. The entire army wintered in Persepolis where we ate, drank, trained and planned for the coming campaign season. Persepolis is a city of extravagant architecture and even a lowly Ionian Greek such as I was allowed to step foot into the palaces of Xerxes, Darius, Tachara, Hadish, Apadana, as well as the palace of one hundred columns."

"On one evening of revelry, the Palace of Xerxes was burned to the ground with its flames spreading to much of the city. We were called to fetch water but saw our leaders adding to the flames when we arrived. Thus we dispensed of the water and found kindling of our own to contribute. Many Greeks viewed the action as revenge for the Persian's destruction of Athens and the Acropolis one hundred years earlier. Others saw Alexander's actions as a confirmation that he did not intend to remain in Persia and we would all see our homes again someday. Most believers in the latter view would be sorely mistaken."

"The Persians deserve everything they got from Alexander for their previous invasion of Greece!" Argos interrupted. Leandros ignored the outburst and continued.

"In early spring the Achaemenid summer capital of Ecbatana became Alexander's goal in his campaign to capture Darius and conquer the remaining Persian Satrapies. It was rumoured Darius fled the Battle of Gaugamela with his surviving generals to the Median city and Alexander's scouts confirmed the Persian King's presence attempting to organize and raise another army from his eastern Satrapies using Ecbatana as a base of operations. Among Darius' generals with him in Ecbatana was Bessus, a royal family member and Satrap of Bactria. Bessus had commanded the Persian left flank at Gaugamela. On our march to the summer capital we learned Bessus had Darius killed and proclaimed himself the rightful successor to the Persian throne. He anointed himself Artaxerxes V and retreated east to Bactria where he attempted to raise an army amongst his allies in familiar territory. Alexander was outraged by this act of regicide and gave Darius' remains full funerary honors. Bessus now became the primary target of our army. Ecbatana submitted without a fight and Alexander utilized the city as a communications centre and treasury to store the Persian fortune looted from Susa and Persepolis."

Upon leaving Ecbatana, Leandros now entered a world completely unknown to us. The world he had just taken us through was barely recognizable other than a vague familiarity with names of large Persian cities. Veterans of the eastern campaigns were only now beginning to return to their homes and filling in the details of Alexander and the east. Leandros had a rapt audience and we all felt we were receiving knowledge reserved for the Gods.

"We pushed further east past the riches of Media and into the rugged regions of Parthia and Aria pursuing the imposter. Bessus was not in a strong position, however, since most of the empire was defeated and his standing in Bactria was severely diminished. Spitamenes, a tribal war lord from Sogdiana, a wild land north of Bactria inhabited by Scythians, eventually arrested Bessus and presented him to Alexander who promptly had the pretender brutally killed according to the Persian punishment for regicide."

"So were you in any battles?" asked Nearchus' brother Argaeus impatiently.

"Let him tell the story," chided Nearchus' mother.

"Yes, I'll get there," Leandros reassured. "To this point, however, I had not really seen the violence of warfare. We had marched for months and the only action the army had seen since my enlistment were by some scout forces. Some of the new soldiers worried that Alexander had already defeated all of our enemies and we would never see combat. That all changed, however, when we entered Bactria and faced the Scythians."

"We crossed the Oxus River and passed through the surprisingly large and bustling city of Maracanda where we reached the northeastern most limit of the former Persian Empire. Alexander wished to shore up his northern boundary along the Jaxartes River in Sogdiana and it was here, at the northern edge of the world, that I saw the human potential for unbelievable violence, as well as the true military genius of our King."

"The Scythians were a frustrating enemy to both our army and to the Persians before us. They could mass a cavalry force quickly, conduct a targeted strike, then disappear into their wild, uncivilized country to the north. Alexander induced them to stand and fight at the Jaxartes by exploiting their urge to avenge the Scythians' historic defeat by the Macedonians under Alexander's father Philip II- resulting in the death of the infamous Scythian King Ateas. Alexander also allowed the Scythians to think they had the tactical advantage over our army. The Scythians cannot be blamed for believing this ruse, however, since most of our lower-level commanders believed it to be true as well."

51

"The Scythian enemy, led by the warlord Satraces, took up position on the opposite bank of the Jaxartes River and intended to fire upon us with his archers as we crossed before meeting us en masse at the opposite bank. I had never been more scared in my life stepping on to an unsteady raft made of wooden planks and inflated cow skin- readying to face a massive force of barbarians screaming as they waited to butcher us on the other side. I was able to suppress these fears and present a stoic appearance- however others did not fare as well. I could hear faint whimpering from several members of my Syntagma and two individuals vomited next to me which brought the wrath of our Lochos' Commander, the Lochagos."

Nearchus and I looked at each other with a smile during Leandros' description; this truly was a hero's tale not properly conveyed in his letters home to us over the years. Argos remained statuesque with an underlying look of immense pride on his face. Our mothers displayed overemphasized gestures of concern as if they were painted on an urn or performing a pantomime routine.

"Alexander ordered the Macedonian army to cross en masse which prevented the Scythians from overwhelming us at any one point with their artillery. Their archers and bolt weapons were too few to effectively stop the mass crossing. The site of tens of thousands of Greeks fording the Jaxartes River at the northern edge of the world was awe inspiring. The Scythians loosed their arrows on us and never had I seen the sky become so engulfed by instruments of violence as it did then. They began landing all around me, making a low pitch whistling noise. Some hit our upright sarissas and lost their lethal trajectory, others grazed helmets, cuirasses and limbs leaving nicks, scrapes, and full impalements. Shrieks began crying out as unlucky phalangites were hit in their shoulders, necks, faces, arms, and chests. One arrow grazed my shoulder, another ricocheted off my helmet and I worried I would not be able to summon the necessary fighting spirit to meet a rested enemy on the opposite shore. Our Lochagos' recognized our demoralized state and began encouraging us and screaming profanities to the enemy which emboldened many of us to join in- some out of frustration in our situation, others out of sheer terror."

"Just as I was beginning to curse Alexander for sending us to inevitable slaughter, his military genius was revealed. He had kept our siege engines and archers hidden in the rear on our side of the river and now unleashed a torrent of death upon the heads of our enemies. It was a remarkable spectacle to behold overhead with arrows and bolts heading towards us and flaming boulders, arrows and bolts raining down on the enemy, all passing each other directly above us. Our barrage of projectiles overwhelmed our foes who began pushing back off the river bank to escape our fury. Alexander's actions not only created a large buffer for us to safely land on the other side of the river, it also heavily diluted the number of arrows and bolts the enemy could muster in their attack. Now we all felt the momentum and morale shift and the river became a sea of blood curdling screams by thousands of Greek soldiers praying to Ares for a chance to cross the river alive and meet the Scythians in battle. Our raft reached the opposite bank and we disembarked to see a demoralized and retreating enemy before us. It became clear that the Scythian cowards were going to withdraw into their rotten, barren country only to fight us again at another time and place of their choosing. Here again, Alexander showed his strategic mastery by clandestinely sending a large detachment of mounted spearmen to cross the Jaxartes several miles downriver and ride round behind the enemy to prevent them from escaping as he knew they would. This flanking action successfully held the fleeing Scythians in a fixed position, allowing the infantry to close with and massacre them."

It seemed as though Leandros was going to end the narrative of the battle at this point without further elaboration. Nearchus, Argos, and I at once implored him to give us more details. It was clear he did not want to go into the particulars of combat but understood the enthusiastic mood his story had engendered in his audience and indulged us.

"Once the majority of the army had disembarked, our commanders ensured we were in proper formation before advancing- despite everyone's eagerness to charge a fleeing enemy. The Commander of our Phalanx, General Craterus, called the Phalangiarch, controlled his various Taxis, each commanded by a Strategos, utilizing various horns and flags. I finally saw the fruits of my endless training when the entire Phalanx formed on the opposite side of the Jaxartes and began marching forward as one. The front lines of the enemy facing us were in a state of confusion owing to their inability to retreat which was being obstructed by Alexander's flanking cavalry. The importance of morale and momentum cannot be overstated in pitched battle and our commanders continuously rallied us to a fevered state as we marched towards the disordered Scythians."

"Because I had shown promise through our march to Sogdiana I was placed fourth in our Lochos column which meant my spear point was part of the initial teeth bourn by the front five rows of our Phalanx. Our Lochagos was first in the column, with junior officers at the eighth and sixteenth positions for best control of the men. The enemy soon accepted retreat was not possible and hurried to form a cohesive front line to face us. They were dressed in thick, long sleeved tunics, some ornately decorated with polished metal. The Scythians wore long trousers and high boots. Their heads were adorned with a helmet that tapered up to a point with flaps hanging down to protect their ears and neck. Their facial appearance was that of a barbarian with long dense beards and bushy eye brows. I could see individual faces now as we neared battle. Both sides were letting out shouts of bloodlust as our skirmishers began loosing their projectiles which added to the enemy's confused state. The Phalanx maintained a steady, deliberate march forward as the barbarians ran at us like a disorganized murderous mob. As the two armies joined battle I felt a jolt back as if two mountains had collided and our forward momentum ceased. I began hearing the shrieks of impaled men and the violent cacophony of screaming and shouting every obscenity known to the Gods. My sarissa point had not yet reached the enemy despite our front line inflicting heavy initial damage. Shortly after the impact, my Lochos mates began pushing me forward and it felt as if I was holding up all the men who were behind me. The only thing keeping me from falling over was the amount of weight I was now exerting on the phalangite in front me. This crush of inertia continued to the Lochagos in front who had the unenviable task of leaning forward and advancing on our enemies. Our Syntagma began lurching forward. We took several hardy steps forward to where I could see the point of my sarissa within striking range of enemy soldiers that had survived the opening charge. Despite being many feet away from the foe I wound my sarissa back slightly and thrust a precise blow to the chest of a Scythian who was preoccupied engaging a Macedonian on the front line. After the initial impact I felt his legs give out from under him which forced the front of my sarissa down as he fell, trapping my spear in between his ribs. I had to give several vigorous pulls to free the point from his corpse. As I did so I saw another Scythian within range and, in one motion, I released my spear from the corpse and rammed its point into the stomach of the second barbarian. He hunched over the spear point as well but this time I pulled it back before his weight could force it down again."

"Sensing the enemy was losing heart, our army took several more steps forward and I now found myself in the second position within my Lochos due to my Lochagos being injured and the soldier behind him being killed. As we moved forward we began trampling over fallen Scythians. Some were still clinging to life as they were trampled by the Phalanx. My boots became saturated with a foul concoction of sweat, blood, vomit, bile, gore, piss, and shit as various bodies laid beneath us with their stomachs speared open and their bowels released. The smell is now what I remember most. The excitement of the moment, coupled with the stench of death, overwhelmed my faculties, forcing me to vomit on the heels of the phalangite in front of me. Being in the first position and engaged in heavy fighting, he did not notice this transgression. After vomiting I became extremely dehydrated and my mouth completely dried up. I began panting and struggled to find breath. Wounded Scythians were clawing at my feet trying to stand themselves up to avoid being crushed. This forced me to begin violently stomping in their skulls with my heel as we continued to march forward. I caved in several Scythian skulls in this manner and, to this day, can recall the way that wicked act felt under my feet. The battle continued in this way for another hour with me impaling several more Scythians and incrementally moving forward over the slain corpses until our line finally met the flanking Macedonian cavalry and the battle was won."

Leandros now attempted to end his account of the battle but I insisted that he describe what happens after such a battle is won. My sentiment was shared by the other males of the audience and Leandros reluctantly continued.

"Once the battle is over, all captured enemy survivors are taken prisoner. For non-Greek barbarians such as these, the army will keep most of the officers for ransom and murder the rest. This ignominious task is unfortunately reserved for the lower ranks of infantry such as me. After the hostilities ended our Syntagma Commander keeps the unit together. The wounded Greeks are carried off, prisoners are guarded and enemy wounded are murdered where they lay with a sword thrust to the throat or back of the head. The Syntagma Commander then decides which of the enemy officers will be ransomed and has them bound and taken to the rear. He then commands his Lochagos' to produce men to promptly murder the remaining prisoners. Some enjoy this task, others incrementally lose their soul with each sword thrust, but disobeying direct orders is unthinkable. I can still remember looking into the eyes of these condemned men just as I stabbed them in the heart or throat. The dead bodies and baggage train are then looted for valuables, although Scythians do not have much by way of baggage trains. Alexander surveyed the carnage's aftermath and personally congratulated those identified to him as having distinguished themselves in battle. He then went right into erecting defenses and laying the foundation for a new city, Alexandria Eschate- 'the farthest'."

"During this time Alexander had dispatched a contingent to quell a small rebellion led by the barbarian Spitamenes- the same barbarian who delivered the imposter Bessus to Alexander several months earlier. The warlord ambushed and annihilated this detachment and exploited his success by waging a year-long insurrection against the inadequately garrisoned Greek cities and forts of Bactria and Sogdiana. Spitamenes now became Alexander's primary target and we waged a hard campaign against the warlord who relied on his Scythian roots through hit and run attacks, feints, and tactical retreats rather than standing to face our army in open contest. The army was frustrated but Alexander meticulously established fortified positions and tribal alliances along the Bactrian-Sogdiana frontier. His tireless efforts eventually succeeded in isolating Spitamenes, forcing open combat between the brigand and a contingent led by Alexander's general Coenus at Gabai near Marakanda. Coenus's forces defeated Spitamenes which eliminated all support he enjoyed from tribal leaders and his Scythian allies. Spitamenes' head was delivered to Alexander by his surviving followers shortly after the battle as a gesture of repentance for siding against the God King. The defeat of Spitamenes signalled the end of organized resistance within the Persian territory and the Persian Empire was totally defeated. Spitamenes' daughter, Apama, was later bequeathed to Alexander's general Seleucus, Commander of the Silver Shields."

"There were hopes within the ranks that we would return home, or at least back to Babylon, soon after Alexander's victory over Spitamenes and his successful conquest of the Achaemenid Empire. The Persian Empire was not enough for the greatest general in history however, especially when another great civilization, rumoured to be even wealthier, lay so tantalizingly close...India- the fabled land visited by Dionysus and Herakles. We endured a grueling winter in Bactria and made ready for the campaign the following year. The men began to grow weary of another conquest so far from their homes. The defeat of Persia had made many among the army rich and their mettle began to soften. The more inexperienced soldiers wished to push on so they too could become weary of combat due to the accumulation of great wealth. Sensing this sentiment, Alexander gave a rousing speech where he declared 'nothing to be more slavish then the love of pleasure and nothing more princely than the life of toil.' He finished this speech by burning his own baggage accumulated since leaving Ecbatana. His words and deeds inspired the men to do the same who then pleaded with him to continue his conquest to the ends of the earth."

"We marched south through the Khyber Pass towards the Hydaspes River into India where we encountered several tribes of strong spirit that marshaled great resistance. Each minor victory against these impoverished savages cost a vast quantity of blood, sweat, and exhaustion from the army...And then the rains came. The rains of this region are as nothing ever witnessed in the Greek or Persian world. An immense torrent of water inundated the army for weeks on end. The individual drops varied from the size of a child's fist to the smallest spray of wet that formed an unending stinging mist that tormented us unceasingly. This constant deluge, coupled with the persistent harassment from hostile clans along our march, took its toll on the army's morale. Under these conditions our clothes rotted, wounds festered and refused to heal, disease was rampant, food spoiled, and marches were agonizing. Despite our suffering, Alexander was in good spirits and rallied us to continue, reminding us that we were walking in the footsteps of Dionysus and Herakles."

"As we continued our march we entered the boundary of the first organized kingdom of India ruled by King Porus. This man was of an enormous physical stature and intended to meet our army in open battle, thus becoming Alexander's new primary target. The two armies met on opposite banks of the Hydaspes River in torrential downpour and a great battle was fought along its bank. It was my second, and last, major battle of the far eastern campaign."

"Alexander conducted numerous feints up river which eventually had its intended effect of lulling Porus into complacency, allowing him to surreptitiously lead a contingent several miles north of the standoff, eventually cross the river and attack Poros' right flank. As Porus received word of the crossing he immediately dispatched a contingent of infantry, chariots, and elephants to meet the flanking Macedonian detachment. As the two sides skirmished outside of our line of sight, the bulk of Alexander's force remained in position along the river's bank, performing numerous crossing ploys to fix Porus' main body, preventing it from assisting in defense of their right flank. Alexander's detachment defeated Poros' right flank and General Craterus now led the main body across the river where our force prohibited Porus' escape and the battle was won."

"Porus and his army fought with unbelievable perseverance in the face of certain defeat, inflicting heavy casualties on our army despite eventually surrendering. It was here, sensing imminent victory, that I foolishly let my guard down and an Indian pike was stabbed directly into my thigh. The pain was so sudden and acute my senses left me and instinct took over. As my assailant pulled his pike from me to deliver a death blow, I grabbed the shaft and pulled him closer where I swiftly stabbed him in the face in a blind fury. We fell to the gore-soaked ground as one and I began to lose consciousness. I lay there, staring into the dead face of my assailant, and used my last seconds of cognizance to tightly tie a piece of leather around my thigh above the wound to mitigate my blood loss. I then stuffed a piece of cloth into the wound and sunk into a dark sleep."

"I later found myself in the surgeon's tent where hundreds of men lay, some writhing in agony, others in quiet shock. The surgeons did what they could for as many Greeks as possible which included occasionally delivering a swift death blow to the back of their heads. One next to me had been gored and trampled by an elephant and was in remarkable pain. No one could believe he still drew breath. Finally, Alexander himself held his hand, prayed to the Gods, positioned the nail in back of his head, and brought down the hammer of mercy, bringing instant peace to the sufferer."

"I later learned that Alexander was so impressed with Porus' personal courage that he allowed the King to retain his realm, subservient to Greece, and became his ally. The battle had a severely negative effect on our army however. Reports began coming in of kingdoms, vastly larger than that of Porus, massing immense sums of men and war elephants to confront our ever dwindling and battered numbers of Greeks. Several instances of mutiny began occurring within our ranks. Some of the differences were reconciled, others were settled through violence in the dark of night. When Alexander wished to lead us further south into India, the army as a whole finally refused. I am ashamed to say that I too was of the same mind as the rest, despite being unable to walk and lying in an infirmary barge along the Indus River."

"He relented to his army's wishes and began travelling down the Indus River, subduing fierce tribes along the way. The surgeons deemed my injury severe and I was to be brought back to Babylon by ship. I wandered in and out of consciousness for the next two weeks but I began to return to life once we successfully navigated the Indus River and boarded sea-faring vessels to return to Babylon via the outer ocean. My expedition home has been a long and arduous one given my permanent injury, but alas, I am home amongst family and friends in the place of my birth and eventual death."

Chapter 6

The room was silent for a few moments after Leandros ended his heroic tale. Argos then leapt to his feet and proposed we all drink to his son's role in the Greek conquest of the world, to which we all enthusiastically complied. Argos continued that he would have Leandros' adventures recorded in the city's archives in the near future. Nearchus shot me a look telling me that our joyous procrastination had come to an end and now must get serious about our situation. Understanding his concern, I proposed a celebratory feast to be made this night and Argos agreed. He ordered the women to market to procure supplies which would give us two hours to talk.

I was finding myself unable to broach the subject despite being willed by Nearchus to the point where I could feel his gaze long after I broke eye contact with him. Leandros perceived the tension between us and asked, "I am back after seven years and I come home to you two morose eunuchs sharing an awkward silence?"

Argos now joined in, looking directly at me, "What's the matter with you?"

Nearchus expelled a sudden burst of twaddle as if it was shot from a bow within his throat, "We are in trouble Argos and we need your help."

Argos saw in his demeanour that whatever vexed us was more than a simple boyhood matter. His face became grave and he tensed up in his chair. "You see son, these two, your cousin in particular, have tried their best to become involved in the basest elements within this city and frequently find themselves in sordid situations."

"Uncle, now is not the time for your tedious lectures, keep quiet and listen to what we have to say for it affects all of us!" I blurted out. My outburst took everyone in the room aback, myself included, for I have never dared speak to my caretaker in that tone before. My desperate behaviour curbed Argos' anger and he now became very concerned.

"Alright, alright, tell us what happened," he urged with a caring disposition.

I recounted the previous night's events, beginning with my summons by Hipolytus, followed by the revelation of Ganymedes' plot, the fight with Theon, the murders, and the escape. After a brief pause, Leandros stood and spoke first.

"This is the state of affairs I return to? Ganymedes was a dreck, a criminal, and a pimp even before I left and now Andrikos is close enough to this villain that he summons him freely by name?"

"I've never spoken to him before last night," I pleaded.

Suddenly Argos stood up and smacked me across the face and shouted, "Shut up you pathetic little shit! You've been begging his favour for years now, like a dog! Now you have it!"

"You are right uncle, and you've always counselled me against it. I didn't listen before but now I see you were right all along," I admitted.

"Don't try and sell me an act of contrition now boy, we're too far gone for that. You speak words of repentance only because of the situation you now find yourself. Had last night's events turned different, you might still be on the path of robbing a fellow merchant like some brigand scum. Maybe even rob me!" These words cut the deepest for it was clear to me Argos was casting me out of his trust and purging me from his familial responsibilities.

"Uncle please! I made a vow last that night that I would alert you of the plot and cease all relations with men of that strain!"

"It is true," added Nearchus somberly. "Such a vow was made in my presence." In fact these words were not broken with Nearchus before the altercation but he knew that supporting evidence coming from him would add needed weight to my case in my uncle's eyes. He was correct and my uncle sat down and moved back from the dark road his emotions were steering him.

"Alright then, we will decide our course of action, for Ganymedes must be either appeased or dispatched tonight. Andrikos is right; this affects all of us, including Leandros, whose name is now ringing the market as we speak- courtesy of our women to be sure. The fact that no one has seen him in years may still be of use, however."

The four of us debated our options ranging the spectrum from killing Ganymedes to prostrating ourselves to beg forgiveness. Leandros wanted to kill his entire network that instant. Argos was concerned about how to navigate the situation in a manner consistent with keeping our family in the favour of the Ilandran ruling factions. Ganymedes was certainly known as a villain but his nefarious dealings inevitably intertwined with powerful economic interests which more than suggested surreptitious alliances with influential Ilandrans.

Argos posited, "Eliminating Ganymedes is the only way forward. Anyone he was working with will publicly renounce him and no one will admit to each other their involvement with his business dealings. Any resolution that leaves him alive will render us vulnerable to furtive manoeuvring by his criminal network with secretive top cover from anonymous influential politicians."

I informed Argos of Ganymedes' two eastern dogs that now habitually heeled at his side and suggested that Pasicrates also would need to be dealt with. "That's now four career murderers we will need to purge. We are only four ourselves with only one of us being trained in combat," Argos concluded.

Leandros now added strategy to the discussion while glaring in my direction. "Andrikos makes a good point, surprisingly, however we have several advantages over our opponents. From what my father says, these two little shits are intimately familiar with their daily routines, we know the size and capability of our enemies, and they will be unaware of all the assets we can bring to bear."

"I can muster support from the Ilandran merchants, maybe three to five men," Argos speculated, seemingly agreeing with Leandros' assessment of the situation. "Several of them already blame Ganymedes' band for stolen wares over the years, some owe me favours. If we can get five to join us in eliminating this blight from our city, we may have a chance."

"His infirmed brother Theon should not escape this scheme," I added. "Allowing him to live will breed a mortal enemy of this family for years to come. I will dispatch him myself after our plan has been executed before word of our deeds reaches his bed chamber."

"That is a secondary consideration at this point. I think we are in agreement as to what has to be done concerning the primary matter at hand. Even if I can convince others to help us, we must decide how best to employ them. From what the boys say, it appears we must take Ganymedes' two foreigners out first before attempting open confrontation. I believe a horse and a good archer can assist in that. Once they are removed, dispatching Ganymedes and Pasicrates should not be difficult with superior numbers. We must also account for the three bodyguards stationed inside the building. Surprise will be vital in eliminating them."

Argos had clearly determined our course of action and the four of us spent the next hour discussing its elements. We concluded our deliberations as the women returned from market. Argos announced he was departing for a short business errand. In reality he travelled to assemble the merchants and give word to Pasicrates that he and I would meet Ganymedes tonight to resolve the situation. We spent the next hour trying to forget about the violence we would commit and made an effort to enjoy each other's company and help the women with our celebratory meal. Argos returned and informed us all was in place and to follow his lead for the rest of the evening.

Dinner was a quiet and content affair with everyone telling stories of the old times and looking forward to new memories together. I couldn't help but think about the strong possibility our family dynamic would be drastically different tomorrow and my mother knew nothing of it. My fellow conspirators all maintained an outward affability that belied similar misgivings about our imminent endeavor. At dinner's end, Argos announced the men would celebrate Leandros' return at a nearby tavern and the four of us stood and solemnly departed my apartment. As we exited I took one last look back through the threshold at my mother and sister, feeling as though it would be the last time they would hold a loving, hopeful disposition towards me.

Chapter 7

Argos led us to an old tavern that he frequented where we met four colleagues from the merchant trade. Antagoras was of solid frame and would prove useful in a fight. Kleomenes' physique would be far less helpful but his slightness would allow him close proximity to unsuspecting enemies. Selagus carried a bow and small quiver that he cleverly concealed under a shoal draped over his tunic. Diocles provided the horse. Argos chose his soldiers well. I knew them all and was familiar with each of their histories with Ganymedes or their loyalty to my uncle. I figured they could care less about my predicament, but held a sense of allegiance to my uncle and were motivated to defend one of their own against a known criminal such as Ganymedes. We all had a couple of drinks to calm our nerves and summon our courage. As per our plan, my uncle and I remained at the tavern awaiting our appointed time to meet Ganymedes while the rest of our party went on ahead to their arranged positions. Nearchus and I exchanged an anxious glance as he passed through the exit and departed.

When Argos and I found ourselves alone in the dimly lit establishment I emphatically apologized for putting the family in this situation and avidly thanked him for taking action on my behalf.

"I'm taking these actions because this affects me, my son, your mother and sister. I believe you never intended to assist Ganymedes in his scheme which was partly why you fought his brother and told me of the plot. But your part in this matter cannot be overlooked or easily forgiven. It pains me to wrest you from your mother but you and Nearchus will need to leave this city for a time after our deeds tonight. I will be viewed as rallying merchants against a plot on one of our own, whereas you will be seen as a murderer and co-conspirator due to your prior dealings with these scum. I warned you this day would someday come and I won't be in a position to help you after tonight."

"The army then?" I sullenly asked.

"I think one tour with the Greek armies would pass sufficient time for you and Nearchus to return to Ilandra with respect once more," responded Argos. "I of course will continue looking after the family. And now with Leandros home, you needn't worry about them."

"And Nearchus' family?" I reminded him. "He's more of a father figure then Priskos ever will be. They need protection as well."

"And they shall have it," Argos assured. "Come, the hour approaches."

We began our journey to Pasicrates' in silence. Argos purposely chose to meet Ganymedes at a time when most were still dining and therefore the establishment's occupancy was low. I entered the tavern to see Leandros on my right gambling in the corner, standing close to the Syrian brute in charge of holding the house money. To my left I noticed Kleomenes talking with a house girl near the Pontus creature guarding the stairs leading to the brothel rooms. Argos and I walked straight to the back where the imp and the colossus stood in front of Ganymedes' chamber. As we approached the expecting colossus Argos informed him, "The boy is staying here. The men will sort this out." The colossus patted Argos down and allowed him to pass into the inner sanctum while I ordered a drink and sat alone near the door to Ganymedes' lair.

Outside of the tavern, Nearchus, Antagoras, and Diocles were around back quietly fastening rope from Diocles' horse to the two support columns holding the outer wall of Ganymedes' back chamber together. Segalus perched himself on the roof adjacent the tavern giving him ample visibility of the battlefield. He had already dispatched a Ganymedes minion guarding the rear alleyway with his bow and now stood ready for his role in the scheme.

My breath hastened, my heart raced as I sat waiting for the calamitous signal of our plan to begin. I finished my cup in one gulp and stutteringly ordered another. My hands were not steady; I felt the concealed iron repeatedly rubbing my outer thigh, constantly reminding me of the coming events. I watched Leandros make several small wagers at dice. He was dressed as a beggar and played the part well. I noticed no recognition of him in the faces of those around him. Kleomenes was now bargaining with the girl, inching closer to the stairs where the Pontus creature dwelled. I began envisioning my mother's reaction to my departure for the army and my insecurities about joining again rose to the surface. Nearchus and I could forge another path in this world but our lack of useful skills would ensure poverty, criminality, or both; and I am not built for those endeavours as Patrochlus and Theon are. My thoughts now settled on Patrochlus, Alexandros and our merry band. How would they fare after tonight? It was possible Patrochlus would replace Ganymedes one day. Eventually leaving them had always felt inevitable and as that hour approached I felt a sense of loss.

As my mind wandered I suddenly heard a thunderous crash come from Ganymedes' lair. Diocles' horse had pulled part of the back room's wall down, partially collapsing the roof while Segalus fired two well-placed arrows through the structural damage into the chest of Meric, Ganymedes' eastern monster, who writhed on the ground in pain gasping for air. My uncle quickly ran out of the rubble and was given a sword by Antagoras. Much shouting and commotion came from behind Ganymedes' door while Leandros immediately stabbed the guard closest to him, took the house money and threw it onto the floor where the few derelicts surrounding him fell to their knees to fight over it. Kleomenes, who was now an arm's length from the stairs produced a dagger and stuck it deep in the side of the creature of Pontus who fell to one knee where Kleomenes cut his throat. This brought forth a shriek from his house girl who he promptly threw aside to make his way towards Ganymedes' door.

These actions occurred so rapidly the colossus did not have time to react. When he gained his bearings to see Kleomenes and Leandros coming towards him blades drawn, he passed right by me to face them. I grabbed the iron blade from my tunic, cautiously walked behind the colossus and buried my dagger deep into his back, severing his spine. He immediately fell limp to the floor where Leandros dispatched him through the neck. The three of us now looked at each other panting, covered in blood and surveyed the establishment. The urchins at the dice tables where quarrelling with each other over the loose coins while the other remaining patrons had fled. Seeing that our rear was clear, we made our way to open the door to Ganymedes' lair.

Leandros kicked the flimsy slab of wood down and we found ourselves in between the two factions who were staring each other down exchanging oaths. Meric's body lay at our feet thrashing from side to side with two arrows protruding from his chest. His apparent inability to breath pointed to one arrow puncturing his lung. Our arrival emboldened our party and dashed all hope of rescue to the three remaining villains. The seven of us now approached Ganymedes, Pasicrates and Druz with swords and daggers drawn. They had overturned the large table to shield themselves from further arrows and now found themselves cornered.

As Leandros approached, Pasicrates revealed too much of himself over the table as he attempted to flee and Segalus put an arrow through his neck. Now only Druz and Ganymedes remained. Druz made a crouched dash towards Leandros who parried and threw him into Antagoras' blade which lodged in his stomach. The eastern snake then stabbed Antagaros directly in the heart with a dagger before Leandros could finish him off with a slash to his temple and both men fell lifeless to the ground.

Ganymedes now threw his sword away and stood up from behind the overturned table with his hands over his head. He began slowly clapping as he understood the futility of his situation and congratulated my uncle on a well executed plan of treachery. He then turned to me, "Had I known the level of deceit you were capable of Andrikos, I would have had you in my employ years ago." Such words would have been as valuable to me as a pronouncement from the Oracle of Delphi only days ago; now they were a stinging reminder of my errant path. "So let us talk of an agreement shall we?"

This question was answered with a swift strike from Leandros' fist, sending Ganymedes to the compacted earthen ground. "Damn you Leandros! Have I wronged you in the past?"

"You threaten my family and our way of life and therefore must be eliminated," was Leandros' cold reply. "And just in case you were wondering, Andrikos here is going to kill that little shit brother of yours tonight as he lays feebly in bed, still battered from his pathetic performance of soldierly." The near sinister way Leandros delivered this macabre message gave me chills and instantly weakened my determination to commit the act. Ganymedes turned to me with eyes that could melt medusa's face clean off and spit on me, "Fuck you swine!" With that, Leandros opened Ganymedes' throat with a dagger which let out a choked gurgle of blood. I noticed a faint smile pass Leandros' lips as the body fell lifelessly to the floor.

The remaining six of us stood in a circle around the last body, all bloody and breathing heavily. "Good work men," Argos declared. "Diocles and I will look after Antagoras' body. Andrikos, you and Nearchus tie up the last loose end." I felt sick thinking the ordeal was not yet over but nodded my consent and walked out of the hole in the back wall with Nearchus. We turned our tunics inside out to mitigate the appearance of violence upon ourselves and covertly made our way to Theon's home. Argos and the others wrapped Antagoras in a small rug, strew his body over the horse's back, and departed via back alley streets.

Nearchus and I walked silently through the darkening Ilandran streets, making certain not to draw any attention as it was still early and people were walking about. All colour had left Nearchus' face and he was in a sweat. "I don't know if I can do this anymore," he admitted as he slowed his pace. He then supported himself against a building wall and vomited.

"It will be over in another minute," I assured him as we arrived at the dwelling. I looked in a window to see an older woman, probably Theon's mother, cleaning and skulking about. I moved to the front door and gently rapped it three times. The woman opened the door a crack and Nearchus and I pushed our way inside. The force of our entry threw her to the floor and she yelled out. Nearchus grabbed her and placed his hand over her mouth while I moved quickly to the back room to find a dazed Theon getting out of bed in the direction of a dagger lying on a table. I closed the distance to him and stabbed him in the side. He let out a scream as I removed the dagger and brought it violently down onto his chest several times. He began grasping at me, unable to establish a firm grip due to the large amount of blood now covering both of us. I fought off his death throws and exited the room where the woman now saw I was covered in the blood of her murdered son and let out another muzzled scream. Nearchus and I looked at each other knowing what had to be done and, given Nearchus' deteriorating condition, I buried the dagger into her heart and carefully cradled her lifeless body to the floor. Nearchus' eyes were now tearing as I took my tunic off and donned a garment from Theon's room.

Nearchus and I again walked silently through the dark streets, coming to our neighbourhood fountain to wash the blood from our skin. I inspected Nearchus after this was completed and wiped away any remaining blood stains. He did the same for me and we embraced as brothers with the knowledge our lives would never be the same. We made our way to my sombre home to find Argos and Leandros sullenly sharing a jug of wine in the dark. Argos looked up as we entered, "Any problems?" Nearchus looked at the ground and I shook my head. "Good, come sit a while so we can discuss our actions tomorrow." I complied but Nearchus announced he would retire for the evening.

After he departed Leandros advised that I needed to watch him. "I've seen the effects killing can have on men not accustomed to it."

"Is that what I saw in you tonight?" asked Argos. "Has my son returned a killer too accustomed to the act?"

"My experiences have taught me a great deal about myself. Most importantly is my knowledge that violent situations do not frighten me. Most men live their whole lives not truly knowing themselves; how they will act when faced with a life or death situation, if they will rise to the occasion when faced with insurmountable challenges, whether they can lead men in battle. I am grateful for knowing these things. Andrikos, to a lesser extent, acted bravely and learned something about *himself* tonight. These experiences have emboldened my natural instincts to protect my family and when facing a villain with murderous designs on those I care for, you will get the result you witnessed tonight. Now, in the morning Andrikos, you will fetch Nearchus and I will help guide him out of the dark corridor he is entering. For it leads to a morbid end if not checked, do you understand?"

Satisfied with Leandros' answer Argos now guided the conversation towards tomorrow and what was to be done with Nearchus and myself. "Tomorrow I will speak to the ruling council about the situation as well as promoting Leandros to be recognized as a hero of Ilandra. His involvement in this night's activities will be concealed. Despite being threatened, you and Nearchus will face scrutiny by the ruling council and possibly receive punishment. I am going to tell you now that leaving this city for an extended period of time is your only option at this point. I am not going to force the path you choose but given your lack of skills, I am strongly suggesting a stint with the Greek army in Ionia under the command of Lord Regent Perdiccas and his General in Asia Minor, Eumenes. Leandros will provide instruction on how best to accomplish this and I will tell the council you and Nearchus have already fled the city. I will also perform the unenviable task of telling your mother of the necessity of your extended departure which will be a more difficult task than staring into Medusa's face. You can take this night to think over your course of action but remaining in Ilandra is no longer a possibility. Tomorrow you and Nearchus can talk it over and assure him that Leandros and I will look after his family despite his father's best attempts to undo it. Leandros and I will stay up till daybreak to ensure no attempt of retaliation is made by any surviving members of Ganymedes' syndicate."

I nodded in compliance, finished my cup and retired to my bed. Sleep did not come easy that night as my mind relentlessly replayed the events of the evening. It finally shifted to the unbearable task of informing my mother of my imminent departure and rationalizing my deeds lest the gods think me a villain and send me to Tartarus. My lack of confidence now surfaced as I was faced with the impending fear of joining the army. Leandros' description of harsh initial training did not bolster my resolve.

Chapter 8

My father was waiting for me at Pasicrates' that night drinking a jug of wine in the back room. Only the body of Ganymedes remained, lying lifelessly in between two chairs that my father and I now occupied. "You had some night," was his salutation looking at the corpse and whistling in acknowledgement of the enormity of the situation. "Your uncle was right, however, this was the only way to ensure the safety of the family and thus he can't be faulted for setting you all on this path. I can't say I would have had the nerve to pull it off but it needed to be done," he concluded as he raised his cup to me.

"I feel sick over it," I confessed.

"It should not be an easy thing to kill a man, for that is what separates us from the animals and the righteous from villains. Your internal pains stem from good morals, despite what your uncle tells you. When the act is committed in the face of great danger to one's self or in defense of those he loves, it is just. Living with the emotional repercussions is a burden you must now bear. Your cousin Leandros didn't look like he has much issue killing any more did he? Well, seven years of warfare can do that to a man."

"And now I am to join the army. I feel I am destined for Tartarus."

"This provides you an opportunity to leave behind your errant path and pursue one of honour. I never diverged from my course of selfishness and irresponsibility and have been barred entry to the Elysian Fields. But remember, simply joining a noble cause does not make one noble."

I woke the next morning not remembering having fallen asleep and experienced the sickening feeling that last night was not some terrible dream. I closed my eyes and drifted back to sleep when I heard a loud scream and commotion in our front room. My heart began to pound as I ran to the noise to find Nearchus' mother covered in blood sobbing in my mother's arms. "What is this?" I exclaimed.

"Nearchus is dead! He opened his wrists in his room last night," my mother replied crying hysterically. The sickening feeling in my stomach now metastasized into a revolting pestilence as I ran upstairs to find my brother's lifeless body lying in a pool of dried blood with a long vertical cut in each wrist. Tears came uncontrollably as I held my face to his and muttered his name several times.

A feeling of disbelief settled over me and the tears ceased. I covered his body in the blood stained blanket and slowly walked across the hall to my uncle's apartment. He and Leandros both had heard the tumult and came rushing out to see me standing in a daze outside their door.

"What happened?" demanded Argos. Words did not form. I weakly pointed in the direction of Nearchus' chamber and the two pushed me aside to investigate. Argos yelled several expletives and was generally angry at the corpse for taking its leave from this world prematurely. He and Leandros entered my apartment and consoled the women, I remained motionless in a chair. When the emotional fervour began to ebb Argos sat the women down and told them a version of last night's events which he deemed most suitable to their fragile ears. "It is important we conceal the manner of the boy's demise so his name is not sullied and Greek funeral rights are bestowed. We will claim he was killed by Ganymedes when I speak to the Ruling Council today."

Nearchus' mother blankly nodded in agreement while my mother looked at me with glassy eyes that I feared could never view me the same way again. Argos pushed my mother over her emotional threshold when he told her I would have to leave Ilandra for an extended period and would likely join the Greek armies. She let out muted sobs as she retired to her chamber and shut the door. Helena remained immobile in the corner, completely overwhelmed by life's cruelties that were once blockaded from our home, but now pervaded its every facet due to my actions. Argos and Leandros departed for the Ruling Council and instructed me to look after the women and children. When they returned they would discuss my future.

I approached Helena and hugged her. Her body remained stiff and did not return my sentimental overture. I released her and she quietly walked into my mother's chamber with Nearchus' mother and closed the door. I understood they blamed my actions and behaviour for Nearchus' death and in many respects probably thought I deserved his punishment. I sat catatonically, staring at my front door waiting for Argos and Leandros to return. I was so unable to think coherently that I would have marched directly off a cliff had my uncle instructed me to do so. I kept trying to open my eyes wider as if to wake from a nightmare.

Argos and Leandros returned from their meeting and brought me up to their apartment. Argos then spoke with my mother while Leandros gave me instructions on travelling to Sardis to include where to stay, which individuals to seek out, what to bring, where to purchase food, where to drink, and where to find decent company in the evenings.

Argos calmed my mother and prepared her for my impending departure. He assured her that while I had made several mistakes in the past that led to last night's events, what transpired was the fault of a villainous network that had harassed Ilandra for years and that my actions were noble. He recommended that she and Helena take all the time they want after I depart to form their final judgment regarding my culpability in Nearchus' suicide but for my final evening with the family, they should put last night aside and enjoy a dinner with our family for the last time. His logic reiterated my coming exodus which brought her back to a low sob but also set her to his purpose. She and Helena would prepare dinner for me and love me this evening no matter what the future held for us.

Argos then escorted Nearchus' mother upstairs and assisted her in preparing Nearchus' body. He instructed her to wait in their front room while he used a dagger to create the appearance Nearchus had been killed in a conflict as oppose to a suicide. Argos instructed me to return to my apartment where both women in my life embraced me with glassy eyes. The three of us prepared dinner and forgot about past transgressions. That evening my mother, Helena, Argos, Leandros and I enjoyed our last meal together. Argos, Leandros and I finished off a jug of wine before I retired and drifted to sleep.

When I woke the next morning my mother had packed all my belongings neatly in a sturdy sack. She was surprisingly calm and collected. Argos and Leandros arrived and all present embraced me and wished me well. Argos shook my hand and Leandros warned me to not stand out during my basic training. My mother waited till all had said their goodbyes to hug and kiss me. "You come back to me," were the only words she could summon and, with that, I crossed our apartment's threshold to begin the next chapter in my life.

Chapter 9

My journey to Sardis was uneventful. My mind wandered along the way from Nearchus' death, my unceremonious farewell to my mother and sister, my insecurities of joining the army, and the loss of my close friends Alexandros and Patrochlus. I was alone and nervous. Upon my entry to Sardis, I had officially travelled farther from home than at any other point in my life.

Following Leandros' instructions, I reserved a room and located an army recruiter. I procrastinated enlisting, however, and decided to get more information about the process and obtain news from the east. The city was large, expansive, and dirty. Its population had swelled since the Battle of the Granicus with countless Greek travellers flooding its streets everyday on their journey east. The city's infrastructure had not kept pace with this influx and evidence of squalor was always in the periphery if not directly in your face. Remembering conversations of several Ilandran travellers as well as Leandros' guidance, I made my way down to Sardis' drinking, gambling, and prostitution houses. This neighbourhood was especially vibrant in the early evening and I entered a small, crowded tavern. I drank my wine quietly and listened to the animated conversations occurring around me. Their main topic was the growing tension between Lord Regent Perdiccas and his general Eumenes, versus Antipater, ruler of Greece and Macedon during Alexander's absence, and his ally Antigonus. Craterus, a well respected general within Alexander's infantry, had also crossed the Hellespont into Greece with ten thousand returning Macedonian veterans and allied himself with Antipater and Antigonus. These competing poles contributed to an ominous mood and I was unsure which army I would be recruited into.

I was suddenly jostled out of these contemplations by the individual sitting to my right "You are not from here are you? Just passing through?" He was of similar age and build as I, his features were noticeably Greek.

"Just passing through," I stutteringly responded, being caught off guard by the stranger.

"Joining the army?" he asked.

I became defensive by this unexpected attention to me and did not wish to indulge his curiosity further, yet was compelled to nod in the affirmative due to his intense gaze. He handed me another cup of wine, "It's on me, friend; my name is Stephanos. I am here to join the Greek armies as well. My companion and I have travelled from Athens but he has grown very ill and has been bed-ridden for several days. This has both stalled our journey and lessened our purse."

"If you are from Greece, why have you not joined the army of Antipater?" I asked.

"Antipater has routed most of the Greek uprisings in the Lamian War and defeated the armies of my city," Stephanos explained. "My father and brother were both killed by Antipater's forces several months ago. My companion and I refuse to fight for his cause and travelled east to join the army of Lord Regent Perdiccas, Antipater's rival and protector of the true successor to Alexander's throne, Alexander IV. If you travel alone friend, you should join your fortune with ours."

"Why do you make such offering to a stranger?" I asked.

"This city is dangerous for foreigners. I have lodged here for seven days and can attest to its perils. My companion's condition worsens and I fear I may be alone by next moon. I only suggest we join common cause to a goal we both share."

"And what are the benefits to me if I accept?" I asked sarcastically.

"Well, I can at least show you the best places to screw in this town," he answered with a smile.

"My name is Andrikos of Ilandra, lead the way friend."

Stephanos was the first Greek I met that experienced Greek civil strife since Alexander's consolidation of the Greek mainland. He was also the first Greek I met that fostered animosity towards another Greek faction within Alexander's former empire for personal reasons. While I suffered through countless impassioned arguments on world politics from my uncle and his associates, Stephanos spoke with a genuine fervour and clarity that intrigued me. He explained how Antigonus, ruler of Asia Minor, had refused Lord Regent

Perdiccas' order to secure Cappadocia on behalf of General Eumenes and allied himself with Antipater and Craterus against the Regent. Perdiccas now sent Eumenes and Neoptolemus, former general of Alexander and current Satrap of Armenia, to confront all elements hostile to the two Kings of the empire in Asia Minor.

"How can a former secretary of Alexander defeat Craterus and Antigonus?" I asked, recalling the numerous deliberations of my uncle's comrades.

"You know my motives for joining this fight. Antigonus is in his sixties and Antipater in his seventies. Both old men are in Greece. Eumenes retains a larger force than Craterus and thus holds the advantage in Asia Minor. Despite his history as a secretary for both Philip II and Alexander, he also held command in India and conducted himself with skill and honour."

I didn't pursue the issue further. It was clear I did not hold the level of knowledge regarding world events as Stephanos and did not wish to further convey my ignorance. We continued drinking heavily with Stephanos toasting to this general and that battle of the Lamian War- all names I had never heard before. We made our way to a brothel where the women were of decent appearance and the accommodations comfortable. I soon found Sardis companionship to be costlier than the average Ilandran fare but did not want to insult our new acquaintances and grudgingly agreed to the transaction. Stephanos and I were brought upstairs after our party of four indulged in copious amounts of wine. Stephanos was by now severely drunk and had pulled off his tunic and threw his woman over his bare shoulder as we walked to the designated room. As we entered, Stephanos carefully threw her down on a bed, turned to me and stated he was happy to have met me and that he never trusted anyone he had not shared women with. This was a strange measure for trust but I certainly understood the sentiment.

We did not have enough money for an extended stay, nor did I want to fall asleep in an unknown brothel. I suggested we stay at my room since we would surely disturb his infirmed companion in our inebriated state. Stephanos agreed but cautioned that while he had paid the owner of their room more money to ensure his companion was looked after, he did not want to leave him alone for such an extended time; thus he instructed we would rise early and see him first thing next morning. Stephanos and I established a rapid bond that evening spurred by drink, women, and similar dispositions. I agreed to his plan and fell quickly to an alcohol-induced sleep after returning from our revelry.

I was roused next morning by my disheveled new companion who urged me to wake and accompany him to his room. We apparently slept later than he planned and he was eager to depart. "I am meeting the surgeon at our quarters this morning," he informed me, pulling me out of bed. My feet hit the floor and I immediately realized I was still drunk. We splashed water on our faces and drank from the bowl provided to me by my room's proprietor and began our journey. The streets contained more squalid images than Ilandra's sordid neighbourhoods and the urchins occupying its filthy thoroughfares were certainly more aggressive to passers-by. A foul odour permeated the crowded streets and alleys on our way short journey. The atmosphere certainly put me in a defensive posture and we were physically pulled on several occasions by destitute locals trying to take advantage of confused foreigners. On one instance, Stephanos struck a decrepit man across the brow and roared, "Do we look any better off than you swine?"

The smell was beginning to turn my stomach when we finally arrived at Stephanos' quarters. The structure was not noticeably more sanitary than the streets outside but it was dry and the doors had sturdy locks. We entered Stephanos' chamber and were greeted with the rank smell of death, causing me to partially gag. "This is Isocrates," Stephanos announced stoically. Isocrates looked as though his soul had faded, leaving his feeble body reciting the machinations of life out of habit.

The surgeon had already arrived and looked up at Stephanos, shaking his head and making the prognosis, "Its pneumonia, he will die tomorrow." Stephanos somberly paid the surgeon a coin and received information on funerary arrangements. He and I remained at Isocrates' side the remainder of the day.

The following day saw the surgeon's prediction fulfilled and I assisted Stephanos with Isocrates' body. He wrote a compassionate letter to the deceased's mother and announced, "I will make preparations for enlistment tomorrow. Tonight, let us drink to his memory." That evening was a more sombre affair than our previous venture and the following morning we enlisted to a training outfit marching east to swell General Eumenes' ranks.

Chapter 10

Stephanos and I met outside the city gates at the appointed early morning hour three days after enlisting. My internal fears intensified in the days leading up to this morning but the poise displayed by Stephanos' determined motivation steadied my outward appearance. His confidence was infectious and I was glad to have met him when I did.

We were to travel east to meet General Eumenes' army in Cappadocia, where he had been appointed Satrap. The march was to be approximately five hundred miles following the Royal Road and we were to be trained along the way; picking up additional recruits from the major cities we passed through. Fifteen men were waiting at the gate with no sign of anyone taking charge. We loitered for an hour until a group of four men approached our throng. As they neared I realized this contingent of men were the most impressive, battle hardened soldiers I had ever seen. Their arrival quieted our chatter as everyone appeared to draw the same conclusion about these demigods.

"Line up!" the largest of them shouted. "Is every man here enlisting?"

Several 'yeses' were muttered by the group.

"Answer the question!" one of them roared from behind our meager line and struck a recruit in the back causing him to fall down and gasp for air. "Get up!" the same brute screamed as he forced the man back to his feet.

"Is every man here enlisting?" the largest of them shouted again.

"Yes!" we yelled emphatically.

"Then form a proper line!" he ordered.

Our gaggle pathetically attempted to assemble ourselves into an orderly formation but again failed. One of the brutes now stood in front of the feeblest and most out of place among us and struck him in the stomach with such force that he keeled over and vomited. The brute then threw him into the vile puddle and pulled him back to his feet.

The largest then addressed us. "You little shits better unfuck yourselves quickly or you won't make it to Cappadocia. I don't care about your personal sob stories and how this is your last resort. I don't care if you think you're some hardened criminal running from your home town. I don't care if you think you're the next Alexander searching for honour and glory. I don't care if you grew up in squalor. I don't care if you're a deranged maniac lusting to kill. I don't care if you have families. I don't care if you think you've had some training in combat. I don't care if you've killed someone. I don't care if mummy and daddy didn't love you. I don't care if mummy and daddy sent you to a school and now you think you know something. I don't care if you're dumb as a sack of bricks. The only thing I care about is providing an army with trained men who are worth a damn so I can get paid."

"My name is Agathon," he announced. "And what you dogs need to understand is that right now your bodies are pathetic and your minds are weak. You're scared. You're useless. You're cowards." He paced as he delivered his warm greeting and now stopped in front of the unfortunate recipient of the stomach blow, who now had pieces of vomit soiling his appearance. "Look at you, you're a disgrace! Are you Greek?"

"Y-yes," he muttered.

"Answer me like a man damn it!" Agathon screamed. His face was so close to the unfortunate soul that saliva was flying from Agathon's mouth into his face.

"Yes!" he yelled in exasperation.

"You're a humiliation to our race and to everything Alexander accomplished. If he'd had an army of emasculated pussies like you we never would have crossed the Granicus. I will be shocked if you're alive in three months." Agathon struck him again in the stomach which brought him to his knees. This time Agathon allowed him to remain in his pool of vomit writhing in pain. This exchange terrified me. Agathon held the most intimidating presence I've ever seen- more so than Meric. It was impossible that he would find merit in my appearance and I thought it only a matter of time before I too was writhing in my own vomit.

82

Agathon continued pacing and stopped in front of a capable looking man in our line. Surely Agathon could not find fault with his appearance. I was wrong. "Look at that embarrassing piece of shit on the ground!" he ordered the unsuspecting recruit. The man looked at the unfortunate soul and let out a small smirk from the side of his mouth. "I think you're going to be dead even before him," Agathon continued. "You have an arrogant look on your face yet I see a pathetic nobody standing before me. Am I right?"

"No," replied the man deliberately.

"We'll see about that," Agathon answered, annoyed the recruit did not give him more material to work with. This exchange further unsettled me because I had already made the assumption that the recruit was superior to me in appearance, and thus in many other facets, yet he too was provoking Agathon's ire. None of us was safe from this man. I later learned the recruit's name was Bacchylides.

"I will tell you the two traits you will need to survive our little journey and become worthy of taking your place within the Royal Macedonian army," Agathon continued. "Work hard and do as you're told. This sounds easy enough but some of you will choose not to heed my words and will suffer for it." I certainly did not plan to be one of them.

"My men and I are all Macedonian veterans of the great conquest under Alexander. I fought at Gaugamela and at the Jaxartes River. Callisthenes fought alongside me at the Jaxartes and continued on to India and the Hydaspes River, returning with Alexander to Babylon. Telemachus and Lasthenes crossed the Granicus with Alexander and fought at the siege of Tyre, the Battle of Issus, and at Gaugamela. These men have accomplished feats of courage and soldiery that none of you will ever amount to." I certainly believed the latter statement, for these men appeared vastly superior to me in every way.

Agathon and Callisthenes were clearly the younger of the four. Their mannerisms and confidence reminded me of Leandros returning from the east. Maybe they knew him. Agathon was the apparent leader of the group. He was several inches taller than me, about twice as wide, and probably eight years older. His body beared multiple scars from sword cuts and arrows. His skin was weathered and worn with pronounced sinews and veins. Everything about him emanated strength and he instantly became a goal to strive for in my mind. I wanted to speak with his command, I wanted to act with his confidence, I wanted to instill fear in men as he did within me.

Callisthenes was smaller in stature but also maintained an imposing demeanour. He was about two inches shorter than I and of the same width. His body resembled a bronze cuirass forged through years of hard campaigning. His face contained sharp features and portrayed a sadistic expression when set to purpose. He took pleasure in his corrective duties and I prayed my dismal appearance did not spark his interest.

The other two men were clearly older but no less threatening in appearance. Their bodies were rigid yet beginning to succumb to age. Their faces forcefully told of a life wrought with hardship, violence and heavy drinking. Their delight in administering pain had luckily waned with maturity and they remained in the background while Agathon and Callisthenes performed their cruel routine.

"From now until you are delivered to the army, your lives will consist of marching, drilling, and carrying your sarissa." Agathon paused while Telemachus brought him an example of the deadly spear. He handled the mammoth instrument with unbelievable ease and dexterity. He held it straight up, then lowered it to the ready, then thrust it forward and back with incredible skill. "If you cannot master this weapon, you will be worthless to the phalanx and relegated to the baggage train with the servants and whores. You!" Agathon shouted looking at Stephanos. My proximity to his target made my stomach kick with terror. "You! Step forward!" Stephanos obeyed and took two steps in front of our line. "Closer you coward! Take this weapon." Stephanos deferentially approached our caretaker and grabbed the pike. He immediately dropped the weighted end to the ground. Agathon's face resembled that of someone witnessing a shocking heresy. "What are you doing! If you drop your sarissa in combat you will screw everyone behind you which may lose the battle! Pick it up!" Stephanos repositioned his grip, picked the spear off the ground and lost control of its momentum, letting the fearsome warhead at the end of the eighteen foot pike almost touch the ground before gaining proper control. No one made a sound in the line. All breathing ceased. This ineptitude was too much to bear for Callisthenes who ran at Stephanos like a rabid dog, knocking him to the ground, and repeatedly striking him in the face while Agathon addressed the line. "If you drop your weapon to the ground you are killing the men in front of you doing the fighting! Your spear point supports your mates. When you drop your point you are a worthless pile of shit unworthy of surviving the battle." Turning to Stephanos he exclaimed, "I should kill you myself and have you trampled by this pathetic formation this instant!"

I wanted to run out and help my new companion but did not have the courage to do so. I willed the maniac to stop but my urging fell on an unwilling participant. Agathon must have been the unintended recipient, however, since he looked directly at me and decided I would be next on his parade of torment. "You! Pick up that sarissa!" I ran over and waveringly held it in a semi vertical position. Luckily my presence took Callisthenes' attention from Stephanos who recovered back in the line. He approached me, exhibiting such a look of disgust on his face that I dared not look him in the eye. He pushed and pulled the sarissa which overpowered my feeble grip and brought the point into the ground. He punished this dishonour with a strike to my stomach which knocked the breath from me and caused me to hunch over the spear. It took my entire constitution to keep the weapon in my grasp. This rare feat absolved me from further trauma and Agathon again addressed the line. "You don't let someone grab your fucking pike and pull you along with it! If someone is close enough to grab your spear they should already be dead!" Now looking at me, Agathon ordered me to thrust the pike forward to which I clumsily complied. "That dismal thrust wouldn't kill a Persian eunuch," Agathon informed the line. "Give Callisthenes the sarissa and get back in formation."

Our battered line had suffered this morning and everyone's spirits were down. Agathon now gave final instructions. "Remember how you feel this morning. If you work hard and do as you're told, in a week you will never feel this way again." We were all given a dull, heavy wooden sarissa to begin our march east along the Royal Road. Our handlers ensured we kept proper spacing and held our spears upright and straight. At random intervals the old men yelled out an order to lunge our pikes forward in a battle thrust and recover them upright quickly. Agathon and Callisthenes circled us like vultures atop their horses and screamed at and whipped those who performed the drill inadequately. The sun now bore down on our fragile line and beads of sweat meandered their way down my face, causing irritable itch and discomfort that could not easily be relieved due to both hands being required to hold my sarissa. I began feeling blisters forming where my toes and heel rubbed against the leather of my worn sandal. Towards the middle of our first day, my lower leg muscles were sore and tight to the point of swelling. This swelling hindered adequate blood flow to my feet which induced an uncomfortable tingling numbness. Towards the end of the first day my thigh muscles could barely raise my legs up to put forth each step. My lower back ached and my arms were past the point of muscle fatigue and frequently spasmed.

I periodically looked at my new mates, Stephanos in particular, to gauge their level of exhaustion. Surely they had to feel as I now did. Most of their faces shouted the same expression of physical agony. I watched as the unfortunate recruit who had vomited earlier in the day now wavered in his footing. He began to wander off the road and collapsed. I learned his name was Labdacus while our handlers punished him. Callisthenes was first on him, screaming in his face and kicking his torso. We were instructed to continue marching and our wayward companion would catch up. Luckily we were only two miles from where we were to set camp for the evening. Our line almost collapsed as one when we were informed of our arrival. Few words were exchanged that night. The only additional energy expended was to consume our allotted grain and water. Stephanos and I ate in silence. His morale had clearly waned yet he did not utter a word of discontent. I was thankful of his resolve since it would not have taken much to convince me to desert our undertaking that evening.

Labdacus and Callisthenes made it to camp about ninety minutes afterwards. He looked like a walking corpse. He was probably not going to make it to Cappadocia. I fell to sleep immediately on the hard ground that evening using my pack to support my head. Our meager rations were not enough to replace the energy I had expended and hunger pains carried me off to sleep.

Chapter 11

We were awakened the next morning at sunrise to the screams and kicks of Callisthenes. My body resisted every effort to rise this early after yesterday's exertion and cried out for food and drink. My eye lids strained to remain open; my neck struggled to hold the weight of my head. As I rose to my feet the swelling had subsided in my lower legs but now a debilitating soreness manifested itself with each muscle contraction. My blisters stung with each step, forcing me to rearrange the leather straps on my sandals. My inner forearms ached where they met my inner elbow from holding my sarissa. It was unclear to me how I would summon the motivation and strength to march for another day, then I saw Callisthenes tormenting Labdacus who sluggishly rose to his feet and my motivation materialized.

Labdacus' lethargy attracted the attention of our handlers and I used this time to limp over to Stephanos. "I'm hurting," was my morning salutation.

"So am I," he whispered looking at Labdacus. "After the first day, however, it is clear that our stamina to endure this march is about average, therefore we must ensure we outperform the bottom half of our line. They can't show up to Eumenes' camp empty handed can they? Listen, we must make a vow to ourselves right now to not waver in our march, to not succumb to our body's demands to quit. If one of us begins to falter the other will come to his aid. The goal is to avoid the beatings."

Stephanos had clearly thought our situation through to a level that my fatigue would not allow and I was grateful for it. I joined him in this vow of survival and felt I would follow him to the River Styx at that moment. Our conversation was interrupted by our handlers calling us to muster. We lined up in two ranks and received instructions for the day. We were to eat, train, and march until sun down. I had a feeling this schedule would repeat itself many times over before we reached Cappadocia.

The morning meal was a paltry affair. Our small contingent carried most of our supplies on mules and would resupply when stops were made to cities along the Royal Road. Eating my mashed grains and drinking my two cups of water did not satisfy my stomach's painful hollowness. I noticed the same look of dissatisfaction from my new mates and I looked to Stephanos, "This is all we are to eat until sundown?" He responded with a glance that reminded me of our newly recited vow.

Morning drill was exhausting. We performed countless repetitions of holding our sarissas upright at the port-arms position, then leveling it and thrusting forward several times before bringing them back to port-arms. These exercises lasted for two hours and brought my forearms past muscle fatigue. My hands began to loosen their grip of my heavy spear. One recruit dropped their spear to the ground during a thrusting exercise. The sound of the heavy pike reverberating on the ground was loud and terrifying since we all knew what it meant. Everyone looked to Labdacus as the culprit but to our surprise it was Bacchylides. He quickly recovered his sarissa off the ground but it was too late. His offense insulted our two older handlers most and they were on him within seconds. We continued our drills as Bacchylides was continuously struck and derided in front of us. Sensing our exhaustion, Agathon now called out rapid orders to thrust our spears continuously. The high rate of repetition became too much for me and I was now on the verge of dropping my sarissa. I questioned how Labdacus could withstand this torture as long as I. Stephanos, observing my descent, encouraged me to remember our vow, "Just a little longer, brother." His words aided my strength for several more thrusts until I heard the deafening sound of another spear hit the ground, and another. We were ordered to halt; those who dropped their sarissas were beaten, Stephanos had spared me the same fate and I felt further indebted to him.

Our handlers allowed us to rest for thirty minutes while they broke camp. The thought of another day's march was daunting but Stephanos' words steadied my resolve. I just had to outlast the lower recruits in our line. After our brief intermission we were called to our feet with sarissas at the port-arms position. As we departed, every step I took was deliberate and forced. I could feel the soreness and tension within my legs like a clamp had been fastened to them. The sting of each blister felt like a dagger rubbing my skin raw. The muscle fatigue within my forearms formed a painful tension in the inner bend of my arm. At first, I kept all thoughts out of my mind and resembled a walking carcass. This strategy allowed my physical ailments to take prominence so I next attempted to envision reaching the end of our march; but such a goal seemed too distant to grasp. I thought about joining the army of General Eumenes and fighting to keep the world under Greek rule; but my inner insecurities surfaced and I did not think myself worthy of joining such a great cause. Finally my mind settled on my family. This pain I endured all went towards the rebuilding of my character in my family's eyes. I thought about returning home to Ilandra triumphantly, gaining the respect and admiration of all. I foresaw my uncle Argos parading me to the Ilandran council, as he did Leandros, to declare me hero of the city and archive my adventures. I visualized the look of pride my uncle, mother and sister would have when speaking of me and when in my presence. I pictured our whole family together again, enjoying the blessings of good health and fortune. This was the stream of consciousness that propelled me through my physical misery, and I would return to this place of warmth and familiarity many times over the course of my hardships to come.

These inspiring musings, or mental masturbations, allowed me to forget my current hardship for a precious interval but eventually a misstep over a large pebble forced me to rebalance my sarissa and my focus rushed like Hermes out of Ilandra and unto the Royal Road of Asia Minor. My body's injuries had been neglected during my cerebral departure and now they shouted at me twofold like a baby crying for the attention of its mother. In my mental absence a new malady vied for my attention- a terrible thirst. We had not drank water since departing camp several hours ago and I was forming collections of foamed saliva at the corners of my mouth. My tongue was devoid of all moisture, my throat was parched, my skin was chapped and a sore was beginning to form on my lower lip. My ailments had brought me back to reality too early, however, since I judged we still had two hours left in our march. My body would not allow my consciousness to flee it again despite my best efforts with each ache and pain grasping at my attention, forming an unbreakable chain between my current situation and my subconscious. I felt the recurring wobble of my heavy sarissa at the port-arms position as my exhausted forearms frequently gave out. I felt the unsteady trembling of my knees with each new step. I figured we now had close to an hour's march left.

I again thought of Stephanos' words but this time I was not fortified by them. I was at the end of my abilities and none of the other recruits had faltered. Surely others were suffering their own collection of torments during the march. Was I at the bottom of our order of merit? I began to feel ashamed that Stephanos would tie his fate to someone so unworthy of it. My ensemble of misery brought the attention of Agathon who was now riding next to me atop his horse. I was panting through my mouth and reached my breaking point. He began insulting me and ordered our line to begin thrusting exercises. Agathon watched my feeble repetitions as each thrust saw my spear point lower closer to the ground. "Do you strike a midget?" yelled Agathon. "Bring that fucking point up!"

But I physically couldn't. Agathon was aware of this and would have the whole line execute the drill until I dropped my sarissa to the ground. I figured I had about ten more thrusts in me. "Keep your point up!" encouraged Stephanos, observing my plight.

"Shut up!" was Agathon's response to his support. Stephanos' words strengthened me to raise the point about two inches higher than my previous thrust, but no more. Agathon looked in sadistic anticipation with each thrust, awaiting me to give him an opportunity to discipline my ineptness. I estimated about five repetitions remained when we all heard the loud, terrifying thud of a sarissa hitting the ground. It was Labdacus. Agathon ordered us back to port-arms as he rode over to the poor soul who already had Callisthenes fast upon him. Labdacus' surrender was followed by another collapse to my right, and another in front of me. Our handlers instituted their punishment and marched us about fifteen minutes farther to the nearest well along the road where we set up camp for the evening.

Words between the recruits were again scarce as we devoured our dinner of mashed grain and water. A cavernous pain remained in my stomach upon completing my meager ration and I feared my body would not have requisite sustenance to complete tomorrow's burdens. With what little energy remained, I lanced three blisters which instantly relieved pressure as they seeped blood and puss. I asked Stephanos how he was faring and he weakly responded to remember the vow. I admitted that I was very close to giving up on the march and was barely saved by his words of encouragement and Labdacus' surrender. I also confessed my fears of not being able to make it to Cappadocia. He reiterated that they couldn't arrive at General Eumenes' camp empty handed and we just needed to survive a little longer. I was fast asleep on the hard ground before he finished the sentence.

The next morning we again awoke to Agathon's screams and Callisthenes' kicks. We were ordered to muster in two ranks and informed we were to eat, drill, march, and camp- a routine that was becoming familiar, however tonight we were to camp outside a moderately sized town. My soreness had mildly subsided but my muscle fatigue was more pronounced this morning. Our inadequate breakfast was provided and my hunger pains worsened. Our morning drills consisted of one hour of spear work followed by a one hour introduction to unit tactics. They formed us up in five-man columns to show how we were to use our sarissas in concert during battle. This was a welcome addition to our training for it allowed several of us to rest as two five-man columns practiced the new techniques. Our two older handlers circled our formation like hawks critiquing individual performances with a small club that could be jabbed into one's side if offense warranted. Agathon shouted movement orders to simulate formational movements in battle. Participating in these manoeuvres gave me a better understanding and appreciation of the importance to keep my spear at the ready at all times. It was the first time I had any infinitesimal notion of what it was like to be a soldier in a Macedonian Greek phalanx. This hour of reduced hardship lifted my spirits and gave my maladies time to heal. My lanced blisters stung less, my legs less sore, my arms less fatigued. When it was time to begin our march I felt a renewed vigour to continue our trek- which quickly dissipated after the first hour. My small surgery on my feet alleviated most of the blister pain and my muscles were slowly acclimating to their new arduous demands; but my fatigue and my extreme thirst remained. My dehydration caused my nascent lip sore to metastasize into a festering legion which I licked incessantly.

I ignored these remaining hardships by returning to Ilandra and basking in the glow and pride of my family. This pleasant fiction was so far from my current reality, yet it comforted my anxieties and removed me from the march. A midday collapse to my right ripped me from my mental escape and I came crashing back to the road and the march. The unfortunate victim this time was a recruit named Rhexenor. Our handlers reacted differently to his failing, however, and they hurried to bring him water instead of punishing him. It became apparent that he was dehydrated to the point of near death and had begun to seizure. Agathon ordered everyone to rest alongside the road and drop their spears. Our two older handlers brought water stored on one of the mules to us and we were allowed to rest for several moments. I immediately laid back against the ground and entered a semiconscious state that induced a mild euphoria. Our hiatus was abruptly ended by Agathon who reached his breaking point on the level of sloth he could witness and we all resumed the march. The rest of the day was divided between my visits to Ilandra and conducting countless spear thrust exercises. No one else fell out of the march and we reached the boundary of Kadoi near dusk. Upon arrival we were called to formation and told we were picking up new recruits the morning after next from the town. We would not march tomorrow and would not begin drills until after midday. This news was welcomed by the line as we were given leave for the evening.

We took our dinner and I noticed the chasm in my stomach had lessened despite our portions remaining the same. This night was the first time anyone had enough energy to socialize after a march and we all sat in three circles of various sizes getting to know each other. My circle consisted of Stephanos, Bacchylides, Rhexenor, and a Theban named Dion. Our banter consisted mainly of sharing a small bit about our background, griping about our hardships along the march, and discussing what to do with our precious night of freedom. Stephanos assumed control of the group and announced we would find women and wine for the evening. No one objected to the suggestion and our group made our way to the sordid neighbourhoods of our temporary home.

It was an easy task finding the right establishment and the five of us took seats around a soiled table. The tavern served both wine and women and was occupied by several disorderly locals and a few female employees of acceptable appearance. Stephanos bought the table the first jug of wine and a loaf of bread. Our march thus far had driven our party ravenous and such provisions had never been more satisfying as they were this night after several days of hard toil. Our spirits were high that evening as like-minded men formed bonds over alcohol and the shared experience of hardship. Stories were traded from our past, good natured ridicules were exchanged, jugs of wine ordered, and house women, recognizing interested customers, now joined us at the soiled table.

Our merriment's crescendo reached a level that now attracted the attention of some of the local patrons. One of which walked directly over to Bacchylides, during one of his many tales of inflated exploit, and assertively stared at him during the account. This abrasive intrusion gave Bacchylides pause to which the patron interjected, "Please, don't let me stop your epic saga of bullshit, boy." His confrontational tone immediately hastened my heart rate and silenced the mood of our table.

"My story is for my mates, stranger. Nor is it meant to offend," Bacchylides responded in a wavering voice while not making eye contact with the imposing man.

"I see bragging nobodies like you come through here often, always ranting about some heroic deed of the past and some nonsensical declaration about what you will do when you the join the armies. Let me tell you something you little shit, I've seen real battle in Alexander's wars, I know what it is to take life in combat. You're worthless and I don't want to hear your man-pleaser spout off anymore glorified nonsense in my town." The man was about forty-five and clearly drunk but held an imposing physique nonetheless. Bacchylides and the rest of our group looked down towards the table as we received our admonishment. His presence overpowered our aura of inexperienced arrogance. Half of me even agreed with his characterization of us when, suddenly, Stephanos stood up to him face to face, displaying a fuming demeanour.

"I've had enough of washed up drunks like you telling me I don't know anything and am not worth a damn. You're fully aware of why we are passing through your insignificant little town, and yet you mock our determination to do our part to keep the world Greek. Remove yourself from our table!" was Stephanos' parting orders to the stranger. His confidence in the presence of a man I considered my superior was inconceivable to me. The local patron was at first shocked, then infuriated with this insult. Bacchylides now stood beside Stephanos compelling my unwilling legs to also stand and move towards the confrontation. Nervously making my way, I witnessed Bacchylides strike the patron in the stomach, causing him to hunch over, while Stephanos struck him in the temple several times. The stranger managed to make a crazed lunge at Stephanos, clawing and punching at his face, while I assisted Bacchylides in bringing the man to the ground where the rest of our party now joined in repeatedly kicking the man until he yielded. Stephanos then spit blood from his injured mouth onto the man, sat back down, and called over one of the house women who were watching the familiar scene from a distance.

None of the other patrons came to his aid nor looked at all interested in the affair. The wine server came from around his post and helped the man up and saw him out. Rhexenor suggested that we leave lest he return with a gang of interested comrades. "Had he any, they would have been here with him. He's a drunk and a fool," replied Stephanos, now turning to his female companion, "And I am not leaving here without getting to know my new friend better." The rest of the evening was spent drinking, laughing and fornicating. The image of the bloody veteran being dragged out remained with me throughout the night, however. His criticism of our table wrung true to me for we had done nothing, nor did we endure anything other than three days of drill and marching. The incident had further elevated my view of Stephanos as well; whereas my reaction to such reprimand harkened me back to uncle Argos and my insecurities, Stephanos stood straight up and confronted such condescending rebukes. My constitution paled in comparison to his and I attributed

95

this to the raw emotions created from the Lamian Wars that now bolstered his confidence and compelled him to action. My past had been a procession of one self-serving act upon another which left me devoid of any emotional affection, familial loyalty being the exception, that could stir me to such bravery.

We clumsily made our way back to camp after finishing with the house women. Our journey reminded me of my countless walks home with Patrochlus, Alexandros, and Nearchus. I felt a sinking feeling as Nearchus' face floated through my mind's eye. I missed him. We passed by several decrepit beggars whom Bacchylides shouted drunken obscenities towards. He was the most inebriated and leaned heavily on Rhexenor as we stumbled our way down winding streets, eventually reaching our camp just outside the town's boundary. Our other mates of the line seemed to be all back and already asleep. My intoxicated contingent ineptly stepped as quietly as possible to our bedrolls around a low fire but Bacchylides tripped over one sleeping recruit, bringing himself and Rhexenor down upon another sleeping victim. This caused a small stir with the two awoken recruits cursing us and Bacchylides laughing uncontrollably as he struggled to regain his footing. With our evening concluded, we all quickly fell to sleep around the dying camp fire. Another night my father would have been proud to be a part of.

Chapter 12

Morning greeted our degenerate contingent with the familiar weight of a hangover and dehydration. Luckily I woke before our handlers felt it necessary to begin our anguish for the day and I lingered near our smouldered out fire to eat a morsel of bread saved from the prior evening and drink what water was available. Most of our line was awake with the exception of Labdacus and my contingent. Looking at Stephanos' bruised eye and fat lip, it was clear which faction best enjoyed our precious evening.

I walked over and nudged Labdacus for fear that his sluggishness would rile the mood of our handlers. My stirring about woke Stephanos and Rhexenor, but Bacchylides remained stubbornly still, looking as though he was screwed into the dirt. Agathon and Callisthenes began making their way over to the throng and it was apparent from their glassy red eyes they had enjoyed themselves last night as well.

"Line up at port-arms!" was Agathon's morning salutation. Our weary line bustled about to recover our sarissas and assemble to formation. "Any issues last night?" Our line remained silent as Callisthenes paced up and down inspecting each recruit. He stopped in front of Stephanos to question his injuries "Where did you receive these fresh wounds?"

"I mistakenly fell last night," was his unconvincing response. Callisthenes immediately struck Stephanos in the stomach which caused him to yell out and hunch over. Grabbing his hair, Callisthenes then brought his face back up to his and repeated the question.

"Where did you receive these injuries?"

"At a tavern," replied Stephanos in a strained voice.

"Who did this to you?"

"No one, I had too much wine and lost my step," explained Stephanos dispassionately.

Callisthenes now struck Stephanos on the cheek and threw him to the ground. "You fought a local townsmen you worthless drunken fool! If your actions cause the people here to bar us from recruiting in the future, you will be beaten to death!" He then quickly inspected the rest of the recruits' bodies to ensure no other had the signs of combat besides what had been put there by our handlers. Callisthenes then stopped in front of Bacchylides who displayed several bruises. "Where did you get these?"

"I received them as punishment from you and Agathon," answered Bacchylides.

"Good, you probably deserved worse."

"The new batch of meat arrives in three hours which means you have plenty of time to drill before our attention moves elsewhere," shouted Agathon. He then instructed us to spread our ranks wide to create enough room to manoeuvre our sarissas. For the next hour we performed every manner of drill that could be devised from Agathon's creative mind. My shoulders began burning from the mundane repetitions and I felt strength leaving my arms. Bacchylides was the first to vomit yet had the sense to not drop his spear- saving him from a violent correction. Next Labdacus began resting the weighted end of his spear on the ground between repetitions which resulted in several strikes to the ribs and back.

Rhexenor now vomited to my immediate left. The sight and sound of this vile action began to rile my fragile stomach. My breaths consisted of open-mouthed panting that made a slight wheezing sound as I struggled to hold my sarissa correctly during each machination. Dehydration prohibited me from properly vomiting so I fiercely dry-heaved on several occasions. Our handlers sensed the deteriorating resolve of our line and increased the intensity of our drills to hasten our complete collapse. They walked the ranks eagerly looking for recruits on the edge of surrender as Agathon called out commands at a rapid pace. When they found a candidate for capitulation they would begin correcting their flawed technique which accelerated their fatigue and led to their knees buckling and spears dropping. Our handlers responded to these blasphemies with severe penalties.

My body was also failing and my technique worsened with each repetition. I summoned all my strength to perform each movement adequately while our handlers' eyes were upon me and briefly rested when they were preoccupied with some other unfortunate recruit. Several soldiers had succumbed to their weakness and I could no longer mask my fatigue. One of the older handlers now took an interest in me and screamed for me to improve my technique. I could not, of course, and was in a losing battle to keep my knees from buckling and my spear off the ground. The commands continued and my sarissa lowered farther to the ground with each repetition. My handler watched in delight as my shoulders and arms failed me and the weighted end of my spear crashed into the ground. I was struck several times, giving me the excuse I needed to collapse onto the ground. A well placed kick to my mid section prompted me to vomit a small amount of an acidic mixture on myself. I lay there, unable to comprehend the myriad of clever insults levelled at the sight of my pathetic posture. My body had reached its breaking point and I gave in to it completely. I had never felt this level of physical exhaustion in my life.

Agathon continued our hellish training session for several more minutes before allowing us to rest. I had been beaten by this day's training and any thoughts from yesterday of crossing some threshold of competence were immediately erased. Agathon ordered us to remain where we were while the new recruits entered the camp. As my senses returned to me I counted ten recruits formed up in a curved line before their new handlers. Agathon fell seamlessly into his first-day routine with the new group of ten victims; berating them, beating them, and insulting them for a good hour. I empathized with their plight, mainly because I knew it did not get better with time- at least in four days' time. I ensured to drink what little water was available to us before we began the day's march as I saw our handlers giving the new recruits spears and forming them up. Our handlers paid little attention to our line during the march so as to devote their full sadism on the new Kadoi cohort. Agathon drilled them mercilessly throughout the day and several fell out of the march to receive their violent punishment.

Despite the weight of my spear, I found the day's march to be somewhat pleasant without our handlers circling our line like hawks shouting excruciating drill repetitions. Our normal distractions absent, I was able to fill my head with all manner of satisfying thoughts. They ranged from the future adventures I was to have in the army, my triumphant return home and the feeling of pride I would someday engender in my family again. I also allowed my mind to wander on to the subject of my old mates, and eventually to Nearchus. I felt such a sense of longing that a hole opened up in my stomach and I began feeling nauseous. What were his final thoughts? Why did he not feel he could come to me first? Finally, I began to consider my last fateful nights in Ilandra and where they relegated me on the spiritual scale of morality. Was I now condemned to Tartarus or the Fields of Punishment? Would I be allowed entry to the Asphodal Meadows where souls of an indifferent nature who have committed no serious crime dwell? Would some future heroic deed grant me a place among the valiant souls of the Elysian Fields? I dared not consider my poor soul would ever be destined for the Isles of the Blessed. I ended this line of thought with the conclusion that my fate lay somewhere between the Fields of Punishment and the Asphodal Meadows and only an act of selflessness or courage could change my destiny.

The next several days all blended together as the new recruits were tormented and our line was left to march in relative peace. After one week the new recruits began showing competence and were brought into our ranks to practice drills and manoeuvres in larger formations. We marched as a cohesive unit for several more days before reaching the city of Gordium. Upon our arrival at the city limits we were called to formation where Agathon addressed our line. "We are stopping in Gordium to pick up more recruits. You will have tomorrow morning off." He then stood in front of Stephanos and added, "If any of you do something stupid and screw up my ability to recruit people from Gordium I will kill you myself!" Agathon's words came as welcome news to our line, especially the newer recruits who had not enjoyed a precious evening since their enlistment.

That night our same group of five was joined by Labdacus and two Kadoi recruits named Diokles and Spear. Spear was given this name by his group of recruits due to his initial competence using the weapon. Spear was tall, handsome and confident. It was clear he was the leader of the two and naturally drifted towards Stephanos as a foreign dignitary would to a king in a room full of beggars. Our enlarged group was not interested in seeing the graves of the famous Macedonians Midas and Gordias as some of our line was eager to do and made our way to the sordid streets of the city's taverns and brothels for some proper revelry.

Our group had taken on Labdacus as a charity case and was now coming to love his jovial, kind-hearted nature. He was quick to tell an obscene joke or drink unbelievable amounts of wine for our amusement. He delighted in our enjoyment and became our group's mascot. While everyone was warming to Labdacus, it became clear the two strong personalities of Bacchylides and Spear were colliding like dueling rams. Bacchylides was noticeably drunk and took considerable offense to a prostitute he favoured shunning his attentions for that of Spear. Spear intentionally exacerbated the situation through a number of taunts after observing the level of anger it produced in his new adversary. The two were close to coming to blows when Stephanos, angry over being disturbed from enjoying the company of his woman, got in between them and forbade any bloodshed. He quickly signalled for another woman to be brought for Bacchylides and ordered him to sit in a seat farthest from Spear at our table.

Towards the end of the night Labdacus had become the drunkest of our clan through multiple episodes of heavy drinking to please his new friends. We all pitched in money to ensure he had a woman for the night and laughed hysterically as he stumbled after her up the stairs. This spectacle calmed tempers between Bacchylides and Spear for the time being and the rest of our group made arrangements with our women to spend an hour our two upstairs before departing back to our camp at the edge of the city. The eight of us stumbled down the winding streets of Gordium that night, laughing, howling, and shouting obscenities before quietly slipping back into camp and passing out on the ground near our burnt out fire.

The next morning our combined line was called to formation so our handlers could inspect us and ensure everyone was accounted for. Agathon stopped in front of Labdacus, who looked like a standing corpse and struck him in the face- knocking him flat off his feet. In the past I was too concerned about my own well being to care about one of our line being punished, but we had all taken warmly to the good-humoured recruit and his violent castigation now engendered strong feelings of sympathy. Labdacus slowly rose to his feet and Agathon promptly struck him in the stomach, causing him to keel over and vomit violently on the ground. We were ordered to ready our spears and open the ranks so several feet existed between each recruit. Agathon then began the day's anguish with countless numbers of spear drills, each imaginatively designed to exhaust our muscles. After ninety minutes, the Kadoi recruits began to fall out of the formation. They were welcomed by the fists of our two older handlers while Callisthenes walked in and out of the formation looking for new candidates on the verge of submission. Agathon made a point to notice all who fell out but kept bringing his attention to Labdacus. Seeing the poor lad was not faring well, he began walking over to him and screaming out orders faster and faster. Agathon's eyes had a look of ecstatic anticipation as Labdacus' technique continued to falter after each repetition. He finally gave up and Agathon beat him senseless. Labdacus had lost the ability to hold his head up so Agathon cradled the back of his head and struck him directly in the face two more times until his faculties left him. Each strike further disfigured his face and splattered blood everywhere. Our day's drills were concluded after Agathon's cathartic battering of our new mascot and we were ordered to stay out of the way while the new Gordium recruits entered our camp.

Stephanos and I carried Labdacus' limp body back to the recruit's side of the camp and rested while our handlers began their now familiar routine of indoctrination all over again. Gordium, being a larger city, produced twenty recruits who all stood in a winding line receiving their first exposure of the torments to come. They were screamed at, beaten, and mocked for about an hour before they were given their sarissas for the day's march. I was worried that Labdacus would not be physically ready for the march but he had recovered well after being given food and water by his mates and we all formed into two sections with the Gordium recruits marching ahead of us, being circled by the handlers like vultures.

The day's march was tolerable for the veteran recruit formation and agonizing for the Gordium enlistees. They were constantly drilled and berated as their bodies experienced the physical hardships of their new normal. After several hours the first of the Gordium recruits began falling out of the march and were welcomed by our handlers with violent censure. At this time I began to notice Labdacus' failings within our formation. He was clearly exhausted and dehydrated and was now teetering on the verge of surrender. I pitied his defeated appearance, having experienced it myself, and felt guilty that our want of drunken spectacle from him the previous night contributed to his exasperated state. I gave him words of encouragement but he was too foregone to be bolstered. He collapsed along the side of the road with his sarissa making a deafening thud. Rhexenor, being the closest, attempted to help him but Callisthenes had already raced to the spot of infraction and knocked Rhexenor over to administer violent castigation. Callisthenes then picked up Labdacus' spear and thrust its blunt edge into the back of Labdacus, steering him at rapid pace ahead to the new recruits' formation. "You clearly don't even deserve to be in the presence of proper Greek recruits you pathetic toad! You will train with the new scum stains until you can conduct a proper day's march!" Labdacus now took position with the Gordium recruits to participate in their excruciating drills for the remainder of the march- a fate intended by Callisthenes to break the man. Several more Gordium recruits fell out of the formation and a dozen ended the day's march with blood stained faces and out-of-joint noses.

Labdacus was forbid access to his mates of the veteran formation at camp that night yet Stephanos and I were able to sneak extra food and water to him. It was clear that his health was deteriorating and was exhibiting dangerous fever symptoms. "He isn't going to make it if he has to drill all day during the march tomorrow with the Gordium recruits," assessed Stephanos. "He may not even make it through tomorrow's exercises *before* the day's march."

"Callisthenes will never grant him a reprieve from his continued punishment and we are not close enough to a settlement to procure him a remedy," I added.

"There was a small village about four miles back along the road, but running an additional eight miles after the march we just had will be difficult," observed Stephanos. "A horse perhaps could make the journey but Callisthenes would never allow such extra labour to be levied on their animals for the benefit of a lowly recruit."

"We could steal it for the night," I suggested. Stephanos thought this idea over but came to the conclusion that it was not feasible due to its proximity to our handlers and the amount of noise it would make.

"I will run it," Stephanos announced. "I could make it there and back in ninety minutes."

"With legs that just marched sixteen miles?" I asked incredulously.

"He would do the same to help one of us."

"Only because we are the only ones that have shown him kindness, besides, he physically couldn't ever do something like this for us. Despite his good nature, our handlers are right, he's a physical disgrace." My body was doing the talking for me. It couldn't bear the further exertion Stephanos was contemplating.

"I would do it for you," claimed Stephanos

"And I you, but…"

"I'm not asking you to join me," interrupted Stephanos. "I will make this journey alone if I must."

Every ounce of my being protested but my loyalty to Stephanos and my enhanced admiration of him compelled the weak response of "alright". We waited till twilight to begin our trek and ran at a slow but steady pace in silence for the first few miles. After the second mile my body began to coast on its own. By the third mile, however, my legs began to cramp and my stamina failed me. I demanded we stop and Stephanos agreed.

"This little shit better appreciate this," I said, panting like a dog. Stephanos didn't reply and sat with a half smile on his face. "I don't know what perverted treachery you are trying to compensate for with this deed, but I'd say we will have achieved access to the Elysian Fields by sunrise."

Our last mile was the slowest and my legs and feet were numb by the time we saw flickering lights ahead of us. Stephanos quietly knocked on a door with a lit window and announced our intentions.

A toothless, decrepit dirt farmer opened the door holding a sharpened farm tool as defense against our unsolicited visit. Stephanos asked to purchase ground willow leaf and bark to assist our ill companion. The dirt farmer had none but led us to another small dwelling and the exchange was made. The procurement lasted a total of ten minutes and my body pleaded with me to delay further strenuous actions but Stephanos willed me forward.

My body began failing after the first mile and I implored Stephanos to adjust our pace to a fast walk for the next mile. He complied on the pretext we would run the next mile, to which I negotiated a slow jog for the fourth. By the time our small camp fires were visible I could run no farther and began walking again. We finally made it to where Labdacus lay and noticed his condition had worsened. He lay by himself, shivering and moaning in a cold sweat. I stoked the small fire next to him and Stephanos administered our hard-fought remedy. He whispered something to the patient and we both took our leave back to the veteran recruits' side of the camp.

The next morning I was surprised to find Labdacus still alive and readying for the day's toil. He was in poor spirits and did not remember seeing Stephanos and me the prior evening. My legs and lower back were aching from the added strain from the night's sortie and I was apprehensive about my ability to complete the day's exertions. Our first hour was spent conducting numerous repetitions with our sarissas. Our handlers then split us with the veteran recruits performing movement drills and the Gordium recruits continuing their sarissa repetitions. I could no longer see Labdacus but observed several new recruits vomiting or falling out of their formation to the unwelcoming hands of Callisthenes.

After the second hour we were told to rest for several minutes before the day's march began. I saw Labdacus had new bruises and fresh blood running down his face and he resembled a walking corpse. I approached him and gave him words of encouragement but he was too exhausted to listen to me. Labdacus again accompanied the Gordium recruits on the days march and they were all once again subjected to arduous spear drills and admonishments. Several of them began falling out of formation and were beaten. My own muscles were on the verge of submission due to the evening's activities and I began to resent Labdacus' weakness. These feelings subsided and returned to pity once I saw he had fallen out of the formation towards the end of the march covered in sweat, blood, and vomit. Callisthenes took pleasure in exercising the remaining weakness from Labdacus' failing body as our line passed him on the road.

Making camp that night, we noticed the new recruits' formation was smaller than when we began that morning. Callisthenes was also absent which did not bode well for those missing. Thirty minutes later he led the battered and broken contingent of stragglers into camp. To my surprise and delight, Labdacus was among them. He was present in physical terms only, however, for exhaustion had erased his mind's ability to recognize people or form words. Callisthenes gave him one more kick for good measure which brought him to the ground where Stephanos and I carried him to our fire. His condition was serious and we tried to make him as comfortable as possible. He convulsed throughout the night and occasionally reached out to one of our hands for comfort. His eyes had the look of recognition and appreciation but he was unable to speak. Sleep finally overcame us all and in the morning Labdacus was dead.

Stephanos internalized Labdacus' death with outrage and a blood lust to kill Callisthenes. It took all my oratory skills to quietly convince him now was not the right time. He washed the blood off Labdacus' frail, battered body and we all gave him funerary rights as best as we knew how. Labdacus was not the only recruit missing from morning formation however as several Gordium recruits had deserted. Agathon was incensed by this act of betrayal and beat three recruits mercilessly who knew the absconders best. These three unfortunate recruits then spent the next two hours performing spear drills while their faces were covered in blood. Each of them fell out of the morning's exercise and the day's march which brought further cruelty down upon them. Two of them were dead the following morning.

*

After several more days of marching and drilling we entered the boundary of Cappadocia. Our line of recruits had become lean and hardened through the many weeks of toil and adversity. The beatings subsided as our competence slowly rose to an acceptable level in the eyes of our handlers. Callisthenes rode ahead of our line to scout exactly where the army was and returned several days later to guide our line to General Eumenes' camp. He brought with him the inconceivable news that General Ptolemy, ruler of all Macedonian territories in Egypt, had stolen the remains of our God King on the way from Babylon to their final resting place in Macedonia. Callisthenes also informed us Lord Regent Perdiccas departed Cappadocia with a sizeable force heading south to seize Ptolemy's Egyptian holdings and recapture Alexander's remains. Lord Regent Perdiccas' contingent included the Silver Shields that Leandros told me about. They were now commanded by Antigenes and Tuetamis.

Argos was right about Greeks soon fighting each other, and Callisthenes' news meant the army we were joining was now at war with a hero of Alexander's world conquest. There was a palpable nervous energy within the ranks on our remaining days' march coupled with a general feeling of contentment knowing our relationship with our handlers was coming to an end. Our line's confidence, built over the hard weeks of pain, deflated rapidly, however, as we neared the encampment and observed the battle-hardened faces of the soldiers within it. I immediately viewed these men as my superiors and could not conceive how they could ever consider me their equal or believe the arrival of our pathetic line could aid their cause in any meaningful way. Their intimidating facial expressions did not convince me otherwise.

Chapter 13

Our handlers were granted access to the encampment and marched us to an open space segregated from the efficient bivouacs of the regular army. We were put in formation with our sarissas at port-arms. Several formidable soldiers approached our line looking as impressive as Agathon himself. It was clear they knew each other since they embraced our handlers warmly as they pointed in our direction with disdainful antipathy. These new intimidators then approached our line, led by a particularly imposing brute, and began inspection. They pushed and pulled, prodded and poked each recruit, some attempting to push us over, others attempting to rip the sarissa from our grasp. The process resembled an auction for slaves or cattle. They smacked a wooden stick over our muscles to determine our solidity and they inspected our mouths and eyes to gauge our health.

Having decided our lot met their basic standard of durability, our evaluators asked Agathon who was weakest among us. Agathon called out several names to step forward. To my disappointment, Rhexenor was included in this unfortunate grouping and they were ordered to stand in a gaggle off to our right. Our evaluators then walked through our formation again and pulled several more recruits whom they believed undeserving of the phalanx. The evaluators made their way towards Stephanos and I, which compelled me to avoid eye contact as if to shirk their notice. Stephanos, however, stood up straight and looked the inquisitor directly in the eye which encouraged the man to move on to me. I ceased avoiding notice and aped Stephanos' confident posture, looking hard into my assessor's eyes. Doing so never came easy to me, especially to a stranger whom I had deemed my superior. After what seemed like an eternity the evaluator appeared satisfied and moved on to the next recruit. Upon completion of their assessment, two soldiers marched the weaker faction away while the remaining soldiers ordered us to close ranks to impart instructions.

"You have been chosen for probationary assignment to the phalanx of General Eumenes, Chief Commander of Lord Regent Perdiccas, Protector of the true Argead heirs to the Macedonian Empire, Philip III and Alexander IV. Perform well and you will be granted the honour of serving in the greatest army in history whose conquests span from Greece to India. Perform inadequately and you will be assigned to the baggage train with the rest of the women, children, and slaves. Display any act of cowardice, insubordination, or dishonour and you will be beaten, imprisoned, starved, and killed. I am Androkles, Strategos of the Taxis with which you will be assigned. I serve at the will of our Phalangiarch, Alcetas, brother to Lord Regent Perdiccas. All in this camp serve General Eumenes. As the Taxis Commander this will likely be the first and last time I address you outside of an official formation. From now on your day will begin and end by the will of your Syntagma Commander and your Lochagos. They have control of life and death over you and you will obey their commands as if they were proclaimed from Zeus."

Androkles departed and four Syntagma Commanders stepped forward to divide us among their ranks. Traditionally, Syntagmas were comprised of phalangites from the same region within Macedon. Over a decade of Asiatic conquests and the division of forces after Alexander's death had diluted their homogeny and created new configurations of Asiatic Syntagmas as well- an unwelcome development to most Macedonians. I feared being split from Stephanos and the rest of our mates and watched the Commanders' deliberations intensely, trying to make out any discernible reasoning that could assist in predicting my fate. All non-Greeks were immediately singled out for the Asiatic Syntagmas. The rest of us were carefully looked over and the Syntagma Commanders began taking turns choosing recruits to fill their ranks. Stephanos was chosen first, followed by some recruits I was not familiar with but looked superior then I. Stephanos' new Syntagma Commander chose again and another round was completed with Dion being selected to another Syntagma. Spear was chosen next for Stephanos' Syntagma and his companion Diokles was assigned to another. Bacchylides was then picked for Stephanos' Syntagma and a pit promptly opened in my stomach at the thought that I may be separated from the core of my mates. Looking at the remainder of the formation I surmised that I and one other portrayed the most favourable appearance so I slouched and avoided eye contact when the unfavourable Syntagma Commander made his selection. Stephanos' Syntagma Commander now selected and I struck a rigid posture and made direct eye contact with the man, willing him with all my nerve to choose me. I assessed his favour lay between myself and one other, yet he finally settled to call me forward. The sigh I expelled was noticed by all as I walked over to my mates.

After the selection process was complete, each grouping was marched over to their Syntagma encampment. Our encampment was identified by our Syntagma's standard containing several banners signifying the unit's honorable participation in the battles of Alexander's conquests. The tents were aligned evenly by Lochos among the approximately two hundred and fifty phalangites assigned to our Syntagma. They were busy conducting all manner of activities to include sharpening weapons, polishing bronze, re-tying leather straps, cooking, shaving, sleeping, conversing, laughing, and gambling. Our Syntagma Commander marched us through the main thoroughfare of tents which garnered deferential salutes for him and condescending leers towards us. Our Syntagma Commander brought us to a small open space near our encampment and was joined by another menacing-looking soldier with severe facial features that were exacerbated by multiple scars and pock marks. Our Syntagma Commander then turned and addressed us.

"I am Lykos, Commander of the Pydna Syntagma. You have been assigned to my unit on a probationary basis until you prove yourself worthy or unworthy. As our Strategos Androkles informed you, if you conduct yourself in any way that I deem unacceptable, you will be punished harshly." Lykos then motioned toward the severe creature standing beside him. "This is Drakon, Ouragos for the Pydna Syntagma. For those of you that do not know what an Ouragos is, he is my voice, my ears, and my hand. He will train the clumps of shit that stand before me into members of a formidable fighting weapon. He will determine who is worthy to become a phalangite within my Syntagma. He will administer my commands

110

which will be obeyed without thought, question or hesitancy. He will mete out harsh punishment for those that do not do as they're told. In battle he will ensure none of you offend the proud honour and tradition of this Syntagma." Lykos then departed to his command tent and left us in the callous hands of Drakon.

Drakon was an old soldier of fifty with the weathered and scarred face of a man in his seventies. His black hair had thinned and grayed through the years, and eyes resembled sunken pools of black. Despite his age, his physique was impressive; standing the same height as myself with tight musculature and broad shoulders. He inspected his new line of recruits before addressing us. "The only thing you swine need to remember from all you have been told today is that you will obey the orders of your Strategos and Syntagma Commander without thought, question, or hesitance. From now on, I am the biggest star in your pathetic sky. My eyes and ears of the Syntagma are my Lochagos'. Each commands one of the sixteen Lochos'. A Lochagos is chosen because of his leadership, bravery, and fighting abilities. They are superior to you pukes in every way conceivable and will be obeyed without hesitation. Your worst fear should be your Lochagos informing me that you are unworthy of the Syntagma. You should go to sleep with nightmares about that potentiality. You should wake up each morning vowing to be the greatest phalangite in the Syntagma to win the favour of your Lochagos."

Drakon had a deep, raspy, threatening voice that came from years of screaming at enemy soldiers and insubordinate phalangites. He paced up and down our line of eight recruits, staring, poking, prodding, pulling and grabbing at various parts of our bodies to determine our physical strength. Drakon then continued his morose introduction. "Since you all know nothing and are probably pissing yourselves right now in anticipation as to what is going to happen next, I will tell you. We are going to march to the Phalanx Quartermaster and draw equipment. Because you all know nothing I will instruct you on its uses and how to wear it correctly. Since you all are worthless I will then drill you into the dirt so that if I decide you are ready to be assigned to a Lochos, you will report to your Lochagos with a modicum of competence. As is usually the case, especially with recruits from the troop of recruiters that brought you here, some of you fools believe the minor inconveniences you endured on your way to this encampment have hardened you into soldiers. I will prove you wrong through the quality time we are going to spend together over the next few days and weeks."

The thought of days and weeks of hard training with this sinister man, of which I had formed a very superior opinion of, opened the pit back in my stomach once again. I thought back to our agonizing days with our handlers and the words of Stephanos that got me through it all. I looked at my new group of mates and assessed myself to be in the lower half. I was going to be one of the recruits everyone else strove to outlast. I was snapped out of this depressing line of thought by Drakon ordering us to follow him in formation to the Phalanx Quartermaster.

We arrived to find a virtual city of equipment and people engaged in every conceivable manner of human activity. It was here that the organization required to manage the chaos of a moving army of thousands began to sink in. Such strategic concepts were as foreign to me as mathematics to an infant. Drakon marched us past the standard issue tent, however, and brought us to another function of the Quartermaster- the holding cells. As we walked past these wretched cages Drakon assured us that he would not hesitate to have one of us waste away here, should we demonstrate cowardice or insubordination. "Some of this worthless scum will be executed; others will die from their inherent weakness. Some are here for less severe transgressions and may yet live to serve this army again. Remember their faces," was his final warning. As I looked at several of the unfortunate inmates I saw battered facades, emaciated stomachs, and utter filth. Some had given up and sat quietly in their cage awaiting death. Others had lost their wits and were yelling nonsensical drivel at us. Drakon stopped at the cage of one poor soul and informed our group, "This is Sagicus. I put him here myself for lack of motivation and insubordination. How do you like it here Sagicus?" The inmate shook his head weakly. "If I were to ever release you from this cage would you again display laziness and disrespect?" The inmate again weakly shook his head. As we exited I observed Drakon's victim to have multiple bruises on his face and body, sallow eyes, hair matted with grime, and the look of pure agony upon him. Drakon's lesson certainly had its intended impact on me.

Our group arrived at the Quartermaster's standard issue tent. Items were grouped together and distributed to us as we passed each station. We were issued our weapons, bivouac kit, and armament. Drakon then marched us back to our Syntagma encampment and ordered us to assemble our recruit bivouac away from our Syntagma regulars because we were unworthy to be in their presence. Drakon gave us a purposefully inadequate demonstration on tent assembly and then sent us on our task to complete our bivouac while berating our incompetent attempts to follow his orders. He inspected our work when completed, gave his blunt judgment and violently tore them down for us to reassemble again. This process continued as per Drakon's design for an hour before he was satisfied with our work. His next class exhibited our inability to correctly don our armament when ordered to do so. Drakon would inspect our line and identify several mistakes such as the miss-tie of a leather strap, an improper tilt of a helmet, the incorrect holding of a shield. These corrections were all dealt with severely and Drakon used a specialized cane to perform the task- he called it his 'motivator.' Next came the order to arm ourselves with sarissa and short sword. Our sarissas came in two sections for ease of travel and screwed together for combat. Our line now stood at port-arms with our assembled sarissas standing upright as our previous handlers had instructed us. Drakon paced through our line and pulled several of our sarissas directly out of our hands, sending them to the ground. His motivator ensured the perpetrators followed their spears to the soil. Having seen this performed several times already I was confident that I would hold my sarissa if challenged. Drakon stopped in front of me and ripped the pike out of my grasp with a vicious strength I had never experienced. My mid-section was greeted with a piercing strike of the motivator, causing me to fall to the ground hunched over my wound.

Drakon now pivoted from malicious instruction to cruel physical drills in full combat kit. It began with the familiar sarissa repetitions although Drakon added several new and creative techniques that hastened our muscle fatigue. After sarissa drills we moved to short sword repetitions. These exercises were new to us and thus we were frequently motivated by Drakon's cane when our form was lacking. The final hour of drill incorporated our lessons with Syntagma manoeuvres teaching us the position of the sarissa, the placement of the feet, the shifting of our weight and our positioning in relation to each other. Drakon purposely added a level of complexity to these drills that exceeded our line's nascent capabilities and regularly motivated us throughout the exercises. I was saturated with sweat under my stiff linen cuirass and a torrent rained down my brow from my helmet. Each bead created a river of itch on my face that I could not easily alleviate because my spear required both hands. I would sometimes sneak my hand in to wipe my brow which frequently elicited a sharp correction from Drakon's motivator.

Drakon ended our torment for the day and it was clear that while our line of recruits had bolstered our physical endurance along our gruelling march to Cappadocia, our ability to employ battle tactics was severely lacking. Our line huddled together within our bivouac after the day's training to eat and converse. The eight members of our contingent were all impressive in stature and mettle which added to my fears of being singled out by Drakon as unworthy of joining the Syntagma and being sent to the rear where there was no honour or glory to be won. Everyone was too exhausted for meaningful conversation but Stephanos did lead the group in introductions. Bacchylides and Spear were still not on good terms and I was too fatigued to participate and feigned sleep. In my semiconscious state I did gather three of the four names of the other recruits- Lycurgus from Thessaly, Philippos of Pydna, and an imposing specimen from Corinth who went by the name Boxer due to his participation in the sport during the last Olympic Games.

Drakon greeted us at daybreak and admonished the disorderly state of our bivouac. A few unnoticed debris fragments were the grounds for the chastisement and several motivating strikes were delivered before breakfast. On one occasion, Drakon had struck me with his motivator along my left forearm which caused what felt like a small fracture. I had been hit countless times since becoming a recruit but this pain lingered and had a debilitating effect on my ability to perform the day's training. I dared not complain to Drakon and fought through the sting that arose from each spear thrust. The pain became unbearable and my thoughts now saw me sitting in a cage among my own filth waiting to die. This notion encouraged me through the painful morning spear exercises until I was finally granted a reprieve as we transitioned to short sword drills primarily using my uninjured right arm. After an hour of thrusting, parrying, and blocking, Drakon called us to port arms and again began ripping our sarissas from our grasp. Some recruits were now able to resist Drakon's violent attempts while I braced for a shot of pain from my forearm. Drakon stood in front of me, grabbed hold of my spear, looked me in the eye and pulled the sarissa with the force of an ox. The pain cut through my forearm like a knife and I let out a loud scream as the spear was ripped from my grasp and landed on the ground. I immediately grabbed my left arm and fell to the ground before Drakon could club me. My reaction surprised our Ouragos and he refrained from immediately punishing my sorry display of soldierly.

"What is this? Why are you crying like a woman?" Drakon demanded.

"I think I have a broken arm from this morning," I hesitantly responded.

Drakon immediately grabbed my left forearm and inspected it. I let another grimace of pain to which he told me to shut my 'man-pleaser'. My arm was a little swollen and severely bruised. Drakon squeezed it in several different places and instructed me to see the surgeon after the day's training was completed. He added that if I hadn't screwed up I wouldn't have been struck in the first place. He then kicked me to the ground. This act of clemency surprised me but I assumed he respected my attempt to conceal the injury and continue training. From the look of his scarred body he'd probably had a similar wound at one point or another. The day's training concluded with movement formations which were still too new and complex for our line to perform properly. Drakon corrected our incompetence with his motivator but ensured not to hit my injured forearm. Upon conclusion of our movement drills Drakon ordered me to the surgeon's tent and to report back to him afterwards.

Stephanos held my dinner for me as I departed and found myself truly alone for the first time in weeks while making my small trek.

My walk was punctuated by the pungent odours of elaborate concoctions as I passed by countless soldiers readying pots over open fires for dinner. I cherished my short amount of solitude and purposely took my time to extend the fleeting moment before arriving at my destination. The surgeon's tent had several patients in line being treated for various training injuries or accidents and a few succumbing to illness. I quietly awaited my turn and observed the interactions taking place. Several surgeons were present and a statue of the healer god Asclepius, with his snake-entwined staff, was in a corner. The surgeon's tent was well stocked with all manner of herbal remedies, bandages, braces, and surgery tools. A young surgeon pointed to me and asked me my name, position, and ailment.

"Andrikos, assigned to the Pydna Syntagma commanded by Lykos, under Strategos Androkles," I replied.

"A real soldier," the surgeon responded lively. "We usually only get injuries from labourers or logistical pukes with venereal diseases from screwing too many whores in the baggage train."

I thought this response odd coming from a doctor but he quickly explained himself. "My name is Philotheos, I used to be a soldier once. I was in over my head, however, and took a blow to my shoulder, cutting a number of muscles and tendons. I couldn't raise my left arm over my head from then on and decided to make myself useful as a surgeon. What Lochos are you assigned?"

"None yet, I am still in training which is why I am here." My unimpressive recruit status quickly lost his attention and he became impersonal and detached for the rest of my visit. As he was inspecting my arm an assistant interrupted him with a small box of medicines.

"Excuse me sir," said the assistant, "I have a box containing the last of our supplies of white and black hellebore, fenugreek, and willow. What shall I do with them?"

"Set the hellebore and fenugreek in the back, we will only use them in emergency," Philotheos ordered. "Take some of our reserve funds and procure more willow from the nearest settlement tomorrow and tell everyone to use it sparingly until we procure a proper supply from the next large city."

"Yes sir," replied the assistant as he quickly disappeared.

After examining my injury he diagnosed me with a broken upper forearm. "Normally I would apply cerate and bound up your arm to prevent its movement. I doubt this would be conducive to your basic training, however, so I am going to give you a removable brace that you can wear for most exercises that will keep your arm and wrist in a favourable position. You are going to be in pain for several more days and you need to wear this brace for at least three weeks. Tell your Ouragos to try and refrain from striking you in that arm for a while, or you could just not fuck up again," Philotheos added with a smile. "See me again in a week," were his departing words.

I returned to our recruit bivouac at a deliberately slow pace to enjoy the last remnants of my solitude. I first reported to Drakon and told him of the surgeon's prognosis. He grunted and dismissed me. I took my dinner from Stephanos and retired for the evening where a welcome audience with my father was waiting for me.

Chapter 14

"My son, a genuine foot soldier in the army of the Kings," my father proclaimed proudly. Iatrokles was sitting in front of Drakon's tent fiddling with his sword and helmet. Despite being a dream, I was still nervous the Ouragos would appear to see me acting as an accessory to the violation of his possessions.

"Not yet father, I still must survive that maniac," I replied motioning to Drakon's tent.

"You will," he assured. "And how does this make you feel?"

"Excited of course."

"Yet you have lingering angst from your last night in Ilandra."

"Yes," I weakly responded while looking at the ground.

"We spoke of what had to be done, for yourself and the safety of the family. The woman, she is what vexes you."

"Yes. I think she was the cause of Nearchus'...act. That and a broken heart."

"And you think both you and he are damned for this action? It is true, you killed those men for the legitimate reason of safety and justice. But the mother was killed as an act of selfishness. A way to protect yourself from implication and public scrutiny. Had you the full conviction of merit behind your actions, you would not hesitate to let her live and publicly defend yourself."

"So it's true?" I asked with worried eyes.

"It's true you made an impulsive and unrighteous decision in the heat of emotional intensity," my father determined. "Other men with more structured upbringing might have made the better choice. She is not blameless for raising such vipers either. However, the whole of your existence has not been characterized with egregious examples of immorality and thus you have the option to even the scales of final judgment with your actions going forward."

"Through courage on the battlefield?" I asked. "I think I will act bravely but I am nervous."

"Through a great many choices. Overt courage spurred by bloodlust isn't going to buy your way into the Elysian Fields.

Courage brought on by love of one's brothers-in-arms and the glory of Greece is another story, however. Although the Fates are always with us, we are ultimately responsible for our own actions when presented with their choices." With that, I awoke to our unpleasant reveille from Drakon signaling the beginning of another day's training.

The next several days blended together. My brace did help alleviate some of the pain in my arm during the short sword and manoeuvre drills but it took every ounce of fortitude to complete our morning sarissa exercises without falling out or dropping my spear. I did so on two occasions to which Drakon rained down motivation on every spot other than my left arm. Others had been falling out too. One recruit in particular, Demaratos, had the misfortune of an unmotivated attitude as well. Demaratos was brutalized by Drakon on several occasions to which he finally exclaimed, "Why don't you break something on me like you did Andrikos so you can baby me through training as well!"

This was especially offensive to Drakon for it impugned his station as an Ouragos- which was unacceptable. He further beat Demaratos and applied restraints to his wrists with his arms behind his back. Drakon then brought Demaratos up to his knees and addressed our line, "I want you to look at this unworthy shit stain kneeling before you. If you are physically weak, I can beat it out of you or I can send you to the rear units. If you are insubordinate in battle, however, you will get your mates killed and I can't have that. We do have a remedy for insubordination and you all saw it on your first day here. That is where this undeserving scum is going to rot for a long time. Demaratos, you are going to be my latest example of suffering to my new recruits, now get up! The rest of you clean your gear until I return." Drakon wedged his motivator into Demaratos' wrist restraints and used it as a lever to steer Demaratos away. None of our line would trade positions with Demaratos now for all the gold in Persia.

In the days that followed, another recruit's body surrendered. Lycurgus from Thessaly fell out of our exercises one too many times and was sent to the rear units. As we watched him depart our line for the relative safety and ease of the rear, there were probably a few recruits who were willing to trade positions with Lycurgus, myself possibly being one of them. Bacchylides suffered a leg injury during this time and was forced to conduct the rest of our training in a cumbersome leg brace which only added to his generally unpleasant demeanour.

It had been a week since my arm injury and I reported back to the surgeon's tent as instructed after the day's training. There were several people ahead of me and I spotted my 'combat' surgeon Philotheos running back and forth looking very busy. There was an older man sitting next to me with a lapel insignia on his tunic indicating he was a member of General Eumenes' Staff. The man was about mid forty with sandy blond hair and chiselled features from years of exposure and toil. He had the appearance of a silent professional, someone who had full confidence in their knowledge and abilities and didn't care if anyone knew it or not. I immediately coveted his impressive poise and assuredness. He spotted me staring at his staff officer insignia, causing me to quickly turn away.

"What are you here for son? Who are you?" he asked warmly.

"I have a broken arm from basic training. I am Andrikos, assigned to the Pydna Syntagma commanded by Lykos under Strategos Androkles."

"Who is your Ouragos?"

"Drakon."

"Oh, that explains it," he responded with a smile. He was the second person who smiled at my injury within the surgeon's tent. A doctor other than Philotheos appeared to attend to the man and he spoke in a low tone so that I could not hear the conversation. The surgeon appeared to be responding to the man in the negative and the man was becoming increasingly angered. A few more words were exchanged with the man cursing the surgeon under his breath. The man then saw me looking at him inquisitively.

"You don't hide your interest in others well do you?" His question embarrassed me and I immediately looked down at the ground and apologized. Seeing that I was still curious as to what transpired he added "That frail little nobody is denying me materials that are essential to an upcoming operation. Materials whose purpose is as foreign to these waifs as a sword is to a woman."

Being caught up in the kindness the man had showed me I suddenly blurted out, "There is another surgeon you should talk to. Stories about front line combat and important missions on behalf of the General's Staff are the key to his heart. Someone like you should have no trouble sparking his interest. I overheard him stockpiling ingredients of a lethal nature last week," I proclaimed enthusiastically, pointing to Philotheos.

"Put your hand down!" the man said in a low but forceful rebuke. "Don't ever point at someone when you don't want their attention." His demeanour quickly thawed after the reprimand. "Thanks for the advice kid, get that arm healed," were his departing words as Philotheos called me to him after seeing me pointing like an excited fool.

"What's the matter? The green recruit can't wait his turn?" asked Philotheos sarcastically.

"I got into a conversation with that man and he asked me who I was waiting for. I certainly did not mean to appear impatient," I explained deceitfully.

"Well let's take a look. You don't seem to be in any acute pain. You've been wearing the brace?" he asked while removing it, poking and prodding the injury. His machinations elicited far less pain then last week and he seemed satisfied with my progress. "Continue wearing it for two more weeks, then return it to me," were his final instructions as I exited the surgeon's tent and made my way back to the recruit bivouac.

The next morning we rose and assembled in formation to begin the day's training. Drakon took his position to address our line and informed us that Antipater's forces had allied with Ptolemy and crossed into Asia Minor from Greece. Our army was to join with the forces of Neoptolemus, Satrap of Armenia and veteran of Alexander's conquests, to meet Antipater's allies in battle. Preparations were to be made immediately and our line was informed that we would all be reporting to our Lochos today. Stephanos and I looked at each other with excited grins as we heard this news. Many weeks of hard march, followed by another week-plus of torment under our Ouragos, had finally delivered us to our units within the Royal Army.

Drakon called out our names, notifying us which Lochagos to report. "Bacchylides, report to Lochagos Cleisthenes; Stephanos, Croesus." I could feel my heart now beating faster as I waited to hear my name called. "Spear, Philon; Andrikos, Croesus." I looked at Stephanos enthusiastically as I envisioned us fighting together in battle. When Drakon concluded calling out our assignments he unenthusiastically congratulated us and dismissed us to pack up our bivouac and report to our Lochagos.

Stephanos and I found our Lochos' bivouac and asked for the Lochagos. We received several unflattering remarks and condescending sneers from our new Lochos mates as we made our way to Croesus. Our Lochos' bivouac was squared away with all tents perfectly aligned and wooden planks between them serving as walkways over the dirt and mud. We found Croesus sharpening his short sword outside his tent. He was solidly built with a black beard that covered his face almost to the bottom of his eyes. He was a Spartan and when his helmet was donned one could not make out any facial features other than a crooked nose and two black eyes which would intimidate the roughest Scythian barbarian. He looked directly at us as we approached, forcing me to avert making direct eye contact with him. It was clear that he was not impressed with our appearance as we stood at attention.

"Lochagos Croesus, we have been ordered to report to you by Ouragos Drakon for assignment to your Lochos," Stephanos announced in his deepest, most deliberate voice.

"Do you know why you have been assigned to me?" asked Croesus.

"No sir," Stephanos responded.

"Because the last two worthless recruits he sent didn't listen and were killed during our pacification of Cappadocia," Croesus explained. "Where are you from?"

"Athens, Ilandra, sir," Stephanos and I shouted at once.

"Athens, your kind is lazy, weak, and spoiled," Croesus stated definitively. "Ilandra? Never heard of it. You two will set up your tents and report to our formation when I return from the Syntagma staff meeting. I am the Lochagos here because I was the most capable soldier in this Lochos when my predecessor fell in battle so

122

you will do exactly as I say or I will have you killed. I fight in the first position of our file and therefore rely on the men behind me to cover my ass. Since you two are relatively worthless you will be in the fourteenth and fifteenth positions when assembled for battle within the Syntagma. Prove yourselves and your efforts will be recognized. Show cowardice and I will personally nail you to a tree to rot." Croesus departed after delivering his initial brief to us and we set about erecting our tents as instructed.

Stephanos and I laboured quietly on our tents while other soldiers of our Lochos ignored us. "No more training, we are real soldiers," I stated with a grin. "We are soldiers in the Royal Army of the Kings."

"We proved ourselves physically but now we are going to be tested mentally," Stephanos replied. "This time we are the two lowest skilled of our line and the rest of our mates know it."

"They were all in our positions at one point, we must do as we're told and act with courage and we'll eventually earn their respect," I said optimistically.

Our celebratory banter was interrupted by two soldiers of our new Lochos. "You two!" shouted the smaller one. "Why aren't your tents finished? You have to finish digging this drainage trench." The soldier threw a pick ax and shovel in our direction and pointed us to the unfinished labour. The larger one kicked me into the dirt as we submissively walked to our latest chore.

"Lowest of the line," Stephanos reiterated with a smirk. We dug for over an hour until Croesus returned and called the Lochos to formation. Stephanos and I took the two last positions which were reserved for the lowest ranks.

"Men, we have two new recruits to replace Tellis and Demeas. They were fools but died nobly- facing the enemy in battle." Croesus then looked directly at Stephanos and I, "I have no doubt they are scared shitless and will do as they're told. We've been given orders from our Syntagma Commander. By now you have all heard Antipater's forces have crossed the Hellespont into Asia Minor. What you haven't heard is that Satrap Neoptolemus of Armenia has refused the direct order of Lord Regent Perdiccas to join his forces with ours and place himself under the command of General Eumenes. Satrap Neoptolemus has been proclaimed a traitor of the

Kings and the army will march east at dawn to commandeer his forces and usurp his satrapy. Upon completion of this task our reinforced army will march west and defeat Antipater's forces."

Our Lochos received this unbelievable news with silent nerve but, internally, all must have been tempering the same storm of apprehension as I was. We were now setting out to face two separate Greek armies while Perdiccas marched on Ptolemy in Egypt. This was not the case of a superior force led by Alexander defeating lesser barbarian races throughout the known world. This was five separate Greek armies, all comprised of the remnants of Alexander's military, fighting each other for control of the world. And then, of course, there was my pitiful presence. I felt like a boy watching grown men engage in mortal combat except I was somehow expected to contribute to the effort. Countless hours of thrusting a spear into the air had not prepared me for combat verse an experienced Greek army.

Croesus dismissed the men to make ready for breaking camp in the morning and called Stephanos and I over to him. Pointing at Stephanos he stated, "You will be in the fourteenth position and your lesser mate will be in the fifteenth. If the battle necessitates the two of you to face the enemy head on, we're in serious trouble. So keep your nerve and listen to my subordinate officers. First Officer Neokles will be at the eighth position and Second Officer Gelon will be in the rear behind you. Gelon has earned his place and he will be on your ass if you fuck up. I will be at the head of our Lochos and if the battle gets to the point where you have to start using your sarissa I will have been long dead and trampled. Keep your composure and you will earn the respect of your Lochos. Act like a coward and Gelon will slit you from neck to undercarriage. Have a good war boys," were his departing words to us.

Chapter 15

As we began our march east to face the army of Neoptolemus, our formation was led by General Eumenes and his cavalry in the same manner I witnessed Alexander those many years ago. These Cappadocian cavalry units, led by Apollonides, were certainly not the Macedonian Companions, however General Eumenes utilized extraordinary resources and care to create a premier cavalry force both out of military necessity and an inherent fear of his Macedonian regulars' loyalties. The Macedonian Foot Companion Phalanx followed, of which my Syntagma marched as one of six making up our Taxis. Our phalanx was comprised of six such Taxis led by the Phalangiarch, Alcetas- brother of Lord Regent Perdiccas. Our Taxis Strategos, Androkles, led on horseback while several Ouragos', including Drakon, patrolled the formation to maintain order. Normally the main phalanx would be preceded by the Silver Shields but they had all marched with Perdiccas south to defeat Ptolemy in Egypt.

General Eumenes' Macedonian Foot Companions were not the homogenous fighting force they once were, with each Syntagma comprised of men from the same region of Macedon. The Foot Companions were followed by our skirmishers and other mercenaries with the quartermaster, baggage train, and artillery weapons in the rear. For the veterans who had years of services, the entirety of their accumulated wealth and families were stowed in wagons and pack mules in the baggage trains. The baggage train of any army was a prized possession to be safeguarded at all costs. Elite scouting units and spies were sent ahead of our formation to establish the size, location, composition, and morale of Neoptolemus' forces, as well as determine favourable ground to conduct the battle. I thought of the older staff officer I met in the surgeon's tent and what part he was now playing forward of our lines.

Our group of recruits first met with General Eumenes at the western edge of Cappadocia and now our army was marching east to meet Neoptolemus' forces. Neoptolemus was close to us since he had already departed Armenia days ago in keeping with the ruse that he was obeying Lord Regent Perdiccas' orders to join his army with ours. Upon our victory over Neoptolemus, we were to appropriate his surviving forces and immediately march west to meet Antipater's army near the Hellespont where they had already crossed into Ionia on their way east to face Eumenes. As our army snaked its way east, kicking up dust and meandering over the length of several miles, I noticed many locals had taken an interest in our formation along the road just as I had with my mates as a child. Children were following our army playing with wooden sticks and sometimes venturing to within an arm's length of us to get a closer look.

This march was different then my experiences under Agathon and Callisthenes. We did not have to hold our sarissas at the ready and constantly conduct thrusting exercises. Our spears were now disassembled into manageable pieces which were easily carried on our back along with the rest of our armament and bivouac equipment. Agathon and Callisthenes's tortures had certainly strengthened my fortitude and I found the march to be quite tolerable which allowed me to leave the road and return to the enthused company of my family in Ilandra. My fictional voyage seemed more palpable since I had survived my recruitment phase and was now a member of the Royal Army marching to defend the Kings against overt traitors to the Argead family. My family was of course overjoyed to have me back in their presence and the lavish baggage train I had returned with was enough to make us wealthy for generations. My mental masturbations carried me through a few hours of the march which brought us to the end of the sixteen mile day where we set up our bivouacs for the night.

The Taxis' camped in a generally contiguous mass with each Syntagma maintaining orderly bivouacs by Lochos. Our Lochos made camp with Stephanos and I pitching our tents at the far end of our bivouac. This position was to last for one night only and therefore was not as robust as the initial encampment Agathon and Callisthenes marched our line of recruits into which boasted full quartermaster and surgeon tents. The majority of our army's equipment would remain packed until we closed with and defeated

Neoptolemus' army. Our Lochos still had not warmed to our presence so the two of us ate and maintained our equipment by ourselves.

"Today's march was tolerable," I stated. "It seems a lifetime since we were vomiting and collapsing out of Agathon's march."

"You were vomiting," corrected Stephanos. "Our bodies have been properly formed, now we'll see if our nerves have hardened to withstand the rigours of battle."

"Do you have doubts?" Stephanos proved to have superior confidence, courage and bearing than I, thus a public statement of uncertainty surprised me.

"A man won't know how he will act in the presence of danger until he comes face to face with it," Stephanos responded.

"You've proven to me on many occasions your resolve. You stood up to that local drunk in whatever piss ass village we were in on behalf of Bacchylides. You dragged me along to extend Labdacus' life by one more day- something I couldn't have brought myself to do on my own. Surely your father and brother spoke to you about the rigours of battle and thus you are as prepared as one can be without firsthand experience. My cousin spoke to me about his involvement in Alexander's eastern campaigns to Bactria, Sogdiana, and India. He echoed your statements about men not truly knowing how they will react when faced with violence for the first time. I think you and I can only look to related examples in our own lives for hints as to our future acts of soldiery and from what I've witnessed, you, of all men inexperienced with combat, should have the least to worry about."

"You're a good friend Andrikos," Stephanos bestowed graciously. "What in your experiences gives you the confidence to speak with such authority on these matters?"

"There was an incident which forced me to leave my home and ultimately make the decision to join the Royal Army," I responded in a low and deliberate voice. "Of the people I know best that yet draw breath, I would only confide in you what I am about to divulge." Stephanos' face took on a serious expression as he motioned closer to me. "I too have shared in the deliberations of which you now speak in preparation of a violent circumstance. It certainly is not on the level to which we found ourselves on this eve, but it has both bolstered my confidence and forced me from my home." Stephanos leaned in closer as I related to him in a low voice the totality of my affairs regarding Patrochlus, Nearchus, Alexandros, Theon, Hipolytus, Ganymedes, Pasicrates, and the rest of Ilandra's cast of characters. Shame prevented me from recounting my actions within the home of Theon or Nearchus' suicide. When I was finished I commanded Stephanos to make a vow to the Gods never to repeat his knowledge of my past to anyone, to which he agreed while displaying a look of both astonishment towards my story and a new-found respect for me.

"You carry the burden of your past well, Andrikos; I never would have guessed you capable of such feats at so young an age. You truly are ready to kill men by the hundreds."

"I don't recite this story to boast, but rather to reinforce your confidence by proving someone who thinks you his superior in every meaningful way has the ability to do what is necessary when faced with impending violence, thus you will rise to the occasion as well."

Our conversation was interrupted by Croesus who called the Lochos to formation to put out instructions for the remainder of the night and tomorrow morning. We were to receive remedial training from Croesus on the verbal, auditory and visual commands of the Syntagma during battle for the remainder of the evening and break camp at first light to continue our march. Our evening drills forced our Lochos mates to intermittently acknowledge our presence; however Stephanos and I certainly did not receive any feeling of companionship from them. I surmised most were waiting to see if we survived a battle with honour before they committed any finite sentiments of goodwill.

The next three days repeated themselves with our marches beginning at day break, lasting approximately fifteen to seventeen miles, making a hastily fortified camp, and casually going over commands and battle scenarios with Croesus and our two Lochos junior officers Gelon, and Neokles. On the fourth day of our march the army remained in place at daybreak and the rumour within our Lochos was that our scouts had returned and the two armies were now aware of each other's presence- being close enough to join battle. The prolonged wait we now experienced was torturous. Final preparation of weapons and equipment did little to stem the tide of nervous energy brought on by the hours of languish. Idle hands may be the seeds of deviance but an idle mind before battle is fertile soil for doubt and irresolution. Stephanos and I sat near our Lochos mates as they discussed different rumours and scenarios regarding the current situation. Our Lochos believed our scouts and Phalanx Commanders were now deciding where best to field the army that provided best use of the terrain to our advantage. This posturing could take days as both armies attempted to out-manoeuvre the other to gain favourable position. It was generally agreed by our Lochos that we would be called to don our full kit and begin moving shortly.

Two more hours passed when suddenly a commotion could be heard in the distance, rapidly moving closer and closer like an audible wave until finally the sound of trumpets and screams from officers to arm ourselves and line up in formation washed over us like the sea crashing on the shore. Stephanos and I had carefully laid out our kit and weapons in preparation for this order to ensure speedy compliance. We ran to our tents and donned our equipment at a furious pace. Having completed this, we checked each other to make certain neither of us looked ridiculous due to a missed strap, untied lace, or some other incompetence that would be seen as an egregious offense by our Lochos veterans. Our appearance was the only display of aptitude Stephanos and I possessed since we had yet to prove ourselves in the eyes of our Lochos. After double and triple checking each other, Stephanos and I took our fourteenth and fifteenth positions within our Lochos file as part of the Pydna Syntagma.

Our army moved as one lumbering behemoth as fifteen thousand men and five thousand horse hurriedly marched to an open plain near our encampment. Veterans near me in the Syntagma speculated that General Eumenes was choosing this specific location to maximize the advantage he believed he held with our cavalry forces that he painstakingly cultivated over many months in Cappadocia at a great cost of resources. Not knowing anything about battlefield tactics, this hypothesis made sense to Stephanos and myself and thus became our belief as well.

Our army seeped into the open terrain like dye dripped on a white cloth. The instruction was then given to assemble in battle formation. Each Taxis spread out forming a phalanx six Taxis wide occupying the middle of our army. I had a very narrow grasp of my place in the larger formation and followed what everyone was instinctively doing until we came to a stop at our assigned place within the phalanx. I was so confused and overwhelmed by the enormity of organization that was taking place I did not notice the enemy forming opposite us. Because I was so far back in the formation my ability see what lay before us was limited. It appeared the terrain opposite our army gradually raised, thus providing the enemy some high ground over our forces.

To the left of the phalanx were mercenary light cavalry and infantry forces from the defeated Cappadocian territories. To our right was General Eumenes and his elite heavy cavalry. Skirmishers and scout cavalry were arrayed in front of our main force armed with javelins, slings, arrows and other light missiles. Within my own Syntagma, Stephanos and I stood perfectly still with our eighteen foot sarissas held straight up at the ready. Being in the rear of the phalanx I truly had an unbelievable view of the forest of pikes arrayed by our phalanx. After the commotion of manoeuvring subsided, a deafening calm washed over our army so we may hear further instructions. As the enemy settled into their position, word circulated through our lines that Neoptolemus possessed a robust phalanx of veteran Macedonian infantry at the centre of his formation directly opposite our phalanx. This news did not bolster my confidence as I recalled Croesus' comment about being in serious trouble if I was required to use my sarissa during the battle. An opponent of hardened Macedonian phalangites might indeed be able to stab and hack their way to me.

I heard a loud set of horns blow with corresponding flags signalling the skirmishers, followed by a cloud of dust being kicked up. Their purpose was to defeat the enemy skirmishers and engage and harass the opposing army to sow confusion and create openings in the line that could be exploited by heavier units such as the phalanx or cavalry. I was so far back from our skirmishers all that could be ascertained was the dust, the occasional missile in flight, and the distant roar of men engaging in mortal combat. An individual scream of either agony or bloodlust could sporadically be heard over the symphony of violence which made me content that I was so far back from the fighting. I immediately felt guilty for thinking such a cowardly notion and a large pit opened in my stomach when we were commanded to move forward to exploit gains made by our skirmishers. This command was greeted with enthusiastic cheers by some and blank stares by others. Stephanos looked back at me and gave an encouraging head nod.

I gauged we were twelve hundred feet from the enemy when we began moving and I could not see whether they were now moving towards us as well. Someone then yelled out, "missiles!" which was followed by several arrows zipping through our forest of pikes. Most were deflected by our sarissas, causing them to lose their deadly trajectory and flail off our helmets and linen cuirasses. Other arrows were loosed with greater skill which caused them to descend on our phalanx at almost a straight vertical trajectory. These well placed projectiles rained down into phalangite shoulder blades, chests, and even a few through the helmet. None landed in this way near me but I could hear screams, some faint, and some frighteningly loud, of soldiers being struck by these warheads.

We continued our march forward and the front line of our phalanx was now closing with the enemy. The dust saturated everything and I could only hear the savage battle being fought fifteen ranks in front of me. As our armies joined our momentum ceased and sarissas from both sides entangled like a wooden grinder of flesh. I could hear the screams of men being impaled while others roared with aggression as if Ares had possessed them. I could hear the Lochos officers of the eighth rank shouting orders and encouraging the men. Gelon and his counterparts at the sixteenth position continually shouted for us to keep moving forward, to keep our formation tight, and to keep pushing. Because I could not see anything in front of me I began focussing on our right flank where General Eumenes and the heavy cavalry were positioned. While the momentum of the phalanx slowed to a stalemate, it appeared our heavy cavalry was making notable gains. They were now in front of our phalanx on the right flank and giving chase to the fleeing enemy cavalry. This site encouraged the men but did not translate into further forward momentum. The enemy phalanx was now using their raised terrain to their advantage which effectively halted any forward progress by our foot soldiers and began moving our Phalanx back. The constant din of screams and weaponry slamming against armor was the most disturbing noise I had ever heard. Both generals chose their positions on the field well and the battle would be determined by who best leveraged their advantages.

The bloody stalemate lasted another hour and the enemy had succeeded in moving our Phalanx back several feet. I noticed Stephanos and I had moved forward in our column in comparison with many to our left and right, pointing to our column losing a number of men. Screams from the front signalled their Phalanx was besting ours and I now began fearing a sarissa point slamming through our rear ranks at any moment. Just as Gelon was becoming more and more frenzied in his appeal for us to hold the ground we were cumulatively losing, General Apollonides could be seen leading his heavy cavalry towards the enemy's left flank like a well thrown spear into the side of the enemy formation. Our heavy cavalry smashed into the left flank of the enemy phalanx which caused unbelievable destruction and prompted their retreat. The enemy phalanx was trampled, impaled, and routed by our heavy cavalry. Our Lochos officers now screamed at inhuman decibels to move forward and seize the momentum. We took several robust steps forward and I began walking over the first of the corpses- both enemy and friendly. Their skulls were caved in from being trampled, their torsos showed signs of impalement or slashes. Some eyes were out of socket, some stomachs were emptied. The macabre carcasses all contributed to soaking the ground with a slippery, reddish-black bile whose smell burrowed into my nasal cavity. I could smell it in between breaths. I could taste the smell in my mouth. It permeated the battlefield, making my stomach sick.

The momentum had swung completely in our favour, thanks to General Eumenes' seizure of the enemy's baggage train and the flanking manoeuvre by General Apollonides, prompting a full retreat and surrender of Neoptolemus' forces as they stood huddled in a mass of terrified confusion. As they capitulated, our army continued to encircle them and an uneasy truce was reached. Emissaries from the defeated foe were sent to discuss the terms of the surrender which greatly favoured Eumenes due to his cavalry's successful capture of the entire contents of their accumulated wealth and families. General Eumenes reached the following agreement with the defeated army: The indigenous Armenian forces would return to their Satrapy and serve the new Satrap to be installed by Eumenes; the Macedonian soldiers and Greek mercenaries would join our army; the non-Greek mercenary officers would be ransomed and the non-Greek mercenary soldiers would be killed. It was later learned Neoptolemus fled the field at the site of Apollonides' cavalry charge with a small contingent of his bodyguard.

It took another hour for the enemy army to be divided and all weapons seized from the non-Greek soldiers as per the terms of their surrender. The Macedonians, other Greeks, and Armenian contingent were all segregated separately under armed guard while our army singled out non-Greek officers from non-Greek regulars. Stephanos and I were still bystanders to all of this activity while our Syntagma stood in formation. Once the non-Greek officers were removed, all that remained were non-Greek regulars from the barbarian territories north of Armenia such as Pontus and Scythia. They numbered about two thousand and were completely disoriented by the massive isolation efforts conducted after their defeat. Drakon, covered in blood and dirt, then called several names forward. Stephanos and I were included. As I looked around the assembled lot I realized we were all the most inexperienced soldiers of the phalanx. We spotted Bacchylides and Spear amongst our contingent and made our way towards them. As we did so Croesus pulled Stephanos and I aside and gave us words of encouragement while assuring us the coming bloodshed would be good for our development.

Drakon assumed the head of our mob and shouted, "Line up! You have been chosen to eliminate the remainder of our enemy. Do not get ahead of each other in the formation and remember your training. If I see anyone hesitate in this duty I will kill you where you stand and you will die with the rest of these filthy barbarians. Leave your sarissas here, you will retrieve them when you're finished. This work is personal and requires the short sword." With that Drakon moved behind the line of new recruits and ordered us to begin our march forward into the mob of barbarians whose escape was blocked by a full Taxis formation to their rear. Our staged battle was of immense entertainment to the rest of the army. Soldiers took bets on the bravery of this recruit or that. Lochagos' used it as a test to determine the soldiery of their untested men. The spirit of our line was strong, with some doing all in their power to not sprint ahead of the formation and bury their sword into the skull of an unarmed barbarian.

I remember feeling uneasy listening to Leandros recount this practice and now felt it cheapened our impressive victory, while doing nothing to bring honour and respect to the recruits. We neared our unarmed enemy and Stephanos, sensing my internal doubts, yelled over the low roar to me, Spear, and Bacchylides, "Don't treat this any differently than warfare. These barbarians will take your sword and kill you with it if you let your guard down. Let us show our commanders that we four our better than this menial task so the next time we are closer to the battle and are not in need of artificial experiences to test our mettle!"

Stephanos' words strengthened my resolve as we closed with the enemy. Some of the victims mustered their courage and charged at our line bare-handed. Others retreated to delay the inevitable, causing mayhem within the condemned contingent. I wondered to myself which way I would be running if I were in their situation. The first man I came into contact with violently lunged at me trying to grab my sword by its sharpened edge, slicing his palms and fingers. He was larger and stronger than I but I managed to brace most of his inertia with my shield while frantically stabbing at his hands, further lacerating them. His enraged scream made me wince as he tried to rip my shield from me with his blood-soaked hands. I exploited this opening by stabbing him low in his side, producing seeping black bile from a punctured organ. He instinctively covered the wound with his hand, allowing me to stab him directly in the chest. My blade got caught within his ribs however and I struggled to pull it back as another barbarian punched me in the side of the face and began biting my sword arm. I let out a scream which alerted Stephanos to my predicament. My assailant's eyes and mouth instantly opened past the point of normalcy while his entire body convulsed. I looked to my right to see Stephanos had stabbed him directly in the back of the neck, severing his spine and dispatching him immediately. Stephanos removed his sword and the corpse collapsed to the ground in a vicious death spasm.

The charge of courageous victims had run its course and all that remained were the multitude of men trying to escape. I looked to my left to see Bacchylides hacking these manic escapees with utter merriment, even laughing at times as blood spattered on his face. Spear was coldly dispatching them with the perfect proficiency his impressive physique evoked. We were now walking over the dead and dying with puncture wounds in their chests and hack wounds on their arms. Many were still alive and writhing in an orgy of agony at our feet. As we moved forward, soldiers were stomping their skulls in with their heels and repeatedly stabbing them to ensure no one escaped our wave of death. One victim began clawing at my legs, digging his nails into my skin. I instinctively picked my leg up as if I had stepped on a nail and brought my heel down on his temple with a violent force that surprised even me. I felt his skull fracture and my heel slightly sunk into his head. I will remember that grotesque feeling for the rest of my life. I dispatched another crawling in my path with a brisk stab to the throat.

I caught up to my first escaping victim with his back still facing me, instinctively attempting to push his way to the back of the mob to escape the slaughter. I stabbed him to the left of his spine which forced him to reach for the wound and fall to his knees. I then hacked the side of his head, feeling my blade break his skull and cut through part of his brain. I killed several more in this dishonourable manner until I reached the last of the men who had nowhere left to retreat. Many fell to their knees, putting their hands out crying for mercy, cursing us in unknown languages or praying to unfamiliar deities. We hacked at their outstretched hands and forearms before stabbing them in the throat and chest.

There were others, however, who didn't act craven when faced with imminent murder. They stood or sat very still and looked their assailants directly in the eye, as if daring us to kill them in this most shameful of manners. One now stood before me and I could not hold eye contact with him. I felt his appearance and demeanour superior to me and I hesitated in delivering the death blow. I didn't think myself worthy enough to kill this man so I yelled to my immediate left for Bacchylides to do the ignominious deed. Bacchylides apparently did not have the same scruples as I and hacked his neck several times until his head became detached from his body. His eyes never left me during this gruesome ordeal and he never let out a scream. I looked at his eyes but not into them during his murder and felt he had defeated me. Even as his head lay severed on the ground it looked directly into my eyes, causing me to look away. Few victims remained in front of me now and I dispatched them with anger and vigour until I had reached the other Taxis blocking the victims' retreat. As our line of murderous recruits completed our dishonourable task, the army cheered for us as if we had lost our combat virginity.

We were all exhausted after the ordeal and my arm was both fatigued and pained due to deep bite marks. Drakon allowed us to pillage the bodies for loot but these pathetic corpses held very little of any value. After about fifteen minutes, Drakon called us back into formation where General Eumenes congratulated his victorious forces with a very abrupt appearance and speech. I was not close enough to hear it but the veterans did not seem impressed with his words or his command presence in front of the formation. No one could deny he had led a brilliant victory, however, and that was most important.

Chapter 16

That night General Eumenes kept in the Greek tradition of celebrating a battlefield victory. He had much to celebrate, for his victory was absolute with little loss of life to our army. The only blemish on the triumph was the failure to capture or kill Neoptolemus, who cravenly bolted from the field at the sight of Apollonides' cavalry charge against his left flank.

The veterans of our army drank heavily around large campfires that evening. allowing myself, Stephanos, Spear, Bacchylides and even Diokles to enjoy each other's company without being hassled by our Lochos' to perform menial tasks. Spear and Bacchylides' prior disdain for one another appeared to have dissipated with time, allowing the five of us to bond over shared hardship and glory. Just as the veterans were retelling inflated tales of the day's battle, our merry band recounted our tertiary role in the victory. We all willingly forgot our adversaries were unarmed as Bacchylides reenacted the execution of one of his victims while mimicking their expressions of terror to the enjoyment of all. Stephanos recalled his part in saving me from a barbarian cannibal looking to bite off my arm which produced wild laughter and a demand to see the wound.

Croesus gingerly made his way over to our band with a jug of wine. We all shut up and stood at attention. "Evening sir," Stephanos and I delivered in unison.

"At ease, at ease," responded Croesus with a faint slur. "Who are these three?" Croesus asked pointing at Bacchylides, Diokles and Spear.

"They are our mates from recruitment," replied Stephanos.

"Did they participate in today's victory?"

"Yes sir, they were directly left of Andrikos." Answered Stephanos. "They served honourably, killing many barbarians."

"Then the five of you popped your cherries tonight. I brought you a jug of wine to share. Enjoy with your mates then make your way to our Lochos fire where you will be officially recognized and accepted into the unit. You three," Croesus snapped, addressing Spear and Bacchylides, "I suggest you do the same."

"Yes sir!" replied the three in unison.

As Croesus stumbled away, Stephanos and I each retrieved cups from our tent area nearby and distributed them amongst our band. Once libations were poured we put our cups up, not quite knowing exactly what to drink to. Bacchylides put forth, "to victory," but Stephanos overruled the suggestion with, "to Labdacus." We all sincerely honoured our fallen friend and finished off the jug feeling we were invincible in the coming campaign against Antipater. Our officers' intent to strengthen our resolve by including us in the slaughter of barbarians did have its intended effect. Tonight was the first time I had thought of Labdacus since his death and it was clear that Stephanos had not forgotten our little mascot either. Thinking of him now made me nauseous with pity so I deliberately put his memory from my mind for the remainder of the evening.

The five of us departed to our respective Lochos' where Stephanos and I found the veterans' intoxication had reached a fever pitch. Three women had been procured either by local vendors or from the contingent of entrepreneurs following our army's movements. They did not appear to be in good shape nor did they seem to be enjoying their evening assignment. Drunk, rough men, too intoxicated to climax, were taking turns with them as they were bent over makeshift tables near our fire. They were being forced to drink wine while being continuously ravaged. One laid still and internalized her discomfort, one let out muttered moans of displeasure after each thrust, the last was crying softly. The scene playing out before me did not arouse any desire to join in.

Stephanos and I approached Croesus as ordered, who promptly called out our presence to the rest of the Lochos. We were received with drunken cheers and pats on the back and from our mates in the same manner as we once did with Labdacus. To the veterans, we were a sort of mascot. More wine was provided to us and Stephanos was escorted to the front of the line to take a turn on one of the women for the veterans' amusement. I felt fortunate that I was not immediately chosen for I had no desire to partake, yet refusing such a demand was not an option. Stephanos, not yet being drunk, competently accomplished his task to the delight of the Lochos. I wondered how he could display such empathy for Labdacus and seemingly none for the poor girl. He no doubt knew he was being ordered by the Lochos to participate and therefore declining on moral grounds would ostracize him from our unit; however, if these were his thoughts, he hid them well.

The rest of the night was a blur as more wine was consumed, songs were sung, respect to the fallen was paid, women were taken, and oaths were sworn. There was not a morning formation the following day as most were hung over with some vomiting out the sides of their tents. I woke up not remembering the last two hours of the night and feeling sick. Croesus walked through our bivouac, looking unwell, to ensure his men were all still alive. He informed us our first formation would be at noon after he had attended the Syntagma staff meeting.

I drank some brackish water, splashed the remainder on my face, rinsed out my mouth, squared away my tent area and readied my equipment for orders to pack up and depart. Stephanos was still sleeping when I received permission from Croesus to visit the surgeon's tent to return my wrist brace and have my bite wounds looked at. My walk through our encampment saw soldiers in varying states of biliousness. Everything was being done at half-speed.

The surgeon's tent, however, was a sea of activity. The casualties from the battlefield that survived the night were being tended to by several field surgeons. Before seeking out Philotheos, I walked through the bay of cots while ensuring to stay out of anyone's way. I saw several injuries of a gruesome nature. Bandages covered in blood, brownish bile, and greenish-yellow puss. Hideous stab wounds and lacerations were freshly stitched. The ground beneath my feet was saturated in all manner of bodily fluids which creating a vile stench. Some patients were crying out in pain, others were drugged with Apollinarix, a powerful sedative and pain reliever made from Black Henbane. Some patients looked scared, others weakly awaited death. Philotheos spotted me and called me over to him.

"How's my young patient?" Philotheos asked. "Are you ready to return your brace?" I removed it while Philotheos began grabbing, squeezing and bending the affected area. "How does this feel?"

"There is still residual pain but it is certainly manageable. I did receive a wound from the battle, however, which I wanted you to look at."

"Really? Let's have a look," Philotheos exclaimed excitedly. My value clearly went up in his eyes now that I had a real battle injury. I removed the makeshift bandage off my right arm and showed him the bite marks. "Ooh, this is nice," he observed smiling. "How did you receive this?" I retold the story to which he produced an ointment made from honey and metal shavings. "I am going to give you a small vile of this ointment and some extra bandages. I want you to change bandages and apply the ointment every day for a week, understood?"

"Yes sir," I responded. Before he could send me on my way I interjected, "Sir, the man from the battle staff that was here with me last time, do you know him?"

"Vettias? Older man, tall, light sandy hair?" Philotheos answered.

"Yes, what do you know of him? Does he come here often?" I inquired leveraging the renewed interest Philotheos had in me now that I was a real wounded veteran.

"I don't know more than the very little he tells me when he requires supplies on behalf of General Eumenes. He never says what it is for or the nature of his work, however he will hint towards secret undertakings on behalf of the army if he encounters hesitancy on our part to provide all he desires. Why do you ask?"

"No reason," I answered, looking to end the conversation and depart now that I had the man's name. "He had asked me to seek him out about something and I wanted to know more about him is all." Satisfied with this answer, Philotheos dismissed me and I exited the surgeon's tent, leaving the groans of pain behind me.

As I departed the tent I assessed I still had time before my Lochos formation and decided to walk around the quartermaster and supply areas of the encampment. Most items were still packed since the army was planning on marching west to meet Antipater shortly after our victory. I saw the holding areas where our prisoners from the battle were being held. The Macedonians and Greek mercenaries had separate bivouacs where they waited to be integrated into our army. They did not appear in want of any supplies and were in good spirits. The Armenian forces were preparing for their return home under the command of a new Satrap assigned by Lord Regent Perdiccas. The barbarian officers' accommodations were not as generous as they awaited the long process of ransom to further finance our army's activities.

Taking my leave of the holding areas I felt a hand touch my shoulder and a familiar voice spoke my name. "Andrikos!" I turned around to see the welcome sight of my old friend from our initial line of recruits, Rhexenor.

"Rhexenor, how are you?"

"Doing well, I have been assigned to the quartermaster," Rhexenor explained. "No opportunities for glory but a good place to establish importance within the army. We are responsible for all the army's possessions to include loot accumulated in the baggage train. Each day I increase my ability to acquire all manner of items. Let me know if you are in need of anything and I'll see what I can do."

"Will do, I appreciate the offer," I responded.

"So how is the phalanx?" Rhexenor asked excitedly. "Did you see action in the battle yesterday? How are our enlistment mates?"

"Stephanos and I are in the same Lochos; Diokles, Spear, and Bacchylides are in adjacent columns in my Syntagma. They are all alive and well. We pretty much occupy positions in the back of our Lochos'; however we were all part of the annihilation of the barbarian regulars yesterday."

"I figured you were there, I was looking for you. We all made sure to get prime viewing for the slaughter. That was a great spectacle, did you kill many of them?"

"We all did- really gruesome stuff." I displayed my wound which only whetted Rhexenor's appetite for more details. I explained what happened while Rhexenor hung on my every word. He clearly did not think killing unarmed men to be an issue.

"If you could speak to your Lochagos to allow me to participate in the next opportunity to eliminate prisoners I would be indebted to you, and am certainly in a position to return the favour."

"Are you sure you don't want to be in the front line during the actual battle?" I asked sarcastically.

"They already determined I am not competent enough for work like that," Rhexenor retorted sullenly. "This would be my only opportunity for battlefield glory."

I didn't bother recounting the ghastly details of what he was asking to be a part of and assured him I would do what I could, to which he heartily thanked me. We embraced as brothers and I took my leave to ensure I was present at the Lochos formation. As I returned to our Lochos I began feeling my initial apprehensions about my part in the battle give way to an acceptance of it as a necessary evil- an inevitable consequence of war. I rationalized that as long as I didn't enjoy it I could be protected from its immoral taint. Others took pleasure in watching the slaughter as sport, while people like Rhexenor were begging to be a part of it. Hopefully I wouldn't be a part of that contingent of murder much longer as my experience grew.

I returned to find Stephanos stirring and most of my Lochos beginning their waking routines. A concert of hacking, spitting, belching, coughing, and flatulence could be heard from our bivouac as my Lochos mates readied for first formation. Croesus returned from his Syntagma meeting shortly after and called us to formation.

Once formed, Croesus addressed us. "Men, we were victorious on the battlefield, we lost two of our brothers but our two new recruits popped their cherry and carried themselves with honor. Although the enemy general fled like a coward, the fight to protect the two kings and preserve all that Alexander conquered continues. Our role is but one of many actions that must take place in order to achieve that goal. As we speak Lord Regent Perdiccas and the Silver Shields have invaded Egypt to dislodge Ptolemy, ally of Antipater and traitor to the kings. They will be victorious just as we were with Neoptolemus yesterday. We have commandeered the Macedon regulars and Greek mercenaries of Neoptolemus' forces and are now incorporating them into our army. We will add one full Taxis of Macedonians to our phalanx and another two thousand Greek mercenaries to be used as light infantry on our flanks. Each Syntagma will see some personnel changes made, to include ours, as we integrate Neoptolemus' Macedonians into our phalanx. Our next fight lies west where we will confront Antipater's forces to secure all Alexander's gains east of Macedon. We will break camp at dawn to begin what we estimate to be a five day march west. Make all preparations necessary for that schedule; as I hear more about how the Macedonian integration will affect us, I will let you know."

As we were dismissed to make necessary preparations for the coming departure I heard several veterans in our Lochos speculating that each rank was to receive a number of the Macedonians because General Eumenes, not being from Macedon himself, did not trust their allegiance to him as a coherent unit in pitched battle opposite another phalanx of Macedon. He was going to dissipate their homogeneity throughout the already mixed Syntagmas of our phalanx to mitigate any possibility of mass defection or refusal to fight. The plan made sense to me, however I was a little nervous that I would have to further prove my worth to new veterans within our Lochos and Syntagma. Since I had already completed much of the required tasks to break camp I laid down near Stephanos' unorganized living space, half watching him toil, half napping. Croesus came through two hours later and briefly introduced to our new Macedonian attachments: Strabo and Brick. Brick was aptly named for he had bulbous, rock-like features, while Strabo appeared to be the brains of the two. They were greeted as coldly as Stephanos and I were and everyone went back to attending their pre movement tasks.

The battle, coupled with the reorganization of the phalanx and impending movement orders, caused that evening to be busy. The entire Taxis seemed to be toiling with nervous energy. Food was eaten quickly while wounds were bandaged, equipment was repaired, weapons were sharpened and bronze was shined. Very little socializing occurred and the entire phalanx retired early that evening to be ready for the morning's march. The horns sounded early at dawn and all soldiers packed their equipment, quickly ate breakfast, and assembled in full marching formation. The day's march was pleasant and my mind was free to travel back home for several hours to enjoy the company of my adoring family, teeming with pride in my accomplishments, despite my reservations regarding the role I played in the recent battle.

We established our temporary encampment that evening, where Stephanos and I were finally invited to sit at the Lochos fire as equals. The two new Macedonians were there as well. Their prestige and experience earned them a seat at any campfire and none from our Lochos was going to say otherwise.

Our First Officer Neokles began interrogating our new Macedonian mates. "Will your coward leader Neoptolemus run to Antipater? Are we going to see him again in a few days?"

"We don't claim a woman from a backwater in Epirus as our Commander," Strabo answered. "He controlled our salary in that uncivilized Armenian shithole- that is all."

"Why did you follow his orders to betray Lord Regent Perdiccas?" Neokles continued. "He is the rightful Macedonian protector of Kings Alexander IV and Philip III."

"He convinced us that you were marching to fight General Craterus," Strabo responded. "General Craterus is the most respected of the living Generals from Macedon. He Commanded the Macedonian Phalanx at the Battle of Issus. He led us at the Battle of the Hydaspes River in India."

"We are marching to face Antipater," Neokles countered.

"General Craterus has allied with Antipater, Ptolemy, and Antigonus," Strabo interjected.

"We march to face the army of Antipater and probably that rat coward Neoptolemus as well!" Neokles snapped. "Will you fight for General Eumenes of Cardia against Antipater from Macedon?"

"We will fight for Lord Regent Perdiccas, protector of the Argead Kings," Strabo concluded. "That answer will have to suffice for now."

A general lull overtook the fire as several small side conversations about the possibility of fighting General Craterus petered out and everyone retired for the evening. Strabo was correct, however. Many soldiers, including non-Macedonians like Leandros, held General Craterus in the highest regard. General Eumenes was smart to disperse the incoming Macedonian contingent; he would always be vulnerable when fighting a true Macedonian general from Alexander's or Philip's campaigns.

The next day's march transpired without incident as our scouting units were again sent out to locate the enemy and ascertain its size, composition, capabilities, and morale, as well as determine the best ground to occupy for the battle. Three days later our scouts returned and Croesus informed our Lochos the enemy had been located. This news roused the men and eased rumours of Craterus being with Antipater's army since he was not reported being seen.

After the following day's march the entire army remained in formation to be addressed by General Eumenes. This was the longest he had been in my line of sight and I strained to obtain a good glimpse of him. He was of slightly below-average height and stature and dressed in the same manner as the Macedonian Generals. He had not adopted the eastern style dress Alexander and some of his close advisors did for fear of further alienating his Macedonian regulars. His face was very handsome, having high cheek bones, good proportionality and complexion. His overall command presence was somewhat lacking in the view of many of the soldiers, however, and his voice was not deep and did not carry well.

"Men," General Eumenes began, "We stand on the verge of facing another enemy of Alexander's accomplishments and his rightful heirs to it. You are all the true and legitimate protectors of Alexander's legacy. The men who lead our enemy may be Macedonian, but they only seek power for themselves. As all of you know, I am not Macedonian and have no designs on usurping Alexander's empire. I serve at the behest of Lord Regent Perdiccas, protector of the two Kings and temporary steward of the realm as directed by Alexander himself. I've been serving the Macedonian cause since I was assigned to King Philip's staff many years ago. I was there, managing the affairs of the Empire through all of Alexander's conquests, always sitting at the right hand of the King. I was there in India where I personally held Command at the Jaxartes and Hydaspes Rivers. I was made a Royal Bodyguard by Alexander himself for my leadership and loyalty. I was there at his deathbed when he gave Lord Regent Perdiccas the Royal Signet Ring, personally identifying him as Regent. I was present at the leadership council after his death where all in the room, including our current enemies, agreed upon Alexander IV and Philip III as rightful successors. We have defeated those who challenged Alexander's conquest in Cappadocia and those who challenged Alexander's final instructions to name Perdiccas Lord Regent just days ago. Now we face an enemy who challenges Alexander's very legacy by claiming his heirs to be illegitimate!" His emphasis on this last line evoked a strong response from the army.

"I am not one for flamboyant spectacle like some of my contemporaries. But I have assembled you here in this way to relay a message from the God King himself, delivered to me in a dream last night." The army now grew silent to the point where one could hear individual breaths being taken. "It was interpreted by our priests this morning to be an acceptance of my stewardship of his army on behalf of his legitimate son and brother. It was an omen for victory." The men burst into a roar, for a favourable omen sent from Alexander himself was undefeatable.

"Men, there are several factions forming as a result of Alexander's death but rest assured, I will always fight on the side of Alexander's true heirs. I will always do all I can to protect them so Alexander IV may one day take his rightful place upon the throne. Those that follow me can always be confident in the same and when you fight our enemies in the coming days you may tell them as the life slowly leaves their body that you fight for Alexander and they fight for a second rate schoolmate of his or his father's!" At this conclusion the men again burst out into cheers, begging to face the enemy at that immediate moment. The men who had doubted many things about General Eumenes just moments ago were now cheering for him to lead them to the Gates of Hades.

The next day was spent in place as our army again sent its scouts and commanding officers out to choose favourable ground to occupy during the battle. Our Lochos passed the time polishing our armour, sharpening weapons, and generally laying about discussing all manner of rumours. Croesus summoned Stephanos and me to inform us that he was moving us up in the Lochos order to move some of the wounded to the rear and to give us further experience. We would now occupy the sixth and seventh positions. This was the first half of the column and would almost guarantee direct participation in the battle. Stephanos and I both thanked Croesus for his confidence in us and were dismissed. Walking back to our equipment Stephanos stated with a smile "You better have my back."

"We are certain to see combat, especially with you at the sixth position," I replied. "That's only one position back from the initial sarissa combatants." The two of us sat back down in silence awaiting further instruction with ominous thoughts of the coming battle now occupying our inner-dialogues.

Chapter 17

An hour before midday I heard the coming crescendo of noise signalling it was time to move into position. Stephanos and I hurriedly donned our full kit and double-checked each other for minor omissions. We then took our new places at the sixth and seventh positions directly in front of First Officer Neokles. As we got situated Neokles expressed his confidence in our abilities and also threatened to kill us if we demeaned our new positions of honour. Once the army formed the order was given to occupy the predetermined ground on the battlefield. Antipater's forces were doing the same opposite us on the Cappadocian plain. General Eumenes headed the right flank with Apollonides and his heavy cavalry while a different Macedonian General named Perdiccas, known as the lesser since Lord Regent Perdiccas' rise to power, led the left flank of light infantry and light cavalry. As the two armies faced each other, word spread quickly from Neoptolemus' former Macedonian phalangites that the traitor general's banners could be seen on the enemy's left flank arrayed directly opposite General Eumenes' position.

An imposing man on horseback from the enemy right flank then rode out front of their formation, up and down the enemy line, rallying his men to a fever pitch. The performance was impressive and certainly had its intended effect on the morale of their troops. Many of our veterans envied the enemy general's inspiring command presence and popularity with his men. Suddenly, a wave of noise and commotion came over our formation screaming, "It's Craterus, it's Craterus!" The whole of the army gasped at the prospect of charging into battle against the greatest living Macedonian General. The Lochagos', Ouragos' and Syntagma Commanders rallied their phalangites, imploring them to keep their resolve and remember General Eumenes' speech the day prior. The junior officers of our Lochos threatened to kill anyone seen hesitating in battle. Their words were directed towards men like

Strabo and Brick, both of whom now occupied our ninth and tenth positions.

The plain which the battle was to be fought on was expansive, and a great distance separated the two armies. After Craterus' inspiring performance he returned to lead the enemy right flank and quickly made a direct charge at our left flank. Our cavalry appeared to have superior numbers, especially our heavy cavalry, but Craterus looked willing to mitigate his inferior numbers with the sheer weight of his leadership by charging his heavy cavalry directly at our light cavalry and light infantry in the same manner of Alexander. General Eumenes and Apollonides then led our heavy cavalry charge directly at Neoptolemus and the enemy left flank. Both of these engagements took place well ahead of our phalanx and Phalangiarch Alcetas ordered us to begin marching forward.

Since I was considerably closer to the front of our line I could see more of the battle unfolding in front of us. Both cavalry engagements occurred far in advance of our line and resembled a mass of bodies, horses, shouting, and dust. We continued marching forward when I heard a loud roar of cheers coming from the left side of the phalanx. As I looked over I witnessed the surprising sight of General Craterus' cavalry in full retreat and our cavalry hot on their heels, slaying scores of fleeing horsemen. A lone horseman from our left flank rode in our direction at full gallop. When he was within audible distance he began shouting "Craterus is dead! Craterus is dead! Craterus is dead!" The phalanx met his cries with cautious excitement, primarily because no one believed the news. The lone horseman rode on past the phalanx towards the right flank cavalry forward of our line to bring word of Craterus' death and the left flank's defeat.

Our pace naturally increased as we heard the news and saw the enemy left flank in full route. Drakon barked out orders for everyone to maintain their spacing and alignment, cautioning us not to get caught up in the moment and do something stupid. As we neared the right flank cavalry assault we could see the enemy begin to take flight and our heavy cavalry lead a full route. This welcome scene bolstered our spirits to the point that it took all of our power to not break formation and bolt at full speed towards the enemy phalanx.

Lochagos' and junior officers were all screaming at the top of their lungs, horns were blaring and drums were pounding over the phalanx's wild screams of blood lust and our desire to take part in the slaughter. A rider from the right flank raced towards our line holding a severed head shouting "Neoptolemus is dead by the hand of General Eumenes!" This unbelievable news provoked frenzy among the phalanx. Everyone was now screaming and begging for their chance to kill the enemy. Drakon was actually whipping phalangites back to keep them in proper formation. This was done out of battlefield necessity, however, since I suspected Drakon appreciated our fanatic desire for bloodshed.

Both of the enemy's defeated flanks retreated to the relative safety of the enemy middle phalanx of Macedonians, now standing as a fortress under direct assault. The news had surely reached them by now and they stood in disbelief at the events that had occurred so unexpectedly around them. General Eumenes sounded a loud trumpet instructing Apollonides and Perdiccas the lesser to pull their cavalry units back to our phalanx as we were now within three hundred feet of the enemy lines. Emissaries from our army were sent to the now leaderless enemy mass with the bodies of General Craterus and Neoptolemus in tow to offer truce if they joined forces with our army. The majority of our soldiers could still not believe the swiftness and proficiency of our victory over one of the greatest living Macedonian generals of the time; yet here we were negotiating a peace without even engaging the enemy phalanx. Whatever our feelings of General Eumenes prior to today's battle, he would now forever be considered a formidable commander of men.

The enemy officers quickly gave their consent to surrender and join the Royal Army of the Kings, still in awe of what had just occurred and grateful for the opportunity to surrender. As our phalanx stood in formation, rumours began flying about the cavalry battle that just ensued. It was said General Craterus fell from his horse and was ingloriously trampled by his own cavalry. Just as we struggled to understand what we were being told, news of Neoptolemus' demise was even more shocking. General Eumenes and Neoptolemus had spied each other during the cavalry charge and engaged in hand-to-hand combat after falling from their horses during the initial clash. Neoptolemus moderately wounded General Eumenes before our Commander was able to hack off his head in full view of all present.

The totality of our victory brought a deafening calm over both phalanxes, despite our cries for blood minutes earlier. Everyone stood perfectly still waiting for our orders and wondering what would happen next. It was discovered that Antipater was not among the vanquished, however, because he had led a large contingent to parts further south and east. General Eumenes allowed our defeated foes to regroup, resupply off the local land, and tend to their casualties- of which there were over a thousand from their cavalry units. The enemy would report to our encampment the next morning for integration into the Royal Army.

The terms of the surrender being reached, our army was marched back to our encampment while the enemy carried out the tasks allowed them by General Eumenes. There was no celebration that evening as there was after our victory over Neoptolemus because the enemy had not yet been dissipated and integrated into our force and General Eumenes did not trust a still autonomous Macedonian phalanx not under armed guard. Provisions were arranged by individual units, however, especially within the esteemed cavalry, to discreetly celebrate the victory with libations. Because we would not be moving tomorrow due to the cumbersome task of incorporating the defeated Macedonians into or army, our Lochos shared a few jugs of wine without wild enthusiasm since we had not played a role in the victory. Our discussions centred around the future and the encouraging momentum we now enjoyed on our way to completely defeating Antipater's forces and securing the Macedonian throne for the true heirs of Alexander. We ended our subdued celebration early and retired for the evening confident in our mission and certain in our prospects of achieving it.

My father was waiting for me that evening, sitting near our burnt out Lochos fire staring longingly at a jug of wine before looking up to see me with a warm smile on his face. "My son the hero," he said, putting his arm around me. "I knew you would succeed."

"Not dying in battle does not make one a hero, father," I replied, only now fully understanding Leandros' words to Argos. "I don't like the word hero, father. My actions during our first battle were less than honourable but I am done denying you your satisfaction as long as we cease to discuss it in the precious fleeting moments I have to speak with you."

"Ha, you and Leandros need to let your fathers be proud of you. It's true killing unarmed, *yet still dangerous*, barbarians is not what you envisioned when you and Nearchus played soldier as children, but you have to earn the right to face a proper enemy in open combat. You did so and now are a valued member of the phalanx. But you're down on yourself again aren't you?"

I nodded sullenly.

"About the barbarians?"

I nodded again.

"You did what you were ordered to do and you conducted yourself with as much honour as one can in such a situation. These things happen in warfare. Your General, he is a good and honourable man is he not? Someone selflessly fighting on behalf of the Kings?"

"Yes, General Eumenes is a good man."

"And do you think him damned to Tartarus because of his command to slaughter barbarian prisoners?"

"No, father."

"And why not?"

"It had to be done, I suppose."

"Then why do you belittle yourself for carrying out what had to be done?"

"I just don't see it as an honourable part to play in the victory. Being on the front line, facing the enemy in close combat, those men are the heroes."

"And you were chosen to be one of these heroes today were you not? You can't help the way the battle played out. You will get your chance. And the women last night? You've been thinking about that as well. Whores on campaign are not exactly the same as the ones in Eurydike's brothel are they? It's good you have these feelings-proves you have noble intentions. But do you think everyone that partook in their pleasure a villain? Even your new friend Stephanos?

"No," I replied.

"And why not? Is it because you know them? What if you knew the girl?"

"I don't know," was my weak response. I always avoided the questions my father was raising. Had my selfish desires contributed to someone else's misery, despite her not openly expressing it?

"Lastly, that officer of the battle staff you met recently- you were right in seeking his favour. Do so again if the opportunity presents itself." With that he looked up with an inquisitive expression on his face as we heard a faint horn blowing. It got increasingly louder before it sounded like someone was blowing it directly in my ear as I jumped out of sleep to find our encampment in a frenzy of action.

The first face I saw in the blur was Stephanos. "What has happened?" I yelled over the commotion.

"The defeated Macedonians have broken their truce and fled. General Eumenes has assembled a crack unit to chase them down while the main force is to conduct a forced march to bring up the rear once we have fixed them."

"Are we breaking camp?"

"No, a rear guard will be posted," Stephanos yelled. "Get your kit on, we're forming up in ten minutes." Stephanos and I did our routine of quickly checking over each other and took our places in the Lochos. The junior officers, Lochagos', and Ouragos' were all screaming for everyone to hurry up and get into position. Within another three minutes the order was given to begin our hurried march. It was approximately two hours before sunrise and I had never marched in such a formation in pitch darkness.

We marched at a brisk pace for three hours before elements of General Eumenes' advance fell back to the main body to inform us the enemy had escaped. It was a sullen march back to our encampment as it was generally agreed that while General Eumenes certainly increased his prestige and reputation as a Commander, our victory was for naught due to the entirety of the Macedonian phalanx escaping our grasp through treachery. It now marched to rejoin with Antipater's contingent uncontested.

"We're going to face the very same cowards again someday, we should have slaughtered them while we had the chance," griped Stephanos.

"But Craterus and Neoptolemus are dead," I added.

"Neoptolemus was a worthless snake," Stephanos retorted. "Not having to face Craterus again is a positive outcome. We still have to worry about Antipater, Antigonus, and Ptolemy, however."

"I'm optimistic that Lord Regent Perdiccas will deal with Ptolemy and we'll have as much success against Antigonus as we've had against everyone else Antipater has thrown at us." Our army returned to camp deflated and was given the rest of the afternoon and evening off. The following morning we broke camp to take up a more permanent position in a better defendable region of Cappadocia, to await our next move.

Chapter 18

Sitting in camp for weeks without further information about unfolding events created a sense of confusion and lowered morale, despite our army's two recent victories- the news of which had by now circulated throughout the empire and solidified General Eumenes' reputation as the preeminent protector of the Kings. Croesus used our stasis to further train our Lochos in formation tactics and exercises. The lull also allowed for Stephanos and me to be better socialized into the unit and come to know our Lochos mates.

One morning Stephanos injured his ankle to the point that he could not put any weight on it and was sent to the surgeon's tent after being derided by Croesus for not paying closer attention to what he was doing. I was chosen to assist Stephanos in hobbling to the infirmary since, according to Croesus, "I practically lived there and was sure to know the way." The surgeon's tent was fairly quiet with the only patients being holdovers with severe injuries from our recent battle with Craterus. Philotheos spotted me enter and called the two of us over.

"What have we here Andrikos?" The doctor asked. "Are your misfortunes transferring to others now?"

"This is Stephanos, he rolled his ankle and cannot put weight on it," I replied.

"Hmm, let's have a look," Philotheos stated with a jovial smirk. He sat Stephanos down and brought his leg into his lap which evoked an audible wince from the patient. Philotheos began his normal routine of squeezing, poking, prodding, and repositioning the affected area. Each machination caused Stephanos to let out grunts of pain to the seeming delight of the caretaker. "Well, I don't think it's broken but you do have a severe sprain. I'm going to give you a brace to wear for the next four weeks and you need to stay off it for the next five days. Good thing we're not going anywhere."

I began to wander around the bay of patients as Philotheos continued his familiar routine and fitted a brace on Stephanos' ankle.

I saw some of the same casualties from my last visit which spoke both to the severity of their injuries and the resolve of the patient. I wondered how I would fare in that situation. Would I conduct myself as honourably as these brave men? My familiar soul searching was interrupted with the materialization of the staff officer, Vettias.

"You again?" he said, recognizing me, "What, do you live here?"

"My Lochos mate injured his ankle and I assisted him getting here," I replied, struggling to retain eye contact.

"Perhaps it is the Fates then," Vettias said cryptically. "What unit did you say you were from again?"

"I serve under Lochagos Croesus, under Syntagma Commander Lykos, under Strategos Androkles."

"I will come seek you out tomorrow," Vettias informed me. "I have need of a young phalangite whose mind hasn't been corrupted with any amount of knowledge yet. Did you fight in the recent battles?"

"Yes sir."

"Did you kill the enemy?" Vettias further interrogated.

"The barbarian regulars," I answered waveringly.

"Well, that will do. Tell your Lochagos I will be speaking with him tomorrow."

"Yes sir."

Vettias continued on to see Philotheos who immediately left Stephanos in the care of a junior surgeon in order to speak with Vettias discreetly. As they walked out of view I saw, what I interpreted to be, the two of them looking in my direction with a patronizing laugh. I returned to Stephanos to find the surgeon handing him a crutch with a brace affixed to his ankle.

"Are you taking him back?" asked the surgeon. "He should be able to use the crutch on his own, just make sure he doesn't fall on his face." The surgeon then turned to Stephanos and ordered him to return in five days.

Stephanos and I managed our way back to our Lochos at a very deliberate pace.

"Who were you speaking with back in the infirmary?" asked Stephanos. "He looked pretty important."

I told Stephanos about my previous meeting with Vettias and my impending meeting with him tomorrow. Stephanos was very interested and seemed genuinely happy at my apparent good fortune.

"The Fates smile on you, Andrikos," Stephanos said warmly.

"I'll inquire into any opportunities for you as well, friend."

"I doubt someone like that has a use for a broke-dick like me," Stephanos joked. "Maybe when I'm back on my feet." As we reached our bivouac Stephanos thanked me for the help and reported his prognosis to Croesus. I requested to speak with the Lochagos after he dismissed Stephanos in an irritated manner.

"Sir, request permission to speak," I stated confidently.

"And what do you want?" Croesus replied. I informed Croesus of my dealings with Vettias to which he seemed very interested. "What does someone from General Eumenes' Battle Staff want with a pathetic nobody like you?"

"I honestly don't know sir, I am just relaying his instructions," I answered stutteringly.

"Well, I hope you told him where to find me," were his parting words.

That night my nervous excitement about Vettias foiled my attempts to retire early and I only slept for about three hours before the morning horns were blown. The next morning our Lochos continued with drills as Stephanos looked on. His ankle was now swollen and blue, preventing him from putting any weight on it. My mind was far from my Lochos, however. During our exercises I allowed myself to wander far from our encampment on some important errand with Vettias. Would he come to our Lochos during our drills and publicly call for me in front of my mates? I wished this not to be the case, for many would hold feelings of jealousy towards me and believe me unworthy, given their years of service and experience. I agreed with the imaginary sentiments I had ascribed to my mates and hoped Vettias would speak with me and Croesus in private. Croesus' words also ran through my mind- why did a staff officer want anything to do with a nobody like me? Vettias' own statement seemed to echo this notion when he explained he wanted someone that didn't know anything. My uncertainty was exacerbated by Vettias' belated arrival, prolonging my inner torment.

157

Dusk was approaching as I lay in my tent impatiently rustling from one position to the other when I heard Croesus summon me.

"Andrikos," he yelled in a deep guttural tone.

I darted out of my tent and exclaimed, "Yes sir!"

"Report to my quarters!" I walked past Stephanos' tent where he shot me an encouraging glance. As I approached I felt fortunate that this meeting was taking place when the rest of my Lochos mates were preparing dinner. The short walk to Croesus' tent seemed like an eternity but luckily none of the tent occupants I passed seemed to notice or care about my summons.

I arrived at my destination to find Vettias seated on an upright log.

"Here he is," Croesus announced. "Are you sure this is who you are looking for sir?"

"Yes Lochagos, thank you," Vettias replied. "I understand your confusion but let your judgment be comforted that it is his very naiveté that I desire. News has come from Egypt which even I am not fully privy to. I have been ordered to make an expedition south of here into Syria and I require an aide with some semblance of intelligence, yet willing to do as he is told at all times. I will have him back to you in short order and your Lochos will be the stronger for it given the experience he is bound to gain."

"My resources are at the disposal of General Eumenes. If someone from his staff requires everything I have to offer, so be it sir." It was rare to see him have to act deferential to anyone.

"I don't require that much, Lochagos, just the boy here," Vettias assured him with a smile. "Andrikos has spoken highly of your leadership and I have no doubt you'll be able to manage during his temporary absence." Croesus looked at me skeptically in response to Vettias' flattery. "I depart tomorrow and will expect Andrikos to meet me at the Commander's tent at sunrise. He will not require his armament or sarissa but will need to bring his tent and short sword."

"He will be there with his required items. Andrikos, you will turn in your armament tonight and will be waiting at the command tent thirty minutes before dawn tomorrow."

"Thank you Lochagos, I can see Andrikos was correct in speaking so highly of you. Andrikos, I will see you tomorrow."

As Vettias departed Croesus continued looking at me with a stern skepticism. Sensing his thoughts I added, "Sir, I swear I do not have any notion of what he wants. My only dealings with him were the two occasions at the medical tent and occurred exactly as I described."

"Hmmph," was his response. "Get your shit together tonight and try not to bring any dishonour on yourself or the Lochos. Dismissed."

"Yes sir," I replied, and departed to gather my armament to return to the quartermaster that evening. Upon completing this errand I visited Stephanos' tent where I relayed to him all that transpired. He again was genuinely pleased at my apparent good fortune. I suggested he seek out and strengthen his relationship with Rhexenor when he returned to the surgeon's tent in five days since he claimed to be in a position to acquire things. As we were talking I realized that I was about to be separated from Stephanos for the first time since our chance encounter in Sardis several months ago, and the two of us embraced as brothers when it was time to retire for the evening.

"You better not replace me," I said, only half kidding.

"Return soon then, there are many in line waiting to take your place."

The next morning I rose before the horns, disassembled my tent, ate some hard tack bread, and drank some brackish water before donning my marching pack and making my way to the command tent. Very few people were awake and stirring at this early hour, with all bivouac fires burnt out and the waning minutes of night perfectly still and calm. Guards standing at attention holding torches could be seen throughout as I neared the leadership areas. They silently eyed my every move until I reached the perimeter of the command tent and the quarters of the high officers. Guards stopped me and demanded I state my business in this area. I explained I was to meet Vettias from the Battle Staff at the command tent, to which one of the guards escorted me. Another quad of guards stood in front of the tent's entrance and my escort passed me into their custody. Since I was so anxious to be punctual I was in fact thirty minutes early and spent the next fifteen minutes in awkward silence until

Vettias mercifully arrived. I followed him to where his gear was assembled and noticed two horses tied to a post.

"Can you ride?" asked Vettias. "I probably should have asked that yesterday."

"I'm no Companion but I am competent enough."

"Good, then pack you gear on that one so we can depart," Vettias ordered, pointing at an impressive mount. I did so and we led our horses out of the encampment entrance. There we were interrogated by the watch commander to whom Vettias briefly spoke with and was granted passage. I looked back at the few flickering lights of the encampment as we mounted our horses and felt like a farm animal let out of its cage, not knowing what to do with itself after a lifetime of captivity. As we started a slow trot Vettias turned to me and asked, "So, interested to know what this is all about?"

"Yes sir," I enthusiastically answered.

"First thing is you will never call me sir, call me uncle for now." You are not to speak to others unless spoken to and you will be introduced as my nephew. Your parents are dead, you are not married and you have no children. We are going to grow out our beards from now until we are finished. We are merchants from Cyprus looking to acquire wares at the upcoming meeting of the Kings and generals taking place in Syria. I realize that doesn't answer any of your questions but you must become the person I have just described immediately and never stray from our story until we are safely back within General Eumenes' encampment. Understood?"

"Yes sir, err yes uncle," I replied.

"Good. Now, tomorrow the army will be informed of disastrous news to our cause of protecting the heirs of Alexander. Lord Regent Perdiccas has been defeated in Egypt and betrayed to Ptolemy through treachery perpetrated by the Silver Shields and Perdiccas' own deputy commander, Seleucus. Regency of the Kings has been granted to two of the conspirators and General Eumenes has been declared rebel and enemy of the Kings. A meeting has been called at Triparadeisus, Syria by Antipater to divide the empire between our enemies and their allies. I have been sent to Triparadeisus to try and influence the outcome as much as possible and report back to

General Eumenes on what is decided. I can't be everywhere at once and will require the assistance of someone with a modicum of competence who does as he's told. So, naturally, when I met you in the surgeon's tent displaying an overt willingness to please me, I decided you would be the right man for the job."

There was a long pause as I processed all that was just relayed to me. Most disturbing was that overnight, I, and thousands of others, had gone from victorious defenders of Alexander's true heirs to outlaws of the Macedonian crown and enemies of the Kings' Regency. After a few moments I gathered my thoughts and responded. "This news certainly complicates things; I am at your disposal sir, err, uncle, in any way that will assist our cause."

"I know you will. So, tell me about yourself, young Andrikos," Vettias commanded. "If I am to be your uncle I should know a little something about you."

As dawn broke I told Vettias of my childhood, my mother, Helena, Leandros, Argos, my father, Nearchus, the wine shop, and life in Ilandra. I of course left out the details regarding Theon, Ganymedes, and Nearchus' ignoble fate. Vettias listened intently, asking questions now and then while keeping eye contact and smiling warmly at appropriate intervals. The idea of someone who I felt so far my superior taking interest in anything I had to say engendered in me such a desire to obey and please this man that I would do just about anything he asked at any moment. The back of my mind told me his kindness was for this result all along but his demeanour and confidence alone would have created a loyal servant of me. My father's early departure sowed fertile ground for the overtures of capable, confident men that showed an interest in me.

Our slow pace continued throughout the morning until we broke for a meal at midday. "Have you heard of Triparadeisus?" Vettias asked.

"No, is it a large city?"

"It's not really a city at all. A Paradeisus is the name given to the decadent pleasure retreats established by the Achaemenid Kings of Persia. There are several Paradeisus' around the empire; at Ecbatana, Susa, Persepolis, Babylon, and a Tri-Paradeisus in Syria. The Tri means it is three times the opulence and size of a normal Paradeisus-which is formidable in its own right. Someone of your meagre background cannot comprehend that such a place could be constructed, let alone enjoyed, by men. If man can create such a place, we do not hold the mental capacity to grasp what Mount Olympus is like. There will be a multitude of factions vying for power through intrigue at this meeting. There will be agents sent for the explicit purpose of countering our efforts. I will teach you how to survive in such a lion's den along the way. Perform well and perhaps there will be a future in this line of work for you- the pay is better and you won't have to dig drainage ditches with the rest of the line units of the army. Tomorrow we'll begin your training along the road and put it into practice tomorrow evening."

We made camp that evening on the outskirts of a small town. As I lay in my tent chasing sleep, my mind raced at a fever pitch thinking about all that was conveyed to me today and what the future would bring. Vettias was correct about someone from such a simple background as I not being able to comprehend the information I had been given, and the world I had been thrust into.

Chapter 19

We began our ride early that morning after procuring several items in the town and having breakfast. Vettias appeared to have an inexhaustible supply of coin that must have been allotted him from the army's treasury by General Eumenes himself. Two hours passed along the road before my 'training' began.

"We'll stay in a proper town tonight with proper food, drink, and women," Vettias assured. "One benefit of travelling with me is that you will enjoy a standard of living unknown to someone like you. It will be hard to go back to the life you knew after our mission is completed. So, let's begin. What are we going to do in Triparadeisus?"

"We are going to attempt to influence the outcome and report the final conclusions to General Eumenes," I said unsure of my answer.

"Correct, but how are we to do this? We'll get to the influencing part later. To be able to influence the negotiations we have to know what is going on. How are we going to ascertain what is going on if we are not in the actual meetings?"

"I don't know," was my uninspired reply. Vettias was starting to move beyond my feeble reasoning abilities the more he spoke.

"Think, Andrikos; in your home of Ilandra, how do you obtain information about an event you did not witness yourself?"

"You ask someone who was there," I answered unsurely.

"Yes, that is how a normal person with benevolent motives would learn of events for which he did not witness. This will be our starting point for today's lesson," Vettias continued in a condescending manner. "When we arrive in Triparadeisus and we are attempting to discover what is being discussed in the inner chamber of the council, will we simply walk up to Lord Regent Antipater and ask him what his intentions are for General Eumenes and our army?"

"No," I feebly responded.

"And why not?"

"Because Antipater is not likely to divulge that sort of information to someone outside of his inner circle."

"That is true. We are beginning to learn, despite not yet moving past the realm of common sense. So should we walk up to someone in Lord Regent Antipater's inner circle and ask them what the Regency's plans are for General Eumenes and our army?" Vettias further interrogated.

"No."

"And why not?"

"For the same reasons it would be unwise to ask Lord Regent Antipater."

"So if we don't ask Lord Regent Antipater, and we don't ask someone in his inner circle, who do we ask?"

"Someone other than Antipater or his inner circle that is privy to the information," I responded.

"Excellent. Now, who would that be?"

"I don't know." Vettias had now pushed me well beyond any previous mental exercise I had been a part of.

"Come now, Andrikos, I'm not going to make this easy for you. There are plenty of invisible people around these men that hear all sorts of things. Servants, aides, relatives, whores- all kinds of people. So, assuming we find someone who is close to a member of Antipater's inner council, what do we do then?"

"We ask them what they know about the information we desire?"

"Incorrect. Why would someone with access to the most important men in the entire world divulge information to a stranger that would surely get him killed if discovered?"

"They wouldn't."

"Then how are you going to get the information necessary to allow General Eumenes and our army to be triumphant in our quest to protect Alexander's heirs? Do you think General Eumenes will obtain all the information he requires by divine intervention? Do you think he has another plan to glean the information necessary to defeat Antipater, Antigonus, and Ptolemy? We are here on behalf of our general, the only leader working solely on behalf of the Kings, to attempt to influence events and quickly report the outcome of this summit. You need to get your head out of your ass and start understanding the immense responsibility General Eumenes has placed in me and I have placed in you."

"I'm sorry sir, err uncle," I said in a fluster. "I assure you the entirety of my mental faculties are being directed to absorbing all you are explaining to me now, perhaps you decided poorly in choosing your aide on this mission of great importance."

"Don't try and garner sympathy from me. I know you are trying, don't let my demeanour discourage you. I am simply conveying the importance of what we are embarking on and identifying the mindset needed to accomplish it. No one as inexperienced as you could know the answers to all the questions I have asked. Just continue learning the tenets I am conveying and understand the importance of our mission. The Socratic Method can be frustrating to the student, just stay with me…So, how do you get someone to tell you something they normally would not?"

My fear of sounding ridiculous gave way to memories of Ilandra where Argos would regularly defeat my best attempts to conceal information about my exploits and my eagerness to perform the same manipulations on my mates. "You could trick them," I said after a short pause.

"Alright, I'll accept that as proof you at least have the ability to think. But there is much more to it than that. First, you must present yourself in a way that your target doesn't feel he or she has committed a transgression by divulging information to you. Second, if your mental ruse is too blatant, you may have obtained some sliver of information in the short term but you will have shown your intention to your target and risk exposure. Never allow your target to know the information you are actually after. Never ask yes or no questions. Never ask direct questions for they divulge your intent to your target. You must always prompt your target to willingly tell you what you seek without them feeling as though you coaxed it from them or had a premeditated interest in it."

"You can tell a story similar to the topic you are interested in and allow the target to reply with a story of their own that relates information about themselves or the issue of interest. You can divulge something private about yourself, real or imagined, to cajole the target to reciprocate by sharing something personal about themselves which reveals information of importance. You can use deliberate silences to entice your target to fill the quiet. You can purport to know more about a subject than you actually do to deceive him into feeling comfortable talking about information he assumes you already know. Bring up different aspects of your desired information at different intervals to obfuscate your objective. Alcohol is always useful as well. The options are limited only by your resourcefulness and the particulars of the target and situation."

"This is all of course before we start to introduce money. We must identify motivations of targets who will have prolonged exposure to information we desire. Money is always a factor but some value their lives over money. Others are too proud to take it, thus introducing it in the first place reduces our chances of the target agreeing to cooperate with us. We cannot assume every target we meet is for sale- but make no mistake, anyone willing to lie, cheat, steal or kill is susceptible to enticement. In addition to what motivates them, it is beneficial to identify something in their lives that makes them susceptible to bribery or intrigue. There are the few targets who are truly moral beings, however, and we may have to manufacture a circumstance in their life for which they will do anything to avoid. This can sometimes involve threatening those they hold dearest. Once we exploit motivations and establish liabilities we should have pretty firm control over their actions and must keep them alive long enough to serve our purposes."

"Still what we practice is an unreliable art. Good practitioners of these skills can usually accomplish their goals efficiently and discreetly. Sometimes, however, when time is of the essence and the importance of our charge is so great, untidy options will present themselves."

"You mean kidnap...torture...murder," I asked. Vettias nodded in response to each.

"Sometimes, but we try to avoid it and always remember the cause at hand. I call it coercion. There is an art to that side of our profession as well, Andrikos, and I will need your assistance in that respect to be sure. For now, let's focus on getting people to willingly tell you things since the better you are at it, the less you will have to resort to cruel tactics. Tonight you are going to apply what I have taught you with unsuspecting patrons and employees in the tavern we stop at."

We continued our journey for three more hours in relative silence before arriving at the medium-sized town of Myrana where we stabled our horses and rented two respectable rooms for the evening. Our amenities provided warm water to bathe in, fresh meat to consume, and offered to wash our clothes the following morning which Vettias purchased for the two of us. I had three articles of clothing to my name after leaving Ilandra and all had been washed very infrequently since enlisting in the army. After our appetites were sated, Vettias inquired into the best source of entertainment for the evening and the two of us walked down the main thoroughfare in the direction pointed out by our lodging's patron. I had pent up nervous energy as we made the short walk to the tavern. I was excited to drink good wine and possibly bed a woman, but vowed to pace my indulgences lest Vettias think me a degenerate. However, what if he was a heavy drinker and thought my moderation unworthy of a drinking companion? I decided I would drink exactly as much as he and mind my tongue for fear of blurting out something absurd in Vettias' presence. There was also the unexplained expectation of practicing the day's lesson on unsuspecting patrons.

We arrived at a standard establishment that was moderately attended with uninteresting patrons. Vettias purposely walked over to the counter where an old, thin man with unkempt facial hair and gnarled skin was serving cups of wine. I followed him to an unoccupied space where I watched him scan the room. He then positioned himself on the other side of me and instructed that I educe from the man standing to my left his name, trade, and immediate family members within the next five minutes. Vettias' sudden assignment caught me off guard and I awkwardly stood next to the target for the first minute while I composed a suitable approach. Looking at the man, I deduced he was a local patron, most likely a labourer or tradesman, who probably had no interest in anything a twenty year old nobody like myself had to say.

"Are you from around here sir?" I asked as confidently as possible. The man didn't acknowledge me. I repeated my question in a more assertive tone. The man turned to me with an annoyed, half interested expression.

"What?" he yelled. Upon my third repetition its silliness became apparent to me and I wavered in my delivery.

"Who are you?" was his terse reply.

"Nobody sir, just travelling through Myrana and making conversation," I answered, hoping he would take an interest and ask a question regarding my travels. He grunted and turned back to his cup of wine where another minute of awkward silence ensued. My anxiety level began rising as I could feel Vettias dissecting every aspect of the pitiful encounter.

"Do you frequent this establishment often sir," I feebly asked, attempting to spark any kind of conversation with the curmudgeon.

"Why the hell do you have a hard-on for me kid?" was his curt reply as he again turned away from me.

"I am travelling with my uncle, sir, and as I have said, I am just making conversation," was my final plea for his attention.

"Go make it with someone that gives a damn," were his final words. With that my mental clock's horn sounded and I looked over to Vettias in defeat. He had a condescending grin on his face and put an arm around me.

"You've got some work to do," was his consolation. "Don't worry, I picked him on purpose. Some targets won't give you anything to work with but I would have started with offering to buy him a drink. Alcohol is sometimes the best lubricant for extracting what a target knows. He clearly is a drinker, thus, that is one of his weaknesses we can exploit. Additionally, that type of man has no enjoyment in his life, thus, I would attempt to join him in complaining about something- like the influx of foreigners, or the price of the mediocre women and wine. If we absolutely needed this target we also could drug his cup and coax him out to the ally where we would have a cart waiting. Finally, every target is different so if I hit a dead end with a local in a place like this, I'd try talking with the women- they are the key to this business. Kindness and money are your best instruments in winning them over. Their line of work inspires little of either. Speaking of which, we'll have to sample this shithole's wares this evening- my treat."

I smirked and nodded at Vettias' proposal, making sure to keep my composure yet seem an agreeable drinking companion. "We'll work on your approaches again many times between now and Triparadeisus, but for now, let us sit at a table and inspect what this hovel has to offer. You are not only going to need to know how to approach haggard strangers with no interest in talking, you are going to need to become an expert with women. I'm sure you and your idiot friends are familiar with the mechanics of sex but taking the time to please a female target, most likely a prostitute, is essential to this trade."

Vettias then motioned for a prostitute to come over to us and whispered something inaudible in her ear which caused her to laugh. She departed our table as he smacked her rear. "A beautiful woman is the greatest gift the Gods ever gave man. Long, flowing hair smelling of perfume; skin soft like the finest eastern silk; tits staring you right in the face- young, healthy and full. Legs like two lengthy, toned avenues leading to a lush haven of pleasure flowing with honey and nectar of the Gods. The women here are nothing like that but you must make them feel that way. You must make them feel like you believe they are Aphrodite's equal. Then of course you tip them a little extra and now you've established a reliable source of information."

I never heard anyone speak of women so eloquently as Vettias- especially thinking back to my Lochos' post-battle celebration. I couldn't guess whether it was genuine or a pretense since Vettias' mental abilities were so superior to me from years of experience and travel throughout the empire. Vettias' prostitute returned with two more of her colleagues to join our grimy table. The three women were of average attractiveness and all seemed infatuated with my tutor. It was probably unlikely they saw men as worldly as he enter their tavern. Two of the women appeared older than I and the third was about my age. It seemed the younger was under the guidance of the other two, much the same that I was to Vettias. As they sat down, one on Vettias' lap, one on mine, and the third in a separate chair, it became clear that Vettias was correct in assuming I knew nothing about women. The extant of my knowledge stemmed from getting drunk, clumsily doing the deed, and recounting my exploits with my mates the next morning. That kind of mindless behaviour might work with the sorry lot at present but certainly wouldn't with the type of women Vettias had just described.

"Ladies, thank you for joining us on short notice," Vettias began. "I promise to make it worth your while."

"They would have been over here sooner but had to tactfully extricate themselves from some pitiable locals with meagre resources," The woman on Vettias' lap replied.

"That is beauty's privilege. Beautiful women can command a lowly sap like myself to wait years for their attention and favour." The three women looked at each other with smirking glances as Vettias delivered a routine he no doubt performed to similar effect countless times in countless taverns such as this. "I am travelling with my nephew and want to teach him how to appreciate and please a woman. I'm hoping you can help me."

"Only if you're part of the deal," the woman sitting in the chair responded, giggling.

"Repetition is the mother of skill, my dear, and I believe one must practice their craft regularly in order to maintain their prowess," Vettias answered with a wink. The three women looked at each other again with a head nod as if they were communicating without words, despite the content of their message being quite apparent. Vettias' appearance and vocabulary were far superior to what our new companions were used to yet his demeanour and mild self-deprecation made them feel as though he was intentionally coming down to their level- which caused them to be further captivated. "So what do you think, ladies, which of you wants to give a lesson to my boy here and which of you want to receive a lesson from me?"

The older woman sitting on Vettias' lap decided that she and the younger girl would learn from the intriguing stranger while the older woman sitting on my lap would teach me there was more to fornication than drunkenly giving some poor girl about three minutes of clumsy thrusting. "Now before we get down to business let my nephew and I enjoy your distinguished company by sharing a jug of wine with you. Nephew, fetch our ladies here some libations," Vettias ordered as he tossed a coin in my direction. I returned with the order and three additional cups, filling each one liberally. Vettias then proposed a toast to his audience, observing it was women such

170

as this that allowed men of an average lot such as himself to live like a king, if only for the evening.

I was careful to let the women do most of the drinking since I still felt under probation by my instructor and our conversation over the first jug involved incessant flatteries, of which Vettias drew from an unending well. It was when the second jug was ordered that I witnessed Vettias subtly change the subject from meaningless flirtations to questions of substance. "Since my nephew and I are merchants, I am curious to know the manner of foreigner that passes through this establishment and is fortunate enough to experience the delicacies within. I am always looking for potential buyers of my wares. Promising contacts would certainly encourage me to come back with a heavy purse and visit old acquaintances," Vettias smirked, passing each woman a coin. What appeared to be an abrupt change of course in the conversation was taken as a natural segue by our now drunk companions which prompted an amusing conversation amongst themselves about the recent clients they had been with; laughing as they recounted names, destinations, resources, and the endowment of their manhood. When it appeared their impressive list was exhausted, Vettias suggested we continue our revelry upstairs, away from jealous eyes, to which our companions were eager to oblige. Walking up the stairs with the remaining jug of wine was the last memory I had of the evening.

Chapter 20

I woke the next morning not remembering how I returned to my bed, and found a fresh bowl of water sitting next to my neatly folded cleaned clothes. I drank down several cupped-palms full of fresh water and splashed the rest on my face, hair, and arm pits. Realizing I could not remember the end of the night, I became nervous that I had committed some embarrassing transgression and hurried to find Vettias to ensure he was not displeased with me. I found him dressed, washed, and looking like he'd been awake for hours as he was cordially conversing with the establishment's purveyor.

"Look who arises from Tartarus," Vettias announced in good spirits. "Learn a few lessons last night?"

"I don't really remember to be honest," I replied, not sure I gave the correct answer.

"I don't think you'll take anything away from a whore like that except venereal disease," Vettias laughed.

"You certainly were convincing in your praise for them last night," I observed. With this comment, Vettias escorted me away from the ear of the owner.

"And hopefully that was the real lesson you learned," Vettias retorted. "I could have one of them screw and kill an enemy of General Eumenes this afternoon if the opportunity presented itself. It's too bad none were fair enough to bring along with us to Triparadeisus to use in our employ. If you cannot remember the end of the evening then you clearly drank too much. Our enemies are waiting for such moments to have you killed if you don't have your shit together. There are larger forces at work which you can't possibly understand, and you will be soon entering a world of intrigue, violence, and complexity."

Vettias instructed me to pack my belongings while he settled our bill, and the two of us departed on our mounts. Vettias did not speak for the first two hours and we travelled in silence. My thoughts focused on his last words to me regarding 'larger forces at work.' If last night had taught me anything it was that I knew nothing of the world Vettias was introducing me to and certainly did not feel ready to enter it facing potential enemies around every corner. I wished for him to speak with me so I could convey my concerns and undergo further training before arriving at Triparadeisus.

Perhaps sensing my inner dialogue, Vettias informed me "Tonight we will try your hand at elicitation again. How did you think you did last night?"

"Not well," I answered.

"I purposely wanted you to practice on a hard target. Tonight we'll have you work on a drunk- it will be easier. There were things you could have done better, however. Yesterday we discussed ploys and mental manipulations to discreetly draw out information from people. You seemed to grasp the concepts but your demeanour was all wrong. It all depends on the person, but your target last night did not view you as an equal, nor did you act like one. When dealing with someone like that you must be confident in your speech and body language. On the other hand, the whores thought me their superior; therefore my demeanour was one of kindness mixed with a little self-deprecation to lighten the mood. Tonight we'll find a drunk for you to talk to. He'll probably give you everything you want to know without you even provoking him to do so. You will also use a guise tonight.

"A guise?" I inquired.

"You will not be Andrikos from Ilandra, you will develop another persona while speaking to your target and will not be allowed to break this ruse the entire evening. Whatever you decide I will uphold throughout the evening as well. I'm also going to expect you to add more to the conversation with our women tonight. You're a good looking enough kid of good enough stock- there is no reason you cannot have them eating out of your hand as I did last night."

I nodded throughout Vettias' instructions and we continued riding in silence for another thirty minutes until my desire to ask about his meaning of the large, dangerous world I would be entering forced me to make further inquiry of my tutor. "What did you mean this morning about my inability to understand the larger world I would be entering?"

173

"Well, I guess now is as good of time as any," Vettias replied after a long pause. He then looked at me very seriously. "I started my military career similar to you, within the army of Alexander's father, Philip II; Just a know-nothing phalangite from greater Macedon doing as he was told. I joined when I came of age after the Third Sacred War made Philip II the most powerful man in Greece. Two years after my enlistment, an alliance of Greek city states, led by Athens and Thebes, opposed Philip and a great battle was fought near the Boeotian town of Chaeronea. It was there that Alexander wrote the prelude to his future glory while commanding a Taxis of the Macedonian phalanx opposing the Sacred Band of the Thebans- a previously invincible infantry force responsible for the legendary defeat of the Spartans at Leuctra under Philip's military mentor, Epaminondas. Fighting within a Lochos under Alexander's Taxis, we shattered The Sacred Band and routed the Greek allies- bringing peace and order to the Greek mainland for the first time in generations. It was here that I first witnessed Alexander's greatness."

I always had a penchant for the retelling of battles and it took great concentration to keep a stoic façade as Vettias spoke of high adventure with Philip and Alexander. Using my new vernacular, I would be a target susceptible to a man like Vettias who could spin tales of epic conflict between historic legends. I excitedly struggled to determine how anything regarding Philip and Alexander had anything to do with me and could tell Vettias understood the effect he was having on his audience as he continued.

"The assassination of Philip II saw Alexander become King of Macedon and General of the army at age twenty. Alexander quickly made haste to establish his authority and carry out his father's plans of Persian conquest. I crossed the Hellespont with his army as a phalangite and fought in the Battle of the Granicus. After the Battle of Issus my Syntagma Commander chose me to become the aid to a General within Alexander's staff named Polyperchon. This position brought me into contact with the most powerful men of the army and I soon knew them all.

After the Battle of Gaugamela and the surrender of Babylon, General Polyperchon summoned me to his quarters to reassign me to a new position. Alexander's chief secretary at the time, the man you now know as General Eumenes, was also present during the meeting, which I thought odd, until General Polyperchon explained his purpose. I was to be assigned to a secretive organization led by Eumenes and unbeknownst to most anyone within Alexander's army. We were to employ any means necessary to execute specific orders from Alexander that could not be carried out within the public eye. This included all manner of information collection against any perceived threat to his leadership within the army, as well as the discreet elimination of Alexander's enemies. Such a position required someone who had demonstrated the requisite skills for the task and absolute loyalty to the King. General Polyperchon had observed these qualities in me while serving on his staff and recommended me for the position. The name of this shadowy group was the King's Hand and any disclosure of its existence was punishable by death."

Vettias' last remark caught me a little off-guard, since he was now divulging the very information whose knowledge by an outsider would spell death for him. Vettias perceived my perplexity and added "Don't worry, this disclosure will not result in anyone's death. You will understand once I have finished."

"The King's Hand was heavily compartmentalized and each element was not necessarily aware of one another, except for a small tattoo located on all members' hip. This mark is easily concealable with any manner of dress yet a small slit can be made into clothing material in case one must discreetly present it to another member as bona fides. It was here that I learned the dark arts, and performed them well, on behalf of the King."

"As Alexander's eastern campaign dragged on and became more arduous, the King's Hand was kept quite busy as Alexander's suspicions increasingly mounted. By the time the army mutinied in India, Alexander had us conduct several large scale purging operations of those he thought disloyal to him. It was during this time, following Alexander's severe injuries received while fighting the Malli tribe along the Indus River, a special meeting was called bringing all leadership of the King's Hand into Alexander's chambers, along with Generals Polyperchon, Hephaestion, and Eumenes. Prior to this meeting no one holding the rank lower than

Captain was allowed into a King's Hand meeting while other members were present. No one knew what to make of this clear breach of security by calling all lower level operatives to congregate at one place but, as we learned, the meeting was convened on the orders of Alexander himself."

"While Alexander's wounds healed he had not been seen by the army and rumours were spreading that he had already died. The image of our God King sitting fraily before us did not bolster our confidence in his ultimate recovery. His skin pale, his face gaunt, his hair stringy and lifeless, his eyes sallow, his body atrophied. Everyone held their breath waiting for Alexander to address this unprecedented gathering of shadow operatives."

"'I have purposely gathered you all here to personally acknowledge the important work you have done on my behalf during our great conquest' Alexander began in a mild and underwhelming tone. 'The lowliest phalangite in this army has the opportunity to display great courage and feats of soldiery and thus be rightfully recognized as a hero worthy of his place in the Elysian Fields. Awards and honours will be bestowed on them, forever cementing their place among the titans of this conquest. The greatest among them will have ballads written in their honour and their names will admiringly roll off the tongues of Greek children for generations to come. The men assembled in this tent will never be praised publicly, nor will your deeds be recognized by anyone outside this gathering. But whose actions are more important to our conquest? The heroic soldier who does his small part in killing a dozen men in battle, or the one of you standing before me that is able to elicit information, eliminate an enemy, or persuade an ally to further our strategic interests without fighting a battle in the first place? I say the latter. I want to instill in your natural human desire for recognition that, despite your lack of public acknowledgement, I consider the work you do to be of the utmost importance to this campaign.'"

"Alexander's speech had its intended effect on all present and his words did more to galvanize our spirit than a thousand public tributes. 'I realize there have been many rumours and foreboding about my health as of late and I intentionally chose to reveal my condition to the King's Hand before even my generals for a very important reason,' Alexander continued, his voice now taking a more serious tone. 'During the worst of my recovery I was frequently in and out of consciousness which allowed me to receive a vision from the spiritual realm.' It was here that I now noticed several of Alexander's diviner entourage standing in the back corner of the tent looking on in statuesque poses. 'The pronouncement of the Oracle at Siwa in Egypt declaring my divine lineage was reiterated to me by my father Zeus Ammon himself last night.' He then turned to his diviners who all shook their heads quite rigorously. 'To the left of my father was Heracles, son of Zeus and patriarch of the Argead House. My father's message, as interpreted by myself and my diviners, was a warning that, although I am his son and will not die from a wound suffered in battle, I too am susceptible to a mortal death by treachery, just as his son Heracles was. Such a fate at this point would be disastrous to the Argead Dynasty and the Greek cause without an established heir. Which brings me to the essence of your presence here today.'"

"The mood of the room was rapt on his every word. The fact that our God King would choose to divulge such personal and consequential information to us was at the forefront of everyone's mind, lurking just behind our poised facades. 'It is with this backdrop that I now call upon the King's Hand to enter the next chapter of its existence,' Alexander announced with a renewed vigour in his voice. 'Your charge has been to defend the interest of this army and its leader. Zeus Ammon has opened my eyes to the narrowness of this charter. Under the order of your King, commanded by Zeus Ammon himself, the King's Hand will swear a divine oath in front of all present that, as of now, you are the divine protectors of the Argead Dynasty. Not just of myself but of my line should I perish. Men, we are returning to Babylon after a decade of conquest. My enemies are slain and subjugated and we will now enter a new phase- one of stability, strengthening of the royal foundation, and eventual conquest of the Arabia, Western Europe and Carthage. The King's Hand will vow to always protect the Argead Line during this time and ensure a member of my blood, the blood of Zeus and Heracles, occupies the world's throne from now until the end of days.'"

"Alexander's speech had prepared us well for this moment, and while no one could conceive we would be protecting his lineage after his death so soon after that day, we all took the solemn oath as prepared by the diviners and in the presence of Alexander, Hephaestion, Polyperchon, Eumenes, and all leaders of the King's Hand. So you see, we ride to Triparadeisus not to further the ambition of some General, but we are fighting a clandestine battle for the blood of Alexander, descendant of Heracles and Zeus Ammon, against those that wish to usurp his rightful succession by Alexander IV. That is why Perdiccas' defeat was so grave and we are racing to Triparadeisus. Both Philip III and Alexander IV have fallen into the hands of those who wish to use them as props long enough to steal control and eliminate them when the proper time allows. We need to ensure that doesn't happen."

Vettias had just imparted more information than I knew how to process at once. I could not form words worthy enough to respond to such a tale. After a pause, only one question seemed most in need of answering. "Why have you decided to involve such a nobody as me in this grand struggle?"

"Alexander's sudden death came as a shock to everyone, including the King's Hand," Vettias admitted. "Since that time we have been racing to get ahead of events and shape them from the shadows across the empire. Antigonus' refusal to obey Lord Regent Perdiccas' orders to quell the Cappadocian opposition was the first sign of insubordination. This ill omen was followed by Neoptolemus' outright treachery and Ptolemy's brazen hijack of Alexander's body. Since then we have been carefully growing our numbers and increasing our reach by placing agents within as many circles of leadership as possible throughout the world. I chose you because I need someone unknown to the world of shadows. You will be able to do things I cannot in Triparadeisus due to my notoriety over the years. I chose you because you seemed like you had a decent enough head on your shoulders, despite being as green as a blade of grass. I chose you, Andrikos, because if you survive this mission, you will take the oath and become a member of the King's Hand."

178

Vettias then purposefully advanced the subject before I had a chance to respond. "As per our plan, we are arriving at Triparadeisus before Antipater due to Cappadocia's relative close proximity. This will give us time to scout the area, establish semi-witting sources of information and identify targets. Getting there early will also allow us to create discreet ways of communicating and obtain separate quarters."

"We are to be separated during our time in Triparadeisus?" I interrupted.

"At times, for the reasons I just described," Vettias retorted with irritation.

"But I am still...You said yourself, I don't know anything," I countered.

"That is what our journey is for. I'm going to teach you how to operate on your own and we will have a couple days in Triparadeisus together before we part ways to ensure we always have a way to securely communicate. If you still feel nervous, take heed in that I need you alive in order to complete this mission therefore I am going to do all I can to ensure your safety."

Vettias had certainly done wonders to build my confidence in *his* capabilities but the revelation that I would not be under his aegis caused my insecurities to boil to the surface. "I submit to your judgment, whatever you think best."

"Don't worry, you'll have the local drunk telling you the size of his dick before this night's over and then you can show yours to some fortunate flower of the establishment."

That evening, it was as Vettias had described and I began to understand the art of elicitation. Working on a soft target, I was able to guide the conversation and take him to the point where he willingly told me personal information such as his affairs, his debts, and his overall self pity. I also fared alright in keeping up my established guise while trying to remember Vettias' as well. Any transgression of memory on this account was mitigated by my target's inability to remember what my name was to begin with. This of course was the point of tonight's exercise- to get me comfortable practicing the principles Vettias was teaching. Vettias reminded me that this drunk had probably told the same story to every regular at

179

the bar over his lifetime but encouraged me on my technique and congratulated me on a good practice session. I found more words later with our women after following Vettias' lead and bedded a girl one year younger than I to complete the building of my confidence for the evening.

Chapter 21

The next few days repeated themselves as we travelled south from town to town, practicing conversational manipulations along the way. Vettias gave several lessons during the days and set me to task each evening with varying degrees of success. He would evaluate my performances, sometimes from afar, other times as a participant in the conversation. I began relating much of what Vettias taught me to the mental exploitations I underwent from uncle Argos. I thought he would be a successful practitioner of the dark arts but he would probably claim to be just a practitioner of good parenting. As my experience grew and aptitude increased, I believed I was reaching the point where I could return to Ilandra and have Patrochlus and Argos thoroughly subjugated by my cunning. This of course was an exaggeration, but I certainly had come a long way since the surgeon's tent where Vettias and I first met.

Our steady progression led us into the prosperous satrapy of Cilicia, through the Cilician Gates mountain pass and into its capital, Tarsus, along the Cydnus River. The ancient city was the site of a Royal treasury which we would have been welcome to draw from several weeks ago but now were considered enemies of the Kings. As we neared its gates Vettias took a serious tone and cautioned me prior to entering.

"We are entering an important city. The presence of the treasury will ensure there are enemies of General Eumenes within. We must stringently follow our guise as Cypriot traders en route to Syria for business. You told me of your friend from youth named Nearchus. That's as good a Greek name as any for you to be called from now on. I will be your uncle Argos. I choose these names to make it easy for you to remember so you can act as natural as possible while we are here. I plan on staying here for several days as a final lesson before we enter Syria. We will stay in separate dwellings and will rehearse communicating discreetly among enemies. Do you understand?"

"Yes uncle," I answered with a smirk.

"We'll start with my quarters and then search out where you will stay," Vettias instructed. "It will be dark soon and I want a full day with you before we start running around at night, so we'll retire early and meet first light tomorrow at a location I will determine later."

"Have you been to this city before?" I asked.

"Yes, during Alexander's initial conquest. We passed through the Cilician Gates and made camp near the city along the Cydnus River. The river originates from the mountains above and thus its water is markedly colder than the surrounding lakes and streams. Alexander caught pneumonia after bathing in it and was seriously ill for three tense days."

With Vettias' instructions conveyed, our horses slowly entered the large city which had come back to life after the noon heat baked its roads and buildings. Vettias began scanning the horizon for the tallest structures to seek shelter for the evening. Having identified a few promising contenders we slowly steered our mounts through the throngs of people. When it became too crowded we dismounted so as not to draw too much attention to ourselves and arrived at a three story building that was clearly a tenement with no rooms available to rent. We quickly moved on to the next building of two stories. The building was indeed an inn with rooms available as indicated by the sign outside. Vettias met with its owner and was first shown a room on the first floor. Vettias requested availability on the second floor for security reasons which seemed reasonable to the owner. We entered the second floor room and Vettias methodically made his way to the single window looking out onto the city. The view was unobstructed and faced north looking out upon a large swath of Tarsus. He shook his head in approval and informed the owner he would take it. The owner nodded and informed us he would take our mounts to his small stable and hurriedly departed.

Vettias waited for the door to close to bring me to the window and explain his intentions for the rest of the day. "This is a good window; it faces the majority of the city with several two and three story buildings in a line of sight. I'm going to tie this white scarf around the shutter of this window and it will be up to you to find a room north of here that allows for visibility of it. Once you have found one, reserve the room and tie this purple scarf around the shutter of your window. Once I see your scarf I will remove mine which is the signal to meet me at the statue of Sandon where we will make plans for the morning. Do you see the monument?" Vettias asked, pointing to a large city square. "It is right there to your left. Try and obtain a room in one of those three buildings to the west of it. You must hurry while we still have daylight. If I am unable to discern where your scarf has been tied, I will leave my scarf on my window. If darkness falls without its removal, meet me here tomorrow and we will try again in the morning. Do you understand these instructions?"

"Yes uncle," I replied and quickly departed at a brisk pace towards the first building suggested by Vettias. Tarsus was of a similar size to Sardis and its roads and thoroughfares were congested with people, carts, and animals. I made it to the first candidate, a two story structure with rooms available. I entered the building and was shown a room on the second floor with a window facing north, thus not visible to Vettias' room. I thanked the owner for his time and declined the room. Moving to Vettias's second suggestion I quickly realized it was a tenement and began a slow jog to the last of the candidates. It was a three story structure with available rooms for rent. The sun was beginning to set and I spoke to the proprietor with a sense of urgency that was not reciprocated. When he finally made it to the third floor and unlocked the door I impatiently walked directly to the window and surveyed my view for Vettias' signal. His building was one of several of similar height and appearance all in a row and I had difficulty observing the white scarf. Finally spotting it, I purchased the room, hurried the old man out the door and tied my purple scarf outside the window. Vettias' white scarf now became the object of my fixation while I anxiously awaited its removal as per his instructions. It remained for an extended period of time until I saw it finally removed. Thus, with our first discreet communication executed, I made a hurried rush for the statue of Sandon.

The city square was spacious and many Hellenistic influences could be seen throughout; from its temple to Sandon, chief god of the ancient Cilician pantheon, to its fountain, to its columned building facades in the Doric style. My nascent instincts concluded Vettias chose our place of encounter well due to the square's high level of foot traffic- making it an ideal location to hide in plain sight and briefly meet someone in the open. Sandon had been equated with the ancient god Marduk by the eastern religions and the Greeks had determined Sandon was the Cilician interpretation of Heracles. The local population appeared to embrace the Greek equation, especially since Alexander's conquest, with many references to the Argead patriarch throughout the monument square.

My assessment of the surroundings was cut short by the appearance of Vettias who congratulated me on my successful execution of his instructions. "Going forward, the white scarf will prompt a meeting between us here. At daybreak I will hang a different colored scarf to identify where we will hold our morning meeting. Tomorrow it will be the white one again. You will hang your purple scarf to signify you received the message and wait for me to remove mine, signalling I am departing to meet you. At that point you will remove yours and depart as well. Tomorrow morning we will conduct this process and meet back here at daybreak where I will introduce several principles throughout the day to ensure you can manoeuvre safely within a hostile environment. Tonight I want you to return to your room and get some sleep. Do you have any questions?"

"Not yet uncle," I replied as Vettias abruptly turned around and disappeared into the throng of people. Our meeting lasted no longer than two minutes and went completely unnoticed by the crowd around us. Vettias' teachings were accelerating my thoughts so completely that my body felt as exhausted as it did back on the royal road marching with sarissa in hand. I returned to my room as I was told, and fell to sleep early that evening.

Chapter 22

My nervous energy caused me to wake an hour before the first cock crowed for fear of missing the signal at the appointed hour. I lay in bed staring at my room's ceiling, scrutinizing every crack and water stain in the cheap mortar. My thoughts settled on Stephanos for a time and what he and the Lochos were doing. Since I believed Stephanos superior to me in many ways I thought him better suited to the task I now found myself set upon and felt guilty that Vettias chose me without meeting him first. I also thought of Nearchus and how many probably wished I had died in his stead. This stream of conscious led me to think Nearchus and Stephanos would have been like brothers had they known each other. They were better meant for companionship than I was with either of them. My thoughts now brought me to the familiar realm of insecurity and self-doubt. I questioned the sanity of the Fates since I felt I didn't deserve to be the one still alive, let alone chosen by a great man like Vettias. Despite all these questions raising my anxiety I dozed off for what felt like an hour but was probably more like sixty seconds. I shot out of sleep as soon as I recognized my dream-like state, fearing I had overslept the appointed time. Dawn was still absent but I got up and took a more uncomfortable position in a chair by the window to mitigate the chance I would fail Vettias by sleeping through his signal. It is always darkest just before sunrise and I sat motionless staring out into a black, cloudless sky enveloping the city below me like a dark blanket. The calm of night was only mildly interrupted with the bark of a dog, the flicker of a lamp, or the shadowy scampering of intermittent people wading through the dark alleys with increased vigour as if they felt unprotected without the sun- like a mouse in an open field.

I caught myself dozing on and off for the remainder of the night until the black began ceding its dominance to lighter shades of grays, before the sun's advance guard cleared the horizon, announcing its imminent arrival with reds and oranges. Several roosters now heralded the procession of colour which I deduced had woken

Vettias if he had not already risen. The city's traffic began picking up by the time the yellow body crested into the sky and I sat focussed on Vettias' window like a cat stalking prey. Finally a glint of flowing white materialized and I immediately took my purple scarf, which I had been clutching for the past hour, and tied it around my shutter, signaling my receipt of the message. I continued watching Vettias' window with an anticipatory grin as he removed his scarf thus completing our clandestine conversation. I quickly untied mine and hurried down to Tarsus' patron deity for my daily lesson.

I arrived first since my room was closer to the predetermined meeting place, and spotted Vettias entering the square several minutes later. He led me to a nondescript corner of the plaza where we stood with our backs against a wall, allowing us to converse unheard and unnoticed yet still be fully aware of the events transpiring around us.

"So you're getting the hang of it?" Vettias asked with an inviting smile.

"I think so."

"Well, your confidence will certainly waver by the end of today. Your head is going to be spinning by the time night falls." Considering my mind was already in danger of reaching its limits of comprehension with all I had learned thus far, Vettias' statement made me a little uneasy.

"So, look around this square. Do you know why I chose this location for us to meet?"

"Because it is crowded and will allow us to get lost in its commotion," I answered.

"Good, but what good does that do if you led someone here who was following you and now they can anonymously hide in the sea of activity?" Vettias countered.

"I, I don't know,"

"When you departed, no doubt excitedly running out of your inn this morning, did you even bother to look behind you?"

"No."

"So you could have led someone to this square and now they are observing the two of us talking without fear of detection. So instead of one person of interest now they have two. Maybe they'll follow me back to my room from here and see who I meet with. Maybe they'll kidnap me out of my room in the middle of the night and torture me until I tell them what they want then kill me. Do you understand where I'm going with this?"

"I think so," I responded unconvincingly.

"We'll see. What if they are only suspicious of you? If you start looking over your shoulder every minute you may identify your followers but now they know you have something to hide which will only increase their interest in you because normal people don't behave in that manner."

"So I don't want to know if I'm being followed?" I asked, thoroughly confused.

"Of course you want to know, but you want to determine it in a way that does not look like you are alerted to their presence. There are ways to accomplish discreet acts while being followed, thus achieving your overall goal and removing suspicion from those that may do you harm. What if you knew you had led followers to a meeting with me, how would you alert me to the danger in a way that would tell me to abort the meeting yet appear innocuous to your shadowers? Finally, what if you are being followed while you are learning the many streets of a new city? How dubious you would look to your followers then?" I stood without reply in hopes he would further elaborate without asking another question. I cursed Socrates under my breath for devising such a labourious method of study. "Now of course there are times when you must flee your shadowers and it doesn't matter if they know you know or not. Other times you can leverage being followed into an advantage by leading them into an ambush."

"We will go over all of these principles in detail today but we'll begin back at your room. What if you are doing everything right? You are aware of your scrutiny, you have not alerted them to your knowledge of their presence, and you are travelling to a location that will allow us to briefly meet one another securely. But this time your followers mean to kill you. If you travel the same way each time out of your room to various locations then your attackers need only choose the best place to lie and wait. In addition to being aware of followers you must also change routes that you take from one place to another. But if you take different routes that do not appear logical to the persons shadowing you, they may assume you are hiding something. Keeping routines is very dangerous in this line of work but you must also appear as though you are not trying to avoid routines, understand?"

I looked at him with a blank expression, for Vettias had succeeded in confounding my meagre intellectual abilities. "Of course you don't," he continued, "but don't worry, I didn't learn all of this in a day either. We'll do some training exercises that will illustrate these principles vividly. Now, show me the way you travelled from your room to this square." I led him through the direct route of narrow alleys back to my room where he took inventory of every twist and turn along the way. We arrived at a small courtyard which had four alleys jutting off of it with my inn residing at the end of one of them.

"So this is where all possible routes to and from your inn converge," Vettias concluded. "This is where your watchers will pick up your trail, either coming or going." He further studied the space, pointing out two store fronts and several windows looking onto the courtyard. "What time do these stores open? How busy does this square get? During which hours is it quiet like it is now?"

"I don't know."

"Of course you don't, but these are the things you must know about a place where you frequently travel to and fro. Planning your travels through this space when it is busy with people will make it very difficult to determine if someone has picked up your trail. However, if it ever becomes crushed with people during the day like Sandon's square, which I doubt it ever would, this could be a good place to lose any followers you may have brought with you this far."

"Now let us return to Sandon using a different path. It is clear why you chose the route we just took because that is the most direct. Now we must find an alternate way that would also make sense to a potential shadower." We travelled to the monument using a different set of alleyways and small roads while Vettias surveyed our surroundings closely. I was unsure what we were looking for but held my tongue for fear of looking more inept than I was already portraying myself. He finally found what he was looking for and stopped at a food vendor along the street.

"Ah hah, this may work," Vettias stated without further elaboration. We entered the venue, which was open at this early hour to my surprise, and spoke with the woman sitting behind the counter chopping food stuffs. "Hello madam, your store is open quite early; is this when I can find most storefronts opening in this neighbourhood? My nephew and I are travelling through and will be here a few days."

"Ha, most shop owners around here are either asleep, drunk, or both," the woman replied. They won't open for another two hours."

"I see," Vettias continued. "And what does your store offer, other than hours consistent to when I rise, that others around here do not?"

"The best cheese in Tarsus," she responded without hesitation. "Been making it the same way here since my great grandmother."

"My nephew and I would like to purchase some." The woman walked to the back of the store and produced the requested item. Once the transaction was made Vettias and I continued our walk towards Sandon's square.

We arrived back in the square shortly afterward and Vettias turned to me asking, "So, here we are. Do you understand what just happened?"

"I will need further elaboration," I admitted.

"We travelled a different, more circuitous route to arrive at the same location to avoid establishing a routine. Someone following would think that odd and thus take further interest in you unless there was a logical reason for your detour. That woman's store offers the perfect alibi. Not only is it open earlier than many of the other stores in your neighbourhood, it also offers the best cheese- that is why you travelled out of your way to get here.

"I understand," I answered, seeing the logic in Vettias' explanation.

"Now that you have a basic understanding of choosing your routes, let us become the shadowers so we may view the target from their eyes." Vettias pointed to a random man buying produce at a cart parked alongside the square. "Let us see where he goes without raising his suspicions. While he's in this square we have the advantage, since he is unaware of our intention and we do not have to move in order to keep an eye on him. Once he departs this square, depending on the roads and alleys he travels, he will have the advantage. If he leads us down a solemn alley where we are the only three pedestrians, then he will have succeeded in isolating us from the crowd, making it easier to discern our intentions. If he sticks to heavily travelled thoroughfares, we will have the advantage of invisibility within the crowd."

We observed the man walk between several produce carts purchasing various items before he began walking down one of the streets jutting out from the square. "That's our cue," Vettias stated. "Let's begin." We kept behind him about fifty paces. As congestion grew we shortened our distance to twenty five paces. As he turned on to a new street Vettias and I would quicken our pace to close the distance, turn the corner to establish visual contact, and then slow our pace again to keep an unassuming interval between us. During our overwatch, Vettias would point out good store fronts to utilize as part of a route or good alleyways to traverse that may separate out potential followers. Once the man stopped at a street side cart to procure more items which forced Vettias and I to stop as well. We were compelled to stand against a wall and pretend we were conversing despite the location for our discussion looking odd and out of place.

"That is also a good tactic," Vettias pointed out. "Making frequent, logical stops while travelling can identify people like us standing out of place. If he were to do this in a desolate alleyway he would spot us for sure. Stopping allows the target natural observation to his front, rear, left, and right while the transaction is being conducted. If you keep to the same routine, however, your followers will not have to actually follow you and can wait to acquire you in a stationary position along your habitual route."

The man finished his transaction and continued along his path. "Every time he is out of our sight is an opportunity for him to pass a message or conduct a clandestine act. If he planned his route correctly, he would have someone waiting for him on the other side of a turn in the road. He could make a left or right, be out of our line of sight for thirty seconds, pass a note to a beggar, or shopkeeper, or passerby, and look completely innocuous by the time we reacquire sight of him. Since this man has no worry of being followed he is acting completely normal to the two of us. I want you to see what *normal* looks like to someone following you. A few days of normal activities and you will look completely ordinary; and your followers will look elsewhere to root out potential agents."

The man made one last turn before entering a tenement building near a public water fountain in the form of some unknown ancient Cilician river god. "This will be my red scarf meeting place," Vettias announced. "Tomorrow morning we will meet here when my red scarf hangs from my window. Understood?"

"Yes uncle," I answered with a smirk.

"Good, midday is approaching, let's find some solace from the sun and some decent food and drink, for we will need our strength. Tonight I have a surprise for you." We found a venue not far from the water fountain that offered mediocre food and wine. Vettias and I relaxed while the midday sun beat down on the city. After finishing a jug we both dozed off for about ninety minutes while the worst of the heat passed by. Upon waking we departed the store and passed the time by walking up and down the streets of Tarsus, becoming more familiar with the city. In the late afternoon we found ourselves entering a neighbourhood filled with brothels- our arrival to this neighbourhood was no coincidence.

"Are we to visit a brothel this early?" I asked.

"It's true, most of these establishments are brothels, but our proximity to the east and the largess of Tarsus yields another type of establishment, one as different from a normal brothel as water from a chamber pot is to a fresh stream. We are going to visit a pleasure house. I'm taking you here for more than just the obvious reasons. Someone as green as you has never experienced, nor could ever afford, a place like this. I need you to be familiar with them, however, for they will be prevalent in Triparadeisus and you will need to navigate them with dexterity and skill. Triparadeisus would be too much for a young know-nothing like yourself without a little practice first," Vettias concluded with a smile.

The façade of our destination was clean and freshly painted. The portico was a semi-circle with four impressive Persian-style columns, each with a bull-head capital. A statue of the Babylonian goddess Sarpanit, wife of Marduk, stood over the pediment, harkening back to the days when Tarsus was ruled by Persians. Vettias said he thought it odd that a Persian Goddess associated with fertility would be chosen to stand over an establishment where conception was not welcome. The sculpted relief of the pediment demonstrated a myriad of sexual offerings available inside. We entered through the wrought-iron security gate manned by an imposing figure dressed in a loin cloth. Crossing the threshold I entered a world completely foreign to me. The luxurious decorations were of a quality and opulence my eyes had never witnessed before. The floor had an intricate tile design of a naked woman. Several marble statues stood throughout the foyer with elaborate tapestries in between. Lavish couches lined the walls with plush cushions and gold trim. The ceiling, lit by several gold lamps, boasted a large painting of sexual positions similar to the pediment in outside. Vettias was right about my simplicity regarding establishments such as these.

We were greeted by the headmaster of the pleasure house, who wore a fine silk robe with several gold rings housing many jewels. He was bald with skin fairer then his age should have allowed due, no doubt, to excessive moisturizing and washing. His eye brows were manicured in the thin eastern style.

"Gentlemen, gentlemen, welcome to The Fair Peach. I don't recognize either of you, is this your first time to our establishment?" he asked, looking at my appearance to evaluate whether I was some poor traveller looking for a more reasonably priced experience and wandered into the wrong place.

"I have been here once before many years ago and now have the pleasure of returning with my nephew," Vettias answered, while putting considerable coin in the man's hand. "We will both take the full offering."

"Of course," our host replied with a smile, and clapped his hands summoning two very young girls of eastern features and exceptional beauty. "Laleh and Nyla will show you to the steam rooms." We followed their slender bodies past the atrium and behind a thick red curtain. We entered a sauna where the two girls instructed us to de-robe and lie face down on the two wooden tables draped in cloth.

The girls departed and two older women entered to provide us a massage. My masseuse had deceivingly strong hands for someone of her stature as she rubbed oil into my now open pores. She certainly left no part of my body untouched, however she did not rub my genitals to the point of completion. After a truly relaxing hour we were given robes and led to the baths. Vettias and I took a quick dip in the cold plunge, which took care of my embarrassing erection.

Next we were brought to the warm baths where two beautiful women awaited us with enticing smiles. We entered the warm bath as our new companions readied their bathing instruments. Both wore jewellery around their waist and neck, and began bathing us with soap and scented oils. The water we sat in was saturated with rose petals while the room burned with sweet incense. After our bath mates finished washing us, excellent wine and fruit was presented while they began giving manicures and pedicures- something my extremities had never experienced. Upon completion of our grooming our bath mates further massaged us. Whereas I could not help but wear a childlike grin on my face, Vettias sat with the stoic confidence of a man who believes himself deserving of such treatment. This symbolized why Vettias brought me here as oppose to one of the many brothels in this neighbourhood, and I strained to ape his composure. This effort turned immediately in vain once my bath mate took me in her mouth with a skill and sensuality I did not know existed in women. Vettias observed my aroused fidgeting and instructed my woman to go easy on me since I was not yet used to someone of her skill and he didn't want me finishing before we got our full money's worth. Both females laughed at my lack of sexual sophistication and my woman ended the rest of our splendid hour together keeping me right on the edge of ecstasy.

After the hour was up six women were brought into our bath chamber. "There's more?" I asked.

"Now it's time for a real lesson," Vettias proclaimed with a smile. "Which one do you want? Might I suggest an older woman with experience? Leave the girls to me."

Each women was more beautiful than the next. I now understood the proprietor's initial reluctance to believe me a worthy patron of The Fair Peach given my simple appearance. I followed Vettias' suggestion and chose one that looked to be older than the rest, maybe all of thirty years old. Out of all Vettias had taught and exposed me to, that next hour was truly the most pleasurable experience of my life. I left The Fair Peach with Vettias a new man, whose eyes were now open to what the world truly had to offer. I felt an inch taller amd there was a determined gait in my step. Vettias noted with a smile. "I have done all I can to ready you for our arrival at Triparadeisus, my young nephew. Even now you look to have matured ten years since we departed General Eumenes' camp. There is still much to learn but I'm beginning to feel confident you will actually survive our journey."

Chapter 23

Night had fallen since our entry to The Fair Peach and my body still reverberated with a euphoric glow from strong wine and carnal pleasure. What was I doing with women before tonight, I wandered to myself? It certainly wasn't what I had just been introduced to by my talented and beautiful companion.

"We'll get some food and wine there," Vettias pronounced, pointing to a nearby tavern and brothel. The impressively furnished establishment was moderately full and looked cleaner than any hole Ilandra had to offer. The women working the floor were all of above average attractiveness and a young man played the lyre in the background, adding to the pleasant ambience. We sat at a sturdy table made of fine wood that had recently been cleaned. Vettias ordered a jug of wine with some bread and meat and the two of us ate in silence. The wine and food were excellent, thus every sense had now been indulged.

"I could live here," I joked.

"Not bad is it? Wait till we arrive in Triparadeisus. Maybe one day you'll see Babylon." During our lethargic conversation I noticed Vettias kept looking at the establishment's working girls, as if evaluating which one to bed tonight.

"More women?" I asked surprised.

"If I call one over here just play along and mind your tongue," were his instructions. "Hmm, what do you think of that one?" Vettias asked, looking at a beauty with foreign features.

"I think she's beautiful, but another woman? Right now?"

"Not for what you think. In fact, if she passes her audition, I can change her life for the better." This last statement was strange and cryptic, even for Vettias. He told me to play along, however, so I kept my mouth shut and awaited the night's next lesson, or surprise, to materialize. I now made a concerted effort to remove the sated grin from my face that I'm sure was a constant reminder to Vettias of just how unsophisticated I still was. Vettias mulled his decision for several more minutes looking at the beauty with an inquisitive eye until finally getting her attention and calling her to our table.

"Good evening, my lady." Vettias greeted with his familiar charm, honed by years of replaying this very moment countless times.

"Hello gentlemen, how may I be of service tonight?" She replied with forced warmth.

"Well, probably not in the way you are assuming," Vettias answered, which brought an expression of annoyance from our table guest as she immediately ceased regarding us as possible paying customers. Someone like her working in a city like this was no country whore willing to hang on Vettias' every word. She had no doubt seen countless men of Vettias' eloquence and prominence, perhaps many who could be deemed more impressive. As it looked like she was getting up to find more lucrative prospects Vettias quickly halted her, holding several coins in his hand. "Of course I am willing to reimburse you for your time with us." Her annoyance only half subsided as she changed attitudes and put on her artificial charm once again.

"And what do you have in mind?"

"I would like to make your acquaintance if you have the time. What is your name my lady?"

"Mara."

"And from where do you hail? Your features are not from Cilicia."

"I am a Scythian, taken as a slave by the Greek conquests. My family was nomadic so I do not hail from any one place except far north of here." Her hair was light brown, not quite blond and her skin was a dark honey from years of sun. She was from good stock with ample curves, green eyes, and above average height. Up until the Fair Peach I would have thought her the most beautiful woman I had ever seen. As I listened to the conversation unfold I was impressed with the confident way she carried herself, despite being younger than me. Her bearing succeeded in causing me to divert my eyes every time she looked in my direction.

"How long have you been here?" Vettias asked in a concerned voice.

"Here? About two years," She responded coldly. "Other places about one year."

196

"Yet none have succeeded in breaking your spirit, that much is quite evident." Mara afforded Vettias the slightest of smiles. On this point she was certainly in agreement with Vettias' assessment.

"My nephew and I are merchants travelling to parts east and south on business. I am always looking for information on potential buyers and sellers of my wares and thus am willing to reward any who may help me in this regard. My nephew and I are not political animals, however the change in tides also washes new clients ashore. By now you've no doubt heard of Lord Regent Perdiccas' defeat and the new Regency of the Kings. Since there is a royal treasury in Tarsus, I wonder who has been recently washed up in this wave of change?" Mara looked a little puzzled by Vettias' ambiguous question. "What I mean to ask is have there been new faces arriving in town on official business? Members of the new royal retinue? Surely powerful and important men like that would find their way to an upscale establishment such as this."

"There have been new men with authority as of late. They are frequent patrons. They are sitting in the far back corner."

"And have you known them since they've arrived?" Vettias asked.

"The two on the left, yes, on separate occasions."

"And did they speak to you about their current positions?" Vettias continued, passing more coins into Mara's hand.

"One is the new administer of the treasury, he claimed his predecessor was appointed by Perdiccas and thus had him executed. The other did not speak much but was clearly an experienced lover." Vettias casually looked in the direction of the men in question and glanced curiously at the quiet one with almost a look of recognition. Since I was facing their table I had a natural view and began inconspicuously studying their faces once identified to us as being of some importance. The quiet one held the same unassuming confident attitude I had admired in Vettias. He had dark features with a noticeable mark on his face, just left of his nose. My attention in him waned as Vettias continued our conversation with Mara.

"So is this really all you desire of me? I grow tired of these questions."

197

"Why so eager to run off to someone less inviting than I? Us sitting here affords you time away from lustful strangers uninterested casual conversation."

"I am positioning myself to gain the favour of my owner, working hard and making money is the way to do that. Sitting around collecting a small handful of coins with pompous asses is not."

"And here I thought I was speaking to someone a little more worldly," Vettias retorted. I had been around him long enough to know when he intentionally makes a provocative statement to catch his target off guard and momentarily glimpse into their true persona.

"What is that supposed to mean!" Mara fired back. It was apparent she didn't suffer fools kindly, thus she considered Vettias' charge of naiveté a direct insult.

"Well there's nothing stopping you from killing your owner in his sleep and making your way north this very night, is there? But of course to do so without support would be a fool's errand, since you would not survive such a difficult journey on your own through Greek territory for long. At least here you have reasonable accommodations and the off chance of meeting nice men like myself and my nephew here."

"Of course I know all this," Mara sneered but Vettias cut her off.

"You're also too smart to set your hopes on convincing some client who walks through the door to fall in love with you and take you far away from here. Maybe set you up in your own apartment, maybe even marriage. Yet you wish to become the favourite of your owner? Become his best earner? Perhaps pretend to enjoy the times he forces himself on you to gain his trust? Men like him don't care about you and will squeeze as much value out of you before selling you to the next lecher who offers good money. An upscale brothel such as this must see pretty new faces in here all the time, and they're only so many rooms in this establishment. One day it will be your turn to make way for the next scared Scythian girl to begin her life of misery within these walls."

"How dare you talk to me like that!" Mara hissed, keeping her voice just low enough to not be heard by any other employees. "You think you can throw a few coins at me so I'll sit here and be insulted? I'll have the guards beat you from this place. Go down a few blocks to some rotted out hole where you can rent a rotted out whore who'll be impressed with your empty flatteries. I'll make enough money tonight to buy your nephew if I wanted to. And here you are claiming to be one of the nice ones. I'd rather spend my evening with some fat slob who pays the bill than an arrogant prick like you." Mara turned to leave but Vettias firmly held her hand.

"Forgive me for speaking so bluntly, but someone who clearly can deliver harsh truths should be able to hear them- especially from someone like myself who has summoned you to our table to make you an offer I know you'll be interested in. I only mean to get your blood up so you remember how upset you are with your current lot when considering what I have to say. My tact was admittedly rude but since we have only just met I misgauged the exuberant fire that exists behind your cold façade- a trait that makes my decision to speak with you all the wiser." Mara sat back down and lowered her voice.

"So are we going to talk plainly or are you going to keep speaking in eloquent circles like some emasculated eunuch in a Persian palace?"

"Very good my dear, you seem to have an aptitude for understanding people. As I said earlier, our trade relies on the gathering of information, especially from powerful men. We are travelling to a place where there will be many powerful men with valuable secrets which I need to further my business interests. You are in no danger of leaving this place any time soon. Would you be willing to continue your loathed profession for a few more weeks under my care in order to gain full escape from slavery and help reaching your homeland?"

"You Greeks and your homelands. My family and most of my clan were murdered. The rest sold into slavery. We don't live in cities like you comfortable Greeks. Greeks ensured I will never have a homeland to return to. What have you imagined in that arrogant head of yours, I jump into your lap like some grateful dog because you're going to take me to the wild northern regions of Scythia? The first tribe that comes across me will make me a slave in the same way I am here, except I won't be wearing eastern silks. At least the majority of the clientele here bathes on a somewhat regular basis." I could tell Mara's unimpressed response took Vettias by surprise and he struggled to maintain control of his target and the conversation.

"So you'd rather stay here?"

"Just as you so pompously put it earlier, what prospects do I have on my own?"

"What if I could guarantee your protection for as long as it's required in return for your help over these next few weeks? After that time you will have my personal pledge of security and a respite from having to sell your body again. This is that chance that never comes. This is the scenario all young whores dream of and all experienced ones won't allow themselves to dream of anymore."

"You sure think me naïve to risk my life with so little information being provided to me! How do I know you're not some slave trader looking to steal a pretty whore for cheap and sell me out to eastern pimps who won't treat me half as good as here?"

"You don't," Vettias answered frankly. "But I'm not here to swindle you or kidnap you against your will. I am simply going to provide you a time and place where my nephew and I will be waiting should you choose to join us. If not, we will continue on our journey without you."

"And where exactly would you be taking me?"

"I am sorry my dear, I can't tell you that until I know you've committed to joining us. If you appear at the agreed meeting place, all will be revealed to you. I thank you for your time and will let you get back to your work. I hope you have already laid a foundation of good will with your employer, you may need to use all of it to steal away at the appointed hour. Shall I tell you where we will be?" Vettias had done a good job recovering from his intentional provocations and made a good sell to the woman at the end using hurried assessments about her motivations and vulnerabilities.

Mara was quiet as I watched her ponder the myriad of angles Vettias' offer entailed and the number of schemes it would require from her end to be successful. In the end, the essence of Vettias' offer was too enticing for a woman such as Mara, who thought herself above her current circumstances which she was not born into. She leaned closer to Vettias with a hushed tone "Alright, where will you be?"

*

The next morning I stood at the fountain where the red scarf beckoned me at dawn, only to find myself alone despite the location being closer to Vettias' room. The rising sun cast long shadows down the small square creating dark abysses where alleys jutted out from the road. No one stirred at so early an hour and after a few minutes I spotted Vettias turning a corner, emerging from the shadows with our two mounts in tow.

"No sign yet?" Vettias asked.

"Nothing. Do you think she'll show?"

"She'd be a fool not to," he opined as he let out a sigh and lounged against the fountain, closing his eyes. "She'll also build up your confidence around beautiful women. You haven't come across many in your life, and it showed these past couple days. They'll be more of them in Triparadeisus so try not to look like a dirt farmer in their presence. Keep an eye out."

"Do you intend to guarantee her security if she helps us?"

"If we survive the ordeal and make it back to Eumenes' camp she will never be told who sleeps with her again. There will be thousands of men she can wrap around her finger in the army," Vettias answered with his eyes still closed. "Maybe it could be you."

"How long will we wait?" I asked, ignoring his last comment.

"Until the streets begin to fill."

"That will be in the next half hour. If she arrives after we depart, she will be in serious danger."

"We can't worry about that. If she manages to escape, any pursuers will no doubt think she fled north. If she is seen leaving with us to the south, our chances of getting to Triparadeisus without incident are lowered. She knows when and where she is to meet us. Her safety is subordinate to our charge of protecting the Argead line."

The sun continued creeping upwards when I saw a shadowy silhouette emerge from a dim alley like a bit of black matter had been released and instantly emitted colour once free of its dark grasp. It was Mara wearing a dingy grey shoal over her head and carrying a small leather pouch. She materialized out of the alley to see us standing at the prearranged location and quickly made her way towards us with a look of anxious determination. There would be no turning back for Mara now, and she had just put her life in the hands of strangers. I jostled Vettias out of a half conscious state and the two of us mounted our horses. Vettias motioned for her to mount his horse and the three of us made a direct line towards the city's southern gate which was intentionally not far from our location.

"Good morning my lady," greeted Vettias. "Keep your shoal on until we clear the surrounding farms. We'll procure you a horse then."

Chapter 24

Our first few nights were spent avoiding towns or inns and making camp away from the road with low, shielded fires. Vettias made several mild efforts to engage Mara in conversation during these first couple days, but did not find a willing participant. She kept to herself, ate little, and spoke even less. Her riding skills surpassed my own from years of hard nomadic life. The third day brought us out through the Cilician Gates mountain pass to the Pinarus River.

"You know where we are boy? Do you know this hallowed ground your mount now walks?" Vettias asked condescendingly. His question made me realize I hadn't known where I was since I left Sardis.

"No," I answered.

"This is the Issus Plain. That is the Pinarus River. I was here over ten years ago with Alexander's army. This battle cut off Darius from the sea and cleared the way for our march on Phoenicia and Egypt, laying the groundwork for the epic final battle at Gaugamela. I remember the weather being brisk and unseasonably cold for the region. Darius had already killed or mutilated our sick and wounded at the town of Issus and positioned himself in between our army and our supply train by the time our two forces met at this river. Parmenion commanded the left wing, Craterus the middle. Alexander led the Companion Cavalry on the right. Ptolemy, Perdiccas, and Coenus, all commanded regiments while Nicanor, son of Parmenion, commanded the Silver Shields."

"The Phalanx did not play a decisive role in the initial fighting, thus I was able to observe the actions of Alexander as I describe them to you now. Darius began with a full cavalry charge against Paermenion's left flank of allied cavalry. Our left held their ground while Alexander personally led the Silver Shields on foot to make a direct attack on the Persian infantry. He succeeded in punching a hole through their line and mounted Bucephalus to lead the Companion Cavalry on our right flank straight at Darius and his entourage of bodyguards. It was at this time our Phalanx joined with

Darius' Greek mercenaries in the center of the line. They fought well and blunted the momentum gained from Alexander's assault. Darius fled in the face of Alexander's charge and was pursued mercilessly by our cavalry, with Alexander at its head. His audacious pursuit proved too ambitious, however, and the Persian's Greek mercenaries proved too obstinate. Alexander's departure enabled the remaining enemy to gain the upper hand and he was forced to break off his chase and come to our aid. The Companion Cavalry eventually returned and smashed into the rear of our Greek mercenary foes, causing their lines to collapse and flee in full route. Our cavalry bore down on them for the remaining hours of sunlight and mass carnage ensued."

Mara had remained quiet but listened attentively to Vettias' narration. As the story progressed her expression became increasingly disturbed, until Vettias' proud retelling of the battle's aftermath appeared to bring her to near tears. "You men and your glory!" she blurted out uncontrollably. "What does it accomplish? The conquered trade one tyrant for another. Families of your defeated ripped apart, violated, murdered or sold into slavery. Dying would have been better than my fate after Greek soldiers occupying Armenia invaded north into our native lands, burning our possessions, killing our men and boys, raping and enslaving our women and children."

"No one denies the horrors that can occur in the aftermath of warfare, Mara," Vettias interrupted, trying to calm her down. "But the Scythian tribes are no strangers to terrible brutalities. I know this first hand from their repeated raids into Macedon and King Philip's campaign against the great Scythian King Ateas." Vettias appeared surprised by Mara's outburst but I suspected he relayed the story to evoke an emotional reaction from Mara which he could begin to exploit.

Mara continued as if Vettias was no longer in her presence. She looked off into the distance and her mind was clearly in a place far from the Issus Plane. "There had been fighting before that day between several of our tribes and the Greek army in Armenia led by the Satrap Neoptolemus. Recent Greek encroachments and the lure of valuable plunder emboldened our men to make frequent raids against new Greek settlements located within our traditional lands. In previous instances our men were able to disappear back into the vast wilderness and avoid open confrontation with Neoptolemus' army. Neoptolemus began pre-deploying several Scythian traitors familiar with our territories near vulnerable settlements to locate our encampment. One of them must have been successful and we were attacked by Neoptolemus' cavalry and his allied Scythian forces from three flanks at once that evening, cutting off all avenues of escape."

Vettias and I now walked our mounts at a slow pace beside Mara to better hear her account and show support for her. "Our men had been drinking to celebrate the successful raid earlier in the day when I heard the approaching thunder from all sides. They grabbed their weapons as the women and children hurried to the tents. I laid under blankets with my mother and two older sisters as we heard hell opening up around us with the knowledge our father was a part of the massacre. Men were yelling obscenities, screaming in pain, and howling with bloodlust. When I lifted a small piece of our tent up I saw my dead tribesmen strewn throughout the encampment and I realized all would soon be lost. The cries of our tribesmen began to wane and turned into something more disturbing- the shrieks of our women and children. Women were being dragged from their tents and stripped naked."

"I began hearing Greek spoken near our tent; our mother grabbed me back under the blanket and covered my sister's mouth to silence her crying. I heard the entrance flap of our tent open violently- our mother held us tighter. The blanket was ripped off and all sense of security was lost. My oldest sister was grabbed first and ripped outside. My mother began screaming and clawing at her to delay the inevitable but the men quickly overpowered her and dragged her out next. My sister and I were carried out last. I was thrown into a gaggle of children and my mother and two sisters were stripped naked in front of us and led to the group of adult women."

I felt my eyes begin to well as Mara continued her horrific narrative. I thought of my mother and Helena being subjected to this cruelty and could not believe Mara's poise and beauty after experiencing such a trauma. Vettias was wise to choose her, if only she could be persuaded to be our ally.

"I now stood within a herd of crying children forced to view their father's and brother's corpses while watching their mothers and sisters ravaged over and over again. I saw my remaining family violently abused as they let out sobs of agony. When it was over some of the women were dead, others lay covered in blood and dirt quietly weeping, completely numb to the world around them. Those that survived were rounded up, reunited with the children, and marched south to the Greek territories in Armenia to be sold. During this chaos I realized my family did not survive the vile assault and I was marched with what remained of our tribe for five days to the port city of Trebizond where I was sold to a prostitute merchant at the age of thirteen."

"I was deflowered promptly that evening by several rough men and many times a day thereafter by those willing to pay good money for the privilege of someone so young. I was later brought to Mazaka in Cappadocia. The proprietor of the brothel was a cruel man and subjected us to frequent beatings on top of working us relentlessly. Three girls were beaten to death during my year there. Fortunately his foul demeanour was not confined to the brothel and he had many enemies. One of which surreptitiously colluded with some of us to have him killed in return for better treatment. After the act was committed, I was sold to a slave merchant who brought me to Tarsus and sold me to the establishment where you met me last week. I was treated well and lived well but always worked towards escaping someday."

"That is the result of your precious Greek glory. Persian glory was just as brutal before the Greeks arrived. Scythian glory between rival tribes can be even worse. The common denominator in these disparate groups is the lust for glory through violence shared by all men. There are hundreds of thousands of stories like mine. Families murdered, violated, and ripped apart. Men like you who fight in these battles and teach your sons to believe the same are the monsters women like me fear every day. People like me are at the mercy of monsters like you and all too often we are used, abused, and discarded like trash."

Tears were running down Mara's face by this point while she looked up to the gods as if imploring them to rectify the injustice that had been perpetrated against her. I did all I could to mask my tears from Vettias who listened stoically to the traumatic story with empathic eyes and body language.

"Mara, there's no question you've endured an undeserved tragedy, especially at so young an age," Vettias consoled warmly. "And while both sides on a battlefield will view their cause as just and their opponents' without merit, some men do fight for a greater good, not just battlefield glory. You have been honest with my nephew and I, allow us to be honest with you."

Mara looked at Vettias with red eyes as if ready to hear another disappointment. "While I intend to help you in every way I promised back in Tarsus, I have not been truthful about our background and who we really are. The boy and I are in fact soldiers fighting for an ideal, as opposed to glory, in the service of General Eumenes, mortal enemy to the villain Satrap Neoptolemus you speak of. In fact, I witnessed with my own eyes the slaying of Neoptolemus at the hand of General Eumenes himself in Cappadocia. Neoptolemus was a traitor and a villain, yet his allies still seek to sow discord throughout the empire which is sure to cause countless more tragedies like the one you've experienced. We travel to Triparadeisus, where these men are meeting to do what we can to thwart their intentions. I have enlisted you to temporarily continue your profession and assist us in this righteous task. The Fates work in mysterious ways. I had no notion of the injustices committed by Neoptolemus on you when we first met. They have brought us together to offer you a chance to exact revenge against his surviving allies who work to this day to advance the interests he fought for. I hope my decision to withhold the full account of my motives does not deter your initial decision to help us and bolsters your resolve since it is now revealed our paths were joined to thwart a common enemy."

I listened in admiration as Vettias aptly used Mara's tragedy to solidify his bond with her and strengthen her reasons for assisting us. It seemed as though the past week had been planned; from his choosing Mara at the brothel, to holding his tongue during the first few days of our journey and allowing her to decide when she was ready to speak, to his seamless ability to join our purposes as if he already knew the tragic story she would tell. It all worked in unison to bring us to this moment where he would secure her undying loyalty for rescuing her from her predicament and offering her a chance at revenge. There was no way Vettias could have planned for this moment and therefore it surely must have been The Fates guiding both of us. I watched Mara as she processed Vettias' words with her beautiful green eyes looking at him with a cynicism usually reserved for those far older and jaded by life's cruelties.

"And what you say is true?" Mara asked with a wavering voice.

"I swear it to the Gods," Vettias replied emphatically. "All I ask is for you to continue your wretched trade for a short while longer, vice the rest of your life in Tarsus, to assist us in gathering information necessary to thwart our common enemies. Once we depart Triparadeisus you will be welcomed into our camp with full acknowledgement of your contribution to our cause from General Eumenes as well as the personal security that status provides. Can I count on your help? You will not get far on your own and will probably end up in a worse situation then Tarsus."

"You have my word," Mara said in a low voice.

The next several days were spent travelling by day and sleeping in small fishing villages along the Middle Sea coast by night. Vettias and I refrained from visiting the local night life out of respect for Mara's past and to maintain the good rapport Vettias had established. Vettias instructed Mara on the way elegant courtesans spoke proper Greek to their patrons. He taught her how to exploit her physical talents, often using me as the example of a hapless client just waiting to tell her everything I knew. Some of these exercises actually brought her to laughter as the two of us played out Vettias' more humourous scenarios. Not surprisingly, Mara was a natural at manipulation. Someone as smart, fiery, and beautiful as Mara had little difficulty bending men to a predetermined outcome. By the time we neared our destination I thought her to be of more value to our mission than myself.

As we approached Triparadeisus, about a day's ride north of Heliopolis, the road became cluttered with wagons carrying every form of product to be hocked in front of the world's most powerful men leading well paid armies of thousands. Our guise was to continue as merchants, except Vettias made the decision Mara would act as our slave to be rented to an interested party at Triparadeisus. Approaching from the south I began to see the sprawling complex of lush parks and lakes intermittently dotted with elaborate palaces, grand thoroughfares, fountains, orchards, and large herds of exotic game animals. Located within the sprawling grounds was the royal retinue flying the Argead Banners, among other lesser standards, with dozens of ornate carriages glittering with gold and jewels in the late day's sun. Extravagant tents stood in this impressive formation housing members of the royal entourage not important enough to be quartered inside the complex's palaces. At the gate of the complex was a large number of lesser buildings resembling a small town which Vettias explained housed the Triparadeisus staff. The landscaped scenery came to an abrupt end past the main gate where a vast army, twice the size of General Eumenes', laid encamped. Behind the army was the hastily erected tent city of merchants either following the army from Egypt or travelling from the surrounding areas to service the abundant need of commodities and comforts of the army.

"There lies our former comrades," Vettias stated, pointing at the army encampment. "These men fought for Lord Regent Perdiccas just weeks ago. Now they are our enemies, under what looks like General Seleucus' banners- a lifelong friend of Alexander and capable general. It appears not even a summit of the successors was enough to tear Ptolemy from his beloved Egypt. I suspect no amount of force would be strong enough now. We'll have plenty of allies within the ranks, however. Just follow my lead and keep your mouths shut."

"And the Royal Banners?" I asked eagerly, unable to mask my excitement of being so close to Alexander's blood relatives.

"The Kings and royal court," Vettias replied unenthusiastically. "There is one royal family member in particular I wish to speak with and she may hold the key to our success before Lord Regent Antipater arrives from Macedon." I did not take the bait of asking him to elaborate, despite Vettias' intentionally cryptic statement. I knew him well enough by now to play along and he would tell me what I needed to know when I needed to know it.

"We will start in the merchant encampment and buy some local attire," instructed Vettias. "I want you both to cover your faces as much as possible and limit the amount of time people see us together. We'll also purchase some fine clothing as well."

Vettias identified several points of interest to me as meeting places as we made our way through the chaotic maze of tents, purchasing our required clothing items and a little food. We continued towards the army encampment with our local garb covering the top of our heads and the lower half of our faces as was consistent with local customs.

"Are they going to just let us in?" I asked, noticing no coherent guard contingent around the army's perimeter like that of General Eumenes' army.

"This is a disparate force of former allies-turned-foes-turned allies," Vettias noted. "Three weeks will not have been enough time to forge a coherent fighting force. We should be able to exploit the confusion long enough for our purposes."

Vettias' assertion was certainly correct as we walked through the chaos with impunity. Vettias negotiated the horde with ease, making sure to avoid eye contact while finding the command tents of Perdiccas' former staff. Vettias instructed Mara and I to stay back as he approached one of the guards to the headquarters section. He whispered something to the first guard who quickly departed, leaving Vettias with his three colleagues. The guard returned with an impressive looking staff officer who signalled Vettias over to him. Vettias shook his hand, voiced something to him and called us over. The staff officer departed before we reached them and the three of us followed him to a small, nondescript tent in a tucked away corner of the headquarters bivouac. He shooed a subordinate out of the shelter that was sleeping and held the flap open for the three of us to enter. Vettias restrained Mara from entering and ordered the snoozing soldier to keep watch over her outside the tent.

"It's for your own protection, Mara," assured Vettias, after looking at Mara's suspecting eyes.

"Hmph," was her only reply. Once inside, the two men embraced like brothers.

"Ox, it's good to see you," said Vettias. "I thank the gods you are still alive. How fare our brothers? How fares the blood?"

Ox looked in my direction before responding. "This is Andrikos, phalangite under General Eumenes, future member of the Hand," Vettias explained.

Ox certainly lived up to his name. The man looked as though he was a close relative of Alexandros, with broad shoulders, large head, and hair everywhere. He grunted in my direction before turning back to Vettias.

"Brother, the cause is in peril. Our army and the Kings have been seized by our enemies with little hope of restitution save for a spectacular military victory."

"Tell me all that has happened between now and your departure for Egypt so I may best understand how to assist our cause during the summit."

Ox looked back at me wearily before turning to Vettias to recount the past several weeks. "Our march south was executed without major incident despite some tensions brought on by Perdiccas' harsh leadership at first and more nefarious causes later. Signs of strain first began between Perdiccas and General Antigenes, Commander of the Silver Shields. Around this time the members of the King's Hand uncovered several individuals working to undermine the morale of the officers and sow dissention. I immediately went to Perdiccas with these allegations and requested approval for a purge operation that very evening. Perdiccas consulted with Seleucus, his primary deputy, before giving his consent. I awoke the following morning, having eliminated the conspirators, to find five members of The Hand murdered in their tents with their throats slit and right hands hacked off. Such a brazen act committed against such a secret organization had to have been perpetrated by a true professional trained in the dark arts."

"Orontes?" Vettias interrupted, somewhat shaken.

"I thought the same, but after discreetly conducting a thorough investigation of our forces with trusted men, I can confidently say he was not in our camp." I sat silently listening to Ox's narrative, excitedly wondering who this new character was and how he could provoke such a reaction in Vettias.

"The remaining King's Hand members continued work with extreme care so as not to jeopardize the identities of themselves, while ensuring no further attempts to sow discord occurred. The situation died down until we reached the city of Pelusium on the northeast border of Ptolemy's holdings near the Great Egyptian River. Scouts were sent out to conduct reconnaissance and speak with the locals to discern the safest place to cross. The army continued south to the identified location and Perdiccas instructed our elephants to enter the river just upstream of our crossing. They were to remain in the river end-to-end until they spanned the entire length, thus ebbing the mighty river's current while the army made its treacherous journey across. The first contingent made it to the other side after great difficulty, but in the process kicked up the loose sediment of the riverbed, thus deepening the river and making it impassable by the rest of the army. Perdiccas then gave the disastrous order to bring the first contingent back and hundreds were swept downriver or drowned because of the new depth of the crossing."

"That evening General Antigenes was incensed by Perdiccas' incompetence and brought Peithon, Satrap of Media and former bodyguard of Alexander, to his cause against Perdiccas. Our unknown dissenters used the ensuing confusion to further sow discord throughout the officer corps. The King's Hand did what we could to eliminate those we could identify through another violent purge and the evening ended with a very uneasy calm. The next morning virtually all remaining King's Hand operatives were found murdered, with their right hands hacked off. The few remaining King's Hand personnel cut all communication and faded back into our normal duties within the army. My position within the leadership staff gave me a vantage point to observe the rest that was to transpire."

"The next evening General Antigenes and Peithon recruited Seleucus to their side and called an emergency meeting with Perdiccas where they stabbed him repeatedly until he lay in a pool of blood within his own headquarters tent. Shortly after, Ptolemy himself arrogantly rode into our encampment with a small retinue. He was warmly received by the conspirators which all but proved his culpability in the coup. I watched as one of his entourage removed his cloak to reveal the face of the traitor Orontes as sure as I am looking at your faces now. There was now no doubt our army had been infiltrated and General Antigenes had been persuaded against Perdiccas early in our travel. Orontes' presence with Ptolemy confirmed who was pulling the strings. Despite being injured by the efforts of the King's Hand, Orontes' shadow group was deeply imbedded in the army and Ptolemy wasted no time utilizing it during the remaining hours of darkness to eliminate known allies of Perdiccas, slaughter the Regent's family, and persuade as many officers to defect to his side as possible before dawn. The next morning Ptolemy proclaimed Peithon and Arrhidaeus, Deputy Commander of the Silver Shields, to be the Kings' Protectors until a more permanent solution could be reached at Triparadeisus. Seleucus was made Commander of the army and Ptolemy returned back to Egypt where his brilliant clandestine manoeuvrings, aided by Orontes, had further imbedded him within his Egyptian Kingdom."

"Thus is the state of events brother. We failed in protecting the Kings' interests and the few King's Hand survivors cannot even communicate for fear of interception by Orontes' forces, which now swell the ranks of this army like a pestilence. Our conversation must be cut off now for fear of exposing you to prying eyes." Ox delivered this final statement staring at the ground dejectedly.

"Look at me, look at me!" Vettias commanded in an angered hush, hoping to bring the defeated man back to his sworn charge. "I need you to set Andrikos and me up in separate apartments within the town of Triparadeisus. I need you to set up the girl inside the main palace harem. And finally, I need you to tell me about our young Queen. Is she what we thought her to be back in Cappadocia?"

"She is, and even more so now," Ox replied with life returning to his manner. "She is emboldened by the current state of affairs and could be persuaded to aid our cause if brought to purpose by the right individual. At this very moment she has moved to take Protectorship of the Kings away from Arrhidaeus and Peithon."

"Can you get me a clandestine audience with her?" Vettias asked excitedly.

"Your first two requests can be accommodated within a few hours. A clandestine audience with the Queen will take longer. Come back in four hours and I will have your quarters ready. Bring the girl as well. If she's pretty enough I shouldn't have much difficulty securing her a place in the palace. I advise you get yourselves lost in the merchant tent city until the appointed hour lest you be discovered by Orontes' men. They will no doubt be among the merchants as well, so keep your guard up."

"And Orontes, can we get to him?"

"Not in the short amount of time we have. He stays close to his new benefactor, Seleucus, and enjoys the security of Seleucus' own bodyguard. They are separate from all other Macedonian forces and guard them at all times. I have no inroads into that inner-circle and developing a source within it will take too long. For now they remain secluded within the main palace's inner sanctums, surrounded by armed sentries awaiting Antipater's arrival. When he arrives they may feel emboldened to move about more freely. Perhaps then we can make a move but not before."

"What of Orontes network? Have you made any of them?" Vettias asked.

"A few, yes," Ox replied hesitantly, apparently ashamed of the meagre amount of information he was able to provide.

"Then we'll start dealing with them as well. We will return to this tent in four hours, brother." Vettias and Ox embraced as we departed, rejoined with Mara, and made our way through the labyrinth of merchants selling wares from every corner of the world.

Chapter 25

The three of us slowly meandered through the cluttered alleys created by the myriad of merchant tents for an hour before finding a venue selling food with enough space inside to accommodate us. Vettias ordered a plate of dates, fruit, nuts, and a little goat meat while asking Mara to go across the alleyway to procure a cheap jug of wine. Vettias looked at me with a smirk as she departed, with eyes telling me he knew I had several questions of him.

"So, what's on your mind?" Vettias asked- letting me know now was a good time to ask.

"How did you know about Mara? About Neoptolemus' involvement in her story?"

"I didn't."

"Was it really The Fates?"

"Not necessarily," Vettias replied with a grin, enjoying the confused machinations his coyness was creating within me. "This business is about gathering as much information on a target as you can before taking a calculated leap. The more information you have, the less of a leap you have to make. In Mara's case, I got a little lucky. Because I uncovered useful information on her beforehand, I only needed a little help. Some may credit The Fates; I say it is preparedness meeting opportunity."

"But did you know her prior to our first meeting?" I asked, still not totally understanding how Vettias had orchestrated the situation.

"I gave my whore a little extra money at the Fair Peach back in Tarsus to identify anyone she knew of from Scythia working as a prostitute in the neighbourhood. She gave a couple of names and I asked her to tell me their approximate ages to find one young enough to coincide with Neoptolemus' tenure as Satrap since Armenia is the nearest Satrapy to Scythian lands in relation to Tarsus. I also knew Neoptolemus had made many forays into Scythian territories yielding a flood of Scythian slaves into Greek-controlled Asia Minor markets. Three names were provided and I chose the one working in closest proximity to the Fair Peach. My whore gave me a general description of Mara and I decided to speak with her while sitting with you at our table in her establishment. Her passion convinced me she was once free but I still did not know the origin of her circumstances. At that point I had collected all the information I could on my target and had to take a moderate risk from then on. Without knowing all I did prior to our initial meeting, I would be taking a significant risk in making such an offer. Had Mara told me a different story, having nothing to do with Neoptolemus, I would have improvised my proposal and hopefully still have achieved the same result, even if the underpinnings were not as strong. If during our initial discussion I did not think her the right fit, we would have moved on to the next name and location provided to me by my female companion."

Vettias again proved his superior intellect and ability to think several steps farther than most.

"And what of Orontes? Who is he?"

"Orontes is a traitor to Alexander and the King's Hand."

"If he is a traitor, how does he know of the Hand's existence? Was he once a member?"

"Yes."

"And he took the oath in Alexander's tent in India with the rest of you?"

"Yes. He was one of our best operatives; very loyal to Alexander and our cause. His devotion became almost too intense, however, and he developed an unhealthy obsession with our King. He began taking Alexander's decisions personally. His behaviour became erratic and on two occasions he lashed out at the King. It was decided that he would be included in the contingent of the army that marched back to Babylon from India through the Gedrosia Desert. Hundreds of men died in that desert. Men who had defeated every army the world could throw at them lay dead in that hellish land. Many of the veterans that made it out of the desert returned different men, having endured unbelievable physical tortures and hardship. Once the army reconstituted back in Babylon, Orontes' condition deteriorated further and it was decided to eliminate him since he knew too much about our existence. For all the faculties he had lost, he retained his operational competence, however, and disappeared into the vast Babylon metropolis before his elimination could be carried out. That was all that was known of him until Ox's claim today. If he is allied with Ptolemy, a powerful ruler with vast resources and ambition in contradiction to ours, he must be considered a powerful enemy indeed."

"Does that answer all of your concerns?" Vettias asked condescendingly.

"The Queen? Did you mean Alexander's widow Rhoxanne?" I asked.

"I speak of the young wife of King Philip III, Adea. She controls the imbecile and had the Argead lust for power instilled in her from childhood. The Argead blood runs deep within her veins as she and Alexander are cousins. Her own father, nephew of Alexander's father, was King for a short time. That is as far as her cause coincides with ours, however, since she has endured terrible crimes against her family by the very people we fight for. She is beloved by the army and has shown willingness to increase her power in defiance of Antipater. It will be difficult, but if she could be turned to our cause she would make a powerful ally."

"How has she been injured by those we fight for?"

"Her father, Amyntas IV, was the son of the Macedonian King Perdiccas III. Alexander's father, Philip II, was the brother of Perdiccas III and uncle to Amyntas IV. Upon Perdiccas III's death on campaign fighting the northern barbarians of Illyria, the infant Amyntas IV was proclaimed titular king and Philip II established as his Regent. Philip II immediately usurped the throne but saw no threat in the child and allowed him to live. Amyntas IV grew to hold a place of great favour with Philip II who eventually betrothed him his daughter Cynane, half-sister of Alexander and eventual mother to the young Queen Adea. Cynane was the result of Philip II's first marriage to the Illyrian princess Audata, whom he married to seal an alliance with the northern barbarian tribes. Once Alexander succeeded his father to the throne, he immediately had Amyntas IV killed to eliminate any male with a legitimate Argead claim to the throne. Adea's mother, Cynane, was permitted to live and raised her daughter in the Illyrian warrior tradition of Princess Audata. This included riding, hunting, and soldiery skills. Adea's mother was a formidable woman respected throughout the Macedonian Empire, and made her move to have her daughter betrothed to the fool after he was made king following Alexander's death. Lord Regent Perdiccas was threatened by such a bold display and ordered his brother, Alcetas, commander of Eumenes' phalanx, to murder Cynane- which he carried out in Asia Minor. Such an act outraged the Royal Army and nearly caused a mutiny. Lord Regent Perdiccas was forced to allow the marriage to continue, thus establishing Adea as Queen. Her official royal name is now Eurydice II"

"Is it possible that a girl who has suffered so greatly by men we fight in the name of could ever agree to ally with us?"

"Adea is a delicate situation. Remember, we fight for General Eumenes, a righteous man who has committed no trespass against the Queen. Both Alexander and Lord Regent Perdiccas are dead and she will need to forget past transgressions and look to who can best help her achieve her goals in the present and future. Nothing is black and white since Alexander's death and despite the past injustices perpetrated against her, we may have arrived at a point where our paths can be joined. A cousin of Alexander with blood of the northern barbarian tribes would make for a formidable foe."

Vettias' voice tapered off with this last statement as Mara returned with the jug of wine.

The three of us ate quietly for an extended period with Mara finally showing signs of an appetite. "The man we met with is going to get you set up in the palace harem within the grounds of the main complex," Vettias stated with a warm tone. "I will need you to elicit as much information from your clients as possible regarding what is being discussed at the summit. You will also listen to what is being said by the others girls in the harem. I want you to identify individuals who appear to have the best access to this kind of information and determine where they are housed, where they eat, what schedules they keep, and who they associate with. The summit will not last too long and after its completion I will do all I can to bring you back to the encampment of General Eumenes where your prostitution days will be over. Do you understand?"

"Um-hmm," Mara answered with a mouthful of dates.

"I will find a way to communicate with you through the harem. You've proven an intelligent and capable ally in the short time we've spent together and I'm confident you can do this."

We lingered at the food tent for over an hour before we departed and took a purposely long and indirect route back to the headquarters bivouac. We found the same guards at its entrance who allowed us to pass after Vettias gave one of them a nod. The three of us entered the same small tent as before and waited about fifteen minutes for Ox to arrive. He did so looking heavily fatigued and in a flustered state.

"I secured you two separate apartments within the staff quarters so you will have access inside the complex," Ox proclaimed in a huff. "They are secluded and will serve your purpose well. I also have a safe house that can be used in case of emergency. I shouldn't have difficulty getting the girl into the palace harem- apparently they are in need of bodies since they have turned it into a brothel for elite personnel attending the summit. Let me have a look at her."

Vettias nodded to Mara and she took off her head covering. I watched Ox's eyes widen as he smiled and looked to Vettias. "Where'd you find her? She'll do. You'll come with me after this meeting. I informed them that I'll be renting you out. Should be no problem getting you back out once we depart."

Mara looked at Vettias who instructed her to put her new clothes on as we all departed the tent to allow her privacy.

"And our Queen?" Vettias asked. "What of her?"

"Arrangements are being made as we speak. I will hopefully have more for you tonight."

"And the identity of Orontes' agents?"

"Davos will arrive at your quarters four hours past sundown tonight," Ox instructed while nodding to the soldier whose sleep had been interrupted by our presence four hours earlier. "You and the boy be there. We'll be ready to move on one of them then. Davos doesn't know about The Hand but can be trusted. He'll take the two of you to your quarters." Davos was two inches shorter than me but had a more mature and imposing face. I estimated he was about three years older, and, as I would later find out, held a generation of more experience than me.

Mara emerged minutes later from the tent looking truly beautiful. Vettias gave her a hug and whispered words of encouragement. I watched as Ox led Mara out of the tent to her new reality within the palace. She kept a stoic façade but her eyes belied the uncertainty and nervousness just beneath the surface. I quietly hoped Vettias intended to keep his promise to her.

Chapter 26

Davos led Vettias and I through the complex's main gates and into the Triparadeisus staff village. The small streets were awash with activity as servants, cooks, musicians, groundskeepers, actors, dancers, stable hands, smiths, and every other profession required to support the Triparadeisus and its royal patrons moved about with determined purpose. Davos first brought us to Vettias' apartment, where he instructed me to get some sleep before meeting him at his quarters with a predetermined knock. Davos next led me to my nearby apartment and I quickly collapsed on a thin blanket strewn about the floor to sleep for a short while.

Father was sitting by the small fire in my room during my nap, enjoying a jug of wine. "I wager you didn't see yourself here back when you were playing soldier with Nearchus," he stated with a smile. I stood up and sat next time him by the fire.

"If Argos and Leandros could see me now," I replied. "I do fear I'm in over my head, however."

"Vettias will take care of you. He knows what limitations your inexperience are capable of. He'll push you but won't allow you to get into too much trouble. There's a lot to learn from a man like that. But that isn't what has been consuming much of your thoughts, is it? It's the girl. Don't hide these feelings if the opportunity presents itself to make them known." There was no use in arguing with a spectre about the true nature of my feelings. Father was right, I had grown attached to Mara and dreaded the throught of further harm coming to her.

"Channel these feelings you have to see your mission completed. She may appear to not need your help but she is vulnerable in her new station with the two of you. Continue to keep her best interests at heart and you will be rewarded."

As my father spoke these last words I awoke, and made my way to Vettias' quarters. I knocked on Vettias' apartment door later that evening after making the short walk to his quarters. Despite the late hour, staff members were still bustling about and loud singing and shrieks of laughter could be heard from the main palace off in the distance. I wondered how Mara was faring within the gilded walls by the intoxicated revellers. Vettias opened the door promptly and pulled me inside. He poured a cup of wine for me and we sat in his sparsely furnished room lit by one flickering candle and a small fireplace waiting for Davos to arrive.

"Did you get some sleep?"

"Yes."

"Good. Tonight may be long depending on the resolve of our captive."

Vettias detected the uneasiness on my face as my mind conjured up all manner of atrocities Vettias' vague statement could entail.

"Don't worry, you'll do fine. Ideally we would take our time, develop some unsuspecting person with proximity to those we wish to uncover and methodically discover identities within Orontes' network. From there we could set several traps for them or use them to uncover additional individuals to eventually thwart the network. Sometimes events demand quicker action, however, and necessity compels us to utilize more blunt approaches."

"Torture?" I asked with a little hesitance.

"Coercion," Vettias retorted. "The less pain we need to inflict the better."

"Can someone's answers be trusted under such duress?"

"You've been listening to too many philosophers. There are those who object on moral grounds and there are those who object because the information cannot be trusted. To answer both concerns I will ask you a set of questions, Andrikos. If Orontes' operatives captured your mother and sister in an attempt to get to you, and the individual we interrogate tonight has information pertaining to their whereabouts, how would you react if he refused to answer your questions?"

"I would kill him," I answered without hesitation.

"A lot of good he'll do you with his throat slit," Vettias responded.

"Then I would stop at nothing to ensure he did tell me what he knew."

"An understandable position to hold. I've no doubt that most would react in the same way. Now, what if Orontes' operatives capture you tonight? Would you tell them what they wanted to know about The Hand and our intentions here?"

"I would do all I could to resist doing so for I believe in our charge and would give my life for the good of my mates in the Phalanx serving under General Eumenes."

"A noble answer indeed, but it is not your life they want," Vettias stated with his usual condescending manner. "It is your information they seek and they will stop at nothing to obtain it. That being said, there are some highly motivated individuals who won't surrender in the face of intense pain. I know that I could not stand up to the very procedures I am willing to use to extract vital information but perhaps you have a stronger constitution then I." Vettias was grinning after this statement since he knew he had succeeded in exposing my youthful idealism. I did not give him the satisfaction of changing my mind, however, despite knowing I too would eventually give in to torture.

"Lastly, what if Orontes' operatives captured you, your mother and your sister? Their interest still lay in your information but instead of applying pain to you they had you watch as they perpetrated it on your family in front of you? Would you tell them what they wanted to know to make them stop raping and beating your mother and sister before your very eyes? You don't have to answer, but be aware, the only way to avoid that horrid fate in this business is to constantly be on guard, constantly be aware of your surroundings, and have a plan to kill everyone you meet. So in your answers, or non-answers as it were, to these three questions you have admitted that you yourself would resort to physical coercion if the cause was serious enough and that physical harm brought upon you or your family would elicit information you seek to keep secret."

Vettias had once again proved a valuable lesson. My silence assured him of my intellectual surrender and provoked him to expand on his point.

"Blindly taking a side you deem to be moral without seriously thinking about all aspects of the issue is not only moronic, it's dangerous."

With this last mental jab we heard a slight rap against the door and Davos entered. "He's away from his room now, he shouldn't be gone long. Taking him as he attempts to re-enter his room will be the best option. There is a dark alley adjacent to his front door. I suggest we use it to hide, drag him into it, knock him unconscious, gag him, roll him up in this blanket, and carry him back here since this apartment is well situated to dampen noise due to its seclusion."

Vettias nodded his head and looked slightly impressed with Davos' command of the situation and sound planning.

"Ox has taught you well," he conferred while looking at me with a smirk. "Lead the way," he ordered as the three of us departed into the dark alleys of Triparadeisus on our way to visit violence on our unsuspecting victim. As we neared, Davos slowed our pace and pointed to the dark alley adjacent to our target's front door. Vettias and I entered the alley as Davos checked if the room was still empty. He pointed out the door to us before giving a thumbs up that the dwelling was vacant. Davos slinked back into the alley and the three of us waited for our prey to arrive.

After an hour our target appeared at the residence looking over his shoulder three times before unlocking the front latch. Davos produced a small wooden club and motioned for us to stay back as he quietly emerged from our dark corner and crept silently towards our target. Davos neared the man, raised the club above his head when the man suddenly turned around and confronted his attacker. Davos brought the club crashing down on the man's forehead, sending him to the dirt. The blow did not fully incapacitate the man, however, and he clumsily struggled to regain his footing. Davos next clubbed the man's temple which had its intended effect of knocking him temporarily unconscious. Vettias and I rushed into the street with the rug, laid it flat and rolled up the inert body. The three of us hurriedly navigated the lesser travelled alleyways with our portentous cargo on our way to Vettias' quarters.

We arrived and carelessly flopped our captive onto the floor. Vettias and Davos quickly unrolled the rug and set the lifeless body onto the sturdiest chair within the room while stripping off his clothing.

"Tie this rag around his groin in case he shits or pisses himself," Vettias ordered Davos.

Davos then expertly tied his ankles to the two front legs, his wrists to each arm, and secured his thighs and stomach to the seat and back of the chair. The rope was thin, wiry and wound tight. Its strength and utility signalled it was fashioned with the intention of acting as a restraint. Davos' speed and proficiency pointed to prior experience conducting this ominous undertaking.

The captive began writhing and moaning as drool and blood dripped into his lap. Vettias ordered me to check outside our room and lock the door as he started smacking the man's face and throwing water on him encouraging him to come to.

"Come on, come on," cajoled Vettias. "Wake up."

The captive did not yet retain control of his eyes as their focus wandered throughout the room. He let out a loud moan and attempting to move his limbs which were firmly secured to the chair. Vettias threw more water in his face and smacked him as he continued to bring the man back to consciousness.

"Look at me. Look at me." The captive's eyes finally settled on Vettias as his senses began to return. A dart of situational awareness passed through his face as the severity of his predicament set in and his body jerked from side to side in an effort to escape. His face winced as the tightly wound rope dug into his wrists. Realizing he was trapped, the man let out a yell which was immediately muffled as Vettias shoved a gag into his mouth.

"Uh, uh, uh, Shhhhh." Vettias calmly instructed. The captive let out another scream that was successfully subdued by his gag. Vettias struck the man in the face which cautioned against further outbursts. "Do I have your attention? I assume you understand your circumstances." The man nodded his head. "Good. I'm not going to waste my time explaining why you are here. I think we both already know the answer." The man did not attempt to respond and took a deep breath while looking at the floor. I will take that gag out shortly, but first I'd like to show you something. Vettias unrolled a leather purse on a table within sight of the captive, revealing several ominous-looking metallic items whose torturous purpose was apparent. As he did so the captive's eyes widened and he reflexively tried to move his limbs again to escape. His eyes began tearing and his breathing became heavy. I remember how calm and congenial

Vettias' demeanour was at this time, despite his cruel intent. It was clear this was not his first time conducting this activity.

"So, you are going to decide how the rest of your time here will transpire," Vettias stated while brushing his hand over the sinister instruments on display; the captive's eyes following his every move. "If you are cooperative, and I believe you what you tell me, I won't have to use these nasty little tools. If you anger me, I am going to stick the gag back in your mouth and begin my dirty work. Being in the business that you're in, you've no doubt thought to yourself how you would react when faced with this exact situation. You've probably been on this side of the discussion before, haven't you? I've often thought about what I would do on your side of this conversation and I came to the conclusion that I would probably break- so I've taken extra care to not get caught. You clearly should have done the same. If during your inner dialogue you thought to yourself that you would be able to take the pain, I am here to make you a guarantee that you can't. If you think your devotion to your cause so great that you will lie to me long enough for death to mercifully end this ordeal- you won't. Unlike many thugs in this business, I am trained in the arts of pain and healing and I will keep you alive and conscious as long as I need you to be. As we begin our journey together tonight, I will estimate you think very little of me right now. In fact, you are probably seething with hate at this very moment and would gauge out my eyes if I gave you the chance."

"As our evening together progresses, you are going to break and you will respect my authority over you and do as I command. I will make a promise to you right now. By the end of your ordeal, you and I will be very close, like brothers in fact, and you will voluntarily tell me all I need to know. I say these things as an act of kindness because all I have explained will transpire. It is up to you how we get there. Normally I have more time with my victims and the whole affair is a little more civilized. I'd play some mind games so you would divulge what you know. Unfortunately for you, however, time is of the essence and I will have to be more direct. You can forgo all the coming wretchedness by telling me what I want to know now. If you do not, our journey of distress will begin shortly. Are you ready for me to remove your gag?"

Davos stood stoically during Vettias' lecture, staring coldly at the captive. I had a chill run up my arm at Vettias' conclusion and did not think myself capable of resisting Vettias' cold, detached method of inflicting pain. I stood motionless, watching Vettias delicately remove the captive's gag and wondering if it was possible for a man to defy such a daunting and hopeless situation.

"Please, please, I don't know what this is about, I don't know who you think I am," the captive pleaded after his gag was removed.

"I'm not going to waste my time with what you and I already know. There are some things I don't know about you, however, and we'll start with your name," Vettias replied maintaining his calm composure. "What do they call you friend?"

"Shifty," the captive exclaimed, still panting and sweating heavily. Vettias looked to Davos who now stood out of the captive's line of vision and nodded his head in agreement.

"And what sort of name is that?"

"I have a tick which forces me to frequently move my body uncontrollably."

"Good, and what are you doing here Shifty?" Vettias continued.

"I work on the Quartermaster's staff." Vettias again looked to Davos who again nodded.

"Excellent. Were you a member of Ptolemy's army or Lord Regent Perdiccas' army?"

"General Ptolemy." Davos again nodded.

"So far you're doing great," Vettias stated. "You've been forthcoming and truthful. Now, who do you receive orders from to conduct operations against known supporters of Lord Regent Perdiccas?"

"What?"

"Hmmm," Vettias uttered threateningly. "You were doing so well. I'm detecting your inner pride attempting to sway you from telling me the truth. Don't listen to it. No man can withstand the journey that lies ahead if you are not forthcoming with me. It is not dishonourable to spare yourself this agony since I've already guaranteed that you will break eventually. This will be your last chance though. I won't ask you again and I expect you to answer me immediately."

"I, I don't know what you're talking about."

My heart began pounding as Vettias motioned Davos to come from behind the captive and firmly hold his torso to the seat while Vettias put the gag back in his mouth. He walked to the table and selected a flat iron rod and placed it in the fireplace. He then picked up a freshly sharpened knife and approached the captive.

"I'm going to let that heat up for a minute which will give you some precious few moments to decide how you want to arrive at the end of your journey with me this evening." Vettias grazed the blade over the man's face as he spoke. Shifty's breathing became manic as he let out a muffled cry for help.

"It's getting warmer," Vettias taunted as he now was grazing the sharp blade over the captive's fingers. Shifty's eyes raced around the room, desperately searching for some elusive saviour that would not arrive. "Ah, just about ready. Hold him tight now Davos because he's going to squirm. Andrikos, come over here and hold his pinky out on the chair's arm."

Vettias' enunciation of my name snapped me out of my overwhelmed trance and I quickly made my way to the captive and asked Vettias to repeat his instruction. "Hold out his pinky." As I went to grab it, Shifty instantly made a panic-stricken fist to the point where his knuckles were turning white. I looked at Vettias for guidance who responded with an annoyed glare informing me he was aware of the development and did not care. I took a strong hold of the man's wrist with my right hand and pried open his pinky with my left hand. As the doomed appendage emerged the captive began writhing and shouting muffled screams to be heard by no one. I watched with trepidation as Vettias took the knife and sawed the man's finger off at the first knuckle. Blood instantly squirted everywhere and the captive yelled and struggled within his restraints. Vettias calmly produced the red hot tip of the flat iron rod and placed it directly on the fresh wound to cauterize the bleeding-evoking further screaming and writhing from our victim.

"You can let go now," Vettias instructed Davos. "Let him be for a moment." Shifty let out a few more muted screams before his breathing slowed and the initial pain of his wound subsided to a manageable level. "You see, you aren't going to bleed out. I'm not going to let you die. I can do that two more times on that same finger before I start moving somewhere else. And believe me, this is a progression. Later punishment will be more creative and painful if you know what I mean." Vettias looked at the man's genitals as he uttered this last threat.

Shifty then started brutishly convulsing. "He's going to puke. Get that gag out of his mouth." Shifty vomited on himself and the floor which made for a disgusting sight as he sat there whimpering, covered in his own blood and discharge. "It's a messy business isn't it? And we've only just started." Vettias laughed as he gently slapped Shifty on his cheek. "We'll have you talking in no time son. Andrikos, clean up this mess on the floor lest someone walking past thinks there's a dead body in here."

I took a rag and went about the nauseating task of cleaning up Shifty's vomit while listening to him quietly sob and sniffle, pleading his ignorance over and over again. My pity and guilt about Shifty's predicament coupled with the stench of vomit riled my stomach to the point where I had to exit the room and dry heave. Vettias and Davos sat in the opposite corner discussing further lines of questioning at a low decibel while I finished up my revolting labour. Once completed, Davos took his place behind the captive and Vettias resumed his interrogation.

"Alright, you've had long enough to decide whether you're going to be cooperative; so let's pick up where we left off shall we? The gag can go back in your mouth at any time, it's up to you. Now, who do you receive orders from to conduct operations against known supporters of Lord Regent Perdiccas?"

"I, I don't know what you're talking about," Shifty responded weakly while avoiding eye contact with Vettias.

'Hmm, alright. Davos, if you would hold him to the chair again. Andrikos please give me some help." Vettias put the gag back in Shifty's mouth and I reluctantly grabbed his wrist. I winced as I pried his wounded pinky out of his clenched fist and could almost feel the pain I was inflicting as Shifty screamed and fought his restraints. Vettias took his knife and sawed off Shifty's pinky at the next knuckle producing another gush of blood. As an added torture Vettias grabbed his protruding pinky bone and wiggled it a little before he again took the red hot iron and singed the wound close. Shifty lost consciousness from the pain and lost control of his bowels producing a stream of urine running down his leg.

"No, no, no, you're not getting off that easily," Vettias stated with a chuckle as he smacked Shifty across the face several times to wake him. As he came to and realized he had not just been in a nightmare he began sobbing and pulling at his restraints once more in vain. "I can keep going until there's nothing left of you. Why don't you do yourself a favour? You know the name I want, just give it to me."

As the hopelessness of his situation set in, Shifty whispered the name Pirus. Vettias smiled and patted the defeated victim on the shoulder while looking at Davos who nodded in recognition of the name. "Very good. And when are you scheduled to meet Pirus again?"

"Please, I, I can't," Shifty uttered in desperation.

Vettias grabbed a small barbed pin from the table and stuck it directly into Shifty's cauterized wound which induced a shrill scream that Vettias quickly silenced with his hand.

"When are you to meet with him again?" Vettias demanded sternly. "I have a lot more pins. This one will stay in there until you answer," he shouted while twisting the pin violently.

"At sunrise," Shifty exclaimed in frustration, panting form the latest penalty.

"Where?"

"Near the butchery within the Triparadeisus staff quarters."

"See, I told you you were going to talk. I am going to confirm this information and if it doesn't produce your contact you will long for the restraint I have shown you thus far. Do you understand? Now, you are going to tell me everything you know about your contact to include what he looks like and what recognition signals you use."

Shifty provided all information required to make contact with Pirus at sunrise and it was decided I would don Shifty's clothes and work with Davos to capture Pirus, since Vettias believed it was Pirus who could provide us high level details on our adversaries. Vettias refrained from torturing the captive for the rest of the night and even fed him as a reward. We took turns keeping watch over him while awaiting sunrise.

230

Chapter 27

Davos woke me before daybreak so we could scout the meeting location before Pirus arrived. Vettias would stay with Shifty, whose symptoms that inspired his namesake were becoming increasingly apparent. Ox would also stop by to give instructions on our meeting with Queen Adea. Vettias took me aside and informed me this was the most important day we were to have together and I needed to have my shit squared away. Kidnapping, interrogation and a meeting with the Queen- it was shaping up to be a busy day. I had concerns whether we would be able to achieve all of our goals at Triparadeisus, especially if Vettias was relying heavily on me.

Davos and I arrived at the intersection of two dark streets where the meeting was to take place in approximately ninety minutes. Davos immediately went to work walking each of the alleys and identifying places to ambush and drag the body. Once he decided where to lay in wait I stood against the predetermined wall wearing Shifty's tunic and facing east as our captive had instructed. A light rain began to fall, which allowed me to plausibly don a shoal over my head- prohibiting Pirus from discerning my facial features. Davos remained crouched down in an alley that gave him a good line of sight to my location, like a predator awaiting prey. I stood in that spot for about an hour, frequently shifting my body's weight from one leg to the next and fidgeting with my hands impatiently. I refrained from looking in Davos' direction but frequently strained to catch a glimpse of him through my periphery. Despite my knowledge of his presence I still could not see him in the shadows, which convinced me our victim would not notice him either. A lone drunkard walked down the small street taking little notice of me. Given Shifty's description, the man was clearly not our target. I abstained from making eye contact lest he take some inebriated interest in me while I clutched the handle of my concealed blade. My stillness emboldened several rats to run down the street, two of which ran over my feet causing me to startle.

I caught myself nodding off when I looked up and saw a shadowy figure cautiously making his way towards my direction. I quickly turned my head to bar him from seeing my face and made several gestures to my nose which was the preplanned signal to Davos that our prey was coming. I could hear Pirus clearing his throat as he neared, and I could feel his gaze against my back. I took a couple of steps in the opposite direction to ensure he would pass Davos' alley. As I did so he called out to Shifty in a hushed tone to which I did not reply and kept walking. He called out Shifty's name louder, but did not finish the last syllable because Davos had struck him in the back of the head with his short wooden club. I turned around to see the man fall to his hands and knees, with Davos standing over him ready to deliver another blow. Pirus looked up at me not comprehending what had happened and I kicked his forehead with my heel causing his eyes to roll back into his head. As he fell to the ground Davos brought a powerful strike down on his temple to ensure his unconsciousness. Davos grabbed Pirus by the hair and inspected his facial expression. Satisfied with his level of coma, Davos ordered me to help him drag the body into the alley. The two of us quickly wrapped the body into the rug, still stained with Shifty's blood, and hurriedly carried it over our shoulders back to Vettias' lair.

The sun was beginning to rise but no one stirred on the quiet streets. We made it back to Vettias' quarters without seeing another individual and barged through the door, violently throwing the rug onto the floor. Shifty made a muffled sound after recognizing our ominous payload and realizing he had directly contributed to his master's current situation. Vettias and Davos rapidly dragged the limp body to another chair on the other side of the room which Vettias had prepared and tied his limbs to it in the same manner as our first captive. Once Pirus was stripped naked and secured, his head hung down onto his chest and blood dripped on the small piece of fabric covering his lap.

Vettias grabbed a bowl of brackish water and threw it in Pirus' face. The captive did not react, which prompted Vettias to smack his face several times while shouting at him to wake. Pirus began stirring and regained hold of his neck while looking around the room, trying to comprehend his new surroundings. He performed the familiar routine of attempting to free himself from his restraints and yelling out. Vettias quickly broke his nose which instructed our new victim raising his voice was not an option.

"I wouldn't do that again," Vettias sternly warned.

"Who are you? What is this? Do you know what you've just done?" Pirus hissed at a muted decibel.

"I don't think I have to tell you that I will be the one asking questions during our cordial discussion." Vettias winked at Pirus with a smile that bore the true contentment I believed he felt while conducting these insidious endeavours. "Andrikos, bring over my little table please." I promptly presented my master with the table bearing his instruments of pain. As I did so our captive's eyes followed me and caught their first glimpse of Shifty's battered façade sitting on the opposite side of the room covered in bruises, blood, vomit, sweat, and urine. His expression became enraged and worried all at once.

"He look familiar?" Vettias asked, pointing at Shifty with a grin. Pirus remained silent as the hopelessness of his situation began to set in. "You don't have to answer that- needless to say I already know quite a bit about you. More than even this pathetic piece of meat knows, to be sure. I will assume you know how this works, so I will spare you my macabre introduction," Vettias taunted as he passed his fingers over his tools of agony in view of Pirus. The look of terror began poking through Pirus' stoicism despite his best efforts. "Your friend here didn't quite understand the situation at first so I had to provide him a minor lesson," Vettias continued holding up Shifty's hand which was missing its pinky. "And I do mean minor. What I am going to do to you if you don't talk may be justifiably called severe. He came around soon enough, and thus, now we have you. Unfortunately, time is not on our side so I am going to have to move fast, despite my desire to verbally spar with someone in your position...Basically, if you don't cooperate in the next couple minutes, I'm going to begin flaying you. I think you're going to talk- what do you think? If I have to put this gag in your mouth, believe me, you are going to beg for a chance to tell me everything you know. Now, shall we begin?"

Pirus sat motionless while his eyes frantically searched for the same absent saviour held within his new surroundings that eluded Shifty as well. "I want to know who you take orders from. I want to know who he takes orders from. I want to know who you give orders to. I want every name in your network." Vettias dropped the sadistically jovial disposition he took with Shifty and became severely hostile with our new captive. Pirus was taking several deep breathes while looking at the floor. "This is the only way you're walking out of this room alive. Consider yourself lucky, you may survive this ordeal. If a colleague of yours were sitting where you are now, they would eventually talk and you would be the one that was assassinated, probably in your sleep. I want that information and I want it now."

Pirus continued avoiding eye contact and remained silent. "Davos, hold him down." Davos came from his position behind the captive and clenched his arms around Pirus' torso, holding it firmly to the seat. "Andrikos, come over here. Pin his elbow down to the arm of the chair." I positioned myself to the side of the captive and locked my forearm into the crook of his arm nervously waiting for whatever horror Vettias was about to inflict. I watched as he took a small, sharp knife from the table and made an incision lengthwise along Pirus' arm starting from his wrist and moving in the direction of his elbow about four inches long. The wound was fairly minor and did not elicit much reaction from the captive. Vettias then made two horizontal incisions perpendicular to the first cut along his wrist and in the middle of his forearm, creating an 'I' pattern. He looked up at Pirus when his meticulous work was done and stated sinisterly "this is your last chance."

Pirus remained silent and Vettias placed three of his fingers along the vertical incision, grabbed hold of Pirus' flesh and peeled his skin back revealing the grotesque inner layers of Pirus' muscle tissue and bone. Pirus let out a violent muffled scream and writhed within his seat. The sight and sound of this action opened a pit in my stomach. Vettias then grabbed Pirus by the face and informed him he was going to begin peeling off the other side of the wound unless he began talking. Pirus screamed and convulsed but his eyes defiantly gave Vettias his answer. Vettias then brutally pealed the skin back from other side of the incision which caused Pirus to let out another manic scream before he lost consciousness.

"Wake him up!" Vettias ordered as he calmly walked towards the small fireplace to retrieve the flat iron rod. "I don't want him to miss this." Davos released his grip around Pirus' torso and began throwing water in his face and smacking him. The captive awoke to the sight of Vettias staring cruelly at him holding the glowing hot rod. "We don't want you to bleed out now do we?" Vettias asked viciously as he placed the instrument on Pirus' exposed muscle tissue. The act produced a horrid smell and Pirus again let out a muffled scream of agony before vomiting. "Get the gag out, let him puke," Vettias barked at me as Pirus vomited over his naked body. The smell of vomit and burnt skin caused me to unexpectedly vomit on the floor next to Pirus which prompted a severe rebuke from Vettias. "Now clean up both messes!" he yelled as I scrambled to regain my composure. He and Davos retired to the far end of the room to discuss further lines of questioning while I conducted the disgusting task of cleaning up vomit next to a bloody, whimpering, beaten man awaiting a cruel death.

Shifty no longer took an interest in his surroundings. He sat motionless, staring at the floor. Vettias examined his injured finger to ensure no infection was taking hold. "Don't think we've forgotten about you boy," Vettias taunted as he retired to the corner to whisper with Davos. When Vettias noticed I had finished my gruesome chore he resumed his position in front of the captive and Davos took his place behind him ready to clutch his torso to the chair again if necessary.

"Alright, you've had some time to think about your options so let us resume shall we?" Pirus did not take notice to Vettias' return and continued staring at the vomit stained ground. Vettias forcefully grabbed Pirus' face and looked him in the eye. "You can try and resist talking to me, but you are going to respect me while you're doing it. When I speak you will look me in the eye or else I will gauge them out. I'm avoiding doing anything permanent for now. Do not do anything that will lesson my restraint. Now, you know the information I seek, let's start with the man who gives you orders. What is his name?" Pirus remained silent but his eyes, still red and glassy, stared defiantly at his torturer. "Davos, Andrikos, hold this piece of meat down!"

Davos and I braced the captive in the same manner while Vettias flayed another four inch swath of skin off the man's forearm, inducing more muted screams of anguish and violent convulsions. Pirus again vomited after Vettias gleefully cauterized the wound. "Shouldn't have ate a big breakfast this morning, huh?" Vettias mocked while gently slapping him on the face. "Andrikos my gentle colleague, please clean this up." Vettias' thinly veiled insult made me a little nervous that he was losing confidence in my nerve. I was also having serious doubts about my willingness to participate in such activities going forward. When my sickening task was complete Vettias angrily repeated the previous question and received no answer. This time, however, even I could tell Pirus' eyes had lost their fiery determination. Vettias stuck a barbed pin into his now eight inch wound and explained it would stay there for the duration of questioning and more would be added. Pirus let out a muffled shriek as it punctured his muscle tissue. As Davos and I braced him for another flaying, Pirus let out one last pain-filled gasp before begging Vettias to cease.

"And is there something you want to tell me friend?" Vettias asked with a smile, knowing he had broken his victim.

Pirus hesitated, causing Vettias to twist the barbed pin, inducing an audible wince. "Nikandros! Nikandros is his name." Vettias looked up at Davos who shook his head indicating this name was unfamiliar to him. "But that isn't the name everyone knows him by, is it?"

"No one knows him, period," Pirus replied in a defeated tone as if he were watching an apparition of himself divulge the prized details and there was nothing he could do to stop it. "You don't find him, he finds you. He lives in the shadows."

"Unlike his boss, who's also here isn't he? He was one of Ptolemy's advisors in his battle staff entourage. But Ptolemy isn't here, however. Nikandros' boss, *the boss*, arrived with Seleucus, posing as one of his staff advisors, didn't he? But the boss won't be leaving with Seleucus. Not if he willingly left the safe confines of Egypt. He'll be leaving with another benefactor. And so will his network. Maybe even you were planning on accompanying him."

Pirus looked up in a startle towards Shifty. His expression conveyed both disbelief that the lowly prisoner would have known this information and confusion as to how Vettias came to know it. I was impressed at the small calculated leap Vettias had made. While Vettias knew Orontes better then Pirus himself, he was unaware of this new Nikandros character. It appeared Vettias had enough information to deduce Nikandros was the second in command and it only made sense Orontes had travelled with Seleucus in some advisory position. Vettias also estimated Seleucus was not powerful enough to best carry out Orontes' grand schemes and he was here in Triparadeisus on behalf of a new, more powerful benefactor. Antipater or Antigonus were the likely candidates. Having as much information as he did already required little reasoning to come to this conclusion yet it had its intended effect on the prisoner.

"Hmm, I'm right aren't I? Don't worry about how we know this. Let's just focus on this Nikandros."

"He is second in command," Pirus confirmed. "He takes all the risks, delivers the orders, and receives the information. You will not know him. He serves in some menial administrative capacity to escape the attention of anyone interested in such matters. He has recently returned from operating inside the camp of General Eumenes." Vettias was not prepared for this last bit of information.

"Describe him. Now! May the Gods help you if you cannot provide me a means to find this man." Vettias' expression denoted he was racking his thoughts for countless nameless faces he may have suspected of nefariousness over the past few months within Eumenes' camp.

"He has dark features, of average build, average height, a number of spots on his skin. He keeps a short beard, frequently travels with a dark cloak. He is a man of few words. His face has a number of pock marks but he is a good looking man. He has one large black mark on the left side of his face. He is not a true believer like Orontes, but Orontes pays him well for his exceptional skills in criminality and brutality. His one vulnerability is women. He will regularly bed prostitutes but is careful not to establish patterns. Normally when in a city for an extended time, like here in Triparadeisus, he will discreetly keep one whore." I paid little attention to Pirus' description at first but as he gave more details a face shot in front of my mind's eye out of the wilderness of my subconscious. It was the quiet man first pointed out to us by Mara on the night of our first encounter with her. I hesitantly pulled Vettias' arm to grab his attention and led him out of earshot of our prisoner. At first Vettias seemed agitated that I would interrupt a captive just as he was cooperating, but calmed down when I informed him that we may know this man.

"This could be the quiet one from the night we met Mara," I whispered. "Think about it. His description fits what Pirus is telling us."

"A lot of people would fit that vague description," Vettias countered skeptically.

"Yes, but Pirus said he was travelling from our camp and he is now here in Triparadeisus. That would place him roughly in the same region of Cappadocia at the same time as us. We met Mara in Tarsus, where one of the royal treasuries resides. Wouldn't he stop there to receive funds, especially since his faction is now on the side of the Kings? Mara said she slept with him. Perhaps she can confirm or deny my suspicion."

Vettias began considering my theory and took a mental account of all the angles that would be involved if what I said were true. "Alright, we will look into this possibility. Say nothing of it now, lest we alert Pirus to this knowledge." Vettias returned to our captive as if what I had told him had no bearing on his line of questioning.

"So you meet with your operatives and deliver what is learned to this Nikandros? And then he supplies this information to the head of your network."

"Yes," Pirus replied.

"I want you to say his name. The leader. Say his name."

There was a pause. As Vettias reached to twist the barbed pin, Pirus let out with a sigh "Orontes."

"Good. And what is Orontes doing here?"

"As you said yourself, he aligned with Ptolemy in Egypt after Alexander's death and accompanied Seleucus here to Triparadeisus after Ptolemy's triumph over Lord Regent Perdiccas. Orontes orchestrated the entire coup."

238

"Why? Why not remain in Egypt with his powerful benefactor?"

"Because Ptolemy's ultimate goals were not his goals. Ptolemy seeks his own dynasty centred in Egypt built upon his legitimate succession to Alexander, the rightful founder of the empire. Orontes has found a new master to serve who shares his hatred of the Argeads and has the resources to ensure their line never inherits the Macedonian Empire."

"Who is this villain?" Vettias shouted. The thought of two individuals whose purpose lay in direct contrast to his sworn oath outraged him. Pirus hesitated answering , causing Vettias to strike his face so hard a bloody tooth was ejected from his mouth. "Who is this swine?! Antipater? Antigonus?" Vettias struck him again causing another tooth to be cast out

Vettias then stabbed Pirus' wounds with several more barbed pins and twisted them to bring forth a gruesome ooze of fluid. Pirus screamed in agony and finally yelled out "The son of Antipater! Cassander! He remains in Macedon while his father travels to Triparadeisus. Cassander has made arrangements for Orontes to serve as an advisor to Antipater's military council but in reality he will be serving Cassander. He will also fund the movement of Orontes' chosen Captains so he can establish his network in Macedon. From there he seeks to plant operatives in every rival's court. He already left several operatives in Egypt. When Cassander succeeds his father, Orontes will serve by his side and together they will attempt to usurp the entire empire through bribery, usurpation, murder, and conquest; while eliminating all remnants of the Argead line along the way. It will begin with the two Kings, who will accompany Lord Regent Antipater back to Pella upon the conclusion of this summit. This will be followed by Alexander's mother, Olympias, who currently resides in her native Epirus since being banished from the royal court by Antipater."

"Why Cassander? Tell me about him."

"He was with Alexander at the beginning, studying and training with him and the rest of the boys from noble Macedonian houses. The two never liked each other, however, and Antipater was unable to convince the King to take his son with him on the great Persian conquest. Alexander's heroic deeds bred greater animosity within

Cassander who remained with his father in Pella, watching his nemesis' name glorified throughout the world. Antipater was finally able to arrange for Cassander to join Alexander in Babylon upon the completion of the eastern campaign. It is whispered Alexander intended to replace Antipater with Craterus and Cassander was sent to establish an ally of Antipater in Alexander's court. Cassander was by this time no more than a distant unpleasant memory to Alexander, yet Cassander had little choice but to hear Alexander's name spoken daily. His father is now an old man and Cassander fully intends to remove all Argead threats to his rule of Macedon. Orontes came to hear of Cassander's contempt of Alexander and searched him out upon returning to Babylon after the eastern campaign. The two united their twisted motivations into a joined purpose and have been waiting for Cassander's succession to further their goals. It is even alleged they were behind Alexander's death in Babylon."

"And you. Why are you a part of this sinister plot?"

"I was a lowly staff officer with General Ptolemy when Nikandros first approached me. I do not hold the hatred of the Argead line as Orontes and Cassander do, but Alexander is dead and we all must choose our sides wisely. What does it matter to me if Alexander IV or that imbecile assumes the throne? Men like Ptolemy, Antipater, and Antigonus are the real seats of power now and I'm not going to hitch my fortunes to an infant and an idiot. If I serve the leaders of my faction well, I will be rewarded accordingly. Nikandros spoke of your faction. He said you were all blind fanatics, doing the will of a dead man, being led by his secretary. I chose my side and thus worked hard to ensure its success. Killing me now won't change the logic of my chosen path, nor those of my colleagues."

I could see Vettias was infuriated by all he had been told but made sure not to take out his anger on the captive lest he become hesitant in divulging more about our adversaries. "You've done well, Pirus, and you withstood my initial questioning honourably. We'll get to your colleagues a little later. Right now I am going to tend to your wounds under the assumption that your initial stubbornness has ebbed and we will talk as comrades. If I determine you are attempting to be less than completely truthful with me, however, the gag will be placed back in your mouth and I will graduate to crueler methods of pain. Am I making the correct choice in doing this?"

Pirus gave a weak nod in the affirmative. "Good. Andrikos, give him some strong wine while I dress his wound."

Chapter 28

The next two hours were spent dressing Pirus' extensive wounds and plying him with strong wine. Pirus was in too much pain to eat the food offered, but continued to be cooperative by giving a detailed list of known operatives within Orontes' network. Davos scribbled down each name, shaking his head when he did not recognize the individual which prompted Vettias to ask more identifying information. After divulging about eight names Vettias ceased his interrogation and re-bandaged Shifty's wound while allowing him to continue to eat and drink. The morning lull caused me to begin daydreaming about my ability to succeed in this underworld of dark arts when a rap at the door startled me back into the situation at hand.

I turned quickly to see Ox barge unceremoniously into the room. His stout physique made the wooden planks of the floor eek with each brazen step. He took a quick inventory of our morose guests and called Vettias into the opposite corner of the room. His lack of reaction led me to believe this was not the first torture den he'd walked into. After whispering a few words Vettias halted him and called me to join the two of them outside in small alley jutting away from our apartment building. Davos remained to keep watch over our prisoners.

"Start from the beginning, I want Andrikos to hear this."

"Everything is set for you to meet with the Queen later this evening," Ox stated proudly. "She is residing in the main palace within the grounds- the same palace where our young whore is currently working. I can get you into the palatial harem as a personal friend to someone from the Battle Staff but it's going to cost you. From there Mara will guide you to the central garden where you will be met by one of the Queen's entourage. You will know her by the white Jasmine in her hair. You will approach her and ask directions to the palatial bath house. She will guide you there and utilize a little known corridor that links to the Queen's palatial suites. Now, you will need to look the part if you are to enter and move about the palace unmolested."

"We have proper garments," Vettias assured.

"And this one?" Ox asked, looking at me. "He looks like he is straight from the stables."

"The lad's been conducting some pretty dirty work the past twelve hours, we'll clean him up."

"You could have Davos," Ox offered, not convinced of my abilities.

"We're going to need Davos' special talents to search out and eliminate Pirus' network. Besides, I have faith in the boy."

"Suit yourself," Ox relented. "Be ready to go at the small tent near my headquarters two hours before dusk. That will give you enough time to clean yourselves up and look presentable. There's a bathhouse that has been set up near our encampment."

"I'm going to need two of your men to watch our guests," Vettias added. "Give Davos what he needs to strike the network while we are away."

"Are we ready for such a bold action?" Ox asked doubtfully. "Such an attack will no doubt rile the survivors, forcing us to go to ground."

"We need to have Orontes' network off balance when the Queen makes her move."

"Just know you will be hunted after tonight. I'll see you in a few hours. Two of my men will be here soon. After tonight you'll need to move your little dungeon over to the kid's apartment to be safe. Go get cleaned up, you two smell like vomit and gore." Ox departed without being persuaded in the likelihood of our chances of success, yet remained earnest in his willingness to do all he could on our behalf.

Vettias and I returned to the apartment where Vettias instructed Davos to spend the rest of the day locating the individuals Pirus identified and learning where they slept, where they ate, and where they screwed. "Don't begin the cleansing until three hours after dusk. Make sure Ox provides you competent men to carry this plan out. When it's over, release your comrades and make your way towards the kid's apartment. We'll meet you there after we finish our audience with the Queen. Make sure your help knows to take extra precautions after tonight."

"You know this is going to set off a war in the shadows of this place," Davos replied indifferently.

"Nothing you can't handle," Vettias answered with a smile. "You should see the overt war I'm going to start tomorrow."

Davos disappeared into the now sunlit streets, busy with staff running around preparing all manner of tasks for the day's palatial functions. Vettias and I sat in the apartment waiting two hours for Ox's prison guards to arrive. Shifty, still tied to his chair, had dozed off with his head lurched over resting on one side of his chest. Pirus, who by now was more than a little drunk, sat calmly in the opposite corner, letting out a quiet whimper of pain every few minutes. A loud rap at the door alerted us to the guards' presence.

"Hey," Vettias called over to Pirus. "No questions for you today, we're going to let you recover a bit. I'm going to leave you two with these guards for a while. I'm going to instruct them to go easy on you, redress your wounds periodically, and make sure you are eating and drinking. I don't have to do this but I am keeping my word regarding your cooperation. Don't mistake my newfound kindness as weakness, understand? When I return I may have some more questions that I expect answered immediately. Alright?"

"Yes, th-thank you," Pirus responded weakly as Vettias and I exited the apartment and made our way to the makeshift bathhouse.

"Ox is right, however; you smell of piss and vomit," Vettias chided. "Let's get cleaned up and changed. Mara will probably want to see a familiar face. Because my face is too well known by many of the people inhabiting the main palace for this summit, I will be travelling in the guise of a local slave tending to my master within the grounds. You will be playing my master- the son of a wealthy merchant here to trade with the world's most powerful men. You are taking me to the palace harem because you like to watch and are willing to give large amounts of coin for your fetish to be enacted. You will ask for Mara because her name has been ringing the grounds of Triparadeisus this morning."

Vettias pushed a heavy purse into my hand as we arrived at the makeshift bathhouse.

"Do you think you can pull this off?"

"You've taught me all you could in the short amount of time we've had together, if I can't rise to the occasion here, I'll never be able to. Better to find out now. Besides, this purse will alleviate anyone's hesitance to believe me."

"Very well, go get cleaned up in there and change- I want you looking the part. I too will be looking the part and will don the local attire, allowing me to have a reason to cover much of my face. I'm also going to forgo bathing so I'll be waiting for you just inside the bathhouse in the character of your loyal servant. My name will be Roda- I heard it uttered by a local slave boy yesterday afternoon and sounds as good as any. You will retain the name of Raman to make it easy for you. When you emerge from your cleansing, we will both have assumed our new personas, understood?"

"Yes Roda, now sit in that corner and wait until I emerge," I ordered sarcastically. Vettias deferentially obliged.

My enjoyable experience lasted about ninety minutes, which gave us two hours before the appointed time to meet at Ox's tent. Vettias and I took a leisurely dinner in a tucked away food stand under a small tent to keep Vettias' face out of public view from unseen agents of Orontes. Vettias passed the time reiterating our plan and going over several 'do's and don'ts' of potential situations that may occur. When the hour approached, we made our way to Ox's side tent where we found him waiting for us inside.

Ox looked us over with a skeptical examination and asked again if Vettias was sure our little ruse would succeed.

"I have faith in the kid, does he not look like he belongs?" Vettias asked.

"Until he opens his mouth," Ox replied. "It's my ass that will be exposed if one of you finds yourself on the other end of a conversation with Orontes, Vettias. You think this kid is going to keep my name out of his mouth when they start making him bleed?"

"I don't think *I* would," Vettias retorted. "That is why we are taking such care to ensure we don't get caught."

"Just remember others are depending on this. We are going to stir a hornet's nest after tonight. Alright kid, your rich merchant father is managing a large deal with the army for the acquisition of needed equipment. I am doing him a personal favour by getting his little shit of a son laid by the most beautiful women in the world at the palace harem. Look at me... You ready?"

"Yes," I answered confidently.

"Then follow me." We departed the side tent and followed Ox past the guards and through the gate leading onto the Triparadeisus grounds. We followed the grand thoroughfare leading past the servant's quarters to the main palace. As we approached, I began to notice the opulent details of the structure that I had not had the time observe since my hectic time spent on the grounds. The dusty earth gave way to well-manicured green bushes, shrubs, bushes, trees, and exotic flowers. Docile game such as peacocks, giraffes, small monkeys, wandered freely throughout the landscape. More dangerous predatory cats laid in comfortable shade chained to large trees.

The foundation of the palace stood fifteen feet above the ground consisting of massive stones painted blue with numerous golden mythical Persian animals. Two immense stone staircases, lined with marble gryphons painted gold in the Persian style, bridged the foundation opposite each other leading to the grand entrance. Ox successfully used his rank to get us past the four guards posted at the staircase and we ascended to the columned entrance hall. The approximately fifty columns were twenty feet high and painted blue with gold capitals and pedestals. Sitting atop the columns was a vast white marble relief depicting epic scenes from Persian mythology. In the middle of the relief was a massive golden Faravahar- the half-man half-eagle guardian of the Achaemenid Royal Dynasty.

The palace was a tiered structure with another level of manicured landscaping on the first roof, followed by another set of columns supporting a second large relief and third level with manicured gardens and trees hanging down onto the second. At the very top of the structure was an open-air, four-walled edifice covered in large relief sculptures brightly painted green and shining in the late afternoon son. Sitting atop each corner was a winged Persian sphinx. A green pyramid-shaped canopy sat atop the rooftop edifice capping off the massive palace. Whereas several of the other conquered regions of Persia we entered were already adopting Greek architecture and customs, Triparadeisus and its mighty palaces retained their unmistakably Persian characteristics of extravagance. Uncle Argos would be at a loss for words in the presence of such a magnificent building.

Entering the great entrance hall my senses were overwhelmed by the elaborate marble patterns of the flooring and lavish ceiling inlaid with gold and jewels. The walls were ornately painted with Persian iconography and traditional art patterns. The front atrium held the largest eastern-style rug containing the most intricate design I had ever seen. Perceiving the bewilderment my surroundings were having on me, Vettias quietly reminded me of my character and to remain in control of my faculties. His nudge snapped me back into persona as a hairless, feminine-looking male attendant approached us.

"Welcome to the Triparadeisus Palace gentlemen, what business do you have here?"

"I am Ponteus of General Ptolemy's battle staff. This is Raman, son of the powerful merchant Nashiram whose name is known throughout this land. The battle staff of General Ptolemy has granted Raman brief use of the palace harem as part of an agreed acquisition compact." Ox completed his introduction by placing several coins in the attendant's hand. "I trust we will have no issues here and you will personally lead us to the palace harem."

"But of course," the attendant replied fairly nervously. "Please follow me." The attendant motioned to his colleague that he would be escorting us and we followed him up a large marble staircase to the second floor. We were led down a long hallway adorned with rich tapestries and marble busts in the Greek style. Our emasculated attendant hurriedly rushed us to the end of the corridor which housed two large marble columns supporting a relief of various sculpted sexual positions similar to the Fair Peach. Two imposing wooden doors with extravagant carvings were opened, giving way to a room luridly decorated with white ceramic tile on the floor and ceiling contrasting the brightly-coloured Persian frescos on the walls. Several plush red couches and full sized-marble sculptures of naked women lined both walls and a marble fountain, calmly spouting cool water, lay in the middle of the atrium. The environment resembled that of the Fair Peach, only grander. Our guide scurried past thick red drapes and quickly returned with the facility's caretaker. He was dressed in the finest eastern silk cloth I had ever seen and his skin was as fair as a newborn child. He had a dark complexion, eastern eyes, and well-kept teeth. He looked a little confused when he saw the reason for his unexpected summoning and immediately looked to Ox as the most important man in the group for an explanation.

"How can I help you today gentlemen?" Ox retold his story to the caretaker who begrudgingly obliged after much coin was presented. Upon confirmation that we would be allowed in, Ox took his leave, escorted out by our attendant, as Vettias and I shared a moment of awkward silence with our new handler. After several seconds I could feel Vettias' thoughts seethe with my inaction and I finally blurted out "I am here for a particular girl of yours."

"We have the world's most beautiful women in Triparadeisus. Which one do you speak of?"

"One known as Mara."

"Ah, one of our new acquisitions. And how have you heard of this one so soon after her arrival here?"

"Word of her beauty and talents are circulating throughout the encampments."

"Of both I can personally attest my friend," the caretaker stated with a depraved smile that instantly made me want to stab him in the throat. "But a woman of this calibre is quite expensive for men who are not part of the Greek leadership here in the palace."

"Money will not be an issue, assuming you name a fair price," I interrupted, under the assumption that would be something my persona would do.

"I see, and may I inquire to your slave's presence in such a place of elegance as this?"

"He will remain with me throughout my time here."

"Hmm, it was my understanding that the girl will be for you alone? There are plenty of whores in the encampments that are better suited for such things, especially with dirty slaves. His very presence soils the character of this harem."

"The girl is not for me, I will watch the two of them."

"But to purchase such a flower of exquisite beauty for a dirty slave is almost sacrilegious."

"She will not be harmed and will be returned to you in good condition- that much I can swear."

"I will have to charge you more, plus the fee for watching."

"Very well," I answered, putting a large purse in his hand. "Now bring her out," I commanded tersely.

"Right away, sir." The warden exited with a newfound sense of urgency fuelled by a heavy purse. He returned seconds later with our girl- adorned in fine silk and smelling of an intoxicating fragrance. My eyes opened wide and I was taken aback by her beauty. I quickly regained my composure and stood stoically next to Vettias who played his role as slave well, deferentially staring at the ground. Mara immediately noticed us but feigned ignorance perfectly.

"She will take you to her room," the warden explained.

"Good, that will be all then," I announced condescendingly.

"Of course sir," he responded and disappeared through the thick red curtain. After his departure Mara gave us the faintest of smiles and led us to her chamber.

Chapter 29

We entered her quarters which were decorated with attractive cushions, rugs, and tapestries. Its cleanliness eased some of the concern I had over her treatment while working on our behalf. She quickly closed the door and hugged me with a warmth I had not detected in her previously. Our embrace lingered just long enough to make me feel slightly uncomfortable before she let go and hugged Vettias as well.

"Ooh, you stink," she proclaimed, releasing Vettias from her grip. "I was wondering when I was going to see you."

"You seem to be in good spirits," Vettias replied. "How are they treating you here? Do you need anything? Is everything alright?"

"As good as can be expected. I would be doing this regardless- at least I am in pleasant surroundings. The men here are rather boorish, however, and certainly don't care to know how to treat a woman."

"So, have we met anyone interesting?"

"An officer of the Silver Shields. His name is Hyllos and claims to be a member of their Battle Staff. He told me of the infighting within the unit over General Antigenes' murder of Lord Regent Perdiccas, Seleucus' betrayal, Ptolemy's theft of Alexander's body, and their Deputy Commander Arrhideaus' new protectorate duties of the Kings. Hyllos believes Arrhideaus does not want this responsibility and the Silver Shields do not support the coming dominance of Antipater that is surely to follow any agreement obtained at this summit. They still hold resentment to Antipater's direct challenge to them while serving Lord Regent Perdiccas' legitimate Regency and blame him and Ptolemy for the current situation."

"You've done an excellent job here Mara, I'm surprised this man would divulge so much to you," Vettias congratulated.

"Greeks don't know what a tongue is for. He's become infatuated with me and I suspect I will see him again." Mara continued to provide Hyllos' general demeanour and his physical attributes.

"Have you met anyone else who might advance our cause?"

"There were only a few other drunken fools who were too inebriated to climax- making for a rough time of it. I won't miss this place when I am through here." Thinking of Mara's mistreatment angered me to no end, but I suppressed these feelings and reciprocated the congenial attitude she was displaying. I thought it the right time to test my theory about Nikandros and inserted myself into the conversation, provoking slight annoyance from Vettias.

"Mara, do you remember when we met that first evening? Do you remember the new head of the treasury you pointed out to us?"

"Yes," she replied, not understanding my line of questioning.

"There was the other individual sitting with him. A man you said you had been with. He was quiet. Do you remember him?"

"Yes."

"Have you seen this individual in Triparadeisus? Has he visited the harem, perhaps taken to a certain girl?"

"I haven't."

"Can you be cognizant of this man and do all you can do determine if he is in fact here? I would recommend looking out for women here who only have regular clients. Perhaps someone that has been rented for long periods of time. Can you do that?"

"There is not much I can do outside of these walls but I will be sure to keep my eyes open."

"How about you Andrikos? Are you proving your worth?" Mara asked with a tone of superiority that belied her youth.

"The boy is coming along quite well," Vettias interjected before I could answer- causing me to feel a little insecure, given how it made me look in front of Mara to be talked about as if I was not present in the room. "Mara, I have a small task for you," Vettias explained as he removed a small parchment, ink, and stylus. Can you write these words to your new admirer as I dictate them to you? I need something that is going to tug on his heart strings." Mara complied and wrote a false message urgently requesting Hyllos meet her immediately because she had been sold and was being moved the following morning. When Mara finished, Vettias rubbed a drop of her perfume on the parchment before rolling it up and placing it back in his small bag.

The three of us lingered for another twenty minutes before Vettias thought it the appropriate time to make our departure. "My dear, we will require one more favour of you this early evening- we will need you to take us to the central palace garden."

As Mara approached her door, she turned around and gave me the softest, most sensual kiss I had ever received and stated in a sarcastic, yet warm tone, "Don't you two forget about me."

She led us back to the atrium where the warden had been waiting anxiously and ran out from behind a curtain when he heard us emerge. "Everything alright gentlemen?" he rushed to ask, while surveying Mara to ensure my slave did not sully his prized property.

"Everything was exceedingly fine, however I have one small additional demand," I stated in an arrogant tone. "I require this beauty to see us out of the palace. Spending those precious few extra moments with her is worth it to me," I explained while putting another small amount of coin in his hand.

"Uh, n-normally we do not let our women leave the premises...But, I can make an exception as long as she comes directly back here so she can wash off that slave's stench," he replied looking sternly at Mara in a way that infuriated me.

"I've no doubt she will see us out and return quickly to her quarters. You may see me again during the summit so be sure to have her ready when I arrive."

"Of course sir," the warden replied deferentially. With that we took our leave through the large wooden doors and followed Mara back down the lavish corridor in the direction of the marble staircase.

"You did great kid," Vettias whispered with a proud smile. This recognition caused a mild euphoria in me as a rush of adrenaline hastened my pace. "You played your part well. I will need you to briefly explain our appearance to our contact in the central garden. Allow me to do the talking from then on, unless challenged by someone before we arrive at the Queen's suite chambers. Mara, my dear, I was right to choose you. In a palace of gilded excess, you are a natural object of grace and beauty. One or both of us will be back to see you soon. Take heart, we will not forget about you."

Mara brought us past the large marble staircase where we found ourselves on the second floor balcony overlooking the grand banquet hall. I looked down onto the large dining tables, each able to hold fifty men, as they were hurriedly being prepared for the evening's festivities. The high ceiling was gilded with gold and jewels while the walls were adorned with tapestries and statues. Continuing along the balcony, we exited the grand dining hall and entered the palace's central garden. This room was at the heart of the palace and spanned its entire height with the structure's central rooftop edifice hovering overhead. It appeared the canopy was opened during the day to allow sunlight into the garden and drawn closed each night. Exotic trees and flowers grew in the middle of the first floor with several peacocks casually strolling about. A number of palace guests loitered in the garden below, enjoying the lush atmosphere. The second and third floor terraces also boasted striking floral arrangements hanging down from above. Mara pointed to a small staircase leading down to the first floor and bid us farewell.

"I should be getting back," she stated sullenly.

"Remember what I told you, we're not going to forget about you," Vettias reassured. She quickly turned and left, perhaps to mask a tear, and Vettias and I descended the staircase into the palatial garden. "Don't avoid eye contact with anyone," Vettias whispered. "You need to act like you belong here. If someone gives you a challenging glance, you need to return it in such a forceful manner as to make them regret questioning your presence in the first place. If someone does question us, you are the personal guest of Ptolemy's Battle staff." I nodded my understanding as we entered the garden to meet our unknown contact. Most of the garden's admirers were too busy looking at the various species of flora to notice us. I did a fairly good job of fending off the few inquisitive glances I did receive at great internal exertion.

Vettias and I walked slowly through the narrow paths landscaped into the garden where we finally saw a girl about my age of unmistakably Macedonian origin. She sat on a small bench examining a particularly exotic flower and wore a white linen robe decorated with a bright purple pattern and ornamental clasps. In her hair she wore two decorative hairpins and a white jasmine flower. My heart raced a little as I approached to make an introduction.

"My lady, may I ask you the way to the palatial baths?" I asked with as polished a Greek tone as my humble upbringing was capable of summoning.

"Its location is difficult to traverse if you don't know the way. Allow me to show you to them." Having executed our recognition signals I quickly sat beside her and explained who we in fact were in a hushed tone. Vettias then apologized for his appearance and introduced himself.

"My lady, thank you for so expertly serving your queen and meeting with us here today. Please lead the way to her suite. Between now and then if we are to be stopped for any reason, please do your best to maintain the guise Andrikos and I have assumed. Are you ready?"

"Yes, please follow me gentlemen. I believe you will find the palatial baths to your liking." We followed in silence as she led us out of the central garden and through several halls and corridors until we reached a set of four marble columns indicating the entrance to the palatial baths.

We entered the bath's main vestibule where several people milled about drinking wine and making conversation. "The corridor we seek is just inside the smaller female facilities. I'll return once I determine our path is clear of any outsiders and we will hurriedly make our way. Wait here and act natural." Vettias nodded his assent and we quietly moved into a dimly lit corner of the atrium.

"Follow my lead when we enter her chambers. I will do the talking. Don't speak unless spoken to. You are about to be in the presence of Argead royalty- Alexander's own cousin no less. You're a long way from the brothels of Ilandra kid," Vettias smirked while putting his arm around me- even he was getting caught up in the gravity of the moment. Our royal guide emerged from the woman's facilities at a determined pace and quickly motioned the two of us to follow her. Vettias took quick stock of our surroundings to ensure he and I had been forgotten by the few conversationalists inside the vestibule. Making the determination we could safely follow, we made a hastened dash through the entrance to the women's side of the bathhouse. We trailed our guide, who quickly darted into a small alcove used to store maintenance supplies. As we did so the three of us froze in place after hearing the carefree laughter of two women patrons approaching. We backed up against the dimly lit alcove wall and held our breaths as the two women neared. The presence of two men in the women's bathhouse facilities would be seen as a great offense and terminate any chance of us meeting with the Queen. The two women passed by completely unaware of our presence, and our guide rapidly opened a hidden door that was constructed to look like part of the alcove's wall. She lit a candle and the three of us entered the dark corridor leading to a stairwell. Closing the secret door behind us we were in complete darkness save for our guide's small candle.

The corridor smelled of mildew and contained multiple unseen cobwebs that I frequently walked in to, causing me to walk up the stairs with my hands out in front me. The stone staircase followed a continuously curving route until it reached an old wooden door whose hinges hadn't looked used in decades. Our guide gave a deliberate knock, denoting a prearranged signal, and the door was unlocked from the other side and slowly creaked open.

An immense man stood in the doorway, with sword drawn, wearing the colours of the royal bodyguard. Recognizing our guide, he hurriedly ushered the three of us in and locked the old door behind us, moving a wooden chest in front of it. We found ourselves in an extravagant circular anteroom occupied by several royal bodyguards and attendants. Perceiving the need to put the brute at ease Vettias spoke first.

"I am Vettias of Amphipolis, son of Nikomachus, veteran of Chaeronea, the Granicus, the Planes of Issus, the sieges of Sidon and Tyre, Gaugamela, The Jaxartes River, The Hydaspes River, as well as the recent battles of succession in Cappadocia. I currently serve the one true defender of the Argead Kings, General Eumenes of Cardia, as an officer within his Battle Staff. I have travelled many weeks, risking life and limb, to stand in this very room to pledge my undying loyalty to Queen Adea and offer assistance against her powerful enemies so she may rightly retain the Argead throne. My colleague is my apprentice in service of the Argead Kings."

The room fell silent as Vettias delivered his impressive introduction. His demeanour always became intensely serious when speaking of Alexander and his successors- underlying the impassioned allegiance he held to the oath taken in India. I hoped to feel as passionate about something as Vettias did to his oath- such passions spur one to accomplish great things and give meaning to one's life.

All in attendance remained silent and cautiously looked towards the gaggle of female attendants huddled on the opposite side of the foyer. Within this group of women, all eyes looked to a singular beauty standing several inches taller than her companions with blond hair, blue eyes, and fair skin. She stepped forward into the center of the room with everyone's eyes deferentially following her. She looked confidently at the two of us as she approached with a poise and grace reserved for royalty despite her apparent young age. I felt obliged to turn my eyes towards the ground in surrender to such self-assuredness. It was clear Argead blood flowed through this young girl as she addressed the two of us.

"Vettias of Amphipolis, I thank you for your service to Macedon's military victories and for your loyalty to the interest of my family. It appears we have both donned guises for this meeting. Let us lift them and speak privately in my chambers."

"As you command, my Queen," Vettias answered, bowing his head. Two attendants opened the colossal double doors, carved with friezes displaying mythical Persian creatures, allowing passage into the royal chambers. The imposing bodyguard who granted us entry to the royal atrium followed the three of us into a large antechamber decorated with distinctly Greek artifacts- no doubt brought from Macedon in the royal baggage train. There were two corridors leading to what looked like a large private dining hall and a bath facility. A larger set of closed double doors was opened by the bodyguard leading to the royal bedchamber.

"It is a great offense for men of your low stature to be allowed in the private chambers of the Queen," Adea stated while motioning us to follow her inside.

"Which is of course why you chose to have this meeting here," Vettias added.

"This place is crawling with snakes thus all precautions must be taken." The bodyguard followed us into the bedroom when Vettias abruptly halted.

"My queen, it is precisely because I agree with you that we must ask to speak with you alone," he implored, while motioning towards her bodyguard. The sentry shot Adea a disapproving stare before being ordered to wait outside after disarming us. As he closed the door behind him Adea motioned us to sit on a plush couch with blue cushions and gold stitching. As I did so I realized this was the most comfortable piece of furniture I had ever sat on.

"My queen, I want to thank you for agreeing to meet us under these circumstances. I…"

"And what makes you think I did not want to have two men who serve under the Phalangiarch Alcetas brought to my chambers to be killed for my amusement?" Adea forcefully interrupted. She spoke with an eloquence resulting from years of study under Greece's best tutors, and a stubborn combativeness that pointed to her young age and northern heritage. It appeared she was not willing to let bygones be bygones- Vettias was going to have his work cut out for him. "Do you think me willing to further the cause of the man who murdered my mother? A woman who surpassed him and his family in every conceivable measure. It's no wonder his brother, the fool Perdiccas, managed to lose his army and his life without a battle being fought. I could have intervened and saved him but instead I spit on his corpse with a smile. He won't be the last to lay dead after crossing me. And this is the faction you come here to entreat me to support?"

"And now you have been brought here to wait for your new master to arrive and take you under his possession until you have served his purposes." Vettias was taking a chance with his blunt assessment to change the course of the conversation. "You've suffered under men who did not have your best interest at heart and now you will be delivered to Antipater to serve as pawn until he no longer has use of you and your husband."

"You forget yourself Vettias, no one speaks to me in that manner," Adea corrected in a half-serious tone. "Let us speak plainly. My husband is an imbecile, Alexander's son is an infant, his widow is from some dirt farm in Bactria, and his mother has been banished to

257

her country of Epirus by Antipater. I alone am suited to act as Protectorate of the Argead line."

"My Queen, I have sworn an oath in the presence of your own cousin, Alexander, to protect the Argead line after his death..."

"Yes, the man responsible for the murder of my father," Adea quickly interrupted again. "I am not naïve enough to shun Alexander because of what he felt he had to do many years ago. The Fates have seen it fit to inexorably entwine our paths so that my only chance for survival is to embrace his blood and side with the faction who wishes to see it continue on the Macedonian throne. That is why I have summoned you here Vettias. Ponteus from Perdiccas' Battle Staff informed me of your allegiance to the Argead cause and your army's defiance of Alexander's self-appointed successors. I need allies who can move freely outside these walls to coordinate the several factions that share your commitment to our cause and can overthrow these pretenders before Antipater arrives within the next few days. Are you such an ally?"

"My Queen, I am at your disposal. Peithon and Arrhidaeus have served Macedon well but have not earned the honour, as you have through your birthright and marriage, to control the Argead Kings. Those that serve the Argead blood have already been working on your behalf to uncover the identities of a secretive organization intent on eradicating the Argead line from this world. We plan on striking a blow to this nefarious group tonight in preparation for you to make your plea of sovereignty over the Argead Kings tomorrow morning before the amenable ears of the Silver Shields and remaining Perdiccan supporters. Winning their support will ensure a majority of the main army follows in proclaiming you Protectorate to the Kings."

"Antipater wishes to take control of Alexander IV and my idiot husband with impunity at the conclusion of this summit. He will learn there is still a member of the royal Argead family willing to stand between him and lay claim to her heritage. Tell me the plans you have made ready and the role in which I am to play."

"My Queen, before this meeting I would be hesitant in making this recommendation, but having had the pleasure of witnessing your grace, determination, and intelligence, I feel making a petition directly to the army may be our best course."

"A woman to stand in front of a Macedonian army to address them? Such a thing is unheard of in our traditions."

"Such an action would add further weight to the importance of our cause. You share the blood of Alexander, you are married to his half-brother, you have the support of the Macedonian regulars, and you have the command presence of a man far older then you. You of all people in this world can stand in front of the army tomorrow and make this case."

"And if I fail?"

"Then you are in only a slightly more disadvantageous position then you are now. Antipater will still be made your caretaker, except now your true intent would have been exposed. Would you be willing to risk that small inconvenience in return for the possibility of ridding yourself from the charge of men who do not have your best interest at heart? To be free to make decisions on your own?"

"You serve your masters well Vettias and have made a compelling argument for bold action. I will choose my words this evening and deliver my argument tomorrow morning."

"I am your humble servant my Queen, however I have one last request. Several actions needed to be taken on your behalf will require the weight of the royal retinue, and I ask that I may be given a royal insignia, to be presented sparingly, when my low status or guise do not grant me access to important people or places. All care will be made to ensure your involvement remains unknown."

"Very well, my bodyguard will provide you with one as you depart. I trust you will be careful not to unnecessarily expose me in any plotting."

"You have my word. It will be used only as a last resort. And your faithful attendant, the one we met in the palace's central gardens. Can you have her in the same place, at the same time, every day, from now until the completion of the summit? This will be our way of communicating."

"Agreed."

Vettias and the Queen discussed the next steps to be taken that evening and tomorrow morning. At the conclusion of the meeting,

Queen Adea instructed her royal bodyguards to see us out through another set of little-used passages to ensure we would not be seen exiting her chambers. We departed the palace through a discreet side door and hurriedly made our way through the servants' quarters in the direction of the Silver Shields encampment.

Chapter 30

"I need to change out of these rags before our next meeting," Vettias announced.

"And who are we to meet with?" I asked.

"We will seek out this Hyllos and compel him to garner support amongst his trusted officers in preparation for the Queen's speech tomorrow. We only have a short amount of time, however, since we will need to be off the streets when Davos conducts his purge of known operatives of Orontes."

Vettias darted behind a row of tents to discard his slave garb and don a more respectable tunic. As we walked through army bivouacs I observed familiar menial tasks and idle conversations conducted by the soldiers which made me think of Stephanos and our Lochos. I assumed he would be the most respected of them by now, and longed to sit beside him at our campfire once again.

Passing the last Taxis bivouac of the regular army, I saw an imposing separate encampment of tents with thousands of polished shields glimmering in the fleeting dusk light. A large banner preceded this line of iron and bronze, proudly displaying the Silver Shields' insignia accompanied by several attached ribbons identifying the many battles where they had been victorious. Unlike the disjointed encampment of the main army, The Silver Shields' entrance was guarded by two older yet imposing soldiers.

"You go up to them and claim you are couriering a message to Hyllos," Vettias instructed while handing me the small parchment with Mara's handwriting. This should get him moving and we'll wait nearby to intercept him. I don't want to use the royal insignia just yet."

I did as instructed, prompting one of the imposing brutes guarding the entrance to depart and deliver the message. Vettias and I sat near a tree under cover of darkness close to the encampment with a good view of anyone entering or leaving.

"Do you think he'll come?" I asked.

"If his lust is how Mara describes he will. That hint of perfume should set him to purpose. The content of the letter is also innocuous- if it is read by someone before it reaches him, no portion of our intent can be gleaned."

"And the Queen, do you really think she will win over the army tomorrow? A girl in her late teens addressing a Macedonian Phalanx is unheard of."

"She's not just any girl and will need no introduction with this crowd. Listen, our odds coming here were never high. General Eumenes knew this, which is why he sent me. Best scenario- Adea is successful tomorrow and takes a more prominent role in the affairs of the Kings ahead of Antipater's arrival. We will then have an ally within the Royal family who will designate Eumenes as Royal General of the Kings, perhaps even Regent. Worst scenario- she fails, Antipater arrives, declares Eumenes enemy of the Kings and takes the Argeads under his protection back to Macedon. The latter potentiality is more likely, in my honest assessment. Even if this were to transpire, at least we would have succeeded in sowing dissention between the royal family and Antipater- albeit at the expense of the Queen. But she is merely a means to the end- the eventual succession of Alexander IV, the legitimate son, is the overall goal. Either way, we will fight on. What are your thoughts?"

"Well, your lack of faith does not give me great assurance. You know I will defer to your judgment on these matters. I haven't progressed enough to have a proper command of the complicated situation you've thrust me into."

"Stop looking for compliments kid, you're doing fine. What are your thoughts on our business last evening in my quarters?"

"Your points were well taken, I was wrong to doubt the effectiveness of the tactics used. I fear my constitution is not strong enough to effectively carry out such a task myself, however, and I undoubtedly could not withstand its torment should I ever find myself tied to a chair."

"Very few can remain quiet, which is the whole point- so don't get caught. Ever. As for your temperament- it will come with time. As I said, it's not something we do often and had you taken to it on your first exposure I would think you a monster from Hades. Now, these

Silver Shield veterans are going to be difficult to manage. Their well-deserved egos must be stroked at all times. They also do not like fighting for those they deem unworthy- which pretty much includes all of Alexander's generals. Perdiccas found this out the hard way. That is the vulnerability I am going to exploit- their unhappiness with the prospect of being subordinated to Antipater." Vettias cut off the last syllable and stared at a silhouette hurriedly making his leave from the Silver Shields encampment. "That's our man, stay back for a moment to avoid giving the impression we mean him harm."

"Pardon me sir, might I have a brief word with you, I know you're in a hurry," Vettias announced deferentially.

"What is this? Remove yourself from my path!" Hyllos ordered.

"Forgive me sir, it is the note you have just received that I wish to speak with you about." The man drew his sword and closed with Vettias.

"What treachery is this? Who are you? Speak or I'll kill you where you stand!"

"Sir, I have been sent on behalf of Queen Adea herself to speak with you about a sensitive matter. My royal insignia bears the truth of my words. All I ask is that we may speak in private for a short while. My apologies for the false correspondence- rest assured it was for your own safety, and that of the Queen's. Mara is not at all to blame either and she is in no danger of being sold or moved any time soon. Manipulating a man's affections is no small transgression, which I hope conveys to you the importance of the message which I bear. Will you delay judgment of me until you have heard what I have to say?"

"Follow me. I will lead us through our encampment in a manner which won't draw any attention. Once in my tent, you will be free to speak openly."

"I thank you sir. With your permission I would like for my associate to accompany us. Come on out kid!" Vettias ordered in a hushed tone. The three of us walked around the encampment and entered a small path leading through the sea of erected tents. My heart rate increased as I walked among the storied soldiers of this famed unit who were milling about in much the same manner as the regular army, save for the air of superiority which was palpable throughout. These men had been with Alexander from the beginning and his father Philip II before that. They were much older than the average phalangite yet looked as though they could crush a normal man's skull with their bare hands- every last one of them. They all made deferential salutes to Hyllos as we traversed down neatly drained alleys and thoroughfares between each row of tents. The most notable aspect of the encampment was the heavily polished silver shields displayed in front of each tent in perfect alignment. It spoke to their sense of pride and reminded all others that they were different, they were better.

We arrived at the Battle Staff quarters and entered Hyllos' private tent relatively unnoticed. It was spacious and allowed for others to sit inside with relative comfort. The dwelling was decorated with a luxurious Persian rug and fine artifacts from the Far East acquired over years of pillaging the Achaemenid Empire. Hyllos took his seat behind an ornate staff table while Vettias and I stood respectfully in front of him, awaiting his permission to speak. He was in his mid-fifties yet held a stature on par with any phalangite half his age. His face had a number of small nicks and scars with leathery skin reddened from years of drinking and exposure. The Silver Shields' attire he wore resembled more a Greek hoplite than a Macedonian phalangite, with bronze cuirass and greaves- allowing for the flexibility needed to perform the myriad of operations Alexander had demanded of them. His intimidating gaze forced me to look at his feet while Vettias did a notable job holding eye contact with this imposing man.

"If you hadn't been sent by the Queen herself you would already be dead. What message do you deliver?"

"If my charge had been of lesser importance I wouldn't dare involve the girl," Vettias assured once again. "Queen Adea has sent me to offer the Silver Shields a way to serve the Argeads without the unpleasantness of subordinating your proud unit to so recent a sworn enemy as Antipater- a man who remained in Pella during the entire Asian campaign. You can help your cause immensely by influencing events before Antipater arrives. Queen Adea respects all the Silver Shields have accomplished on behalf of her cousin Alexander and of

Macedon. She is prepared to give your leadership unrivaled authority within a hierarchy that grants her increased power over the Kings and names General Eumenes as Royal General of the Army. General Eumenes has always paid homage to the great deeds of the Silver Shields and would view your esteemed unit as an autonomous partner in defense of the Argeads. This is more than can be said for any arrangement involving Antigonus, Antipater, Ptolemy, and Seleucus- a man who has traded the princely life of toil as your former Commander, for the slavish acquisition of possessions under Antipater and Ptolemy's yoke."

"You fawn over our storied history yet have such little faith in our ability to provide for our own interests- as if we are a helpless lamb being led to slaughter. General Arrhidaeus, our Deputy Commander, is the new Regent of the Kings and our Commander, Antigenes, is the slayer of Antipater's enemy, Perdiccas. Why do we need the assistance of a young girl who's barely bled for the first time?"

"It is true your position is not without pieces to play, but this game is stacked against you. The Silver Shields have incurred the wrath and distrust of those who travel here to determine the fate of the world. Your loyalty to the Argeads poses a threat to Antipater's future goals. In addition, while you may have struck an accord with Ptolemy in Egypt, your faction has fought and defeated two armies of Antipater. His first act will be to take the Regency from General Arrhidaeus and any final agreement made by him will marginalize the Silver Shields and lead to your ultimate disbandment. All the Queen asks is for you to speak with as many officers within your ranks that you can trust to support her bid for power tomorrow. While the Queen cannot risk putting any pledge in writing, I am here to give you her word that the Silver Shields will retain and increase their position of prominence and act as official guard of the Argead Kings."

Hyllos sat calmly listening to Vettias' convincing offer with his hand stroking his chin in a contemplative expression. Vettias had both paid homage to the reputation of the Silver Shields and offered a path forward that increased their respected position within the Macedonian Empire. It remained to be seen whether he could get over the egregious offense taken by involving Mara into the scheme however.

"You serve the Queen well and her offer points to her firm grasp of the current situation, despite her age," Hyllos responded with a hint of sarcasm denoting his belief that Vettias himself was the father of this strategy. "The Queen will need to succeed in her actions tomorrow before others will be comfortable supporting her openly. How will she get her message out?"

"She will address the Macedonian Army tomorrow after morning sacrifices," Vettias said in a confident tone. Making such a radical pronouncement to a man like Hyllos would not have succeeded if any hint of doubt could be detected. Hyllos' eyes widened at the mere thought of such a sacrilege before he relaxed his expression and retook his contemplative pose. "In addition, her allies have identified a surreptitious group of operatives whose purpose is to abolish the Argead line of Kings and remove all supporters to it. The Queen's agents mean to move against this cabal tonight in preparation for tomorrow."

"She's certainly confident in her abilities. Such a drastic action will no doubt put her in a very vulnerable position if she fails- one that I would not have the Silver Shields follow in."

"A failure on her part will be hers alone. The Queen has left it to you to decide if she is successful in winning over the army. If, in your opinion, her plea has failed to move a requisite number of the army to her side, you can remain silent and no one is the wiser of your motives. She only means to have you lay the groundwork ahead of time with like-minded officers so they will support her if she is successful."

"The Queen is wise to provide a way for us to support her that does not leave us vulnerable in the aftermath of a potential failure. Given the small amount of effort on our part and the potential gain to our objectives, you may discreetly tell her that the Silver Shields will make no promises but stand ready to support her if she is successful. I will make necessary arrangements this evening with officers I can trust. I am ordering you to clandestinely establish contact with me as soon as the Queen's position is secure, is that understood? This

266

should not be any trouble for you given the circumstances of this first encounter."

"I will seek you out sir at the earliest moment that it is safe to do so."

"Good; my squire will show you out."

Upon exiting the camp Vettias decided to speak with Ox and make final preparations before returning to my quarters and to awaiting Davos' return. By now he would have started his purge so our meeting with Ox was to be short. We travelled through the main army's encampment unimpeded until we reached the leadership's bivouac. Vettias hung back while I spoke with the guards to summon Ox. He waved us through as we followed him into our familiar small tent. Ox arrived a few minutes later looking tired and dishevelled as he sat on a storage crate waiting to hear an update from Vettias.

"Brother, we've been busy," Vettias began. "After I set you to purpose, we will have done all we can to further our cause for tomorrow. Then, the fate of the Argeads will rest on the gentle shoulders of a teenage girl."

Vettias performed his familiar routine of being purposely vague for the effect of his audience. Ox was not amused and was too tired for theatrics. "What are you getting at," he asked slightly annoyed.

"Queen Adea is to address the Macedonian Army tomorrow after the morning muster and sacrifice to the Gods," Vettias announced with a satisfied tone.

"You aren't serious," Ox replied with shock. "She's only a girl, Vettias, this isn't a game. You're playing with our lives and will get us all killed- including her!" Ox caught himself before graduating to an outright yell for fear of being heard and lowered his voice to a hushed roar. "I hope there is a greater plan behind this looming blasphemy. A girl, addressing the Macedonian Army, are you mad?"

"Brother, I understand your misgivings but you yourself know what she is capable of. You know the blood she bears and the loyalty she inspires with the army. I would not recommend this course had I not met with her and witnessed for myself her beauty, her oratory, her passion. As we speak Davos is eliminating a number of Orontes' operatives, the Silver Shield officers are with us if she can deliver a rousing speech. All that is left is for you to rally Perdiccas' former officers tonight and convince them to support the Queen tomorrow. The Perdiccan contingent, combined with the Silver Shields, will be more than enough to sway the requisite number of soldiers within the army to support her- all before Antipater arrives. I need to know that you're with me, brother. The hour draws near and we will need to cease all communication after tonight. If she fails in her discourse you can decide to remain silent and we will find another road to achieve our goals. But for now, The Fates have delivered this young Argead to us and we must act before our enemies are too powerful and entrenched to remove. Can I count on you to rally the Perdiccan officers?"

Ox was not fully convinced but begrudgingly acquiesced to Vettias' impassioned plea. "I'll rally the officers, but we will not make a move unless she can pull it off. See you tomorrow, brother."

"Just one more thing, my friend," Vettias added. "I will require use of your safe house within the staff quarters. My current apartment will not be safe after tonight."

"Instruct Davos to show you the way tonight. It has a line of sight to the boy's quarters and will suit your purposes." The three of us departed the tent set to our purposes- Ox to rally the Perdiccans, Vettias and I to meet Davos and move our prisoners to my quarters.

Returning to our makeshift prison, we knocked on Vettias' door and were let in by Ox's sentries. Both captives were asleep and appeared to have fresh blood running down their faces. "You didn't rough them up too much did you?" Vettias whispered.

"Just the amount we were told," one of the goons replied.

"Good, are you ready to begin?" I was confused by the conversation until Vettias loudly walked in the room, waking the prisoners and berating the two guards for mistreating our 'guests'. The sentries apologized profusely as they obsequiously slunk into the corner of the room and Vettias tended to the victims' facial wounds with a wet rag. Our two guests seemed genuinely happy to see their former torturer-turned-saviour, which caused me to remember my initial doubts about Vettias' promise they would become very close in a short while.

"Get some sleep until Davos returns," Vettias suggested. My eyelids were heavy and I fell rapidly to sleep in the corner of the apartment curled up on a thin blanket on the floor near the fireplace. Father was standing in the corner of the room looking at our two prisoners.

"What are your thoughts regarding these two poor bastards?" He asked.

"I find I don't enjoy inflicting such pain on prisoners, if that's what you mean," I replied.

"But to Vettias' earlier point, you could be moved to such acts if properly motivated. If the life of your mother or sister was involved. Maybe Mara as well. Do not be too quick to judge Vettias on his apparent eagerness in this matter. For him, his oath and that half-breed King may evoke similar emotions as would someone who was close to you being in danger." I remained silent while my father's words sunk in until I was awoken by the entrance of Davos to our room.

He had several stains of blood on his clothes and bore several red marks over his body and face. It was clear he met some resistance during his purge. His demeanour was calm and his face remained expressionless. Vettias called me over and the three of us quietly conversed just outside the apartment.

"Were you successful?" Vettias asked in a serious tone.

"For the most part," Davos replied without emotion. "The names we were given have been eliminated, some more discreetly than others. Not all were alone however due to our time constraint, so we made sure to kill those with them as well. A couple of unknown associates got lucky and escaped. There's no way of knowing whether they were part of Orontes' network but we must assume he knows by now. Some of the situations got a little ugly; I lost three of my men tonight. We took care to dispose of their bodies, however, so Orontes will not know their identities."

"And what of those that lived? Were any of you seen by anyone that survived?"

"I can't say for certain so, again, we must assume Orontes knows the identities of at least one of our men."

"I agree. Alright Davos, you did well tonight. From now on we will enter a new phase of our operations. We can no longer operate with the anonymity we enjoyed the past week. We are going to ground. First we will move these two to Andrikos' quarters. I suspect Pirus may be of further use but Shifty is approaching the end of his utility. Davos, do you have a place we can securely dump him?"

"That shouldn't be a problem, tomorrow evening will present the earliest opportunity to do so."

"Good, now I'm going to go over how we move forward after this morning. The Queen's speech is going to set the army encampment on fire. Large fissures will open and tensions are going to be high. The ensuing chaos will provide us opportunities as well as challenges to successfully operate. Davos, I will need to meet with you twice a day going forward. You will be my conduit to Ox. You will pass messages between us as well as receive new instructions from me. Once in the morning, once in the early evening. The location of our first meeting will take place at the small wine vendor's tent closest to the main army's encampment. During the meeting you will communicate any news from Ox, receive new instructions, and I will inform you of the next meeting location. In case of an emergency where one of us needs to set a meeting immediately, either of us, Andrikos included, will tie a white scarf on the window of the butchery where you two picked up Pirus. This means we will need to ensure we pass by this landmark a few times each day while accomplishing our tasks. The initiator of the emergency will wait for us at this apartment since Ox has found me a new one. Do you understand your instructions?"

"Um hmm," Davos answered dryly.

"Alright, let's move these two over to Andrikos' quarters."

We wrapped the detainees in separate rugs and loaded them into a small cart while Davos squatted in between them with a dagger pressed to each of their heads. They were informed if either of them screamed out, both would be killed instantly by Davos. Vettias and I each took one handle of the cart while Ox's two goons walked several paces in front and behind us for security. The circumstances reminded me of uncle Argos and I pulling our merchant cart back from the Ilandran road market. Our current cargo made me think of how far from that reality I was.

Our short trek was without incident as both victims complied with their instructions either out of fear, capitulation, or both. Upon arriving, we carried our captives up the small flight of stairs to my quarters and tied them to two separate chairs on opposite sides of the room. Vettias instructed the sentries to resume watch over the prisoners while Davos guided us to Ox's safe house and slinked away into the dark night like a hungry viper looking for its next prey.

"We'll make our way to the army encampment a little after an hour past dawn," Vettias instructed. "I'm getting some sleep until then, I suggest you do the same."

We both shut our eyes in separate corners of the sparsely furnished room and stole a precious few hours of sleep before our big day.

Chapter 31

I woke to the callous shaking of Vettias, who hurried me out the door as we made our way to the morning army formation. The temperature was cool and the activity within the staff quarters finally died down with nothing to show for it but debris in the streets and burned-out fire pits. We arrived at the end of the ritualistic sacrifices and managed to get lost in the throng of thousands observing the rites. Some soldiers were paying close attention and mentally trying to connect to the Gods through the ceremony. Others were in attendance because their presence was mandated by their officers. A large wooden platform had been erected several feet in the air to enable all observers a line of sight to the events. Several men sat on the shoulders of others or on make shift stands to echo what was being said to the rest of the audience too far away to hear the ceremony. Vettias and I manoeuvred our way close enough to readily see the activities taking place on the platform and were just in ear shot of what was being said directly. The many relay men aided our comprehension if a word or two could not be discerned over the low din of thousands of soldiers engaged in quiet small talk. Standing on my toes I could just make out the polished armour of the Silver Shield formation standing prominently in the front rows to the right of the stage.

As the sacrifice wound down, the low din of conversation increased in volume so that Vettias and I could no longer hear words spoken from the wooden platform. I strained to see and hear what was transpiring while Vettias appeared less interested. At this moment the sun poked through the clouds to illuminate the grey morning sky and a slender figure dressed in full battle armour, combining Macedonian and Illyrian styles, ascended the platform. Those soldiers whose attention was not in the direction of the platform continued their casual conversations, while a wave of silence eventually washed over the army as everyone became aware of the Queen's presence. She wore polished bronze greaves reserved only for the wealthiest of Illyrian warriors. Her tunic was pure white with bright purple stitching along the hem and sleeves. Over her tunic was a bronze cuirass in the Greek hoplite style, except it was cut for a female. A purple cloak flowed over the shoulders of her cuirass down to the back of her calves. Her bronze helmet was in the style of Illyrian elite hoplites with mandibles covering her ears and cheeks and a blood red plume standing straight up from its crest. Borrowing from the God King himself, two large feathers, dyed in purple, adorned her helmet, adding to her royal air. A curved Thracian sword was sheathed at her hip and she held an Illyrian curved throwing ax in her right hand. She manoeuvred up the platform dexterously, despite wearing heavy armour for so young a girl, and wore her equipment as aptly as any phalangite. The able first impression her appearance made on the army could not be overstated. I looked over to Vettias, who had a half-smile denoting immense pride in the young Argead. She clearly passed the first test and no one in the army dared criticize her right to stand in front of them. All remained silent as she motioned to speak.

"Fellow Macedonians," she began with a soft and unsure voice, "Many of you here have travelled from the plains of Anatolia, to the sands of Egypt. From the palaces of Mesopotamia to the harsh lands of Bactria. From the exotic Kingdoms of India back through the arid deserts of Persia." Her voice did not travel far but was echoed by the many criers repeating her words. Thus far no passions had been stirred within her audience, however.

"You conquered all that opposed you and showed the enfeebled Achaemenid Satraps how real men slay their enemies on the battlefield." These bold words struck the right tone and elicited strong shouts and applause from the army. She deftly waited for the outburst to subside before continuing. "You fought as one during the unbelievable triumphs of the greatest campaign of conquest in history; The Granicus, Issus, Tyre, Gaugemela, The Jaxartes, and The Hydaspes. You did so not for bloodlust, although vanquishing one's enemy in combat is invigorating, you fought for my kin, Alexander, and you fought for the glory of Macedonia and Greece." Again, the army broke out into loud applause- our Queen knew her audience and was playing them like a lyre.

"My fellow Macedonians, it pains me to see the fractures that have emerged since Alexander's death. Just weeks ago the army that I stand before was split on opposite sides, ready to combat each other in open conflict. Other battles have already been fought to the north and many good Greeks have been killed. What a shame it is to have survived Alexander's world conquest only to be run through by a fellow Greek on territory that was already spear-won." The army grew quiet as the weight of her words resonated with all in attendance. "It is this very reason that I, a mere woman, take this unprecedented step of addressing the greatest army ever to be assembled. But, my fellow countrymen, as you know, I am no *mere* woman. Macedon does not create *mere* women; for we are the only women in the world that give birth to true men!" Shouts and yells reigned out as she made this last point and several in the crowd started chanting her name. She played off this well by taking her speech into a loud crescendo. "The blood of Alexander flows through my veins. The blood of his father, Philip II, my grandfather, flows through my veins. And Alexander's brother, Philip III, I call husband." The army burst into a loud roar which Adea waited several minutes to subside before continuing.

"The family history I give is already known to most of you. Allow me to speak briefly about the other side of my lineage- one not known to most Macedonians. My mother's mother hailed from lands north of Macedon in the untamed hills and forests of Illyria. Illyrians have a proud warrior history and proved bitter foes of my grandfather Phillip II. The blood of Illyria flowed through Philip II by virtue of his mother and served him well during his fight against them. Those of you old enough to remember the Macedonian campaigns in Illyria know I speak the truth. In Illyria our women are expected to fight alongside our men and my mother's mother, Audata was no exception. Audata, daughter of the great Illyrian King Bardyllis, was a fierce warrior princess before she was given as a bride to Philip II. My grandfather, father of Alexander, a legendary Macedonian warrior in his own right, and his warrior princess Audata, gave birth to my mother Cynane. Cynane was unmistakably raised a Macedonian but Audata always instilled in her the Illyrian warrior ethos." The audience remained silent, in rapt attention to the story being so expertly told by such a young girl. Vettias nodded his head like a father watching his daughter bring honour to the family in her own right. "Cynane was given to Philip II's nephew, my father, Amyntas IV. Since my birth my mother instilled in me the Illyrian warrior ethos just as her mother had done with her."

"I tell you these things not to impress you but to impress upon you that the Argead Queen that stands before you is no *mere* woman and certainly no stranger to the skills of war." At the conclusion of this sentence she took the Illyrian throwing axe she had been using as a speech aid and raised it in a throwing position. All eyes of the army now focused directly on the Queen as she threw the axe with incredible agility directly at an upright wooden support beam of the platform approximately twenty five feet away. No one could believe what they had witnessed. There was no arc to the axe's trajectory. It was thrown in a deadly straight line throughout its flight. The axe seemed to twirl through the air at reduced speed until it was buried deep within the wooden beam. None spoke for a second as her spectacle was processed by the army. The stillness remained until a shout finally rang out, "All hail Queen Adea!" which provoked wild applause and shouts of encouragement.

Vettias looked to me and exclaimed, "She has them! This is the moment, come on girl, take them now!" Adea again waited for the excitement she had ginned up to subside before revealing her true purpose for addressing the army.

"Countrymen, There are those who think me unworthy of the charge I now hold as Queen of Macedonia." Jeers and boos were yelled towards the unnamed villains. "It is true, it is true. These cynics served Macedon well many years ago but did not contribute to your great accomplishments in Asia. They wish to marginalize me, use me for their own purposes, and tell me I cannot speak on behalf of my own husband." More slurs could be heard as the army became incensed that any Macedonian could doubt their precious Queen, especially someone who did not fight in the great campaign.

"Tell us who these cowards are so we may kill them!" demanded the crowd.

"My countrymen, they make great haste to come to this very place and take control of the Argeads. I speak of none other than Antipater and his regime of allies." The crowd fell silent from its previous fever pitch as the weight of what she was now asking sunk in. I looked over to Vettias who had an uncharacteristic look of worry on his face. Perhaps sensing the same, Adea continued. "This man does not care for you, he does not care for Alexander, and he looks to begin his own dynasty through his son, Cassander- a mere boy who never marched one step in Alexander's army." The crowd still remained quiet. Vettias frantically looked in Ox's general direction and towards the Silver Shields. Neither were showing signs of support. Adea continued. "This man Antipater, who only crosses into Asia after the battles have been won- an old withered man who has to get up and piss five times a night lest he wake to a wet bed. A man who willingly pays the wages of Macedonian veterans returning home, yet refuses to give those who remained to fight what is due to them." This last accusation struck a chord since many veterans were owed money, especially the Silver Shields. Grumblings could now be heard in their precincts which gave hope that an eruption of support would ensue.

"And does this man travel to Triparadeisus to pay your just rewards? No, he travels here empty handed with intentions to undo all you have fought for. I speak now to the Silver Shields and all veterans who demand what is rightfully theirs. I, Queen Adea of the Argead House, descendent of Heracles and Zeus Ammon, hereby decree that, if you support me as your rightful Queen, I will quickly provide all back wages to whom it is owed!" Her promise was the final catalyst needed to break the deadlock. The Silver Shields burst into wholehearted support for the Queen. This was followed by the Perdiccan officers and their units around Ox. Finally, three quarters of the army were shouting Adea's name and swearing their allegiance. She had won the day yet Vettias did not look pleased. I shot him a confused glance to which he replied, "She doesn't have the money! We need to speak with her at once, come with me. That attendant better be sitting in the palatial gardens at the proper hour."

Vettias and I exited the crowd which was still energized from Adea's powerful speech and made our way to our new safe house. Vettias ensured we took a circuitous route, making several stops to purchase food and minor items, in order to determine whether we were being followed. When Vettias was satisfied we were not under watchful eye, we entered the safe house and locked the door behind us.

"We'll wait a few hours and then see our contact in the palatial garden. Adea did a superb job but I fear she may have promised something she cannot deliver- that would undo all we've accomplished thus far. Ox and Hyllos will organize their factions to consolidate the gains made today. We'll visit Mara first so we can get in the palace. Tomorrow she should have some info regarding the mood of the palace. There's no doubt Seleucus is incensed and will be working with Orontes to salvage what they can before Antipater's arrival."

Vettias and I finished the portions of food we had purchased in relative silence and stole much needed sleep for the next few hours.

Chapter 32

When the hour approached, Vettias and I again donned clothing to support the guise of a rich merchant's son and his slave. We took an indirect route on our way to the palace to ensure we weren't followed and had little trouble passing through the guards who were reminded of our previous visit with a generous donation of coin. As we ascended the large stairway into the grand entrance hall, our familiar palace attendant received us.

"Good afternoon sir," he announced in a semi-condescending tone. "I was under the impression your previous visit was going to be your last. We are not in the habit of letting individuals unaffiliated with the royal retinue frequent access to these halls." His demeanour left a small window of opportunity that I seized upon through the confidence of the persona I was now inhabiting.

"I need not remind you that I am chief representative and son of the man who supplies the majority of food, slaves, and whores in this palace. I don't expect this to be my last visit here either." Vettias' teachings had served me well. It would have been impossible for me to make such a rebuke in the halls of a Persian palace before our time together. The attendant looked towards one of his colleagues before relenting.

"Of, of course sir, v-very well. To the harem once again?"

"Lead the way," I commanded sternly.

We followed the attendant up the marble staircase and down the extravagant corridor before arriving at the harem entrance. Vettias quietly informed me that I was to meet with Mara alone while he waited outside. Before I could respond we were transferred to the custody of the harem's warden and our attendant quickly returned to his station downstairs.

"I have come for Mara once again," I declared arrogantly. The warden looked disparagingly at Vettias' appearance before answering. "She will be for me this time. My slave will wait here."

"Ah, very good sir. Might I suggest he wait in a more private room away from any customers coming and going?"

"Very well, now bring me the girl."

"Right away sir." The warden departed the atrium and Vettias gave me an approving head nod. I still was unsure why he wasn't accompanying me but did not have time to quietly discuss the matter before our beautiful accomplice graced our presence.

"You look more beautiful than I remember my lady; shall we?" As she took me by the hand I glared at the warden condescendingly, "That will be all." She closed and locked the door behind us as we entered her chamber and sat on the lone couch together. We awkwardly hugged and she waited for me to speak while her eyes were asking why Vettias was not with us.

"Vettias thought it best for me to meet with you alone since your caretaker dislikes his presence. You are still our only plausible way into the palace. How is everything?"

"Good, his clothes smell anyway," she replied with a smile. "Everything is tolerable here. I am starting to learn there are ways of uncovering information without saying a word." She grinned at the confused look she had triggered. "There are many places in the harem that can be used to listen to the conversations of others. Some of these nooks were built intentionally; others are inadvertent details of the structure. Can you imagine the incessant spying of Darius' concubines all vying for his favour? Nothing of use has been learned yet but they will prove valuable for our purposes."

"That is great news, Vettias will be happy to hear about this development. A great power shift is afoot and surely all that pass through here tonight will be speaking of it. Vettias wants you to be aware of who is saying what and their positions within the army or royal retinue. And don't forget to listen for the quiet man."

"Not a problem, but enough about Vettias." Her comment made me blush. I was only invoking his name because I did not feel worthy dictating orders to this stunningly beautiful woman on my own. "Is that all you have to say? You can't leave now, that effeminate monster outside will think I have displeased you. You have paid for a proper visit- stay a while, let your slave wait for his master," she added as she leaned closer to me on the couch. Her forwardness hastened my breathing and I felt a rush of warmth in my loin. I found myself in the unfamiliar situation of having intense feelings for a woman prior to any intimate relations. This was not for an absence of emotion on my part; rather no woman ever took an interest in me, let alone a beauty such as Mara. When I thought of her my stomach ached to think of the life she had endured. As she motioned closer, my eyes diverted to the floor. She pulled them back to hers by placing her soft finger caringly on my chin. "Do you not want me?"

"Nothing could be further from the truth, Mara," I quickly replied, almost angry for how absurd her assertion was. "What a question from someone as astute as you. I can't bear the thought of you in this gilded prison suffering abuse by men who care nothing of you. I want not just you, but to take you from this place and always protect you from the cruelties of this world. But I can't. I have no means to do so. My only shreds of worldliness stem from what Vettias has taught me. But you've heard these words before. Beauty such as yours inspires men to move mountains to win your affections- men more worthy of your favour."

"What if I see in you something different than the drunk powerful men who want me when their lusts run high, then discard me when it is inconvenient to keep a whore around? What if I believe what you have told me regarding your feelings and see in them an authenticity lacking in the hollow overtures of rich and powerful men. I do not hail from luxurious halls occupied by women of leisure. I am a Scythian. We live on our horses and sleep in our tents on the harsh northern Steppes. I do not seek the protection of a man that can provide me my every material desire. Such excess would do nothing but remind me of my time as a sexual captive in a golden cage. I understand Vettias is using me to achieve his ends and I do not begrudge him for it. I agreed to escape with him because of what he promised at the end of this summit. I know he does not care for me afterwards. But I know you do."

She motioned closer to kiss me as my heart raced. It was not the soft kiss of yesterday but rather an impassioned testament to her feelings. I returned her enthusiasm and finally felt what it was like to embrace someone you love. She forcefully pulled me on top of her and removed her silk robe. Her blond hair flowing over her young, healthy breasts was the most arousing sight I had ever laid eyes on. I hurriedly undid my tunic and lifted it up to enter her. As I did so, she grabbed me and pulled me inside her. All prior feelings of pleasure paled in comparison to what I felt at that moment. A pulsating warmth engulfed my body with each thrust. She gyrated her hips in unison with mine, causing my ecstasy to now be concentrated in the tip of my penis. Anticipating my climax she told me to finish inside her. Before she completed these words I collapsed into her arms releasing my seed into her warm vessel. For several minutes I lay there motionless, with my cheek against hers, taking slow deep breathes as my body struggled to regain its faculties after a powerful shock to its senses. Mara did not say a word and lovingly stroked my hair and back. Beads of sweat slowly trickled down my forehead-finally breaking the carnal-induced coma I had entered.

As I raised my head from her bosom I felt as though I had emerged from a dark abyss with the light of the room's window causing me to squint my eyes. When they came into focus I saw Mara's beautiful green eyes looking into mine with a warm smile.

"Is it possible you could hold the same feelings I hold for you?" I asked, still recuperating from the greatest experience of my life.

"Shhh. All I have told you is true. Just relax and enjoy the rest of our time together." I obeyed and rested my head back in the safe warmth of her bosom to further draw out this unexpected moment of pleasure. After another ten minutes, the vision of Vettias skulking in some closet awaiting my return finally stirred me to action.

"Vettias will be expecting me, I should probably go."

"I know."

"The events of this morning may hinder our ability to see you regularly after this. I won't let Vettias forget you.

"I know you won't. Tell our benefactor I said hello," she added with a smile as we both dressed back into our cloths- hers now wrinkled into a small pile on the floor. As I turned to open her door she grabbed my shoulder and pulled me to her. "Vettias will know what has happened, don't let him talk you out of your feelings." We kissed one last time before she saw me out.

"Everything to your liking I trust sir?" the warden asked deferentially.

"Yes. If I am to require an escort out of the palace it will be from the girl."

"Yes sir, however palace custom prohibits harem girls to escort visitors. I'm afraid last instance was a special circumstance and I will insist on one of my eunuchs escorting you out of the palace." I was nearly unable to summon the energy required to assume my pompous tone given recent events and took a deep breath before replying.

"That is wholly unacceptable. I shall be highly displeased if you deny me the few remaining precious moments I have with the girl," I barked while putting a generous amount of coin in his hand.

"Sir, please, I do not wish to anger such a generous customer... I am beholden to my masters as your slave is to you. Please do not put me in the position of either offending you or incurring severe penalties for disobeying their rules."

"I appreciate your situation, unfortunately my position is firm. You have succeeded in conveying the trouble this will cause, however- this should take care of it." I placed another generous donation of coin in his hand and he relented.

"Please have her back quickly," were his final words.

Mara walked Vettias and I to the stairs leading down to the garden and bid us farewell. As we walked to meet our royal contact Vettias shot me an inquisitive glance.

"Successful meeting I presume?" he asked sarcastically.

"It was. All was communicated to her and we engaged in light conversation for the rest of time to bolster our ruse."

"Yes, quite convincing," he replied with a broad smile. I purposely kept quiet for fear of confirming Vettias' assumptions. Our girl was sitting in her predetermined seat and led us through the palatial baths and up the secret stairwell. The Queen's chief bodyguard unlocked the door and granted us entry to her private atrium. Our welcoming was certainly different from yesterday; for her suite's atrium was filled with bodyguards with swords drawn at a heightened alert level. Their eyes followed our every move.

"I come to congratulate the Queen on her successful address and discuss next steps," Vettias announced in a formal tone befitting our surroundings.

"Come, Vettias, let us speak in private," the Queen commanded after emerging from her sea of female attendants. Her chief bodyguard led us into her chambers and closed the door as he departed.

"My Queen, allow me to formally congratulate you on a magnificent speech before the Macedonian Army. After our meeting yesterday I knew you would rise to the occasion; but even I could not imagine the poise, grace, and command presence you were able to summon. There is no doubt you have won the vast majority of the army over."

"Thank you Vettias, you are too kind. I am humbled by such praise from an experienced soldier as yourself. But you still have concerns, yes? Give them voice so I may allay your misgivings." I could not believe the composure this young girl possessed, especially when talking to someone as impressive as Vettias.

"My Queen, you are as perceptive as any diviner. I am concerned about your ability to provide payment to the Silver Shields and other veterans of the eastern campaigns. If this promise is not made good before the month is out, all of the gains you made today could be for naught."

"You men and your pitiable notions about the capabilities of women." Her confrontational tone took us both aback. "Do you think because you have not instructed me as to what my next actions should be I am therefore incapable of making decisions for myself? After I assisted in Perdiccas' demise, many of his surviving supporters took up position in the Phoenician city of Tyre where his former Admiral, Attalus, is presently in command of eight hundred talents of gold from the royal treasury located there. Dispatches were sent to him long before *you* showed up and he is expected to arrive at Triparadeisus within the next few days. I sincerely thank you for your help in my plans but they were set to purpose long ago."

Vettias was clearly surprised by this news. I could see his mind processing all he had been told and trying to comprehend all the angles the Queen's actions now opened. "Admiral Attalus travels here? In the heart of his former enemies? He won't get out alive." He opined.

"That may have been true before this morning, but make no mistake, he will ride into Triparadeisus as unfettered as if he were Alexander himself now. I will name him Regent and he will defer to my judgment in running the empire. On the morrow I will summon Peithon and Arrhidaeus to my chamber to depose them as stewards of the Kings. I'll then march the army south to Tyre and have them paid before the month is out. From there I will name Eumenes Royal General of Asia and re-invade Egypt to wrest control of the Satrapy from Ptolemy and recover Alexander's remains. Our army will then triumphantly march the two Kings to Babylon where they will centrally manage the empire under my supervision. Attalus will sail the fleet and a number of veterans back to Macedon to assume power there while I will assign my allies as new Satraps throughout the empire. Antipater, Ptolemy, Seleucus, and Cassander will be condemned to death while Antigonus will be allowed to retire with honour to a Macedonian farm – never to be heard from again. Oh, and in case you were wondering, the murderer Alcetas will also be condemned. I trust these plans meet your approval?" she asked condescendingly.

Vettias was clearly at a loss for words by the boldness of the Queen's actions. I could not tell if he was more shocked from finding fault with her course of action or from the blow to his pride due to the Queen's refusal of his further guidance. Either way he chose to not make an issue of it now. "My Queen, once again you have shown your superior intellect and leadership. I commend you on your boldness thus far and pledge my undying support to further your ends by any means you see necessary."

"For now I want you to allow these events to unfold and await my next summons. That will be all for now."

"As you wish," Vettias replied while bowing deferentially and making his way to the door. As she was about to let us out some unseen force came over me, imploring me to address her.

"Forgive me my Queen," I began while bowing.

"It speaks!" she replied as I felt the intense gaze of Vettias' angry stare.

"There is someone, a woman, who has assisted us in our efforts to further your position while in Triparadeisus who may require your benevolence in the near future. Like you, her family has been taken from her and has survived many abuses since."

The Queen looked at me curiously, as if wandering why a nobody deemed himself worthy to speak in her presence- let alone ask a favour. "Please, continue."

"We had rescued her from a life of torture in a brothel and she now provides us information on your enemies within the palace harem. She has been promised a reprieve from this life once we have safely escaped Triparadeisus and I ask as your humble servant that, if something were to happen to us where we could not fulfill this promise, you would show mercy and bring her within your royal retinue as an attendant?"

"You must truly care about this girl if she spurs you to ask the Queen of Macedon to intercede on her behalf."

"She is very important, my Queen, and will serve you loyally and faithfully."

"Very well then boy. What is her name?"

"Mara. A courtesan in the palatial harem."

"Luckily for you I have a soft spot for women who are abused by men- especially those working on my behalf. Yes, your cause is just and I will take the girl if you cannot."

"I thank you, my Queen."

Vettias and I exited through the side of the palace and made our way back to my apartment to check in on our captives. "What the fuck was that in there? You think because you got your dick wet you can badger the Queen of Macedon on behalf of some whore? I don't know what God took pity on you in her chamber but you could have ruined everything we've worked for. Do you know how temperamental she is? Do you know how carefully I've chosen every word with that brat to affect her actions? And still she goes off and puts some grand scheme in motion that imperils everything! And then you come along petitioning her about some puppy love horse shit? I let you fuck her as a reward for your good work thus far, and this is how you repay me? If you do something like that again I'll kill you myself, do you understand? After all I've taught you you're still as susceptible as ever to some wet hole with pretty eyes...Pathetic!"

285

I had nothing to say to Vettias' admonishments. He was right, but I didn't care. It didn't change one strand of feeling I held for Mara.

Chapter 33

We entered my apartment to find our captives with fresh wounds courtesy of their handlers. To my amusement they appeared overjoyed to see Vettias enter the room as they now equated him with a respite from Ox's two thugs. Vettias sent the two goons out of the room and began carefully dressing their wounds and providing them food and drink.

"I can't be here at all times, but rest assured no harm will come to you in my presence. That is, of course, as long as you two continue to be cooperative. I don't have to worry about that at this point, correct?" The two eagerly shook their heads like dogs competing for the affections of their master. "Good. I have some good news. Since Shifty has acquitted himself to my satisfaction and has reached the end of his utility, I am going to transfer you out of here to more comfortable accommodations. When we depart Triparadeisus I will release you on your own cognizance. You see, I am a man of my word. Andrikos, please untie Shifty and bring him out. He will be transported to our safe house."

Shifty was weak on his feet and smelled horrid as I assisted in getting his clothes on and walking him outside. Pirus looked at us with pitiable eyes as the underling was seen out. The two guards were waiting in a small alley and appeared to be expecting our arrival. They grabbed hold of the prisoner and smiled at me as I moved to return to the safe house. I turned back to watch as one guard stabbed Shifty through the throat while muffling his mouth and holding his head as his body fell lifelessly to the ground. I can't say I was surprised by the violent act and I now understood the look Pirus was giving us. Subconsciously I knew this was how it would have to end for both prisoners, I was just happy Vettias did not make me do the deed. Returning to the safe house I found Pirus and Vettias engaged in a cordial conversation in between slurps of warm soup and wine by the captive. Vettias had apparently informed Pirus of the morning's development.

"How is Orontes and Seleucus going to counter the Queen's bid for power?"

"Orontes will place an operative in Adea's retinue if he hasn't done so already. Seleucus will use his staff officers and bodyguards to ensure his safety until Antipater's arrival. He will barricade himself in the palace and send runners out to Antipater informing him of events an implore him to make haste. By now Orontes will know I have been compromised and realize there are clandestine forces at work in opposition to his own. He will order Nikandros to begin kidnapping suspected Perdiccan supporters and torture them mercilessly until he extracts names. If he finds me alive he'll have me killed for cooperating with you after first making me divulge information about my captors."

"Then I suggest you go your own way when I release you," Vettias replied.

"Ah yes, my promised release," Pirus muttered sarcastically.

"What about this Nikandros. How do you initiate contact with him?"

"Normally through scheduled meetings. I was supposed to meet with him after speaking with Shifty. My absence will have alerted Nikandros to my demise and he will be suspect of any attempt to initiate an unscheduled meeting. As I said, you don't seek him out, he finds you."

"Alright, we'll continue this later. Andrikos, the hour grows near to meet Davos this evening."

"Y-you are pleased with me, yes? Y-you will tell my guards to treat me well, yes?"

"I want you to think about how I'm going to find Nikandros," Vettias replied in a non-committal tone. "Andrikos, the hour approaches."

The two of us exited the apartment and Vettias instructed the guards to refrain from harming our captive until our return. We took two separate and very circuitous routes to make absolutely certain we were not followed to the meeting location. Despite our indirect courses, we still arrived early to the wine tent across from the main army encampment. We occupied a table in the far corner that was not visible to passersby.

"I may have overreacted after our meeting with the Queen," Vettias conceded after sitting in silence for several minutes. "My anger lay more in the Queen's recklessness than your pitiful outburst of childhood infatuation. That being said, you did fuck up. You understand that, correct?"

"Yes," I answered solemnly, looking at the ground.

"We are going to be little more than bystanders for the remainder of our time here. I fear she's in over her head despite her uncanny ability to inspire the army. She was certainly right about one thing, however- she is no *mere* girl. We'll do what we can in the shadows but if she cannot sustain the full weight of Antipater and Antigonus' arrival, you and I are leaving." After my scolding I didn't dare ask about Mara but would certainly ensure Vettias had a plan for her if we were to make a hasty exit. Davos then causally entered the tent and took a seat at our table.

"What news within the army," Vettias asked.

"Factions are emerging. Seleucus is trying to rally his supporters within the officer corps and hold what he can until Antipater arrives. So far, the Queen's position remains secure. There's something else, however. Two of my men went missing today. These two assisted me in our purge last night. We will have to assume Orontes has them."

"And if that is the case, we must assume Orontes knows who you are. You will have to lay low for the next few days. Andrikos will serve as conduit between myself and Ox."

"Agreed. I will take up at the kid's apartment with the prisoner. I made sure my men were not aware of my relationship with Ox or with the two of you. They cannot provide Orontes enough information to foil our objectives. May the Gods have mercy on them- Orontes surely won't."

"Andrikos," Vettias announced while turning to me. "Davos is going to return with me, you will bring my correspondence to Ox, understood?" I nodded. "Davos, tell the kid when and where you were to meet with Ox again."

"In thirty minutes, at the army encampment's latrine ditch. He'll be there."

"And when you see him," Vettias added, "inform him of all the Queen has told us. Alert him to Davos' missing men and instruct him to remain vigilant over the next few days. Instruct him he is to conduct only passive collection and elicitation. I don't want him doing anything overtly operational. We'll continue our liaison through you, understood? Alright, I think we're done here. Andrikos, meet me back at the safe house when you are finished. Do not bring a tail back with you- make sure you are clean before you approach. Davos will remain at your apartment. As much as it pains me, the Queen's actions have forced us to wait and hide for the next couple days."

I had little trouble traversing through the army encampment and finding Ox at the latrine ditch. The army was in a greater state of confusion now than it was when we first arrived. Hardly anyone gave me more than a second glance as I made my way through the endless rows of tents and saw Ox's broad back looking out over the dozens of phalangites relieving themselves. Our conversation was brief and cordial. It was the first time I felt he was treating me as an equal and not some kid caught up in events too big to comprehend. He shared Vettias' outrage over the Queen's irresponsible behaviour, and agreed remaining unseen and vigilant was the most prudent course of action. He bid me farewell and I returned to our safe house after navigating an indirect path, stopping to purchase jugs of wine and food stuffs along the way.

Vettias was sitting at the table, drinking a jug of wine and staring distantly at the wall. It was clear he loathed the position he found himself in- shut out of decisions, marginalized by a teenage girl, forced to watch events unfold with me in a meagre apartment as opposed to shaping them from the shadows. This was the cause of his recent outburst towards me- the understanding that he had been relegated to insignificance by the very person he had sworn an oath to protect. He passed me a cup as I sat beside him.

"Well, at least *you* can still navigate outside this prison. Orontes will have determined I am here by now. It's just a matter of time before one of his agents spots me. You will continue to see Mara and liaise with Ox so I can stay abreast of events. Davos won't get out of this place alive- not if Orontes has one of his operatives. His utility has just run out."

I watched as Vettias had consigned Davos as a lost cause within the space of a minute and hoped events would not someday relegate me to this fate in his eyes. We remained in relative silence for the rest of the evening, getting drunk off the wine I had purchased.

The next three days I repeated this routine of meeting Ox in the morning to communicate and receive information, return to the safe house, and meet him again in the early evening. Ox informed me that the Queen kept to her word and deposed Peithon and Arrhidaeus as Regents. Arrhidaeus seemed relieved, whereas Peithon was outraged and began working on behalf of Seleucus within the army. Tensions were running high between the two factions and Ox feared the army was on the verge of open conflict. During the afternoon of the third day, Vettias and I were awakened from an afternoon nap by a loud commotion in the direction of the army encampment.

We donned our local garb to cover our faces and made our way to the source of horns blowing and soldiers running about. As we neared the sea of activity we could make out a small entourage moving through the masses on horseback. It was Admiral Attalus, triumphantly trotting through the army- just as Adea predicted. The fact that he was able to do so, while being officially considered an outlaw by the current regime, spoke to the fluidity of the situation. Attalus gave an impromptu speech to the army before continuing on to the palace to be received by the Queen.

"You're going to see Mara tomorrow morning after meeting with Ox," Vettias ordered. The thought of being alone in her chamber shot a jolt of warmth to my loin and brought a smile to my face. Luckily Vettias was too busy observing the spectacle to notice the effect his pronouncement had on me. "Alright, let us return and hide in our hole lest someone recognize me," Vettias suggested in a deflated tone.

The next morning I met with Ox as scheduled and he explained how Attalus' arrival emboldened Adea's faction and several instances of violence had broken out over the evening. He suggested Adea act now and address the army again to take advantage of the shift in momentum and provided several more names of key figures within the Seleucus and Antipater faction for Davos to dispose of. After departing the latrine ditch I made my way towards the palace. I noticed an invigoration in my gate as the image of Mara's hair flowing over her naked body taunted me. Approaching the entrance I noticed an increased guard presence which I attributed to the heightened level of tension, both outside and inside the palace.

One of the guards had recognized me from my previous visits and quickly moved to stop me. "Not a good time to get your dick wet kid. We are on high alert with orders to prohibit anyone not on official business from entering."

"I understand your concern, which is precisely why I am to be allowed entry." The guard looked perplexed at my authoritative answer until I presented him the Queen's royal insignia. "I am here on official business as commanded by the Queen herself. I would appreciate you accompanying me through the entrance hall and informing the attendants that I do not require an escort either."

The guard let out a conciliatory grunt after inspecting the insignia. "Alright, follow me." He led me up the large staircase and informed the attendants that I did not require an escort. They looked at me with antipathy as they consented to my entrance. I shot them a condescending glare and hurried up the marble staircase, down the opulent corridor, and entered the palatial harem.

The warden seemed startled by my presence since the palace was now highly secured. Before he could organize his thoughts to possibly come up with some excuse why I was to be barred entry, I quickly commanded him to bring Mara.

"Y-yes sir," he replied, still in a confused fluster.

"Good morning my lady, I hope I did not wake you this early in the day," I stated as the warden produced Mara, who looked very fatigued.

"No trouble at all sir, please put such silly thoughts from your mind- especially coming from someone who treats me as well as you. Follow me," she replied with a warm grace. She locked her door behind us and we embraced. The smell of her hair and curves of her body instantly shot a warmth of heat to my loins- propelling me to remove her silk robe. She grabbed my hands while looking me in the eyes explaining she had been *working* all night and asked my forgiveness for not being able to be intimate with me now. At first I felt rejected and thought her feelings for me had paled in comparison to mine towards her. I then remembered what she had to endure here and felt guilty even thinking of such a selfish notion. I embraced her again and assured her she had nothing to apologize for.

"Will you be content to lay with me for the next hour until it is time for you to leave?"

"Of course. How I've ached for your warm embrace these past few days. The thought of others with you is almost unbearable. Soon we will be together away from this place and free of these monsters."

"Yes, I eagerly await that day," Mara replied while stroking my hair on her bed. "I also have some news for you. There was much to learn over the past few days." Mara's talk of business snapped me out of the lustful trance I had entered while laying with her. It made me realize, at that moment, I didn't care about our mission or the fates of the Argeads. I just wanted to lie there with her forever. Feelings of guilt overcame these irresponsible ideas and I returned to being Vettias' underling once more.

"I heard news of the quiet man," Mara announced with considerable satisfaction. "Another girl within the harem was speaking with a friend and I overheard her describe him just as if he was standing before us- all the way down to his birth mark. She explained that she is escorted to his quarters each evening within the palace, in the heavily armed wing of Seleucus, and returned each morning. She did not go into detail about his schedule or where to find him, but he is here."

"Did she say his name?"

"No, but now that I know she is his woman, I can casually elicit more from her."

"Yes but please be careful. This man is no doubt probing her for people asking too many questions. You may be successful in getting her to unwittingly divulge something to you but he may see more in it during a cross examination."

"I will be careful. In other news, the palace has become a battleground between the factions of Seleucus and the Queen. There are rumours their bodyguards have already combated one another on several occasions within the palace walls. You'd be wise not to wander around after your departure and exit the palace with great haste."

"What about Hyllos?"

"He has visited me each night and wishes to purchase me. I told you he has fallen for me." This development was unsettling and I would refrain from telling Vettias lest he decide this possibility presented a way for him to renege on his pledge to her.

I remained with her until our hour was up and begrudgingly exited the harem. I allowed a harem eunuch to escort me out of the palace lest a soldier from Seleucus' retinue question why I was walking about unsupervised. I returned to the safe house and informed Vettias my suspicions about Nikandros were correct. He praised my instincts and instructed me to inform Ox at my next meeting with him. "I think we should pay our guest a visit over at your apartment to see what else he can tell us about this 'quiet man.' That will give us something to do to pass the time."

Chapter 34

Vettias and I carefully made our way to my old quarters and gave our predetermined knock on the door. We stood waiting impatiently since no stirring could be heard within the apartment. Vettias knocked again and still no answer was received. He looked at me gravely and unsheathed his short sword tucked under his cloak. I did the same as he kicked the door in and we entered with swords at the ready.

All sources of light had been extinguished and the room was dark. A narrow band of sunlight let in from the open door allowed us to slowly comprehend the scene which we were entering. A strong stale odour permeated the room. An object hung from the ceiling, half in the light and half in the shadows- it was one of Ox's guards. A noose was around his neck tied to a ceiling beam and his stomach was slit open horizontally with his entrails and bowels emptied onto the floor beneath his dangling feet. Vettias hurriedly closed the door and lit the single remaining log in the fireplace to create a flickering source of light in the room. I backed away from the hanging corpse directly into another large swaying object. I startled and turned around to see the guard's colleague hanging from another rafter in the ceiling. His face was contorted into a grotesque expression and his body was stripped naked. There were letters carved into the man's stomach. As his body swung in and out of the flickering light of the fire I made out the bloody name V-E-T-T-I-A-S.

Vettias walked over to the carving and put his hand on my shoulder. "This is Orontes' doing. If he got this far, the two of us are no longer safe." I turned away to look for our captive while Vettias continued to examine the gruesome corpse. I found Pirus' body still tied to his chair in the far corner. He bore several more injuries to include a gash across his throat so vicious his trachea and spinal cord could be seen. Blood stains led down from the gaping wound and collected in a dark pool in his lap. His wrists were red and bloody, speaking to his agonizing struggle due to the intense pain inflicted on him. I looked back towards Vettias in the dimly lit room and noticed something move from the shadows in the opposite corner. Slowly the black entity began to take form into the shape of a man. As it moved forward I yelled out "Vettias! Behind you!"

Before I could finish the words the attacker was on him. My exclamation succeeded in turning Vettias round to face the man, giving him a chance to blunt the initial strike with a quick sword parry. The two entered a mortal embrace, forming an amorphous silhouette of violence where I could not discern where Vettias began and his attacker ended- making it impossible to dispatch the villain with my sword. I raced to Vettias' aid and grabbed his attacker's sword hand so fiercely my fingernails ruptured his skin. The fiend let out a gargled scream as Vettias was able to free himself enough to head butt the man several times. The attacker still was set to murderous purpose, however, and I bit his wrist out of desperation- causing him to scream out and drop his weapon. I then jumped on his back like a parasite, wrapping my legs tightly around his waist and choking him with my arms. My added weight, coupled with his inability to breath, caused the man to let go of Vettias and fall to the ground. His arms flailed wildly, trying to punch and pry me off him. His riotous thrashing came to a sudden end as Vettias buried a dagger into his heart- causing his body to become a lifeless mass on top of me. Vettias pulled the corpse off and extended a hand to pull me up. I declined, however, choosing to lie on the floor and pant for several minutes.

Vettias allowed me to recover as he inspected the rest of the apartment for any other clues. "Davos is not here, we have to assume Orontes has him. I don't recognize this man- one of Nikandros' underlings to be sure. You have one more minute and then we're leaving, understood?" He circled back over me and extended his hand to pull me up. The two of us exited the murderous scene at a brisk pace, heading towards the Silver Shield encampment.

"We're going to Hyllos. He's the only one that can hide us now. We have to assume Ox is dead. If Orontes has made his move, then he must know Antipater is close at hand."

As we approached the encampment, with their recognizable polished shields all in a row in from of their tents, Vettias quickly scribbled on a parchment, sealed it, and handed it to me. "Instruct the guards to courier this letter to Hyllos immediately. Show them the royal insignia as proof of your urgency. Go, quickly." I obeyed and continued on with Vettias to the prescribed meeting location where we took up seats and ordered a jug of wine to fit in with the rest of the patrons.

"It will not be safe to enter the palace from now on," I surmised, hoping to provoke Vettias to discuss our plans for Mara's safety.

"We'll operate out of the Silver Shield encampment for as long we can and take our leave of this place if the situation becomes too dangerous." His response did not inspire faith that Mara's wellbeing was at the forefront of his concerns. I now was put in the position to force the issue.

"And Mara? How will we get her out of here?"

"With great difficulty, if at all. I made her a promise to do all that I could to help her and my ability to do so was severely hampered by the Queen's actions and Orontes' attack on our interests. Remember, all of our personal concerns are subordinate to our mission. We serve a purpose greater than ourselves and I am bound to the sacred oath of the King's Hand."

My eagerness to reject any answer Vettias gave that did not have a plan to save Mara stirred rebellious thoughts regarding the fact that Mara and I had taken no such oath. What difference did it make whose family the new ruler came from if it meant a life of torment for her and a longing abandonment for me? I thought better than to voice these arguments lest I lose the support of the man whose approval I so closely relied upon.

"I knew when I chose her she would prove a skilled practitioner in manipulation. I did not realize the biggest victim of her charms would be the one who aided in bringing her to our cause in the first place," Vettias continued.

"I don't understand. Is it wrong to hold empathy for one that helps our cause? To hope for her escape from this place in accordance with our pledge to her?"

"Your position does not come from such a place. It is something deeper. You have become infatuated with her and believe you now love her. Your time with her in the harem was my gift to you but you must realize she is no *mere* girl either. She is not a helpless victim idly waiting for some man to save her. She is looking out for her own interests, and rightfully so. It was her plan to seduce you to gain a reliable champion for her wellbeing should we become unable to safely free her of bondage. The same as she has done with Hyllos. Knowing this, I allowed you to receive the fruits of her seduction, not realizing they would work so well and you would campaign on her behalf to the Queen of Macedon herself. She clearly chose her champion well."

Was it possible Vettias spoke the truth about Mara? A pit opened in my stomach at the chance her loving words spoken to me at such a time of intimacy would prove false- a ploy to influence my actions on her behalf. My contemplative silence provoked Vettias to continue.

"You do not have to wait long for my reasoning to ring true. If we risked all, and were successful in removing her from this place, she would leave us at the first opportunity she no longer needed our protection. That being said, I too wish her happiness and have every intention of keeping my word. Your outburst with the Queen, while foolish, may have provided her the path required for her escape and the man who travels at this very moment to meet us is the one who will be in the best position to secure it."

The thought of her permanently with the Queen's entourage back in Macedon, made possible by the actions of another man, was unsettling. But there was truth in Vettias' words and I would hold my tongue until her fate was known. I also decided that, no matter Mara's true feelings for me, I would ensure she was safe. These difficult reflections were interrupted by the arrival of Hyllos- looking unhappy with the two of us. He looked around the venue and briskly sat at our table.

"What took so long to make contact with me? The army dances on a dagger's edge and is ready to erupt in overt mutiny."

"Forgive our latency sir, events had precluded us from doing so. I have two issues to discuss with you. One involves our wellbeing, the other involves the girl's." Hyllos made a facial expression indicating his anger that we were in any way aware of his dealings with Mara. "Agents of the Queen's enemies have struck out at her interests last evening and the boy and I are no longer safe. We are here to place ourselves at your mercy and request you provide security for us within the Silver Shield encampment, away from inquiring eyes, until the summit's conclusion so we may continue working on behalf of the Queen's interests."

"And the girl?" Hyllos asked, apparently unconcerned with our plight.

"Yes, Mara. I rescued her from a life of sexual slavery and brought her here to further the cause of the Argeads with the promise I would do all I could to ensure her eventual release from bondage. I fear the actions of the Queen and her enemies have inhibited my ability to make good on our promise. The Queen has agreed to take her on in her retinue if we are unable to free her from the harem. My humble request is that you see this happen since the boy and I can no longer enter the palace safely."

"The girl is coming with me and will take up lodging within our baggage train."

"It appears you are in no need of our help with regards to Mara and I wish you the best with her. She will serve you well as she has done the Queen. I ask you to take into consideration when choosing whether to grant our first request that you would not have met such a fare beauty if not for the keen judgment of myself to bring her here in the first place. The Fates saw it fit for you to meet her and rescue her from a life of misery but they used me as the catalyst. Will you consider that?"

"There is a storage tent located in an area few have access to within our encampment. You two are not to leave it or speak to anyone for any reason, understood? I will bring you food and drink personally each day until we break camp- and then I do not want to see either of you again. Now follow me."

"You're benevolence is thoroughly appreciated. Please lead the way." Hyllos led us to an obscure side entrance through the Silver Shields encampment to the storage tents within their quartermaster bivouacs. Hyllos spoke to a supply officer who ushered us into a twenty-by-forty foot pavilion and showed us to an area boxed in on all sides by two carts and several large crates stacked on top of one another.

"You are to remain here. No one will have reason to come across you in this storage area. Food and drink will be brought to you. I am stationed directly outside if there is an issue. You are to see me first when you are to use the latrine ditch. Other than that, you are not to leave this tent."

"Very well, thank you," Vettias replied. "I do have one question, however."

"Yes?"

"Captain Hyllos has instructed us to depart upon the conclusion of the summit and we have every intention of doing so. Our mounts have become unavailable to us and we are in need of two new ones. We will of course reimburse you for their worth plus provide fair compensation for your effort in assisting us. Is that a transaction you are able to broker?"

"I'll see what I can do," was his terse response as Vettias and I settled in to our new surroundings for what looked to be a long time.

"It looks as though we were able to secure Mara's relative freedom after all- albeit as the property of a powerful captain within the Silver Shields. It's certainly an improvement from her current lot, however, don't you think?"

"Perhaps, until he grows tired of her and discards her like a piece of worn leather. She deserves better than that," I replied dejectedly.

"If your feelings truly do extend beyond lust for her than you should take comfort in her new circumstances. Hyllos can provide her more than you can and appears to have legitimate feelings for her as well. This was the best outcome. You will soon rid her from your mind and refocus on the effort at hand. I don't make this cold prediction out of antipathy; rather I speak as a forty-four year old man who has had his share of love and loss. I can tell you the intense nausea feeling will pass and you will be able to push her from your thoughts over time. I stand by my assessment that her feelings communicated to you were intended to influence you to act on her behalf- not out of sincere compassion. She chose you probably because she knew these ploys would not work on me."

I did not respond to his latest rant. Mostly because I did not know what to say or feel other than I wished nothing more than to hold Mara in my arms again. The next twenty four hours passed slowly as

Vettias and I sat in our boxed-in area of the storage tent. A meagre amount of food was brought to us twice daily and we were allowed to utilize the latrine ditch as necessary. Our quartermaster caretaker decided to take our bribe and secured us two mounts that were tied close to our tent. On several occasions I studied the peculiar machinations of Vettias, whose inner personality had difficulty remaining dormant after being marginalized to irrelevance by recent events. He paced back and forth, frequently talking to himself under his breath. This brooding spectacle was interesting for about an hour until sleep came to me. I woke up several times that night to take stock of my surroundings and ensure Vettias was still in our assigned quarters. We slept-in late that morning, ate our provided meagre breakfast and continued to sit and wait.

Father came to me during my morning bout of sleep and sat on a crate across from me. "She's got you now doesn't she?"

"What am I to do?" I asked, exasperated. "Shall I sit back and watch the woman I love be taken from me by someone who cares not for her? He'll eventually discard her for sure."

"All plausible assumptions. But, if your feelings are so strong for her you must do all you can to ensure she is looked after. The Silver Shield's baggage train may be her best chance for now, but nothing says you can't rescue her again shortly thereafter. I made the mistake of neglecting your mother and my children and I do not want to see you live with the same regret. I was not there for you to provide the guidance and advice all boys require from their fathers- but I am here now. If for nothing else, you saving Mara will allow me to know that while I did not do right by my own family, at least my existence spawned someone who was able to help another woman in need. That may just be enough to effect a positive situation for me in the afterlife."

"And now we have arrived at the crux of the matter. It is certainly true I have cherished this added time I have spent with you and would happily do it for the rest of your life with no expectation of contentment since I had lived irresponsibly. But I do ask you to consider the point that you have a chance to make my existence mean something greater than the continuous coveting of base pleasures and indolence."

I awoke after these words and lay in my makeshift cot for some time afterwards reflecting on what my father had told me. When the sun reached its highest point of the day, rustlings could begin to be heard within the Silver Shield encampment. Vettias and I looked out of an open seam of the tent to determine the cause of the sudden activity. Soldiers were making their way out of their bivouacs in the direction of the road running north and south. Seeing the confusion had occupied all soldiers around our tent, Vettias and I decided to make our way to the disturbance as well. After we walked out of the Silver Shield encampment Vettias asked a soldier what was transpiring.

"Antipater approaches at the head of a Macedonian army."

Vettias and I continued following the mass of people in order to gain a better vantage point. Dust could be seen being kicked up by the approaching monolith spanning many miles in the distance. Facing north along the road we could see a massive army snaking its way along the road towards Triparadeisus with Antipater and his bodyguards at its head. The army stretched many miles in the distance to the point where its end could not be determined. Vettias and I continued observing the army until it broke from the road and set up camp on the west side, opposite the palace compounds and encampments of the main army and the merchant tents. Several officers within the Seleucid group of onlookers began corralling the soldiers in order to restore order to the gaggle- sending them back to their units' bivouacs. Vettias and I hurriedly returned to the Silver Shields encampment and snuck into our holding area before our caretaker returned.

"She is going to have to be strong now. Damn her impatience and Orontes' treachery. I should be by her side. The sycophants surrounding her now know nothing of strategy. You be ready to leave here within a moment's notice, understand?" Vettias poked his head out of a seam in the tent and barked at our caretaker. "You there, tell Captain Hyllos I demand a meeting with him." Vettias' demeanour was uncharacteristically condescending to the man, as if he was attempting to find scraps of relevance through making our caretaker feel beneath us. Our caretaker was not one to be cowed by a stranger, even one as polished as Vettias. As a member of the

Silver Shields, he had seen too much to bend to the whims of two nobodies such as ourselves. "You there!" Vettias shouted more forcefully. "What I have to tell Captain Hyllos is of great importance to him. Don't be the reason he does not hear it in time to take necessary action." Vettias' rephrasing appeared to strike more of an accord with our caretaker who slowly walked over to a squire and sent him on his way to summon the Captain in question. After sending the boy on his way he looked at Vettias with an expression that sarcastically asked if he had any more orders to command.

"Even their quartermasters are arrogant pricks!" Vettias complained to me once he returned to our proscribed area of the storage tent. "Hyllos is our only ally capable of reaching the Queen at this time. I must inform him of the way in which to discreetly speak with her." My time spent with Vettias in the storage tent offered a window into the man's personality. He was not always the stoic, confident, decisive man I had known over the past months. He was susceptible to impatience, anxiety, and feelings of inferiority- all driven by his inability to control events around him that were crucial to the oath he had sworn. He continued pacing back and forth, replaying countless scenarios and angles in his mind and occasionally talking to himself. He seemed off-balance and unstable- an ominous sign given the serious situation we found ourselves in. I could not be counted on to further our goals in such a hostile environment without the valuable insight his years of experience could provide.

After several more minutes Hyllos entered the tent, looking perturbed by his summons as usual and sat on a crate while the two of us stood at attention. "What is the meaning of this summons?" he asked in a pompous tone.

"Sir, by now you are no doubt aware of Antipater's arrival at the head of an army from Macedon," Vettias began.

"Everyone knows this," Hyllos replied, annoyed.

"As such, it cannot be lost on you that all we have discussed, the very reason the Silver Shields shouted out publicly for Queen Adea, is at risk if Antipater is able to successfully advance his agenda. The Queen is strong but she is young and, at times, reckless. She requires the kind of counsel only someone like yourself can provide. Your position in this army allots you the ability to make a formal request for an audience; however, I wish to inform you of another, more subtle way to speak with her that will shield you from prying eyes in this time of intrigue and mistrust."

"Alright, get on with it," Hyllos commanded, still unimpressed. Vettias described to Hyllos that he should overtly enter the palace using his position to see Mara. Then use the staircase into the central gardens where her attendant would be waiting for him. As Vettias spoke, a realization came over me that I was looking at the man who would be taking my love. Mara couldn't possibly love us both, yet her detached description of Hyllos' affections conjured an image of her talking about me in the same light. All this was compounded by the fact this man was so far my superior I could not contemplate a reality where I could possibly be allowed to walk away with such a beauty. I also thought about how inconsequential my plight was when compared to the enormity of events transpiring around us.

"She must waste no time in combating his legitimacy. She must leverage his inability to immediately pay the army. She must hold a meeting with the commanders of the army today to ensure their men are ready for action at a moment's notice. She must also understand that she may lose in her bid for power and may need to escape. I can make arrangements for her to leave this place unmolested and bring her to the army of General Eumenes." Hyllos listened courteously to Vettias' pleadings and stood up when he had heard enough.

He stood up during a natural pause in Vettias' rant and moved towards the exit. "I will do what is in the best interests of the Silver Shields," was his curt reply. Vettias motioned to further make his case but, seeing the futility in it, bowed graciously and said no more. He watched helplessly as Hyllos departed.

"That son of a bitch is going to play both sides," Vettias announced in a defeated tone. "The fools! Antipater will see to it the Silver Shields are relegated to obscurity so they cannot pose such a threat to his designs in the future. I've had enough of this. There's nothing more we can do. We're leaving tonight."

Chapter 35

We spent the remainder of the day waiting for night to fall. Dinner was brought to us one hour before dusk, which we ate in silence. Vettias continually looked out the seam of the tent to determine patterns in our caretaker and the other soldiers around us. As dusk approached Vettias began discussing his plan of escape, how far we would ride on the first night, and the estimated time it would take to link back up with our army. During this discussion our caretaker entered our storage area and, upon confirming visual contact with us, waved in several armed soldiers with swords and short spears drawn. Vettias and I jumped up and drew our swords but found ourselves quickly surrounded by eight capable men.

"What is the meaning of this? We are here under the protection of Captain Hyllos himself!" Vettias announced in a defiant tone.

"It is under his orders we have been sent to ensure you continue to enjoy his hospitality," our caregiver replied sarcastically. "I recommend you relinquish your weapons and cooperate with my associates here. Apparently you two are in very high demand."

Vettias nodded at me and we both laid down our arms. The armed men approached us and tied our wrists behind our backs and sat us back down on our makeshift beds. As I was seated the thought of being tied to a chair undergoing worse punishment than what was given to Pirus now consumed all my thoughts. I immediately felt a deep sense of regret for participating in his torment. My breathing increased and I began having a panic attack. Our guards laughed at my lack of bearing until Vettias calmed my nerves with words of encouragement. We sat silently in detainment for several hours. As the time passed, our guards' numbers dwindled until only two men remained. Sleep eventually came over me as the futility of escape settled in. I was awoken two hours later to the image of Captain Hyllos nudging me.

"Wake up kid," was his cold instructions. I rose to find our guards had all vanished and Hyllos untying our restraints. His attention then focused towards Vettias.

"The Queen has lost the day. The army and the Silver Shields have sided with Antipater after much coin and land had been promised."

"I knew she couldn't win a bidding war with him, she-"

Vettias was cut off mid-sentence, "this is not a back and forth conversation. As far as anyone is concerned, right now you two are waiting to be transferred to General Seleucus' custody. Apparently you were requested by name as part of the agreement. I am only helping you because Mara forced me to swear an oath to her that I would free the two of you from certain death. You owe your lives to that woman. My advice is to mount your horses and don't look back. General Antigonus has been assigned General of Asia and will be ordered by Lord Regent Antipater to lead this combined army against General Eumenes. The royal family is now firmly under Antipater's control and will accompany him back to Macedon. A death sentence has been placed on General Eumenes as well as the both of you so if I see you again you will be killed. That is all, take comfort in the knowledge the girl will be looked after."

Vettias let out a defeated sigh as Hyllos exited. We hurriedly gathered our belongings and made ready to depart.

"We're walking our mounts out of here now. There is still a lot of ground to cover in enemy territory before we are free of this place. Hyllos was right, we owe Mara our lives. Had we not just been freed, Orontes would make sure we suffered before finally killing us." Vettias' words had a chilling effect on me as we began walking our mounts out of the Silver Shield's encampment. I lost my nerve at the mere thought of such torture just hours ago. I could only imagine my reaction when faced with imminent pain while strapped to a chair.

The latest developments spurred the entire army into a bevy of activity which allowed us to exit unchallenged. Upon departing the Silver Shields' encampment we entered the vast city of tents of the main army. Here too, most soldiers were moving at determined paces to and fro. Vettias and I were highly vigilant of our surroundings while avoiding eye contact with anyone lest we draw undue attention to ourselves. We walked with our mounts on either side of us while we remained in between them to screen ourselves from sight. The end of the main army encampment could now be seen and the main road lay tantalizingly close.

As we passed by the last rows of tents a hooded man, not looking in our direction, walked down a perpendicular row of tents several yards in front of us. Vettias had been looking in the other direction and I purposely made a loud cough to grab the hooded man's attention so he would show his face to us. As I did so time appeared to stand still. He slowly turned towards us while still guarding the majority of his face. The moonlight glanced just enough off his profile to reveal a large black mark on his face. The same mark of the quiet man from Tarsus. Seeing my eyes widen with recognition, he quickly closed the distance to us as I grabbed Vettias' shoulder to warn him. Vettias now saw the impending collision and unsheathed his sword. The man was still ten feet from us and began a throwing motion in our direction. As I unsheathed my sword I witnessed Vettias hunch over holding his torso. He fell to the ground while gasping out the name 'Nikandros'.

Finally comprehending what had happened, I turned and faced our assailant who continued his bolt towards us and wound his arm back ready to deliver another projectile. I quickly smacked my horse's hind quarter which sent him charging towards my assailant's direction- causing Nikandros to drop his throwing knife and unsheathe his sword. I now found myself face to face with the infamous villain. His black facial mark was readily visible in the moonlight. His eyes were pale blue and squinted with murderous intent. His hood had fallen around his neck, revealing blonde hair that had been clumped into thick locks in the style of northern barbarians. I thought him to be of Illyria as he raised his sword hand in preparation to strike.

He delivered a hard blow which I feebly blocked, causing me to move backwards several feet. I now fell back on my training as I blocked several more strikes with great difficulty. It became immediately apparent Nikandros' skill far surpassed mine with the short sword and he gained further advantage with each attack. I was fighting for my life and saw myself losing within the next few sword thrusts. I was continuing to back up and finally fell over a tent spike. Nikandros leered at me with a gap-filled smile in the full moon light as he raised his sword to deliver the final blow. The two of us locked eyes, when suddenly his eyes widened and his mouth opened. I looked down his torso to see a bloody sword blade sticking through his chest. It was violently removed and my mystery saviour grabbed Nikandros by the hair and slit his throat. His neck emptied onto my face and torso, covering me with a torrent of blood. Nikandros' body was thrown to the ground and the figure standing before me was none other than Davos.

My emotions quickly went from relief to horror at the thought of Vettias lying dead several feet away from me. I raced to him before Davos could say a word. I found him still breathing and in intense pain.

"There may be more coming, we've got to get out of here," I implored.

"I don't think I can walk," were the only words Vettias could muster without further wincing. I turned to Davos with eyes beseeching him to do something.

"We need to get him out of here! Come with us, there's nothing for you in this army now," I exclaimed.

"Wait here a moment," Davos instructed as he ran back into the guards' bivouac area. He returned with a red hot poker left in one of their fires. "Hold him down," Davos ordered as he removed the throwing knife and applied the hot metal to Vettias' puncture wound, eliciting a loud gasp. "Get him on the horse, you've got to travel south- it's too dangerous to ride past Antipater's army camped along the road to the north. Get him south to Heliopolis by sunrise and I'll meet you there when I can."

Davos and I carefully lifted Vettias up onto his horse, provoking several loud groans of pain. Fortunately he had enough strength to hold on to his mount and trot at a slow pace. Davos and I embraced and he reiterated to find shelter in Heliopolis by sunrise.

We began our journey south and every movement of Vettias' horse aggravated his freshly cauterized wound. We continued at that pace until an hour after sunrise, finally arriving at Heliopolis. I rented us a room and discreetly found a surgeon to attend to my mentor. The surgeon drained the built up bile and puss and properly dressed the injury. I sat with him throughout the morning and waited for Davos.

Sitting there alone, I sat back and reflected on the past several weeks and my time with the man who now lay unconscious before me. Vettias had certainly introduced me to an entire world of knowledge, danger, and adventure. For that, I would give my life to ensure he recovered. For now, I would wait for Davos. I also took an oath of my own that night- to the Gods and whoever else cared to hear me. I vowed to find Mara, no matter how long it took.

Chapter 36

I cared for Vettias without waver over the next few days. I provided him food, water, and attended his wound following the instructions the surgeon supplied me. Vettias had regained only intermittent consciousness during this time and it became clear he would be in no condition to ride anytime soon. My goal then was to procure some manner of wagon to be pulled by his horse, allowing him to lie in a comfortable position. This of course would hinder our speed of travel, meaning we would be seriously delayed in delivering our information, so decided I would wait for Davos to arrive and take the information to Eumenes myself. I would explain that Vettias was being transported by Davos, who had been an indispensable asset to us in Triparadeisus, and thus should be allowed to continue to serve on in our army. My hopes now rested on Davos being alive and able to meet us in Heliopolis. I decided to give him two more days. If he did not show by then I would begin the arduous journey to Eumenes' camp with Vettias myself.

Fortunately, Davos arrived the following day with two comrades who also managed to escape. I informed him of my intentions and instructed him to bring Vettias to our encampment where he would be provided a means to continue his work and given protection from Antigonus' forces. Davos informed me the Kings would accompany Antigonus north in his task to destroy Eumenes, while Antipater's son Cassander was made Antigonus' Chilarch, or deputy commander, as a check on any grander aspirations. The alliance was cemented through marriage. Antipater would betroth his now widowed daughter Phila, wife of the slain Craterus, to Antigonus' young upstart son, Demetrius, whom he was grooming as a successor to an eventual Antigonid dynasty. Neither spouse was particularly pleased with the arrangement but this was the price for some semblance of peace in the Empire- no matter how fleeting. Davos also informed me the Silver Shields were ordered to the ancient Achaemenid capitals of Persepolis and Susa to escort the vast contents of their treasuries to points back west. They were chosen for this labourious task no doubt to keep them from making trouble for the next several months. The thought of Mara travelling almost two thousand miles away from me produced a noticeable grimace on my face that Davos surely took note of.

Davos and his companions agreed to deliver the wounded Vettias to General Eumenes' army and I readied for my departure. I had a six hundred mile solitary journey ahead of me and I dispersed the majority of our remaining funds to Davos for incidentals needed while transporting the patient. With what coin remained, I readied my horse, thanked Davos for saving my life, bid my mentor farewell, and departed north towards Cappadocia.

*

Spending long days on the road allowed my imagination ample time to travel back to my home in Ilandra to the adoring embrace of my family and friends. Had enough time passed for me to return without my previous transgressions spoiling my fictional moment of triumph? What was the theme of the totality of my time in the army thus far? Was it something that they could be proud of? Was I proud of it? Would Argos and Leandros think it noble? Argos once told me it would be a shame to fight other Greeks on territory previously conquered by Alexander. But I believed we were fighting on behalf of Alexander against those who would usurp his great victories for their own interests. If that was the narrative, I certainly had much to be proud of- for I had openly fought and shed blood in defeat of these factions; in addition to working within the shadows to steer events in the Argead's favour. Alexander's speech in India to The Hand, as related to me by Vettias, rang true in that someone who is able to affect the course of an enemy army has done more for his cause then his army's most valiant warrior.

Despite our failure in Triparadeisus, Vettias and I were successful in sowing discontent between the factions of our enemies- albeit at the expense of a teenage girl. My instincts assured me she would again take her chance to rise to prominence in the near future and I did not envy those who tried to control her.

311

I also thought of Mara during much of this time. The thought of her believing Vettias and I had left her, while viewing Hyllos as her saviour, made me sick. But was it not true? I felt my life would not be complete without someday telling her that I did all I could to keep our promise and leaving with Hyllos was the best solution we could muster at the time. Vettias' consolation was correct, however, in that she was much better off in Hyllos' baggage train and I hoped she could keep his attentions long enough for me to find her. But if she believed Vettias and me to have left her, would she even be happy to see me? What if she did eventually develop feelings for her false saviour? What if Vettias was right and she only used me to further her own ends? I determined I did not care the answers to these questions. I would seek her out and if she chose to reject the life I could provide- so be it.

I refrained from visiting brothels for the first two weeks of my journey despite still having enough money to do so. My celibacy was an extension of the decision Vettias and I made to refrain from such pleasures while travelling with Mara. Since my time alone with her in the palace, I felt she was mine and began to view any thought of another woman as an affront to my new found love.

As I neared the boundaries of Cappadocia I found that I had out rode news of Triparadeisus and was now a solitary light of knowledge travelling through enemy territory while harbouring precious intelligence. I reflected on all that had occurred since my departure from Ilandra almost a year ago. Agathon and Drakon took a weak clump of shit and sculpted my nerve and body into hardened rock. Vettias had molded me from a know-nothing boy into a confident young man capable of manipulation, guile, and stealth. These skills and experiences, coupled with my prolonged absence from my Lochos, would allow my character to be reborn into a poised and capable man in the eyes of those who would now come to know me. I started holding myself in higher esteem in relation to strangers I met along my journey and began to comprehend the deep pool of self-assurance, filled by privileged knowledge, which Vettias frequently drew from. While I found I still retained my inner insecurities, I was pleased to see them remain at bay when interacting with those I now felt my subordinate.

312

I began eliciting the army's precise location from prostitutes and fellow taverners during my evenings to better adjust my route and ensure I arrived at our encampment as soon as possible. After about twenty days of hard riding I saw the familiar bivouacs of my army in the distance along the Royal Road. Excitement boiled up in me at the thought of seeing my Lochos mates again. Stephanos' image came across my mind's eye, his face eagerly awaiting my return. This happy forecast suddenly brought feelings of guilt for having become so close to another in the same way I had once enjoyed with Nearchus. I began feeling nervous for my impending meeting with General Eumenes, and started rehearsing how I would present myself to my army's leadership. I was still nobody in their eyes and I would need to draw upon all Vettias had instructed me to make a confident first impression.

I neared the encampment's entrance and approached the four guards. "I am Andrikos, phalangite in the Phalanx of General Eumenes, serving under Lochagos Croesus, as part of the Pydna Syntagma led by Commander Lykos, subordinate to Strategos Androkles. I have returned from a mission assigned to me by General Eumenes' Battle Staff and have pressing intelligence that must be communicated to our leadership immediately."

I delivered my address in a confident tone and maintained eye contact throughout. Having passed this first test, one of the guards escorted me to the headquarters bivouac. My escort conferred with the leadership's bodyguard contingent who took custody of me and walked me into our army's headquarters pavilion. I was ordered to wait just inside the entrance while the bodyguard deferentially whispered to one of Eumenes' staff officers that I had arrived. I stood awkwardly but confidently while awaiting my summons and took stock of my surroundings. I estimated the army had been in this location for several days since the encampment was fully unpacked and the pavilion was decorated with Persian rugs, marble busts, ornate chairs, couches and sweet smelling incense. The majority of the battle staff huddled around a massive oak table with a large map unrolled on it. Several attendants stood stoically along the inner perimeter of the tent- ready to execute any command barked at them.

I was snapped out of my scrutiny by the guard who returned and brought me before the battle staff. I stood at attention while the other men made themselves comfortable to hear the day's latest news. Sitting amongst them in a commanding oak chair was General Eumenes. He was slight in stature with handsome facial features that were beginning to wane through high levels of stress and hard campaigning. His hair was beginning to thin and was prematurely grey. He wore armour similar to that of the Macedonian Companion Cavalry and was flanked on one side by Apollonides, Commander of his Cappadocian Cavalry, and his confidant and fellow countryman Hieronymus on the other.

Apollonides provided a powerful military weapon and Hieronymus was the only man Eumenes could trust in a crowd of Macedonian rivals. Eumenes' appearance was meticulous, without one strap out of place or one area of brass unpolished. His eyes were very alert and his manner was of someone who took a keen interest in every minor detail around them. His mind was totally engaged in the matter at hand and struck me as someone who cut no corners. These traits aligned with what was needed of a Royal Secretary- as well as a competent leader who had already defeated General Craterus.

I stood at attention in front of these impressive men and recalled the time I stood awkwardly in front of Ganymedes. So much had changed since then and I ensured to quickly take command of the situation. "Pardon the interruption sir, I am Andrikos, Phalangite serving under Lochagos Croesus, as part of the Pydna Syntagma led by Commander Lykos, subordinate to Strategos Androkles. I was selected by Vettias, officer within your Battle Staff, to accompany him to the summit at Triparadeisus. I bring urgent news of this event."

"Phalangite Andrikos," Eumenes began. "Where is Vettias?"

"He was severely injured during our mission and is being transported here by those who have supported us along the way. I rode ahead to ensure you received the information we uncovered at the earliest opportunity. Sir, if you will allow me, I am prepared to divulge the entirety of our mission so you may understand all that has transpired."

Eumenes took a deep breath and ordered everyone to depart the headquarters tent with the exception of Hieronymus. Once we were alone he looked at me with a smile, "None of them are aware of our little organization. If you travelled with Vettias you must have some story to tell. How is he? What happened? Speak, boy."

"He was stabbed with a throwing knife sir- an operative of Orontes, who is now in the employ of Cassander. They have arrived at common cause in eradicating the Argead lineage."

"Orontes? Alive? Working with the son of Antipater against the blood? You do have a story to tell. Spare me no detail and start from the beginning."

I began with our journey to Triparadeisus, explaining Vettias' tutelage and ensuring I communicated the importance of Mara. Eumenes was heartened to hear Ox had survived Egypt and saddened by news of his supposed demise in Triparadeisus. The revelation of Orontes and Cassander gave him pause in the same manner it did Vettias. My disclosure of Nikandros operating within his ranks prior to our departure angered him. He took the news of his assigned executioner, Antigonus, travelling north with the Kings, as well as could be expected and I could see the strategic machinations already turning in his mind even before I had finished retelling my account.

At my conclusion, Eumenes congratulated me on my service and instructed me to keep the remaining operational funds for myself while approving an additional bonus to be paid from the army's treasury. When asked if I had any requests to make, two immediately jumped to mind. First, I ensured to impart to him the importance of Davos' role in Triparadeisus and requested he be allowed to take the oath of The Hand and continue his work as a member of our army. Second, I requested the approval to seek out Mara should our army come into contact with the Silver Shields. Lastly, I asked the general for permission to serve with my Lochos again, at least during the coming battle with Antigonus' army. Eumenes was quick to grant my first two requests but was hesitant to grant me leave back into the Phalanx for he wanted to continue utilizing me as one of his operatives. My respectful reply was that he would be gaining an operative of even greater skill with the arrival of Davos and once we defeated Antigonus I would take the oath with a healthy Vettias in attendance. Eumenes begrudgingly agreed to my last demand on a temporary basis and dismissed me back to my Lochos.

"You are not to discuss any of this with anyone other than myself, is that understood? It goes without saying the existence of The King's Hand will remain a secret; however, I am also ordering you to remain silent about Antigonus' approach. The army will be informed of our coming struggle when I deem it necessary."

After delivering my mount to the quartermaster, I made haste to return triumphantly to my Lochos after a long absence. All weight had been removed from my legs and I approached as if I was walking on air. Rather than rushing in to seek out Stephanos, however, I controlled myself enough to report to Lochagos Croesus before finding my friend. I began preparing in my mind how I would approach Croesus and announce my return. Having settled on the right words and posture to assume, I entered our Syntagma bivouac and eagerly approached our Lochos' file of tents. Fears lingered about my mates resenting my absence but were allayed by the fact there were no major battles fought since my departure. If pushed on this issue, I could make the case that it was I who had put himself in harm's way while the rest of the army sat and waited for news from the south. I had no intentions of making such an antagonistic claim without being thoroughly provoked, however.

Croesus was speaking with Second Officer Gelon when I approached and stood at attention waiting to be recognized. Gelon spotted me first and pointed Croesus in my direction with an amused smile.

"Look who decides we are worthy enough to be graced with his presence" Croesus announced irritably.

"Sir, phalangite Andrikos reporting as ordered upon completion of my task assigned by the Battle Staff."

"Yes, yes, your special task. And did you anger those on the Battle Staff? Why have they seen it fit to release you back into the Phalanx with us lowly peasants as opposed to the headquarters tents of our fearless leaders?"

"I chose to return to my Lochos as opposed to accepting the offer to continue working for the battle staff at this time. I cannot explain all that led me to this decision but, suffice it to say, the coming weeks and months will be difficult and I wish to confront them with my Lochos mates. It was neither my wish nor my order to be separated from this Lochos and I intend to take my place back within it if you'll allow me."

Croesus was noticeably impressed with my reply and a mild look of respect passed across his face. He looked at Gelon who shared the Lochagos' look of surprised satisfaction and gave a slight nod. "Alright phalangite Andrikos, report to the quartermaster and draw your basic issuance of weapons and equipment. Erect your tent at the end of our file. Welcome back."

I could not hide the smile which forced its way through my best efforts to maintain a stoic façade- ruining my near perfect interaction with Croesus- a man I held in high regard. I raced through the tent city towards the quartermaster issuance pavilion and traversed the familiar stations, picking up all required weapons and equipment, before making my way back to my file. As I turned to leave I ran into an old friend. I spotted Rhexenor speaking with a colleague off to my right. I approached my old friend and startled him in mid-sentence.

"Andrikos!" Rhexenor exclaimed. "Where have you been?"

"If you are finished with your business here I wish to speak to you in private. I will tell you of all that has transpired."

"Of course, of course," Rhexenor replied, motioning his colleague to depart. "Come to my tent, it is nearby."

I followed Rhexenor through the winding maze of storage pavilions, holding areas, prisons, and personal tents of the quartermaster bivouac until we arrived at his quarters. His tent was measurably larger than the average phalangite and it was clear he had benefited from his time in the quartermaster corps. He had a quality Persian rug on the ground, two intricately carved wooden chairs with plush cushions, and an impressive couch. He had a bigger baggage train than those who fought to secure it without lifting a weapon.

"You clearly have been doing well my friend. What army did you vanquish to acquire such impressive booty?" I asked sarcastically.

"You should see the women I have access to," he responded with a smile. "Just let me know and I'll be sure to procure one for you."

"Yes, I may call on you for such a service in the future. In fact, it is precisely your abilities in these matters that I wish to speak with you. I have been granted a sum of money from the army's treasury and wish to have someone I trust ensure it is transferred to my account and begin the process for setting up a baggage train.

"Of course!" Rhexenor exclaimed, jumping at the chance to help a fellow recruit who had actually seen combat. "Don't worry, I will make all arrangements. This is what I do. Processing a sum of money is much easier than actual items of value. I once had someone try and requisition a twenty foot long banquet table. You remember your promise to me, however; you'll get me into the contingent that eliminates barbarian prisoners in the future, right?"

"Yes my friend, I will do all I can."

Having taken my leave from Rhexenor after a warm embrace, I hurried in the direction of my Lochos file to reunite with Stephanos. Entering my unit's area, I saw him speaking to a small group of Lochos mates- leading the conversation as if holding court. I came up behind him and tapped him on the head.

"You still finding people willing to listen to your lies?" I stated loud enough to elicit laughter from those seated around him. Recognizing my voice he stood up, turned around and knocked me over, forcing me to drop all of my issued equipment and fall to the ground. He stood over me smiling broadly while pulling me up to my feet and embracing me.

"Look who returns to tell tales of Persian palaces and eastern women!" Stephanos exclaimed to the cheering of those assembled. "After you get set up I expect you to speak to your Lochos mates about your travels and adventures," Stephanos proclaimed while accompanying me to the end of our tent file to assist me setting up my gear.

Chapter 37

I happily reintegrated into the familiar routines of Phalanx life over the next few days. General Eumenes did not address the army regarding our outlaw status so I refrained from speaking to my Lochos mates about my adventures- pleading my inability to do so under direct order from Eumenes himself. This only whetted their appetite and Stephanos begrudgingly accepted my silence but commanded me to reveal all there was once I was allowed to do so.

After three weeks I was summoned to the command tent by a squire and once again escorted into the presence of our army's leadership. Only two men stood before me, however, Eumenes and, to my amazement, Vettias- looking to be in good health and spirits. He smiled broadly at my arrival and motioned me to come forth and be embraced.

"How have you arrived here so soon? Your wounds, are they..? I wanted to wait with you but..."

"You did just as you should have and I have told General Eumenes as much," Vettias assured. "Our leader tells me you have chosen to renounce the life I've provided for you and return to your lowly position as a phalangite? You never cease to spurn my lessons," he joked. "To answer your question, the first two weeks of our journey were a huge pain in the ass. Davos earned his weight in gold pulling my broke dick around Syria in some beggar's cart. Luckily my wound healed to the point where I was able to once again ride. We pushed our mounts to their breaking points for the next two weeks and made it here last evening."

"I jest about your noble decision to remain with your mates but I am serious about The Hand needing young, capable operatives such as yourself. You and Davos have proven yourselves and have been afforded the opportunity to take the oath of The Hand to become an official guardian of the house of the Argeads".

"And the coming battle?"

"You will be allowed to take your place within your file once battle is joined. Our army is marching west tomorrow to the city of

Sardis. There we will request an audience with Cleopatra, sister of Alexander. If Antipater and Antigonus have usurped the Kings, we will bring Alexander's mother and sister on our side. The army will be informed about our outlaw status and coming fight with Antigonus this evening. You will be allowed to remain with your mates during our march. Return to the command tent after General Eumenes addresses the army; you will take the oath then."

"Yes sir," I replied and departed to my Lochos. During my walk, I was overjoyed that Vettias was back and healthy. I was also heartened that two men whom I held in the highest regard were actively recruiting me to join an organization, founded by Alexander himself, whose goal was no less than the protection of Alexander's rightful heirs. My thoughts turned to whether I still wanted to join such a group. If the last three months were anything like what my life was to become, I doubted whether my constitution could withstand such pressure. Would I be the one flaying enemies of the Argeads or sawing off fingers? Would I find myself one day tied to a chair enduring unspeakable tortures? A violent death was more than a possibility for me in the Lochos to be sure, but at least I enjoyed the universal bonds of my brothers-in-arms. In the end, my Achilles' heel, the need for older male guidance and empathy, won my inner dialogue and I decided I would be the man Vettias and Eumenes wanted me to be. My life would have a cause greater than battlefield glory or the pursuit of wealth. I would serve the men I looked up to and whose affections I sought. Tonight, my life would have a greater meaning.

Upon returning to my bivouac Stephanos grabbed me and brought me into his small tent. "Alright you little shit," he accosted me with a smile. "I want to know what is going on."

I looked at my most trusted friend, returning his grin and took a seat on his flimsy bedroll. Knowing General Eumenes would be addressing the army tonight I ordered Stephanos to take a vow of silence and motioned him to move in closer so I could speak at a low decibel. I avoided discussing anything regarding The Hand and ensured my narrative conveyed my actions were done on behalf of our army. I omitted details involving Mara, Orontes, and our dirty business with Pirus and Shifty. I did speak about my audience with

Queen Adea, our experience with the Silver Shields, Antipater's arrival, our escape, and Antognus' march north. I also included my time at the Fair Peach, which almost caused my dear friend to faint with envy. Our time in Stephanos' tent reminded me of my family rapt on every word of Leandros except I could not tell my friend all that had transpired- which made me wonder what sordid details my older cousin omitted during his recitation. I concluded my tale with my triumphant return to Eumenes' command tent and reciting all that had occurred to our general.

Despite having to leave out large segments of my story, Stephanos was still exuberant for me and my good fortune for experiencing such adventures and returning unscathed. "But I still don't understand why you were chosen for such an important task. Surely others are more qualified to do such actions," Stephanos asked without malice.

"It is *because* I knew nothing that I was chosen. The Fates saw to it that I met my mentor in the surgeon's tent on two occasions, one of which was during your brief infirmity. It could have easily been you had you broken your arm back when Drakon was drilling us mercilessly. In fact, there were many times during my absence that I thought you would have been a better choice."

"Don't belittle yourself. A lot of good I would have been with a rolled ankle."

"I thank you friend, and again, I implore you to honour your vow of silence. General Eumenes will address the army tonight and inform us Antigonus One Eye has been made General of Asia and given custody of the Kings. He marches as we speak towards Cappadocia to face this army for supreme control of Asia."

Stephanos appeared pleased we would face our enemies in the field again. The unbelievable defeat of Craterus by our army had created a strong sense of invincibility among the phalangites. If we could defeat an army led by the most respected and capable general to survive Alexander, surely we could defeat a force led by a man in his late sixties who remained in Anatolia throughout the great conquest of Asia. Stephanos embraced me and we departed his tent to perform our menial tasks before being called to formation.

After two more hours the horns could be heard calling the army to formation. The Strategos' motioned to their Syntagma Commanders, who in turn barked at their Ouragos', who then yelled at their Lochagos', who screamed at us to take their proper places in formation. I had missed the sense of security induced by the crush of my mates standing shoulder to shoulder in formation. Before we had all settled I called to Bacchylides and Spear, whom I caught glimpses of several files down from ours. They responded with elated smiles and mouthed words informing me we would catch up later tonight. A hush now came over the assembled army as General Eumenes approached. My absence from the Lochos pushed my position within it towards the back, precluding me from seeing Eumenes and having to rely on heralders repeating his words to hear his address.

"Men," Eumenes began with a loud and confident voice. "Who among you doubts that we fight for the true Kings of Macedon?" The army remained silent at the rhetorical question. "Who among you would accept our cause unjust because a usurper deems it so? Who among you can claim I do not ensure my men prosper under my leadership? Who among you believes me illegitimate to lead you because I am not of Macedon? Does that fact not make me the most trustworthy to protect the Kings' interests? I have no illusions about where my future lies. I do not seek to be King. I do not seek a dynasty. My sole purpose is to serve the Argead line and ensure their rightful place as Macedon's monarchs sitting on the throne of the Empire Alexander conquered. We find ourselves in the unpleasant situation of fighting those we called brother just one year ago. Make no mistake; upon the defeat of their leaders we will call them brother again."

"Men, you are all aware of Lord Regent Perdiccas' loss in Egypt. The rightful Argead Regent was murdered under treachery by the very men whom our former brothers are now being led. I have served the Argead cause since the time of Philip II. I have been at the side of Alexander for every battle, every siege, every march, and every victory from Ionia to India. As one of his seven most trusted bodyguards, I was in the room the moment our God King died. I wept for him on his deathbed. I personally witnessed Alexander give

Perdiccas the Argead signet ring. And this is the man our enemies murdered for their own purposes? It is these usurpers that now condemn this army. It is the same men who call us outlaws. I ask you again, do these accusations, made by these men, deem us villains?" As Eumenes posed this last question the army cried out in disgust for the new regime.

"I ask these questions not to bolster my own sense of self but to instill in you the confidence required to face down the false accusations levied on this noble army. As we speak, these usurpers have sent an army north from Syria to face us in open contest. We defeated the army of the fiend Neoptolemus. We bested the army of Alexander's most respected general, Craterus. And what will you say when an army, led by a decrepit seventy year old who did not accompany us through Asia, decrees your cause is unjust, illegitimate, unlawful?"

The army now let out a thunderous roar of defiance to our approaching adversaries. Eumenes had won the army for now. It remained to be seen how loyal the Macedonians would be to the Cardian once the infamous Antigonus One Eye arrived at the head of a twenty-five thousand man Macedonian army with the two Kings in tow.

"The army that truly fights for the Kings will not sit idly by and wait for the usurpers to decide when and where we are to do battle, however. We will travel west to Sardis to enlist the support of Alexander's sister, Cleopatra and, by extension, Alexander's mother Olympias. Lastly, men, know that your commander does not allow his army to be the helpless victim of external events. As I speak to you now, measures have been put in place that will ensure Alexander's heirs assume the throne of the empire. You have done all that has ever been asked of you, and more. I could not be prouder of each of you. Sleep well tonight, for we depart at first light."

Despite ending on a less inspired note, the army was ready to follow Eumenes to Sardis and face Antigonus in open battle. Eumenes departed and we were dismissed back to our bivouacs. Spear and Bacchylides were waiting for me at my tent and the three of us embraced with Stephanos smiling widely in the background.

"I thought your Lochos succeeded in getting rid of your worthless ass," Bacchylides joked. "Stephanos has been talking about some important mission you've been on for the past three months. I figured you just ran away because you couldn't hack it."

"You look a little weak; can you even handle a sarissa anymore?" Spear added.

"Come find out," I replied while gently pushing my more intimidating companion. "Too bad we are to march tomorrow. When we get to Sardis we'll be sure to do some proper celebrating of my triumphant return."

"This one must tell you of the women he's had in the east," Stephanos interjected merrily.

"Oh you better, loverboy," Bacchylides commanded. My two comrades departed towards their file's bivouac and I made my way towards the command pavilion. Guards escorted me to a small guarded tent where Eumenes, Vettias and Davos were waiting for me. Davos and I embraced warmly and were instructed to kneel. Two hooded diviners, dressed in white linen robes with blue and gold embroidering, came forward burning incense in front of Alexander's royal diadem and sceptre.

"Davos of Thrace, Andrikos of Ionia, do you come here of your own free will?" Eumenes asked in a serious tone.

"Yes sir," Davos and I replied in unison.

"Do you come to take the oath of the King's Hand, the Argead Protectors?"

"Yes sir."

Eumenes motioned the diviners to begin the ritual.

"His Excellency, Alexander III of Macedon, from the house of Argead, descendant of Herakles and Zeus Ammon; Freer of peoples, Slayer of tyrants, Builder of cities, wrote these words in his own hand, guided by the instruction of the Gods, two years ago along the Indus River. Those who have taken this oath before you have sworn their lives in protection of Alexander's heirs. Many of whom have made that ultimate sacrifice."

"Davos of Thrace, Andrikos of Ionia, do you hereby swear to the Gods, in the company of those assembled, and in the presence of the diadem and sceptre of Alexander, that the members of the Argead house are the true and rightful heirs to the Macedonian Empire?"

"I do," Davos and I answered.

"Do you hereby swear to the Gods, in the company of those assembled, and in the presence of the diadem and sceptre of Alexander, to sacrifice your lives in service and preservation of this stated belief?"

"I do."

"Do you hereby swear to the Gods, in the company of those assembled, and in the presence of the diadem and sceptre of Alexander, to faithfully serve as a member of the King's Hand?

"I do."

"Do you hereby swear to the Gods, in the company of those assembled, and in the presence of the diadem and sceptre of Alexander, to obey all orders from your superiors without question; to assume The King's Hand's objectives as your own; and to never divulge the existence or goals of The King's Hand to anyone who has not taken the oath under punishment of death?"

"I do."

"Then rise, Davos of Thrace and Andrikos of Ionia, as official and recognized members of the King's Hand."

Before Mara I had never took anything seriously in my life. I had no great piety or reverence towards the Gods. I did not believe in anything, save for the love of my family, which could stir me to action or to accomplish great feats. I always envied men who believed in something that compelled them to subordinate their own self interests. Responsible men such as Nearchus and Argos; driven men such as Vettias and Stephanos. As I affirmed the words of the oath I experienced a feeling of exhilaration come over me. I internalized every word and vowed to live by the oath I had sworn. When instructed to rise I felt as though I was now a man of worth. This was the culmination of my coming of age since leaving Ilandra, since joining the army, since facing men in combat, since my time with Vettias, since meeting Mara. I would now live my life with this knowledge being at the forefront- guiding my actions and bolstering my confidence at all times. I felt compelled to run and speak with all that had been a part of my life in the past- to show them the man I had become and would now be.

Davos remained stoic as usual- I wondered what, if anything, could bring this man to emotion. My eyes met with Vettias who stood smiling proudly at me and motioned me over to embrace. "Congratulations kid, you made it. There's a good deal more to do and I expect much from you. Come to my quarters afterwards."

"Yes sir."

After being congratulated by General Eumenes and embracing Davos, I followed Vettias to his quarters. He poured two cups of uncut wine and we drank in comfortable silence for several minutes. "We're going to start seeing infiltration in the coming days and weeks. There are probably operatives of Orontes in our midst as we speak, so you and Davos will start working for me in the same manner as if we were in Triparadeisus. Just because we are safely out of there does not mean you can't wake up in your tent staring up at an assassin's blade. I still have a few operatives within this army but the majority of my people travelled with Perdiccas and most have not returned. You and Davos will work in coordination as needed but will be compartmented from the rest of The Hand until events necessitate otherwise. I will allow you to participate in the coming battle with Antigonus, despite my better judgment, so don't do anything stupid- like dying. We'll revisit the issue of your position within the army after that time- it may make sense for you to remain within your Lochos but I will make that determination later."

"This business with Cleopatra is a gamble and smacks of desperation on the part of Eumenes. I watched him try to engineer a marriage between the Princess and Perdiccas almost two years ago and it ended in a debacle. The female members of the Argead family are a difficult bunch to say the least. Alexander's mother was a Princess from Epirus when she married Philip II. It is the peculiar tradition of Epirotes that the surviving woman of a slain man becomes head of the house until the maturation of her first born son. Olympias was tantalizingly close to having a major role within the Macedonian Court but Alexander was already sixteen years old at the time of Philip's assassination. That explains why she has been so prevalent in Macedonian affairs as mother of the King and, now, as Dowager to Alexander IV. This Cleopatra, being the widow of her husband, King Alexander I of Epirus, tasted this rare instance of female leadership for several years as Regent of that land. Her decisions will still be influenced by the looming presence of Antipater in Cappadocia traveling back to Macedon, however."

"Our biggest concern between now and the coming battle will be General Eumenes' ability to hold the loyalty of the Macedonian regulars. At this point, he has held their wavering loyalty through military victory and generous allotments of land and acquired wealth. Ironically, his very success in these matters, especially against Craterus, has fostered resentment among many Macedonian officers within the army. They are weary of fighting for a non-Macedonian and, paradoxically, the more success he has against their kinsmen, the more resentment they hold. So, in addition to countering infiltration from enemy operatives, you are going to be keeping an ear out for surreptitious rumblings from the Phalanx. Any sedition rising to the level of potential desertion or treachery must immediately be reported and their leaders identified."

"I am to be a rat against my own phalangites?" I asked, somewhat surprised by Vettias' instructions.

"You are to support The Hand in uncovering and rooting out enemies of this army- the rightful protector of the Kings," Vettias responded forcefully. "Is Antipater not a Macedonian? Antigonus? Orontes? These men will stop at nothing to eliminate this army and the Argeads to further their own goals. We stand as the last bastion of Alexander's legacy. This army is the only force between these usurpers and the total destruction of the Argead House. Now, let us discuss how we are to meet. You will inform your Lochagos to designate you as your Lochos' liaison to the quartermaster."

"I don't inform Croesus of much," I interjected sarcastically. "I ask permission."

"Discreetly tell him it is an order from me and if there is an issue let me know and I will speak to him."

"I may know someone that can assist in providing a secure meeting location," I replied, eager to utilize Rhexenor, my one useful connection within the army.

"That may be of use down the road," Vettias replied. "For now, meet me at the surgeon's tent at dusk three marches from today, understood?" I nodded and returned to my tent to prepare for the morning's march. If I thought I had begun to understand the convoluted world Vettias had thrust me into since Triparadeisus, our discussion that night proved otherwise- more Argeads, more treachery, more battles to worry about.

Chapter 38

Our march the following morning began promptly at daybreak. It felt good to be with my mates again, although my thighs and calves definitely suffered from lack of exercise. Despite this inconvenience, our pace was swift yet manageable- allowing my mind to wander. The fact we were marching west to Sardis, a city teasingly close to Ilandra, brought an excited gait to the march. The realization that, with each step, I was travelling farther from Mara dampened my enthusiasm, however. Vettias' instructions to report members of the Phalanx on charges of sedition also lingered. My first official orders were unsettling but the oath I swore and the overall goals of The Hand allowed me to rationalize this potentially disloyal act. These inner struggles occupied my thoughts for the first few days of the march. Nights were spent as they had been before my departure: preparing dinner, tending to equipment, and sitting around fires speaking with my mates. Our Lochos had absorbed two Macedonian regulars from the defeated army of Neoptolemus but, thus far, they seemed content. The fact we were to face an army in control of the Macedonian Kings did not sit well with us- even non-Macedonians, but most believed our cause was just.

Dusk arrived on the third day and I began my walk to the surgeon's tent to meet with Vettias. Croesus had no issue assigning me to our Lochos' quartermaster detail and none of my mates suspected anything of it. I had little to report to Vettias other than my mates' concerns combating the Kings' army and he advised I begin utilizing my contacts within other Lochos' to expand my awareness of the Phalanx's sentiment. He also allowed me to employ Rhexenor's ability to find us a secure area within the quartermaster bivouacs to use for all meetings going forward. The next two weeks passed in much the same manner, and I had fully settled back into the routines army life- with the notable exception of my new duties as a member of The King's Hand.

On the fifteenth day of the march along the Royal Road, our army arrived at the Satrapal capital of Sardis. We established an encampment just outside the city limits in full view of the Satrapal Palace. General Eumenes had sent runners ahead to alert Cleopatra of our arrival and he ensured everyone had thoroughly polished their armour the night before. Our trumpets blared, our banners were proudly raised, and the army executed several impressive manoeuvres involving complex movements within site of the palace. General Eumenes remained at the head of our army in full battle regalia atop an impressive mount with his top cavalry and infantry generals to complete the regal pomp and circumstance.

Upon conclusion of our prominent display, all Ouragos' and Lochagos' ensured each Syntagma bivouac was perfectly aligned and all individual tents were assembled correctly. General Eumenes proceeded into the city on horseback at the head of a small delegation of his inner circle to include Apollonides and Hieronymus. Our army held a great celebration that evening in honour of Alexander's sibling- complete with wine, women, and meat. Stephanos assembled Rhexenor, Spear, Dion, Bacchylidus, and myself to enjoy our own private celebration.

Our low status in the army ensured we did not have first pick of any of our celebratory offerings and Stephanos proposed slipping out of the encampment to raise a cup and bed a 'proper woman' at our old establishment in the city where Stephanos and I first met. All of us agreed with the idea but Rhexenor was the only one in position to ensure the plan's success due to his many contacts accumulated over the past year. We eagerly followed our connected comrade through the quartermaster bivouacs and out a back alley unseen by our fellow revellers.

The five of us quickly jogged the short distance between our encampment and the city gate, grinning with excitement the whole way. Once we entered Sardis we casually made our way towards the familiar neighbourhood. An air of delight hung over our merry band as stories were told, insults levied, and exaggerated tales of glory recalled. The city was bustling with the arrival of our army and the streets were swelled with all manner of people looking to benefit from the presence of thousands of potential buyers of their wares. Despite our nondescript clothing, we were constantly being haggled and hassled by beggars and merchant alike as we giddily waded through the sea of people.

We arrived at our destination and found the establishment filled to capacity, precluding us from sitting at a table. We shouldered our way through the patrons and occupied a portion of the bar. We passed several hours drinking wine and raising a cup to each other's inflated stories. I fended off several questions about the particulars of my absence and succeeded in describing it in such a way as to lose the group's interest. As the crowd began to thin we occupied a vacated table and took inventory of the tavern's offerings. As I scanned the room a familiar face caught my eye sitting at a table in the back corner- it was our former tormentor, Callisthenes. He was alone and speaking with a prostitute sitting on his lap. His sharp facial features rapidly brought back the image of me hunched over myself laying in a pool of vomit. Stephanos was sitting beside me and noticed my fixation.

"See one you like?" he asked with a grin.

"I see someone you might be interested in meeting again," I responded cryptically, eliciting a questioning look from my mate. "Look to the back corner, the man sitting with the whore over there." Stephanos squinted his eyes and examined the designated portion of the tavern. I watched as his eyes grew wide with stunned recognition before narrowing again in an angered stare. I immediately regretted alerting Stephanos to his presence and tried to talk him out of his apoplectic state. He ignored my words and shooed my hand off his shoulder in an incensed manner. His gaze could not be deterred while the rest of our group now took notice of Stephanos' enraged condition.

"What's the matter with you? The tail here isn't that bad," Dion asked jokingly. Stephanos did not respond.

"Hey, is there a problem?" Spear inquired.

"I'd like to raise a glass to our fallen friend Labdacus," Stephanos announced sullenly. His furious monotone created unease among the table as everyone now looked at me for an explanation. "Put your cups up, damn it!" Stephanos commanded. Everyone did as instructed. "To our fallen comrade Labdacus. A kind, yet hapless kid who was always quick to raise a cup or defend a mate. May his murderer one day remember his name again." The table drank to our departed companion and continued looking at me for an answer.

"Callisthenes is here," I announced solemnly, nodding in his direction. The news startled my table mates as they all jerked their necks around to spy the bane of our recruitment.

"It is that bastard," Bacchylides confirmed. "Should we order him a drink," he asked sarcastically.

"How about some hemlock?" Spear replied.

"How about I walk over there and stab him through his throat?" Stephanos added in a grave voice. His disturbing tone drew the attention of the table for it sounded as though Stephanos was serious. He had not removed his eyes from the old soldier since first spotting him.

"Hold on," I interjected with hushed forcefulness. "You're not seriously talking about killing him are you?"

"If you don't think he deserves to die then why don't you go disappear for another three months and be done with it?" Stephanos snapped. An uncomfortable air settled over the table. No one said a word in response to Stephanos' barbed retort. He had never spoken to me in that manner nor did he look remorseful about it. "I don't tolerate injustice when it is in my power to right it. You once cautioned me against a hasty revenge back on our recruitment march and I begrudgingly heeded your words then. Now heed mine- I will avenge Labdacus tonight- in Sardis, and one of us will not make it out alive. I'll do it alone if I must."

The mood of our band changed once the reality settled in that Stephanos was dangerously serious. The ramifications of such a brazen act sped through the minds of all seated while I furiously tried to summon Vettias' powers of strategy to formulate a plot that would shield us from discovery. I quickly realized the shadow business was quite difficult without the benefit of time and a heavy purse.

Looking around the table I deduced my mates were not having better luck producing a workable plan. Bolstered by my newfound confidence developed over the past three months, I took charge of the situation in the hopes that talking through our current scenario would generate the best way forward.

"Alright, first of all, if we are going to do this, we need to talk it through before Stephanos jumps over this table and makes a mad dash at one of the most lethal men we've ever met in our lifetimes," I began confidently. My bearing quickly brought everyone's attention to me in eager anticipation of a solution. Stephanos remained in his murderous trance, however. "That means you too, Stephanos," I snapped- forcing my friend out of his daze. "You've set us on this path and we're going to need you to keep your wits about you. A lot of good you would have done Labdacus if you confront Callisthenes head on in a drunken rage and he kills you where you stand- which you and I both know is more than a good possibility. So bring your eyes inward and join the discussion." My command presence surprised my mates, who willingly submitted to someone taking charge.

"He is drinking and with a woman- both facts will ensure his mind is distracted. I would initially recommend barging into the whore's chamber upstairs while he is predisposed but there is a guard who would hamper those plans. Killing the guard would be easy enough but that would alert everyone in this tavern to us and our army would surely find out. We need to determine where he will be most vulnerable between here and wherever he will retire for the evening. I say we wait until he is finished with his whore and discreetly follow him out of the tavern." I found myself speaking to a rapt audience as my mates, including Stephanos, looked as if I was divulging the secret knowledge of the Gods to them.

"Ideally we would study the route he takes home tonight and determine where best to ambush him tomorrow. Since we have only this evening to execute our plan, however, we will have to decide where best to dispatch him as events unfold. As I'm sure I don't have to remind you, Callisthenes is no ordinary target. He has the ability and motivation to kill several of us at once if we don't do this right. Therefore we need to stagger our formation and ensure the right people are conducting the right jobs. Stephanos and Spear- you two will be at his rear directly following him and ensuring to stay at least fifty paces behind. Rhexenor, Dion and Bacchylides, you three will accompany me on parallel streets. I will give the final signal to strike which means Spear and Stephanos need to immediately close your distance to him and deliver a violent first blow. The rest of us will be on him seconds later. Does everyone understand?" Everyone nodded in agreement, still looking confused as to how I was able to take charge and deliver a viable plan so quickly. I decided to cease speaking about the plan's particulars lest my mates became too confused.

I instructed everyone to reduce their intake of alcohol as we watched our target proceed upstairs with his woman for the night. We sat in relative silence for the remaining hour it took for Callisthenes to emerge from the girl's quarters. I had given some final instructions to the table prior and everyone appeared ready to take action. Callisthenes did not depart the tavern upon descending the stairs leading to the brothel rooms, however. He gingerly walked towards the bar and ordered another jug of wine. Spear and Stephanos continued inconspicuously observing our target while Rhexenor, Bacchylides, Dion and I positioned ourselves outside the tavern ensuring to remain in the shadows to avoid notice once Callisthenes departed.

"When he comes out we're not going to know which direction he will travel in," I explained. Therefore, we will split into two groups and parallel his movement while Stephanos and Spear keep an eye on him. We will run ahead at each intersection ahead of his movements. As he passes that intersection we will run on to the next one. Whenever he makes a turn down an alley towards one of the teams- that team will then walk in front of him, keeping approximately a fifty pace distance. The other team will follow in the rear behind Stephanos and Spear and begin running parallel to his new route. I will be watching the operation unfold and when I give the signal of a loud drunkard's cough, Stephanos and Spear will strike while the rest of us close in on their position to assist. Everyone understand?" All nodded and we continued to wait in silence for another half hour.

The door to the tavern finally opened and Callisthenes emerged slightly stumbling. He passed by without noticing our gaggle, followed by Spear and Stephanos ensuring to keep a safe distance. I nodded to them as they passed, and our group began to stalk our prey. Rhexenor and I ran down one perpendicular alley while

Bacchylides and Dion ran down the opposite alley. Rhexenor and I made a left at the end of the alley and continued running down the parallel street until we reached the cross section. There we waited, until we observed Callisthenes continue staggering down the parallel street. Determining he continued on his straight course, we ran down our street, keeping parallel with Callisthenes, until we arrived at the second intersection.

We waited about two minutes until we saw him continue staggering down the road. We again ran to the next intersection and waited. I thought to myself that the current alley we were looking down would make a perfect ambush point due to its lack of light and beggars. As Callisthenes came into view once more, he turned left in the direction away from Rhexenor and me and towards Bacchylides and Dion. We held our position until Stephanos and Spear followed him down the alley. We briskly ran in their direction and stopped at the intersection which Callisthenes had just turned from to determine if he was going to continue walking straight or make a turn. I observed him make a right turn so Rhexenor and I also made a right and ran down the road Callisthenes had been travelling to stay parallel with him and pick him up at the next intersection.

The road Callisthenes now travelled was desolate and would suffice for our purposes. Applying logic to Callisthenes' route, I determined it would not make sense for him to turn right again in the direction of Rhexenor and I and decided to force the issue on the current road Callisthenes was travelling. I instructed Rhexenor to continue the course while I ran ahead two city blocks, made a left down the perpendicular alley, and made another left so that I was now on the same road as our target walking in the opposite direction towards him. He was about fifty feet in front of me and I began coughing loudly to alert Stephanos and Spear to close their distance and strike. I watched as they picked up their pace and hoped they would time their strike to coincide with the rest of our party making their way down the perpendicular alleys to intercept Callisthenes all at once. I continued coughing and staggering to both keep Callisthenes' attention on me and to ensure all of my mates heard the signal.

As we all neared the target, I grasped the handle of my blade under my tunic. Callisthenes now yelled to me to get out of his way and I acted as though I was too drunk to comply. He yelled several more times until his breath was cut off mid-syllable. I looked up to see Stephanos had stabbed him in the back. The old soldier didn't go down easily, however, and faced his attackers with sword drawn. He lunged at Stephanos and Spear with such ferocity it knocked them both backwards. Despite the wound, his skill with a blade far surpassed any three of ours at once. I quickly closed the distance and saw the rest of our band running down their respective alleys through my periphery. I stabbed him in the back again, which provoked a loud shriek. He turned and knocked me to the ground. As he moved to deliver a death blow Bacchylides stabbed him in this side and Dion kicked him to the ground. Rhexenor, having never experienced mortal combat, now came upon our victim and wildly slashed at him like some giddy child torturing a helpless animal. Callisthenes was very close to grabbing our weaker friend to the ground with him before I pulled Rhexenor off. The sinister look of joy on his face was disturbing. Callisthenes' injuries now overcame him and he laboured to regain his footing. I kicked him several times, sending him back to the ground where he now saw six familiar assailants standing over him with murderous intent.

"What do you villains want?" he exclaimed.

"Vengeance," Stephanos replied somberly. "You will remember his name...Labdacus... Say it...Labdacus!"

"Who?"

"Say it!"

"La-Lab-dacus," Callisthenes responded weakly.

"Let the confusion over this name be your last living thoughts. Say it again!"

"Labdacus."

"Now say good night." Stephanos leaned over our former tormentor and stabbed him through his neck- dispatching him instantly.

"We need to get back to the encampment immediately" I reminded our band. "Now!" My words snapped everyone out of the moment and we began running in the direction of our army's location.

Everyone remained silent as we slowed our pace and neared a side entrance to the quartermaster bivouacs. Some support soldier was skulking about and Rhexenor spoke with him briefly before we entered our army's encampment and retired for the evening.

I had trouble sleeping that night despite being overly tired. I had conflicting thoughts about our action as well as lingering guilt. While I grieved at Labdacus' death and wanted to see justice done on his murderer, Callisthenes was an honoured veteran of Alexander's army. Labdacus was nothing compared to this man and he did more for the Greek cause then any of us ever did. I believed him to be overly cruel and sadistic yet he did produce hardened recruits ready to take their place among the remnants of Alexander's army. And then there was the way in which we killed him. It was not a fair fight- none of us could ever hope to win that. We stabbed an inebriated man in the back- hardly an honourable death for someone so accomplished. Rhexenor's behaviour also disturbed me. I would remember it and apply it to all future dealings with him.

Finally I dwelled on how easily I followed the will of Stephanos that night to do something I wouldn't necessarily have done on my own. My command presence and decision making certainly impressed my mates, however- I had Vettias to thank for that. But while my leadership was in line with my new persona- born in the fire of combat, Vettias' teachings, and Alexander's oath; blindly following someone to do murder was certainly not. I vowed to never let myself be led like that again. Sleep finally came as I began to think how close I was to Ilandra.

Chapter 39

The following morning we received word we were to remain camped outside of Sardis for the next several days. This news was welcome since I would use it to ask Vettias for a favour- a pass to visit Ilandra for a night. I estimated it would take two days of hard riding to cover the sixty miles separating Sardis and Ilandra, which would give me one night with my family before having to turn back around the following morning to ensure I was not left by the army. Coincidentally I was scheduled to meet Vettias this afternoon and I would humbly ask his approval.

Stephanos did not bring up the events of last night and did not make an effort to speak to anyone that morning. His behaviour led me to believe he was having second thoughts about his actions. "Everything alright?" I asked once we were alone.

"Of course, why?" he replied, slightly agitated by the question.

My silence and concerned expression brought him out of his foul mood and back to being my closest friend. "About last night, you know I didn't mean anything by my outburst towards you. My constitution cannot handle helpless people suffering injustice. I apparently have not gotten over his murder. I think I needed vengeance to help myself get over it. We'll see."

"Don't worry about it, we all knew your blood was up last night. I may be gone for a few days while the army camps here." Stephanos raised an eyebrow indicating he assumed my absence would have something to do with my cryptic new duties with the battle staff.

"It's nothing important, I don't expect to return with any stories for you this time." I finished my morning tasks and made my way to the quartermaster bivouacs to meet Vettias. He began the way he normally did by asking me about any information I had heard or seen, followed by some light criticism about my lack of new news. He again instructed me to expand my reach within my Syntagma to which I nodded in agreement and anxiously awaited him to finish.

"What's on your mind? Something more important to you than the task at hand?" he asked, a bit annoyed.

"I-I have a small favour to ask," I began weakly. "We are two days ride from my home, I…"

"You want permission to go home," Vettias interjected, finishing my sentence.

"If you didn't think it would have too much of a negative impact on our operations here?" I added deferentially. "The Gods know when we will be this close again and it would mean everything to me if I could spend one night with them and deliver the small amount of wealth I have acquired since departing.

"Working for The Hand does have benefits but you have only been away from home for one year. There are men here who've been with Alexander from the beginning. Men who've been away from their families for over ten years. Some of them will never see their homes again. Many have already made that sacrifice. And you ask to take leave of this army for four days?" Vettias' response lowered my expectation of a favourable answer. "I'm going to tell you what- I will allow this, only because my family died before I could see them again and this could be your last shot. You will depart Ilandra the following morning, understood? If you get any feelings about homesickness I will make sure you wake up to an assassin's blade in the near future. Acquire a mount from your friend with the quartermaster, turn in your tent equipment and inform your Lochagos that I have ordered you to depart for four days."

After hearing the answer I wanted I departed quickly so Vettias did not have time to change his mind and ran to seek out Rhexenor. My friend was still on a high from the rush of last evening and was eager to help me. He paid me out the money I had deposited within the baggage train and provided me a sturdy mount to borrow on my short trip. After informing Croesus of my new 'orders' from the battle staff and returning my equipment to the quartermaster again, I bid Stephanos farewell and rode hard west out of Sardis towards the Ionian coastline. From there I would pick up the Ionian Road and head south to Ilandra.

Travelling along the Royal Road for the better part of a year instilled a new appreciation for road construction. A road that was not properly drained, or built with inferior materials, made for much hardship during travel- especially for an army. Although the Royal

Road ended in Sardis, my journey was comfortable with the Ionian Road holding up fairly well in most places.

It was already late morning and I had several hours to make up if I were to arrive early enough the following evening to make my stay worthwhile. The noon sun beat down on the back of my neck and caused my mount to perspire greatly. I was overjoyed to be so close to home as I passed the familiar flora and fauna of my country. Fig trees and grape vines now occupied either side of the road and the unmistakable smell of sea air filled my nostrils. My mount was not the swiftest runner but was built for long hauls at moderate speed. I rode throughout the remainder of the day and about two hours into the night- making it all the way to the great coastal city of Ephesus where I secured lodging for the evening.

I departed one hour before dusk the following morning, heading south along the Ionian Road. Familiar looking merchant carts could be seen at daybreak and I passed several travellers along the way. My thoughts turned towards my long-envisioned triumphant return, and I reminded myself who I now was and how I would now act with regards to those that knew me from Ilandra. My hard riding paid off when I saw the faint silhouette of Ilandra about two hours after noon sun. Entering the city limits, I dismounted my horse and travelled along the many back roads and alleys to avoid being noticed. Arriving on my street I tied my mount outside of Argos' wine shop and entered to find my uncle half asleep behind the counter.

"One jug of your finest wine please," I stated, grinning widely. Upon recognizing me Argos jumped out of his seat and ran over to me and embraced me.

"Andrikos! What is this? What are you doing here? Is everything alright?" His expression now turned to concern as the thought of something negative having happened passed through his mind.

"Everything is fine uncle," I assured him. "Didn't your court of political advisors at the Ilandra marketplace inform you the army of Eumenes now camps at Sardis?" I asked sarcastically. "I guess I out rode the news. Anyway, since we are so close, my good standing within the army secured me a pass to visit my beloved family for one night before returning tomorrow morning." I no longer struggled to maintain eye contact and I spoke with my new command presence. I noticed a look of pleasant surprise in my uncle at my newfound confident demeanour.

"It sounds as though the army has done you a great service. Your mother is going to faint if you walk through her door so let me go in first and tell her the good news. We will have a great feast tonight in your honour and you will tell us of all your adventures."

"Dinner will be at my expense tonight and I will not accept 'no' for an answer," I replied as he departed into my apartment.

"Alright, alright," he responded with a smile. "Just stay here a moment."

Moments later I heard the expected shrieks coming from within my apartment- signalling it was time to enter. As I did so my mother darted at me and aggressively hugged me while crying.

"My baby, my baby," she whimpered repeatedly. I never enjoyed my mother's frequent displays of affection growing up, but they paled in comparison to the emotional assault I found myself receiving. I did my best to return her love yet remain my new stoic self. I looked up during the barrage to see my sister Helena standing several feet away with tears in her eyes. She knew better than to interrupt our mother giving one of us affection- especially after so long a period had passed. Our eyes met and my eyes began tearing as well. She was so much older and more mature than when I departed, yet managed to look even more innocent than before. After allowing mother enough time to have me to herself, Helena joined our embrace and we remained in the threshold of our apartment that way for some time. Argos stood in the corner and allowed his brother's family to enjoy this special moment without interruption.

When my mother finally got hold of her senses, she declared a feast would be prepared tonight and ordered Argos to the market so she and Helena could sit and enjoy my presence. Argos complied and announced he would tell Leandros to return home. I tossed him a small coin purse and reminded him dinner would be my treat this evening. As we sat down I was subjected to a flurry of questions delivered in rapid succession. Eventually I was able to communicate to them I was only here for the night- I was staying safe and I would return home as soon as possible. News of my imminent departure did

341

not sit well with my family, but they were able to couch this disappointment for the time being.

"Andrikos, we have wonderful news!" Mother announced. "Your sister is to be married to a successful merchant. Someone who is kind of heart and has the resources to take care of her. It is because of your cousin Leandros that such a husband could be secured for our Helena. His status has been elevated since your uncle had him declared hero of Ilandra and his tales were recorded in the annals. He is now both a treasure to this family and to Ilandra. His good work has brought prosperity to our family and he is now in a position to ensure your safe return home."

This was all good news; however, I had mixed feelings about Helena's coming marriage. I was not there to act as patriarch during her courtship and now she was to become the possession of another man. She no doubt heard over and over how lucky she was by our mother and she did appear pleased with her new situation, so I acted satisfied as well.

"And Nearchus' family, how do they fare?" My question was answered with an awkward silence for many moments.

"Nearchus' father Priskos continues to be a drunkard and squanders all of their money on taverns, dice, and women. Nearchus' mother tells me her son Argaeus is spending too much time with those two *friends* of yours Patrochlus and Alexandros. Nearchus' family owes a great debt to your cousin and uncle for treating them so well over the past year". Her morose description of Nearchus' family situation opened a pit in my stomach. How much resentment did his mother hold for me? His father? What were my own family's thoughts about my culpability after a year of reflection? Thinking of these questions was too jarring so I decided to put them from my mind.

Argos returned after an hour with an armful of dinner items accompanied by our family's new benefactor, Leandros. He was well dressed in an impressive blue cloak with gold embroidering over a new white tunic. His sandals were constructed of fine leather that showed no sign of wear- pointing to his ownership of more than one pair. His hair was combed and displayed a healthy sheen- pointing to an improved diet. His limp was less noticeable- pointing to further healing or a more concerted effort to conceal it. All in all, he gave off the air of importance.

"How's our family's newest hero?" he asked as we embraced. "I'm impressed your standing within the army is such that you have been granted a special pass. I could never get away with that. You're not deserting, are you?"

"Of course not!" I exclaimed. The very thought of something so grave was unthinkable. "I depart tomorrow morning. The army of General Eumenes makes camp outside of Sardis at this moment."

"Yes, yes. But you are all now outlaws; deemed so by Lord Regent Antipater and his General Antigonus."

"Yes, the situation is most grave," Argos added. "Greek fighting Greek. It's not right and makes a mockery of everything Alexander, and men like my son, fought for."

"Enough of this political gossip!" my mother interrupted. "I don't want to hear another word of it. Especially not while Andrikos is here with us. Argos, give me what you have procured."

I noticed the items Argos purchased were all of fine quality and I doubted my small purse could have purchased such choice sundries. Argos noticed my examination and handed me back my purse. "No one expects you to pay for your own celebration."

"It's not about tonight. This was to be a tangible contribution to the family. I lived here too long without fully contributing in the past and I am going to change that. In fact, while you are all here, I carry a meaningful contribution for this family- to include Nearchus' family." I produced my primary coin purse which contained what remained of my pay over the past year plus my recent bonus from General Eumenes. "It adds to a respectable sum and this is the proudest moment of my life to be able to present it here to you all who mean the most to me. You can't conceive how frequently I've dreamt of this day. It will be a grave insult to neither allow me to pay for this evening's feast nor to bestow the fruits of my past labour onto this family. Don't worry, I have not made myself a beggar with this act of generosity. I still have enough to get by."

All present were amazed by the way I now presented myself. Argos and Leandros looked at each other with a proud nod. My mother's eyes teared again as she could once more be proud of her son. Helena saw in me someone she could look up to again and Argos saw someone whose praises he would be proud to sing at the Ilandran market- not one but two 'heroes' to boast about. And there was no confusion that he would in fact make me a 'hero' in the eyes of any Ilandran that would listen.

We all remained in the kitchen area to help with the cooking. I recounted my story with the army thus far, but left out any mention of The King's Hand for fear of Argos standing in the city square and heralding my involvement for all of Ilandra to hear. My mother performed her obligatory pantomime routine of concern while hanging on my every word. The stoic pride I saw in Argos during Leandros' tales now crossed his face again at my story. Everything I had imagined all came to fruition that evening. We sat down for an incredible dinner of lamb just slaughtered that day, a stew made with fresh vegetables, ripe fruit, and excellent wine. We all stayed up well into the night before my mother and sister retired, leaving Argos, Leandros and I to finish off the last jug of wine.

"I can't tell you how proud of you we are," said Argos. "The difference in you is stark. You left an irresponsible brat who was lucky to get out of this town alive. You've returned in just one year's time a man. Your mother speaks the truth in that Leandros has achieved a position which will allow you to return to Ilandra unmolested by any who would bring up the past. Perhaps your successes will be recorded in the annals of Ilandra. I wish I could say the same for your idiot friends, however. After Ganymedes' departure, there was a vacuum of power within Ilandra's criminal underworld. Your two former acquaintances were too young and stupid to take it over, so several elements moved into the void. There has been a severe uptick in gang violence over the past year, which has settled into an uneasy truce of about four factions. Do not try and contact them while you remain in Ilandra this evening- is that understood? Your cousin and I spent the better part of the past year unsullying your good name and a new association between you and them would ruin all of that."

"Now, regarding Nearchus' family upstairs. That swine Priskos continues to make his family suffer. Leandros and I have helped them along but we've come to the decision that everyone would be better off without him. Arrangements are being made and he will not return from his next fishing expedition in Ephesus. As for his brother Argaeus, that boy needs a kick in the ass and Leandros and I will sit him down after his father's *accident* and explain that he is now the patriarch of the family. If that doesn't work, Leandros and I will beat some responsibility into him. So there you have it. Life continues without you here in the city of your birth, and we will all anxiously await your permanent return."

The three of us finished off the last of the wine, warmly embraced, and retired for the evening. I had a feeling of surrealism lying in my bed again after so long an absence. I truly was a different person now, and I felt disconnected with the boy who slept here for nineteen years. The liberal amount of wine ensured I fell to sleep effortlessly that evening and my family was all there to see me off early that morning. There were conflicting emotions between the joy of my surprise visit and the knowledge that my family would not to see me again for some time. As I mounted my horse no one had a dry eye. I departed Ilandra and began my journey back to my new life.

Chapter 40

Along my journey to Sardis I had the sinking feeling I was riding back into a cauldron of fire with Antigonus' vast army marching towards us at that very moment. I was to participate in the third great battle of Asia Minor between Alexander's generals and each step of my mount brought me closer to it. Could our enemies survive another defeat by General Eumenes? There was the real possibility that if we won this next fight, our cause will have been vindicated and the Argead's would take their rightful place on the throne. Did my oath oblige me to defend their interests forever? If their position was secured could I not return home after my enlistment and begin to finally contribute to my family's fortunes? I was hesitant to bring up the issue to Vettias because one should never ask questions he does not want to know the answer to. I began feeling a little guilty since I had only just taken the oath and was already thinking of being relieved of its charge.

I arrived back at our encampment to find our situation had changed little in my absence. Vettias had instructed that I meet him the evening I returned in our regular space provided by Rhexenor. Since I returned at dusk I went straight to the meeting location to avoid being delayed by any Lochos business. He was waiting for me, looking slightly annoyed, as I entered the tent and sincerely thanked him for his acquiescence in my short trip home.

"Yeah, yeah. You're back now and there's a lot of work to do. Cleopatra has predictably rejected Eumenes' offer of an alliance so everything now relies on the coming battle with Antigonus. The decision has been made that, since we have been deemed outlaws and are no longer in control of any territory, we will pillage the coffers of all we come across on our march towards Antigonus. This way Eumenes can keep the money flowing to the army in order to keep the Macedonians on his side long enough to defeat our enemies and gain access to the Royal treasuries again."

"We are to raid territory within the empire? Like brigands?" I asked, disheartened.

"For now. These Macedonians need to be properly compensated, especially since we do not have control of any Argead within our retinue. It's a dirty business but history is written by the victors and once we have defeated our enemies, little will be mentioned of this necessary unpleasantness. Besides, Antipater has done far worse in Greece itself during the Lamian Wars. If we can turn enough people against Antigonus by proving his inability to protect them from us, we may further our position significantly by the time battle is joined. Since we've remained in place for several days, the chances we have been infiltrated are high. You and I will meet every other day now until informed otherwise by me, understood?"

"One last thing before I let you leave. As in every battle, there is a chance we may lose. Normally in these internecine conflicts, the victor will avoid routing the losing side and integrate the surviving Greeks into their army. If this occurs I don't want you playing hero. You get yourself out of there and wait in the nearest settlement from wherever the battle is to take place. I need you alive now and your life is worth that of the rest of your Lochos to me, understood?"

I nodded in agreement and departed to the quartermaster supply tent to redraw my bivouac equipment and armament. Lack of sleep and four days of hard riding had brought on exhaustion and I had entered an unconscious daze while pitching my tent when Stephanos approached me.

"You don't look good; I thought you said your task would not be anything interesting."

"It wasn't," I replied after his presence brought me back to reality and motioned for him to come closer. "I was granted a four day pass to return to my home," I divulged in a low tone. "You mustn't say a word about it to anyone."

"You lucky dog, did you see any old flames?"

"If I had one in the first place I surely would have. This was strictly a visit to see my family and begin my long road of atonement with them. Four days hard ride has brought me to the point of exhaustion- so get down here and help me with this tent." Stephanos smiled and assisted me in constructing my sleeping quarters. At its completion I bid my friend good evening and collapsed onto my bedroll.

The army remained in Sardis for several more days before the order was given to depart the following morning. Our march along the Royal Road was brisk. We stopped at several cities along the way to commandeer their treasuries and the valuables of wealthy inhabitants so General Eumenes could continue paying the army and potentially sow discontent among the people of the empire Antigonus was nominally in control of. This tactic was unsettling to many, as we were stealing from those who we wished to rule. I used Vettias' logic to rationalize our actions and it did have the effect of keeping the Macedonian regulars content for the time being. General Eumenes went so far as to write vouchers for those unlucky individuals who were coerced into making generous 'donations' to our cause. After the requisition of one city's loot, we would send advance scouts out to the next several urban areas to ensure they could not hide their possessions. We meandered on and off the Royal Road for two months, filling our army's coffers along the way.

During this time, Vettias discovered Antipater and Antigonus' tenuous alliance was fraying, with Cassander deserting our one-eyed adversary and returning to his father, who had by now arrived back in Macedon. Vettias assessed Orontes would have also followed his new benefactor back to Pella as well.

Our old Perdiccan alliance was not fairing much better. General Eumenes wrote numerous letters to the scattered remnants of Perdiccas' court, most notably his brother Alcetas and Adea's ally, Attalus, imploring them to join with us and make common cause against Antigonus. Both refused to serve under a non-Macedonian general and put their own self-serving designs ahead of the overall war effort.

I continued to keep Vettias informed of disgruntled sentiment among the army as well. The more ardent of these subverters were quietly disappeared, which tempered my decision of divulging more names to Vettias in the future unless I was certain of the risk they posed. On one occasion I was summoned by Vettias to a nondescript tent one night away from our main encampment that was guarded by a contingent of General Eumenes' bodyguards. It appeared Vettias' internal operation was bearing fruit as I entered the dwelling to observe an unfortunate stranger on the receiving end of a *discussion* with Vettias and Davos. He had been worked over pretty hard already and looked to be in bad shape.

"This pile of shit is a tough one to break," Vettias stated in his usual content demeanour while performing such acts. His confidence belied a hint of exasperation, however, in the fact that he may not succeed in extracting what he wanted to know from the victim. "There's a plot a foot within our ranks and this son of a bitch knows about it. Don't you!" Vettias yelled as he struck the man for what looked like the one hundredth time and motioned to Davos who was standing stoically to the side, holding a sharpened dagger. Vettias was noticeably frustrated and violently stabbed the man's wrist through the bone and out the other side- getting the point stuck in the arm of the chair. The victim let out a quiet scream, muted by his gag, and began losing consciousness.

"Shit, I hit his vein," Vettias stated as he struggled to remove the dagger's blade from the wooden arm of the chair. "Andrikos! Grab the iron from the fire outside. We need to cauterize this wound. He can't bleed out yet. Damn it!"

Vettias' flustered state alarmed me and I worried our victim had a real chance of expiring prematurely. I clumsily ran out of the tent, grabbed the heated iron and handed it to Vettias who untied the victim's arm to cauterize both ends of the wound. This painful procedure evoked little reaction from the victim which only increased Vettias' flustered state. He began smacking the man and throwing water on him in an attempt to coax him back to consciousness. His breathing stopped and his head slumped lifelessly over his chest. Vettias had killed him through blood loss.

Vettias looked first to Davos with an expression declaring his awareness of the incompetence he had just performed. He next looked at me with an expression of regret having shown ineptitude in front of his pupil. "He knew something, damn it! Antigonus has infiltrated this camp. Before he clammed up he mentioned someone on our Battle Staff was in talks with Antigonus' agents. I let my emotions and pride get the better of me tonight. Let that be a lesson for you, Andrikos. Both of you return to your quarters. I'll clean up here."

Chapter 41

After surrounding and pilfering the ancient city of Ancyra along our route of banditry, our army departed the Royal Road and headed south in the direction of Cilicia to meet the approaching enemy. Several days marching south brought reports from our advanced scouts that Antigonus' army was near. We remained in place close to a settlement called Orcynia for two more days awaiting final movement orders. Our army occupied a large plain to best capitalize on our superior cavalry force. On the third morning a nervous calm had descended over our ranks as all could sense the violence of battle was imminent. We were ordered to keep our armour and weapons at the ready and to ensure no one wandered too far away from their bivouac. Stephanos and I sat with our Lochos mates passing the time around a fire engaging in trivial conversation. I sat propped up against a tree half asleep, contently listening to the quiet banter of my mates, when suddenly I came crashing awake by the sound of our horns blowing. We all looked at each other in confusion while Croesus ran over and screamed at us to ready for battle.

As we scrambled to comply, rumours began flying that Antigonus' army had surreptitiously occupied several foothills overlooking our plain and now held favourable position for combat. This was not a good omen for the coming struggle and I began to fret over the prowess of our adversary if he could so successfully outmanoeuvre our general. Our Lochos scurried into formation within our Syntagma, which took its place within our Taxis. Horns continued blaring and banners waved furiously to arrange all of our units into proper formation. Again, our countless hours of drilling paid off, allowing our army to align itself in short order and giving us enough time to face our enemy before they commenced their surprise attack.

Stephanos had shown impressive leadership during my prolonged absence and was rewarded by occupying the fourth position in our file- his sarissa would be one of the first five spear points to engage in battle. My position had moved back considerably since our battle with Craterus and I now occupied the ninth position, directly behind First Officer Neokles. Second Officer Gelon remained at the rear position and Croesus continued to lead from the front. General Eumenes and his cavalry occupied the right flank. After our battle with Craterus our horses were now the world's most feared cavalry force since Alexander's famed Companions.

The army lurched forward in lumbering unison as we began our march towards Antigonus. My position within the Phalanx limited my ability to view our adversaries but my above average height allowed me to witness the terrifying sight of elephants in the distance. Their presence had an unsettling effect on our troops, especially among those who could clearly see and hear them. Our officers began scolding the men to regain their nerve and reminded us Alexander defeated such beasts in India. Antigonus remained in his advantageous position atop the foothills and began to rain arrows and bolts down on our approaching army. Their prevalence was more than we experienced during our previous two battles, and their impact was more violent due to the favourable trajectory Antigonus' high ground afforded. Thus far, General Eumenes had not convinced me our chances for victory were good.

Antigonus' opening volley had a demoralizing effect on our army, who were still frazzled from the unexpected call to arms just twenty minutes prior. Our forest of sarissas aided in deflecting a good deal of the murderous projectiles but many found their mark. We held our small shields up to protect ourselves as best we could but screams could be heard from unfortunate phalangites on the receiving end of warheads. A multitude of arrows were landing all around me. Most of them had been deflected by our spears and erratically slammed into my shield arm, helmet, cuirass, and face causing several nicks and scrapes that drew blood. Their sting was painful, forcing me to advance forward cautiously with my head turned to the side in a wincing pose. Out of the corner of my eye I watched a phalangite two positions ahead of me in the adjacent file receive an arrow directly through his throat. He dropped his sarissa instantly and fell to the ground. His surviving comrades had no choice but to continue marching forward, trying as best they could not to trample him. As I passed him I saw he still drew breath and had enough wits about him to try and protect himself with his hands. Phalangites towards the rear of his file who had not seen him fall would inevitably walk right over him. This terrible occurrence was reenacted dozens of times around me, further hampering my warrior spirit.

The phalangite directly to my right now took an arrow through his left shoulder. Its close proximity allowed me to hear the warhead slam into his body and tear through his flesh. The man cried out but retained his footing as I tried to assist his balance as best I could. His wound did not seem imminently lethal but caused him unbearable pain. He screamed in agony directly in my ear, drowning out all other noise. After two minutes he was able to relegate his uncontrollable outbursts to more manageable grunts of anguish. I assessed his injury would prevent him from delivering the necessary force behind his sarissa thrusts that was required against Antigonus' Macedonian regulars.

The endless wave of projectiles continued as we neared our enemy. Antigonus' army began marching forward and came into effective range of our projectiles. The shrieks of his several dozen elephants could be heard by all the army now and had their intended effect. Their skin was coated with bright war paint to add to their fearsome appearance. Three men sat atop each- one mahout held the reigns while the other two rained down arrows and javelins on our army. During one spell of staring at these magnificent machines of war, I felt something slam into my shield arm. Its impact forced my forearm back towards my chest and a second later I felt the most intense pain of my life. I looked down to see an arrow sticking through my left arm. Its warhead had punctured my skin, scraped off my bone, and exited the other side. The warhead was mercifully brought to a halt by my linen cuirass. I let out a scream of pain like I had never done before. The phalangites around me, including Neokles, quickly inspected my injury and deemed in non-threatening.

"You'll be alright kid! Break the shaft and pull it out!" Neokles yelled over the cacophony of war. While Neokles' words were encouraging, his instruction could not be executed without considerable effort. The severe sting immediately brought a sickness to my stomach and all motivation left me. I would also have to break and remove the arrow with my right hand, which was preoccupied holding my eighteen foot long sarissa, all while I was maintaining the phalanx's increased marching pace. The viciousness of my situation overwhelmed me and I vomited on myself and Neokles in front of me. He barked more words of encouragement but my mind was not alert enough to hear him.

My thoughts now turned to nothing but my own survival. My feet kept pace with the army- seemingly on their own. My mind left the battlefield. I ached for Stephanos to pull me out of the melee; for Vettias to save me from this torment. More phalangites fell to arrows around me but I did not have the presence of mind to help them. My vision narrowed and I saw my family. I wanted my mother to hold me as my reality narrowed further, as if I was looking through a small tunnel. Mara now entered this small space. Her expression was sombre as she saw my ability to save her fading.

The severity of her potential fate succeeded in bringing me out of my internal delusions. My sight returned and in one uninterrupted motion I held my sarissa against the right side of my torso with my right arm, pinned it there with the assistance of my chin, grabbed the arrow with my right hand, wedged the arrow's point against the left side of my torso, and snapped the back end of the arrow off. I winced at the shot of incredible pain as the shaft ripped a larger tear in my skin. Having broke the feathered end off, I felt its splinters rub against my bone as I pulled the remaining shaft through my wound and dropped the subject of my torment on the ground. This action relieved the acute pressure on my wound, producing a more manageable throb of discomfort. I readjusted my sarissa and slowly gained cognizance of my surroundings.

As the two armies neared, it was clear Antigonus meant to counter our phalanx with his elephants, which he positioned in one single rank ahead of his phalanx in the middle of his formation. Two phalangites within my Lochos had succumbed to Antigonus' murderous volleys, and I now occupied the seventh position. I was close enough to see the back of Stephanos' head and he appeared to be unscathed. Javelins now came flying in from Antigonus' skirmishers and elephants as we closed with the enemy. The combined thunder of their approach shook the very ground as their pace hastened to trample us. Our front five ranks lowered their sarissas in preparation for the impending rush.

Our men released blood curdling screams in the face of this onslaught and braced for impact. The ground shook violently as the beasts collided with our first row of spear points, bringing our forward progress to a halt. I felt the familiar crush of men as seven ranks of phalangites pushed against me and the men to my left and right closed in on me, hindering my ability to hold my sarissa properly. Several of the elephants' momentum was stunted by well placed spear thrusts while the majority charged forward, snapping sarissas or forcing them away from their path. The first of the elephants now reached our front rank and began kicking and thrashing our men. I watched in horror as several Lochagos' were trampled over and gored. Their bodies resembled bloody, mangled cloth as their bones had been crushed and their carcasses lost all rigidity. Some had their entrails ejected from their mouths or from open wounds due to the force of the elephants' charge.

More were making their way forward, impaling and crushing men from the second, third and fourth ranks. Croesus had succeeded in gouging out the eye of the elephant attacking directly opposite our Lochos. The beast's injury blunted its charge as more pikes stabbed its stomach, face and underbelly. The creature finally turned back and began trampling men from Antigonus' phalanx, prompting its rider to hammer a prepositioned stake into the back of its neck- killing it instantly. The elephant fell face first into the enemy phalanx, crushing several phalangites and throwing its riders to the ground to be trampled. The elephant to our right began making headway against the two Lochos' it was engaged with however. The beast was four ranks in and violently swinging its massive tusks to and fro- goring and killing men from several adjacent files. Another phalangite from our line was killed in this way causing Neokles to fall back into me. The animal was so close that I felt its hot breath upon me exhale from its wild trunk that was littered with cut marks and arrows. The monster made it so deep into our phalanx that phalangites from either side of it began stabbing at its powerful torso with their short swords. Several of these strikes punctured vital organs, causing the elephant to fall to one side in submission to its wounds. Had it fell the other way I would have been crushed instantly. Our men mercilessly stomped in the skulls of the animal's riders who had fallen with it to the ground.

Despite all this, our phalanx managed to keep its fighting spirit high. Several more elephants were either turned back or killed, while others managed to annihilate entire Lochos' of our Syntagma. I had forgotten about my injury during this orgy of carnage but was painfully reminded of its presence once it became time for me to lower my sarissa and engage the coming onslaught of Antigonus' phalanx- who were now charging in behind the holes opened by the elephants. The exertion required to effectively thrust my weapon induced a throb of anguish in my arm with every strike. This new wave of death brought even more butchery as thousands of fresh phalangites began thrusting their spear points at our reeling ranks. Our exhausted and battered Syntagma began losing ground to our rested opponents and dozens of our men were being impaled all around me. Our Taxis' Strategos, Androkles, screamed at our Syntagma's Ouragos' to ensure each Lochos' Second Officer stopped the movement backwards and began pushing with all of their might so that the men in front would be forced to hold their ground. If we could hold our position just a little longer, I was sure our superior cavalry would succeed in flanking our enemy, allowing us to push forward and defeat them.

Only Croesus, Stephanos, a Macedonian, and Neokles stood between myself and the front line. Being in the fifth position, my spear point was now actively engaged in the battle. The crush of the army behind us, pushing vociferously to hold our position, was so great that I was pressed completely up against Neokles' back who, in turn, was in similar position against the Macedonian in front of him. I felt as though I could be suspended in air between the men in front and back of me had my feet been lifted off the ground. I fought on as best I could, however, and never stopped thrusting my sarissa despite the pain of my arm and my limited ability to see where my point was striking. The ground was covered in blood, vomit, gore, piss, shit, and some substances I had never seen before. They mixed to create a slippery slick of stench that added to my nausea. Trampled bodies were strewn all around me- some corpses were as thin as a wool blanket and as grotesque as anything from Hades.

Croesus and Stephanos were fighting with the skill of Achilles at the front of our rank. Both of their spears had snapped and Croesus was hacking through a sea of enemy sarissas with his sword while Stephanos was stabbing over his shoulder with his broken sarissa, impaling the enemy with its splintered edge. The sarissas from the remaining three positions behind them assisted in protecting them and fending off the enemy.

The severity of our situation produced an enraged frenzy among our men, and I thrust my spear with blind fury knowing that each strike was keeping my best friend alive. I managed to kill several enemy phalangites as our army's newfound passions succeeded in blunting our retreat and allowed us to take several steps forward, seizing ground from our enemy. Our momentum grew and our army shouted blood curdling oaths at our assailants. It was at this time a spear point grazed Neokles' face, opening his right cheek and fracturing his jaw. He reflexively turned from the blow to look me straight in the eyes as his disfigured face spat blood all over me. His severely broken jaw had become dislocated and, combined with his wide open cheek, produced a ghastly façade where the lower half of his face lost all form with his tongue partially hanging out of the gaping wound. The gruesome injury was not fatal, however, and he quickly spun back around and continued fighting despite losing the ability to speak coherently.

Although many spear points were slicing my shoulders, upper arms, and parts of my face, opening several gashes, the renewed motivation of our phalanx increased my hopes of a victory- if only we could stand firm a little longer. Where was our damned cavalry? Why had they not flanked Antigonus' phalanx by now? I was so enmeshed in the fighting that it was impossible to see anything happening more than ten feet in any direction.

Suddenly, members of our army began shouting that General Apollonides had fled the field! No one near me could see for themselves if this disastrous news was true but it had the effect of instantly changing the momentum of the fighting. We began losing ground once again and this time our rear soldiers could not push hard enough to stop it. Enemy spear points were striking in from seemingly everywhere and it felt as though the whole world was crashing in around us.

The enemy made further inroads and other Lochos' began to collapse to our right and left. This left Croesus and Stephanos surrounded on all sides by enemy spears and swords. I watched as Croesus was stabbed repeatedly before succumbing to a spear thrust and dropping to the gore-soaked ground to be trampled. Stephanos was now in front and risked the same fate. Neokles, still fighting heroically despite his ghastly wound, pulled Stephanos backwards as our army continued falling back. Stephanos slashed and cursed our enemies while being dragged backwards, and looked like a bloody mess with unbridled rage in his eyes. He was covered in bruises, gashes, open cuts, and gore. His breathing was erratic while screaming oaths at the top of his lungs. Neokles now jumped into the first position and threw himself with abandon on our foes. Stephanos and I were now together, fighting side by side- just as we always imagined. I had dropped my sarissa, which was unbroken and thus too long for the close-in battle, and wielded my short sword with reckless abandon. The sarissas from the men behind me succeeded in giving us cover as we hacked at the enemy with our blades.

More of our Lochos' began collapsing as I watched Neokles succumb to numerous stab wounds and fall in front of us. Our spear points began disappearing around Stephanos and I which left us dangerously exposed to the oncoming rush of the enemy phalanx, who by now were motivated with the sense of imminent victory. I turned around to see our army in full flight. I grabbed Stephanos, who was still hacking away at opposing spear points, and pulled him back to retreat- only to realize we were too close to the front line to escape in time. I saw an enormous elephant carcass and darted under it, dragging Stephanos with me. We lay there as first Antigonus' phalanx, and then his cavalry, ran over our fleeing comrades, massacring them by the thousands.

Stephanos and I were panting so heavily I worried enemy soldiers would hear us. After a few minutes my heart rate slowed and I vomited on the ground next to me. I glanced over at my dearest friend looking as though he were bleeding out of every pore. I was able to calm him down so that he was no longer attempting to leave the safety of our hiding place to continue fighting the enemy. An army in full route is no time for heroes, and I did not want to lose another friend as close to me as Stephanos.

"We cannot be captured here, we have to flee this place as soon as we get a chance," I exclaimed, still out of breath. Poking my head up I looked to see Antigonus had lost control of his army and they pressed hard in pursuit of our fleeing forces- making the battlefield an empty scene of death and carnage. Words have never been voiced or written that fully described the apocalyptic scene Stephanos and I gazed upon. Thousands of men lay dead in the most horrible manners imagined: trampled, impaled, stabbed, speared, beaten, clubbed, lanced, and hacked. Hundreds of men squirmed and crawled through the vicious chaos looking for aid, praying to the Gods, or moaning in agony. Their machinations brought a lifelike quality to the sea of death and added to its horrific macabre.

My thoughts now focused on finding Vettias and rejoining what remained of our army to receive care for our wounds. All vestiges of authority I had known over the past year were now shattered, and I felt naked without the comfort of feeling a part of something greater than myself. We remained hidden under the dead elephant for another hour before all remnants of Antigonus' army had moved on from the field in pursuit of Eumenes.

"We should have stayed and fought like soldiers, instead we ran like cowards," Stephanos mumbled sullenly. "What would the Spartans think of us? Neokles pulled me away and held off the enemy so that I could escape. I let him. He no doubt walks among the amber grains of Elysium, with all others who fought admirably. He deserves that honour. What honour has the living earned?"

"Now who pities themselves unnecessarily?" I retorted after Stephanos took a reflective pause. "Who fought more admirably? The phalangite who took an arrow and died before the battle is joined? Or a phalangite in the fourth position who held his ground and butchered our enemies by the dozen? A phalangite who, by the end of the battle, was in the first position and was so covered in his own blood that he resembled a creature of the underworld more so than a man? There is no question Neokles is a hero and will be remembered as such, but do not take away from your own herculean effort on this day. There is no doubt you will be made an officer in General Eumenes' reconstituted army."

"Your praise of me is too kind and your optimism for the future is too foolish. We are beaten. There is no army to reconstitute. Those that survived have been absorbed into General Antigonus' war machine. Whereas before today, General Eumenes was an outlaw with an army; now, he is just an outlaw- if he's even still alive. The antagonists of my father and brother have won the day. I will have to live under their rule knowing I fled when facing them in open combat."

"My praise of you is merited and my assessment of our future prospects is based on the knowledge that there are larger forces at work. There is more at stake than which usurping general holds Regency over the Kings." I stopped myself before I divulged too much but luckily Stephanos was too introverted in his own depressed world at that moment to pay attention. As we sat there, deciding whether it was safe to depart, a large contingent of cavalry raced towards the battlefield. They flew no banners and I assumed they were aligned with Antigonus and continued hiding. They drew closer to Stephanos and I, heightening my fears we would be found. As they neared I began recognizing faces within the cavalry squadron. I stood up and recognized General Eumenes himself at the front of the detachment. Realizing I was amongst allies I nudged Stephanos to stand up and we were noticed by several of the cavalrymen.

"You there!" one of the officers yelled out to us. "Where does thy swear allegiance?"

"To General Eumenes, the true protector of the Argead Kings!" I exclaimed. The officer looked to his colleagues who shook their heads, indicating they did not know whether to believe us or not.

"Which unit do you serve?" The officer interrogated.

"We proudly serve under Strategos Androkles, within the Pydna Syntagma led by Lykos, serving under Lochagos Croesus!"

"I vouch for these phalangites!" A familiar voice now yelled out, angling its way towards the site of questioning. My spirits were raised as I saw Vettias make his way towards us atop a horse and looking down at me with a proud smile. "Look at these two! Is there any doubt they have not contributed to our cause and served General Eumenes honourably? How much blood have you shed on this day?" Vettias yelled as he chided the cavalry officer.

"Forgive me sir, but in light of Apollonides' treachery, no one can be trusted."

"Provide them mounts," Vettias instructed, to which the cavalry officer complied. Stephanos and I mounted the provided horses while the contingent dismounted and began gathering the dead into two large makeshift pyres. "Davos, post!" Vettias shouted. "Escort these two to the nearest settlement to receive care from a surgeon. Give them three days rest and bring them to the rally point, understood?" Davos nodded and led us away from the battlefield while the cavalry contingent continued their work in preparation of honouring the war dead. In this way, Eumenes had denied Antigonus the honour of performing this sacred act- usually reserved for the victors of a battle. His gesture stated for all to witness that though he had been beaten through the treachery of a subordinate, his will had not been extinguished. As the three of us galloped away, it was clear our struggle with Antigonus was not over.

Chapter 42

We followed Davos north at a deliberate pace. The rush of battle had departed us, and our wounds increasingly made their presence known. Each stride of my mount educed a shot of sting in the several open cuts I bore on my sides, arms, legs and face. My puncture wound on my left arm emanated a persistent throb of pain throughout our ride. I looked over to Stephanos, who looked as though he needed all his remaining strength and consciousness to stay atop the animal. He maintained an expressionless stare down at the mane of the horse for the duration of our journey. A terrible thirst now came over me and I motioned for Davos to stop and give us a drink from his bladder of water. After two hours teetering along the edge of consciousness and coma, our debilitated party arrived at a small settlement.

Davos made arrangements for us to reserve a dank room with two rotted wooden slabs serving as beds. Stephanos and I collapsed onto them while Davos departed to find a surgeon. I went in and out of consciousness for the next hour. Each time I fell to sleep I was brought back to the battle field- to the exact moment when our ranks collapsed and a dozen spear points came raining down on me. Each point had a hideous face that was screaming at me while projecting blood. All I could do was cower on the ground with only my bare hands for protection. As the crazed spear points came striking in to deliver their death blow, I would startle awake with a mild yell. I looked over to find Stephanos unconscious but breathing, and I lay back down wondering what was keeping Davos. This unpleasant routine continued several more times until the last time I awoke in a cold sweat into the arms of Davos and what appeared to be a medical attendant. The stranger's simple appearance did not inspire my confidence in his abilities, however. He looked to be about seventy with wrinkled skin and several teeth missing. Davos held me down as I observed the old man stitching an open gash in my side. I looked over to see Stephanos naked and asleep with several sets of stitches throughout his body.

"Your friend will be alright," Davos reassured me after noticing my concern. "He's lucky we got him help when we did. He's lost a lot of blood. He may not be able to ride with us in three days' time."

"We're not leaving him, that is final," I snapped, evoking an amused smile from my older and wiser colleague. I laid back down and felt the jab of the surgeon's stitching needle. "Watch what you're doing old man!" I hissed after wincing from its painful prick.

"Just hold still boy," he replied, seemingly unphased by my order. "I've got a lot more work to do and I don't want you coming apart at the seams."

Davos provided me some strong wine and I eventually fell back to my nightmares. The recurring dream was so tangible it deceived my mind into believing I was on a perpetual battlefield, always on the losing side, and always being ran through by screaming spear points. I startled awake each time, thanking the Gods it was just a dream. It was evening now and Stephanos lay asleep in his bed while Davos slept on a flimsy chair with a bottle of wine on the ground beside him.

A persistent fear lingered over me and I felt as though the decayed door to our room would fly open at any moment- ushering in phalangites of Antigonus' army carrying screaming spears echoing the cries of the battlefield. I felt physically and mentally weak. I felt as though Agathon would cut me in two had I reported to his formation of recruits in my current pathetic state. Visions of my former tormentor floated through my mind's eye, scolding me to stop feeling sorry for myself. After ashamedly listening to him berate my masculinity, I was finally motivated to get out of bed, splash water on my face, and take another drink from Davos' jug of wine.

"You're awake," he stated behind half closed eyelids. "You should continue to sleep. We're leaving the day after tomorrow."

"I'm through sleeping for now, there's nothing but death waiting for me on the other side."

"Reliving the battle? Sometimes that can't be helped. It looked like the two of you were in the middle of a real butchery back there. Anything you want to talk about? Sometimes it helps to speak to someone familiar with what you are going through."

"You act as though Hades himself could not force you to show weakness or fear- as if you could rip a suckling babe from his mother and cast him into the chasm of Mount Taygetos like the Spartans." I was admitting to Davos that he was better suited for this business and thought it a waste of his time to be sitting here with Stephanos and me.

"It gets easier with time. You do have to possess a particular constitution but I've seen nothing in you that would preclude your future success in this business. The taste of alcohol is not appetizing to children. Through maturity and the emulation of those they revere, alcohol becomes pleasant to the drinker. It will get easier the more you learn from Vettias and work with me. Now, this phalangite over here, who is he?"

"He is my closest confidant. A friend from my first day of recruitment."

"Can he be trusted?" Davos inquired.

"He can indeed, however he knows nothing of The Hand."

"He was in pretty bad shape. It looks like he'll live, but we have three days hard riding starting tomorrow. General Eumenes will retreat to the mountain fortress at Nora in eastern Cappadocia. He will remain there with his closest supporters and will release the majority of his surviving army until events are more favourable. Vettias believes The Hand should focus its efforts within the court of Antipater in Pella. His age and deteriorating health may provide an opening to further our goals and enable General Eumenes to depart the Nora fortress. Are you going to be ready to depart tomorrow morning?"

I nodded, took another drink of wine and fell back to sleep for the remainder of the evening. Father was waiting for me, sitting at the foot of my meager cot.

"Now nothing can prevent me from voicing the intense pride I have in my son. Even you will relent and confess that your actions in defense of your army have been noble. Now all that is left for my redemption is for you to save that girl."

"Yes father, but she is thousands of miles away from me. There's nothing I can do in this condition."

"The afterlife puts the concept of time in perspective. I've no doubt you will accomplish all I know you to be capable of. You've already achieved so much and I am immensely proud of the man you've become. Now you must wake and continue on your noble path." I woke to see Stephanos limping around our small room gathering his clothes.

"Where's Davos," I asked.

"He is readying our mounts. Who is he? Why are we here? Why is he helping us?"

"He's an assistant to the battle staff. He was assigned to look after us in recognition of my efforts in Syria. He is to escort us to General Eumenes' encampment. Apparently it is in an impregnable fortress somewhere in Nora, Cappadocia. It is a three days ride from here. Do you think you are up to it?"

"I'll be able to keep up. I would rather lose fighting for a cause that is just than claim victory supporting a man who cares nothing for Greece. If General Eumenes chooses to continue fighting our enemies, then I will do all I can to assist him."

Our journey was easy enough through Cappadocia with the three of us keeping low profiles due to our continuing outlaw status. As we approached the mountainous retreat at Nora, Davos pointed to a craggy summit with a faint walled structure chiseled out of the rock. A light smoke could be seen slowly billowing from the fortress, signalling its occupancy. Its small size belied its impressive stores of water and grain but it was clear no sizeable force could reside there for any period of time.

We followed the winding path up the mountain before arriving at the thick gates of the southern wall. Several men stood atop its ramparts looking down on us with bows and arrows at the ready. The ancient citadel looked to have been there for centuries and its state of decay pointed to decades of vacancy. Its height atop the mountain, the narrow path leading to its gates, and its ability to house large amounts of food and water, allowed the stronghold to repel a foe of any size with only limited manpower. Davos announced our presence to the sentries, prompting the massive doors to lurch open.

We entered the bastion to find a crowded sea of activity as a small contingent of our once great army toiled to fix Nora's dilapidated construction and build new structures to house the large amount of horses occupying the cramped space. Many others were efficiently removing the imposing accumulation of horse dung to guard against an outbreak of disease. A sentry escorted us to a simple building within the fortress that now served as a command headquarters. A sarissa stood upright on top of the headquarters with a freshly severed head sitting on its point. Davos explained that General Eumenes not only buried our war dead but also managed to track down and murder the traitor Apollonides, whose head now resided atop the spear.

The headquarters' guard element opened the door and took custody of us as we entered to find several officers of the battle staff flanking General Eumenes while standing over a large map of Cappadocia.

"These three have just arrived and claim to be members of our army," the sentry announced.

"That will be all, thank you," Vettias instructed the guard while sitting in the corner of the small room. General Eumenes looked up at the three of us, noticing the poor physical shape Stephanos and I were in. Recognizing me, he walked over and embraced us.

"Gentlemen, these two are but thousands of phalangites that fought valiantly for our cause and yet return to this desolate fortress despite their severe injuries. If I had a full army of these devoted young men, our current situation would be very different. What manner of wealth do they have waiting for them here in this shit hole? What comforts and luxuries are to be found here that these two cannot obtain in the outside world? What future reward is guaranteed to them for risking life and limb to serve with *outlaws*? This is the calibre of men that is required to defeat our enemies and ensure the Argeads take their rightful place on the throne of Alexander."

Receiving such high and unsolicited praise from General Eumenes himself made Stephanos and I feel quite uncomfortable. I struggled to keep eye contact with all in the room and stood stoically during our leader's speech. Upon his conclusion, I felt my new persona would be compelled to say something competent within the presence of such an impressive group of men.

"Your praise is too kind sir. We have done our duty in support of this army and its goal of protecting the true Argead successors to the throne. Far better men did the same or more who now lay dead for a cause greater than themselves. Your resolve to continue leading us in this noble endeavour has inspired us to continue to serve this army."

I ended my response there, satisfied my words had their intended effect. Vettias gave me a nod and General Eumenes appeared pleased. "Sentry! Show these two to the infirmary so their wounds can be properly attended. Come see me when you are well, understand?"

"Yes sir," I replied as we were led out.

The infirmary occupied a small warehouse within the grounds and was sparsely filled with people nursing relatively minor injuries. This spoke to how many of our army had perished and how few actually made it to our stronghold. An attendant looked very surprised at the state Stephanos and I were in and eagerly brought us to a cot for examination. He seemed displeased with the quality of work that had been done on us by the decrepit old man and hurried to find the head surgeon.

"Andrikos! Is that you?" a familiar voice rang out from across the room. I looked up to see Philotheos' face beaming at the opportunity to work on real war wounds from someone he knew since a recruit. After gently embracing, he examined our injuries and became agitated. "What dirt farmer did this to you?" he demanded, touching a particularly gruesome gash on Stephanos' side that was haphazardly stitched by the old man. "You're coming apart at the seams, kid. We're going to do something about this immediately," he diagnosed, while his attendants ran around furiously making surgical preparations. We were plied with strong wine and given a willow bark mixture that tasted horrid, but succeeded in numbing the pain while the surgeons re-stitched our wounds and properly dressed them. We were ordered to remain on our cots for the next week to allow our injuries to heal properly.

During this time Davos wandered in and out of the infirmary to check on me, and Vettias came to visit each day with a disposition of a concerned father. My thoughts settled on my family for a time, and I began to question whether I made the right decision returning to such a futile situation. I also thought of Mara. She was thousands of miles away from me in Persia and my stomach ached at the thought of leaving her in Hyllos' custody. I reaffirmed my personal vow to rescue her there on that flimsy cot, atop a rocky crag, in the middle of Cappadocian mountain ranges.

On one morning I woke to find Vettias sitting at my side. He smiled after my eyes settled on his and put his hand on my head. "How are we feeling, hero?"

"I think the life is returning to my limbs" I replied confidently.

"Good. Our work is only just beginning and your newly recited oath demands attention. You and I are to depart this fortress when your wounds allow it. Antigonus' army is approaching and will have Nora under siege in short order."

"What will happen to the people who remain?" I asked, concerned for Stephanos' safety.

"Nora will withstand the siege, although the horses may begin having some issues. Regardless, we can better help those left behind on the outside."

"Where are we to go?"

"Macedonia," Vettias responded with a smirk, knowing his answer would have a heavy effect on me. "The Hand has someone deeply imbedded within Antigonus' court. Now that Cassander has returned to Pella, presumably with Orontes, we are to travel there and assist our operative in whatever way we can to alleviate pressure on our army here. So get some rest hero. I will call on you when it is time."

Vettias exited the room and I continued to lie on my cot within the infirmary. I looked over to Stephanos who was still asleep. The thought of leaving him again so soon did not sit well. Especially since every step Vettias and I took in the direction of Macedon brought me farther from Mara and any chance of ever saving her.

I felt I barely had time to reflect on all that had occurred since leaving Ilandra before Vettias was already ushering in the next chapter of my increasingly interesting existence. I was to walk in the city of Alexander. I was to set foot in Greece- the ancestral home of my family and all peoples of Ionia. I assumed whatever was to occur there could not compare to the harrowing events I had already experienced thus far. However, I knew never to assume anything when Vettias was involved. In two days' time Vettias appeared at my bedside dressed for the long journey.

"So, you ready hero?"

I nodded my head, bid farewell to Stephanos, and followed my mentor out of Nora for the next phase of my education.

Made in the USA
San Bernardino, CA
11 May 2015